Lifeblood

Lifeblood

The 11th Percent Book 3

T.H. Morris

Dedication

This book is dedicated to Amanda Hoey, Jon Lowery, Jared Mingia, and Brenda Jarrett, four people who are proof positive that blood ties sometimes expand past one's family unit.

Acknowledgments

The third go round! Book number three in The 11th Percent Series! THREE! It's a crazy and humbling thing to know how far this path has unfurled. And it's still only the beginning! But I'd be more than remiss, and a little egotistic, if I said I got this far alone. I started this journey with a tight core around me, helping me in any way possible. And that core has not diminished. It has only grown! Family is always a backbone in the system; wouldn't be here today if not for them. My beautiful wife Candace has been in my corner from the word go, and remains so with a kind word and gems of advice for any and all avenues. Love you, darling! Dzintra Sullivan, despite her diverse and hectic creations and schedule, always has time for a kind word and a share, like, or encouraging comment. Patti Roberts is simply the best of the best, with her keen eye for capturing what imagery will most fit the theme, plus her unwavering support and kindness. Elizabeth Wyke is always a ray of light. Jared Mingia, Jon Lowery, Amanda Hoey, Brenda Jarrett…you know how much you mean to me. I dedicated this book to you, after all! I also cannot leave this without mentioning Cynthia Witherspoon, my creative tag team partner, and Tracey Durbas, who always captures my creative endeavors via pastry or sweet delicacy. She, too, is a maven in that regard. The list goes on from there…to name everyone would be a book all by itself. You guys are simply the best.

Contents

Nuptials and Nuisances

Jonah had to admit that this was a very happy day. The afternoon air was pleasantly mild for late August, the sky could not have been bluer, and the sunlight couldn't have been brighter. The sunlight reflected its dazzling illumination in the metallic surface of a pond that was overlooked by many people, including Jonah himself.

As he surveyed the scenes of nature, everyone else was focused on the center of attention. With a mental shake, he turned his own gaze back to the subject at hand. It was a wise thing to do, seeing as he was one of the focal points.

He was one of seven groomsmen to his good friend and former co-worker, Nelson Black, who was just about to complete his own personally-made vows to his fiancée, Tamara Madden. Jonah's mind had wandered as Nelson read them. He was familiar with them, after all; he'd helped Nelson write them.

Nelson and Jonah met at a burdensome staff meeting at the accounting firm of Essa, Langton, and Bane. They were fast friends because of the fact that the two of them seemed to be the only ones in the entire firm that maintained an awareness of life outside of their job. Nelson was also one of the few people Jonah trusted enough to reveal his writing aspirations, and Nelson did not hesitate to encourage him to actively pursue the craft. They'd never lost touch despite Jonah's departure from the firm due to the politics and nonsense.

Nelson had been busy during that time. He met Tamara at the mall one day, and then became an almost permanent fixture in the shoe store where she worked. Jonah didn't recall all the details in between that time, but Nelson had proposed to her after five months of dating, and she'd accepted instantly. Enter

Jonah, who was jarred from a nap one afternoon by a phone call from Nelson after he'd finished a strength test with his best friend, Reena Katoa.

* * *

"Hello?" said Jonah.

"Jonah? Jonah, is that you?" came Nelson's anxious reply.

"Yeah, Nelson, it's me. What's up? Everything okay?"

"No! Well, yes, everything is okay, great in fact—I popped the question, and Tamara said yes!"

Jonah's fatigue faded completely. "Great, man!" he exclaimed. "Glad to hear it!"

"Yeah! Are you willing to be a groomsman?"

"Really, Nelson, is this a question? Of course I'm willing!" Jonah told him.

"Thanks, and, uh—I also need your help."

Jonah laughed. "What, you mean beyond being a groomsman?"

"Yeah, beyond that. See we've decided to write our own vows, and I know Tamara's will be epic, but—"

"Now, Nelson," said Jonah, incredulous, "I *know* you aren't asking me to write your vows—"

"No!" said Nelson in a voice that was almost as panicked as it was scandalized. "I know what I want to say! I do! It's just that—it needs editing, shaping—well, you're the writer, and I am about as talented in writing as I am in parasailing, in other words, not. But I have a feeling that if I screw this up, it could very well be as dangerous *as* parasailing, so—"

Nelson's rambling was so jumbled and desperate that all apprehension Jonah had about assistance with the vows evaporated. This conversation alone proved that Nelson needed all the help he could get. That thing that Nelson said about screwing up being as dangerous as parasailing was inaccurate. If Nelson tanked in front of Tamara and her friends and family, it might prove *fatal*.

"Alright, alright, alright," relented Jonah. "I'll help you."

* * *

So after every detail was perfected and after the clandestine moments Jonah spent shoring up Nelson's shaky words were done, here they all were.

There. Nelson completed his vows without a single hitch. Jonah chose to gauge the success of the words by the tears that fell from the bridesmaids' eyes.

Even Tamara got choked up, but Jonah could tell she fought back the sobs so as not to ruin the pristine state of her makeup.

The pronouncement was made, this kiss sealed the deal, and the ceremony was done. Jonah and company were the inaugural citizenry to meet Mr. and Mrs. Nelson Black.

Happy that this part was over, but cognizant of the fact that they were a long way from finished, Jonah readied himself and interlocked arms with his designated bridesmaid, who was one of Tamara's older sisters. Her face was blotchy due to tears, so Jonah supplied her with a handkerchief. They joined the procession and took the short walk indoors to where the reception would take place. Before seating himself in his designated spot, Jonah nodded to Reena, who had agreed to come with him as friends since he had no date (Reena had suggested that he ask Vera Haliday, another of their friends, to come with him as his date, but Jonah had paled and shot that down).

He knew he was going to owe Reena big for this. She abhorred dressing formally, and only tolerated it for her job. She preferred tank tops, sweats, and sneakers—basically anything she could guiltlessly splatter her beloved paints on. Today, however, she'd made a concession, and looked quite pretty in a sleeveless black top and pants to match, with her black hair and its usual scarlet highlights pulled back in a tight bun. Concerning her outfit, Jonah counted his blessings. A dress or skirt was out of the question.

Tamara's sister noticed the acknowledgement, and glanced at Reena appraisingly. "Is that your girlfriend?" she asked quietly.

Jonah stifled a snort. "Um, no," he answered. "She's just a friend."

"She's a beautiful woman," Tamara's sister coaxed. "You might not want to let her get away. One of the men in here might snatch her up."

Jonah politely grinned and nodded, preferring not to tell her that the chances of Reena being picked up by one of these men was about as unlikely as Nelson's ability to handle his wedding vows by himself.

In the reception setting, further speeches were made. The last of which was by Tamara's father, an extremely thin man that somehow still managed to be intimidating. Then the well-wishers came in droves. After a great deal of socializing, Jonah found himself next to Tamara, who had beckoned him close, as if to confide a juicy secret.

"Jonah," she said quietly, "I wanted to thank you for helping Nelson with his vows."

"Huh?" said Jonah, who then silently scolded himself a second later. "I mean, what would ever give you that idea?"

Tamara laughed and pushed a strand of brown hair out of her face. "Jonah, Nelson is really high on you; always complimentary. He tells me all about how good your writing is, and he—" she cast a glance at him while laughed with his mother, "—I love him dearly, but he is hopeless at writing. You should see the Valentine's card he got me." She closed her eyes and chuckled. "Sweet, but I know he couldn't articulate his feelings like that without help. And I thank you for it."

Jonah sighed, relieved. "You're welcome," he conceded. "For the record, though, they were all his words. I just kind of fine-tuned them."

"I know they were." Tamara smiled. "He'll probably want to dance again; I see he managed to prise himself from his mom."

Indeed, Nelson joined them minutes later, clapping Jonah on the shoulder and taking his wife's hand.

"Alright, Jonah!" he said brightly. "Tam, I wanted another dance—"

"Congratulations to the happy couple!" cried a voice from behind them.

That familiar voice made the happiness in Jonah dim within seconds. He turned and looked into a face that he hadn't seen in over a year, but hadn't missed. One quick appraisal, and he saw, with a narrowing of his eyes, that not one thing had changed. Standing there, with the usual flawless strawberry blonde hair, French-tipped nails, and of course, the skimpy, risqué dress, was Jessica Hale.

"Hey, Jessica," said Nelson, much more successful at concealing his disdain than Jonah ever would've been. "And thank you."

"Not at all!" Jessica flashed a smile that did not reach her eyes to Nelson and Tamara. Then her expression fell on Jonah. The smile didn't slip, but her eyes hardened. "And if it isn't Jonah Rowe."

She extended her hand to him for appearance's sake, but Jonah smoothly escaped touching her by running his hand across the condensation on his glass.

"Well damn it, would you look at that," he said as he gave his hand of mock annoyance. "Sorry."

Jessica's eyes flashed, but she withdrew her hand and turned back to the newlyweds. "Here you are," she said, placing a chocolate-brown box in front of them. "A wedding present. Quaint, but quality."

She turned on her heel and began to mingle. Jonah turned deliberately to Nelson.

"What—the—*HELL* is she doing here?" he demanded.

Nelson took a deep breath. "She said she wanted to come long enough to bring a gift. Said she would leave right afterward."

Jonah glanced at Jessica, who wasn't anywhere near the three exits. "She's here to replenish her stores of gossip," he grumbled. "But she'd be hard-pressed to find anything in here."

Tamara leaned in with interest, and chimed in as soon as she got an opening in the conversation. "So that's Jessica, Nelson?" she asked. "The easy, politicking brown-noser from your job?"

"Well, I wouldn't say easy—" said Nelson in an attempt to be delicate to his wife, but she waved her hand.

"Save it, sweetie," she muttered, observing Jessica's less-than-conservative outfit. "That dress and that demeanor say it all. She's probably the type of woman who'll unbutton her blouse halfway and flirt without shame just to get out of a task she doesn't feel like doing."

Jonah and Nelson looked at each other. How could Tamara have been so spot-on?

"It's a good thing it's just her," said Jonah after a minute. "Would've been worse if she'd had her manservant Anthony with her. But she is still a problem, even when she is alone—"

"Well, the two of you needn't worry," said Tamara, who rose with her hand still clasped with Nelson's. "This day has been perfect thus far, and it will *remain* so. If, by chance, she sees fit to infringe upon said perfection, she will have me to deal with. And my mother. And my sisters."

The mere thought of such an unbalanced confrontation was enough to refill Jonah with lightheartedness and mirth. "Why don't you two go release the tension with some dancing?" he said laughingly. "I've got to get back to Reena."

He turned from them and headed to Reena's table. Halfway there, his path got barred by Jessica. Her face was a lesson in condescension.

"So, Jonah, I hear that you've enrolled at a university in some backwater town in the northeastern part of the state," she drawled. "Workforce that inflexible about letting you back into it?"

Jonah's irritation rose as if it were sentient and recalled how it was always at the surface at the sight of this bitch. "Not that it's any of your damn business," he replied, "but the bookstore where I was employed is undergoing extensive repairs from structural damages. My boss has seen fit to rest, recharge his batteries, and take things slowly. I don't have any trouble with the workforce, thank you very much."

Jessica's eyes surveyed Jonah hungrily; she enjoyed getting a rise out of and pushing the buttons of other people more than anything in the world. "Huh. Well, I said a while back that your grand plans would fail. You seem to be adhering to my affirmation."

Jonah hung his head in mock resignation. "You got me there, Jess," he said in a small voice. "But seeing how your assets have yet to get you to the top, I see that you are still compliant with *my* affirmation."

The smile snapped off of Jessica's face. With a smirk, Jonah brushed past her and continued on to Reena.

"Hey again, friend," Jonah said, and plopped down next to her.

Reena turned to him and grinned. Jonah could see that she was wearing her Jarelsien and selenite dampener, which nullified her ability to read people's essences. Jonah was thankful she had it. With all the warring energies in an emotionally -charged setting such as a wedding, she'd be subject to collapse. Seeing as she already had experience with that, no one was interested in a repeat.

"I wanted to tell you before I forgot," he told her, "Tamara's sister told me, in all seriousness, not to let you slip away, because one of these guys in here could pick you from the bunch."

As expected, Reena laughed out loud. "She needn't worry," she said, "but it was awfully nice of her to be concerned for my virtue. By the way," she frowned slightly, "who was that skank who hopped in front of you?"

"Oh, right," muttered Jonah, irritated. "Remember me telling about Jessica Hale, from the accounting firm?" He told Reena all about Jessica Hale; the duplicity, the charm, the politics, the backstabbing, the skimpy skirts.

Reena made a wry face when Jonah was done. "So *that's* that woman," she grumbled. "Little twit. You know that I have no love for women who attempt to advance themselves using their bodies. Does she take pleasure in making all women look bad with her actions?"

"Jessica takes pleasure in a lot of things best not repeated here," replied Jonah. "But have no fear. Tamara informed me and Nelson that if Jessica caused any disturbances, she would sic her mom and sisters on her, and then scour the scraps herself. She was adamant that this day remain perfect."

Reena smiled. "Ah, love. The emotion that will make people go full-blown primal."

Jonah raised an eyebrow. Both Reena's tone and smile were wistful. But then a suspicion reared itself in his mind. "Were you ever in love, Reena?" he pried.

Reena took three bites of her salad, chewed deliberately, and gulped down half of her water before she answered. "Yes. It's been about seven, eight years ago now. Julia Gallagher. I met her at Ballowiness—that's the local rec center in Rome. We were both really intelligent and really athletic. All these guys wanted her, but she never showed any interest in them whatsoever. After a couple weeks of friendship, she told me that those boys did nothing for her because she wanted *me.*"

Reena stopped speaking, and resumed her contemplation of her salad. But Jonah was hooked now; Reena rarely spoke on her past.

"Wasn't easy, I take it?" he asked unnecessarily.

Reena glanced up at Nelson and Tamara once more, and then returned her eyes to Jonah. "At first, it wasn't as hard as you might think," she answered. "It wasn't like we were always together or anything; she went to the Trand High up I-40, coincidentally where Trip does most of his substitute teaching now," Jonah snorted, "and I went to Caulfield High, the rival. We'd act like we were sworn enemies at meets, and then meet later at night in the town square or at Ballowiness and spend hours together. It was great…every second of it was great."

Reena laughed softly, but ceased shortly thereafter. Jonah allowed her time to collect her thoughts, and then plunged once more.

"What happened?"

"I messed up, Jonah," said Reena without hesitation. "I snuck a letter in her car one time. Lodged it in the steering wheel cover. Unfortunately, her *dad* was the one driving it that day."

Jonah winced. Reena caught the expression and nodded.

"Yeah, it was like that," she told him.

"So what did her father do?"

"Simply put, he went nuclear," Reena replied. "He sent Julia to some fundamentalist bible camp. Paid for her to get therapy in Raleigh. Branded me scum after he found out how my family did me. Funny thing, though? Julia didn't stop seeing me. She even smuggled her phone into the stupid camp to talk to me at night. So her dad went below the belt. She'd gotten accepted into Princeton. It was no small feat, and it was her one-way ticket out of Rome, N.C. Her dad told her that if she didn't break up with me, he wouldn't pay the tuition."

"*Are you frickin' serious?*" demanded Jonah.

"Oh yeah," said Reena. "But even then, she refused. She was willing to go to LTSU to stay with me. She was going to blow off the Ivy League for me."

Comprehension dawned on Jonah. He didn't know how he knew, but he did. Reena looked at him, which was enough to confirm his suspicion.

"You set her free."

Reena nodded. "Hardest thing I've ever done, next to losing my uncle. I told her that I'd always love her, gave her this ring—," she extended the last finger of her right hand and revealed a ring with a smooth surface that showed two female symbols joined at the stem, "—and told her to never lose faith in love."

Jonah was stunned. "Profound words for an eighteen-year old," he commented.

"I'm a profound woman, Jonah," said Reena.

"So how come you have it back?" asked Jonah. "That ring, I mean. I've never seen it before."

"You wouldn't have," Reena muttered. "I just got it back two weeks ago. Julia sent it back to me, with a note attached that said that she hadn't lost faith in love, but she found it in the traditional way. She has some job in finance in Princeton, and she's also married, with a daughter on the way."

At that moment, Jonah got summoned by someone for a conversation. He held up one finger. There was no way in hell he was going to leave Reena so bummed out and raw. Not when everyone else was elated.

"Was she trying to imply that she was going through a phase?" he questioned.

"Seems that way," said Reena quietly. "But whatever. It's in the past. What do you always say? It was what it was."

Jonah didn't buy that Reena was over it, but he felt like he got all that she was willing to give. He glanced at that ring. "I remember your ability to get people's essences off of objects," he said. "Did you get any of her essence off that ring before you cleansed it?"

Reena looked at the ring and sighed. "I don't like being this way, Jonah," she told him instead of answering. "Sometimes, I feel like if I could drop it, I would. I'd give anything to be…normal."

"Now hold on Reena—" began Jonah with disbelief, but Reena interrupted him.

"Think about what I said before you respond, Jonah," she said in a calm tone. "I do not mean my being gay."

Jonah frowned, but then his expression cleared. "Oh," he said. "You mean being an Eleventh Percenter."

He knew that Reena had it rough. Her ethereality was a little different from his own (which had complexities that he still didn't understand), or their other best friend, Terrence, whose ethereality was almost purely strength-based. In addition to her preternatural speed and cold-spot ability, Reena was also a very powerful essence reader, and had to take certain measures to keep that sensitivity from overwhelming her. She was quite adept at it nowadays, but it still had to be a hassle at times.

"You don't need to think that way, Reena," he said in a consoling tone. "You're fine just the way you are, friend. I'm sure that there is no one at the estate who would want you any other way. Everyone looks up to you; you're one of the leaders at the estate! And besides," he waved an impatient hand, "what the hell is *normal* anyway? Who can define what that is? Don't you worry, Reena. Follow your own advice, and don't lose faith."

Reena smiled faintly, and took Jonah's hand and gripped it. "You're a great friend, Jonah," she said. "Terrence, too. Speaking of Terrence, do you know when he is returning from Maui?"

"Oh yeah," said Jonah quickly. "Five days from now. He promised to come back and cook us all the dishes he sampled there. But never mind that now. I want you to cheer up, Reena! What do I have to do to help out with that?"

Reena's eyes widened slightly. "Anything?"

"Sure," said Jonah without thinking.

Her expression went devilish. "Then I want you to go up there and do that stupid line dancing they've got going on right now. It just started, I was watching."

Jonah's determination faded. "Are you serious?"

"Uh-huh," she replied simply.

"But I can't dance!" protested Jonah.

"Then you're in luck," snorted Reena, "because half of the people up there are too drunk to do much better than you."

Jonah shook his head. "Reena, you don't want to see me dance," he warned her. "You'll lose all respect for me."

"Not possible, Jonah," disagreed Reena. "We've been through too much. You *did* say you'd do anything."

Jonah couldn't say anything. Reena nailed him. But it seemed that he'd had the desired effect. She no longer looked somber. In fact, she looked as if she anticipated seeing Jonah provide comedy on the dance floor.

Whatever.

"Fine, Reena," he relented. "But there's one thing. I know that I owed you for dressing up and coming with me. If I do this, we're square, right?"

Reena sat back in her chair. "Depends on how amusing this is," she replied. "Now as they used to say, go cut yourself a slice of rug!"

2

Movin'

On to the next task. Nelson's wedding was in the books, and he and Tamara were on their way to the Poconos for a two-week honeymoon. Jonah, meanwhile, worked in an urgency of his own as he busily packed the remaining items he planned to bring with him to the estate.

"Never thought I'd be doing this again," he muttered to Reena as he zipped his gym bag. "I feel like I'm back home, nervous as hell, packing for undergrad."

Reena slung another of Jonah's bags onto the couch and relaxed her weight on the side of it. "In many ways, you are doing just that," she replied. "New life, new things."

"Thankfully, it isn't *all* new," said Jonah, more than relieved by that fact. "I know the people I'm living with, and I know where I'm staying. It's just being back in college again—with kids."

"Jonah, it's not like you're forty years old in a class of eighteen-year olds that are barely out of pampers," she deadpanned. "And just think—Bobby, Liz, and Douglas go to LTSU as well. They'll help you fit right in. Liz was overjoyed when she found out you would take her suggestion."

It had been Liz Manville's idea that Jonah enroll at LTSU after his place of employment got pulverized. Jonah did it with very little protest, and he was anxious to get started in the Creative Writing program there. Also, he'd be an official full-time resident at the Grannison-Morris estate with his friends. Jonah also couldn't forget that it was a welcome distraction from what he'd recently experienced in the city. He'd come face to face, yet again, with Creyton, but that time, he was in a cunning disguise and had gone by his first name, Roger. Since Creyton had been disguised, he had easily infiltrated all their lives, and they had unwittingly provided almost every detail he needed to go through with his plans—

Jonah gave himself a mental shake. Why was he thinking about that now? It was over and done with. Plus he'd need all his wits about him on this new phase of life he was about to take.

"It was very nice and thoughtful of you to sublease your apartment to Nelson and Tamara," said Reena.

"You have no idea," said Jonah, thankful of the excuse to put his mind on other things. "I know that they will only be here a year at most, but Nelson was living in an efficiency studio; basically a glorified bachelor pad. You should have seen his face when Tamara asked to come back to his place the very first time. I'm doing him a favor, but he deserves it. Well, we'd better head on out now, friend."

Jonah wrote a quick note for Nelson and left it on the kitchen counter for when he and Tamara returned from Pennsylvania. Then, after he tied up some loose ends with the landlord, he and Reena were off. Jonah had been steadily moving his stuff for the past three weeks, so the two gym bags in his trunk were the only things left that needed transport. There would be no usage of the *Astralimes* today, as Jonathan did not allow that power to be abused, so road trip it was. That was completely alright with Jonah, because the scenery on the highway, the sight of the quasi-urban buildings giving way to fields and trees, and the pleasant conversation with Reena whittled away the time most satisfactorily. Indeed, in no time at all, they were off the highway and at 927 Jay Houston Road, where their friends, Bobby and Alvin Decessio, resided.

"This is the address, isn't it?" asked Jonah, who uncertainly pulled into the driveway.

"You really think I'd let you get it wrong?" said Reena with narrow eyes.

"Oh yeah—of course not."

"Let's go on in. Terrence will be showing up any minute, and of course, Bobby and Alvin will want to see you."

When Jonah and Reena stepped out of the car, their muscles felt full of gratitude for being released from the space. Jonah regarded the Decessio home, and took in every detail.

It was a two-story brick house that was comfortably placed between a white house on the left and an aquamarine house on the right (Jonah wondered momentarily what that owner of the latter had been thinking). The porch was spacious enough for lounging, which put Jonah in mind of Fourth of July grilling and comfortable birthday parties. He had been raised in a small, five-room home, and had spent his adult years either in dorms or apartments, so he could see why Alvin, Bobby, and Terrence, who had been adopted into the family at thirteen, loved this house so much.

Jonah and Reena made it about four paces when they heard a shout of welcome from the family room, followed by the front door banging open. Bobby was out the door first, followed by his older brother Alvin, and they were followed by two people who could only be their parents.

Mr. Decessio was tall and burly, like an athlete who'd retired, but had taken the steps necessary to not go to seed. It was no mystery which parent Bobby took after the most. Mrs. Decessio was a slight-framed woman with a friendly face that was lined, but not hardened by any means. She vaguely reminded Jonah of some of the women his grandmother had been friends with in her church when he was younger. As the four of them came to greet him and Reena, Jonah noticed something else: Bobby had gotten his father's bulk, but his mother's height.

"Jonah!" said Bobby exuberantly. "Reena! 'Bout time you got here! How are you?"

He took Jonah's hand in both of his and shook vigorously, while Alvin gave Reena a hug. Mr. Decessio shook Jonah's hand next, and regarded him with interest.

"It's nice to finally put a face with a name, Jonah," he said. "Terrence, Bobby, and Alvin have told us all about you. So is it true that you're going back to school?"

"Yes, sir," said Jonah. "I'm getting back to my writing."

"Oh," said Mrs. Decessio with sudden interest. "So you're going into the Creative Writing program. You had better keep focused in there; Bobby has told me all about how that woman who teaches it is quite a distraction."

She threw a stern look at her youngest son, who stared back innocently.

"Mom, what's the problem with noticing a good-looking, single, older woman?" he asked.

"I'll answer that," muttered Reena. "Liz."

Bobby face went red. "Shut up," he managed, but soon, all of them were laughing.

"How are you doing, Alvin?" asked Jonah.

"Doing well, thanks," said Alvin in his usual preoccupied-sounding voice. "And also," he added in an undertone as they stepped up the steps to the porch, "Bobby is way off. Calling Professor Rayne *good-looking* is a tragic understatement. She is *gorgeous.*"

Dear Lord, thought Jonah, *I need to hurry up and meet this woman myself.*

They all seated themselves in the chairs on the Decessio porch, where Mr. Decessio eyed Jonah once more.

"So Jonah," he said, "where did you grow up, exactly?"

"In a town named Radner, sir," responded Jonah. "It's in the northeastern part of the state, about twenty minutes from the state line."

"Huh," said Mr. Decessio. "Can't say I've ever heard of that place."

Jonah snorted. "I assure you, sir, no one has heard of Radner but the two hundred people who have resigned themselves to live there," he said.

Bobby looked at Jonah like he'd grown an extra limb. "You grew up in a town with only *two hundred* people?" he demanded.

"Yeah," said Jonah, who widened his eyes in dramatic fashion. "Kind of makes Rome—with its population of five thousand people—seem like Nirvana, huh?"

Everyone laughed again, and Jonah randomly turned his head so as to crack the slightly stiff muscles there.

His face froze in that direction.

At the street corner, which was visible from the house, was a very tall hooded man. He was so tall that it seemed like the top of his head was almost level with the bottom of the stop sign. Jonah blinked, but in that space of time, the man was gone.

"Jonah, what's wrong?" asked Reena.

Jonah's gaze remained on that spot, despite the fact that there was no longer anything to see there. "Nothing," he lied. "I—I just thought I saw Terrence."

"Nope!" called a familiar voice. "Because I'm right here!"

They all turned, and the weird occurrence vanished from Jonah's mind. Terrence was there, with a big grin on his face. He was clad in khaki shorts and a Hawaiian shirt almost as bright as his grin.

Everyone made a beeline for him, and there were hugs all around. Terrence laughed and seemed to brace himself so as to avoid being knocked over by the six people invading his personal space.

"Where did you come from, boy?" demanded a grinning Mrs. Decessio. "We were out here to greet you!"

"I know!" said Terrence mischievously. "I told the driver to pass by the house! I paid him extra to make a loop and drop me off a street over so I could sneak up on you!"

"You BUM!" laughed Bobby. He and Alvin grabbed Terrence's shoulders and practically marched him up the porch and into the house.

* * *

Terrence regaled them for hours on end with stories about the vacation. It was obvious that he enjoyed the rapt attention from everyone present. Terrence was giddy as hell as he described everything in great detail, using his deeply tanned hands to animatedly accentuate the most exciting points. Jonah couldn't help but feel a little jealous of his friend for two reasons. He had never even been on the western coast of the United States, let alone Hawaii. And he also knew that Terrence, who ate enough to feed a small football team, had undoubtedly tried every cuisine that was available. Hell, he probably had two helpings of everything. Despite that, he hadn't gained one pound to show for it. Terrence actually looked *thinner* than he had the last time they'd seen him. Jonah just couldn't understand how someone could have such bulletproof fat cells.

"You would not believe the people that just stay for weeks on end," said Terrence with incredulity. "I mean, my brother and his family do that, of course, but he a retired, rich football star. Some of those other folks, though—they ain't famous or anything. Just retirees and whatnot."

"I wouldn't mind retiring there," said Mrs. Decessio longingly. "Just think, Arn; going to Hawaii for two or three whole months, and staying in one of those vacation rentals. Would be nice to get away from where everyone knows everything about you."

Mr. Decessio smiled. "Now Connie, we've been here thirty-four years, and haven't ever had bad experiences living here."

"No, we haven't," conceded Mrs. Decessio. "Relocating from New Jersey to here was a great decision. But there isn't anything wrong with changing things up every now and again."

Reena, who had been born in Hawaii and lived there for several years before her family relocated to Virginia, thumbed through Terrence's pictures with interest, while Bobby grilled Terrence about sports.

"Well, they do have rugby there," Terrence remarked.

"Rugby?" said Bobby, raising an eyebrow in skepticism. "Did you play some?"

"What do you think?" Terrence asked. "Lloyd wouldn't have had it any other way. It's pretty sick and painful without those pads they have in football."

Bobby's eyes narrowed. Jonah knew that if anyone questioned his beloved football, there would be hell to pay. Damage control time.

"We all know that the awesome vacation opportunity was only a small part of why you went," he said to Terrence. "So how did the reconnection go with Lloyd?"

"Oh," responded Terrence, and some of the elation replaced by seriousness. "We had plenty of time to talk. It turned out that he didn't share many of the opinions his parents had about me. It was a breath of fresh air to voice our views on things without that man and woman there to influence them."

Terrence took a deep breath. It was clear to Jonah that his adoptive parents' treatment of him was still a sore subject.

"Anyway, he told me that now that he had his own wife and kids, he was pleased with his life and didn't want any more bad blood," continued Terrence. "He wanted us to have the chance to be the brothers as adults that his parents didn't let us be as kids. So all is well, and the ill will is gone."

"That's good to know, son," said Mr. Decessio. "I appreciate the fact that Lloyd was mature enough to feel that way."

"Besides all that," said Bobby, whom Jonah was glad to see had been successfully distracted from the football jab, "you get to have four brothers now!"

"No complaints there," snorted Terrence. "Family's growing by the second. Hey, Mom, what's good for dinner?"

Shortly thereafter, the majority of the conversation ceased due to the Mrs. Decessio's glorious meal of baked chicken, crescent rolls, potatoes, and salad, topped off with apple cobbler and vanilla ice cream. Reena happily partook in the chicken, salad, and potatoes, but respectfully declined the dessert. Jonah, Terrence, Bobby, and Alvin had no such reservations.

"Man, I shouldn't have eaten like that," commented Jonah. "I feel like my system still hasn't fully recovered from that wedding food."

Reena cast stern eyes on him, but she made no comments. It was a celebratory dinner, after all.

"Wonderful, Ma, as always," said Bobby, who rose from the table and kissed Mrs. Decessio on the cheek. "Now if you'll excuse me, I'm going to go change into some looser pants, and then play some Madden."

He left, and several minutes later, Alvin did, too. Reena offered to help with the dishes, but Mrs. Decessio, a self-proclaimed "kitchen general," kindly passed on the assistance. So Jonah, Terrence, and Reena retreated to Terrence's bedroom, which was upstairs, and opposite Alvin's.

Jonah hadn't ever seen Terrence's room at his home, but it just looked like an extension of his room at the estate: Clothing strewn on the floor, across the bed, and across the weight bench near the window, an eclectic assortment of CDs that featured his beloved alt-rock and metal bands, a closet that appeared to be bursting at the seams, and, plastered across the wall near the bed, was the grinning depiction of his beloved Duke Blue Devils.

"Don't ever leave me alone in here," scoffed Jonah. "I'm liable to burn that damn thing."

Terrence flopped on the bed, and regarded the poster with reverence. "If you manage to succeed," he replied, "I have another one in the closet, and two up in my room at the estate."

"Oh great," said Jonah, shaking his head. "Just great."

"It's great to be home," said Terrence as he rested his eyes.

"Really?" said Reena. "After being in Hawaii, you're glad to be back in *Rome?*"

"Don't get me wrong," said Terrence, whose eyes were still closed. "I adored Hawaii. Adored everything about it. But I don't think I could do those two, three month vacations like rich folks do. Just seems like the novelty would wear off."

"Speak for yourself," said Jonah. "I would force myself to grow accustomed to extended vacations if I could afford them."

"Well publish some of those books you've got, and Reena and I could follow you everywhere."

"I wouldn't have to if you pitched an idea to the Food Network," retorted Jonah.

Terrence flung a pillow at him, which sailed past his head and landed awkwardly on the edge of the chest of drawers near Terrence's window. Jonah reached for it, which allowed him to glance out of the window for a moment.

He saw the tall figure again. The man was at a different sign this time, and unless Jonah was mistaken, the figure, even from a distance, had his face trained in his direction.

Jonah blinked, but this time, it had no effect. The man wore a dark duster (which was odd by itself, seeing as how it was midsummer and there wasn't a chill in the air at all), and he was also hooded. Unlike Jonah's previous encounters with hooded, faceless figures, this person *did* have a face. The bottom half of the man's face was covered, similar to an old west bandit or something.

The figure also seemed tense, as if he fought the urge to lash out and attack someone or something. Jonah almost went into Spectral Sight (that was how he'd known something was up with Roger way back when), but he didn't. Terrence and Reena would know for sure that something was up.

"What say you, Jonah?" said Terrence's voice from somewhere. "Jonah?"

"Uh?"

"*Jonah.*"

It was as if someone slapped him, but then Jonah realized that he'd been hit with another one of Terrence's pillows.

"Huh? What?"

"I asked if you were up to playing some Madden with Bobby," said Terrence. "You were completely zoned out."

"Yeah," murmured Jonah, who chanced a glance out of the window again, but saw no one. "Sorry."

"You alright, man?"

"Oh yeah, of course," said Jonah hastily. "I'm great."

But then Jonah noticed, with a trace of apprehension, that Reena didn't have on her dampener, which meant that his essence was susceptible to reading. She gave Jonah a look that said, *No, you aren't alright,* but Jonah wasn't going to comply. Not today, at least. This was a happy occasion, and he wouldn't mar it with thoughts of suspicion and alarm.

"I'd love to play some Madden," he said with conviction. "It'd be just the thing to change the mental pace."

Jonah, Terrence, Reena, and Bobby spent three days at the Decessio residence, partly because Terrence wanted extra time with his parents, and partly because they were such pleasant company that no one really wanted to leave any sooner than that. At times, Jonah caught himself just observing Alvin's and Bobby's interactions with their parents; that whole "nuclear family" dynamic. It was also so admirable that they treated Terrence like another son. Like he'd been there all along, and hadn't been taken in as an adolescent. Jonah had only had his grandmother, and she was as wonderful a woman as could be. But her great qualities never extended to Jonah's extended family. To this day, they were pretty much strangers to him. This must be what a true family unit entailed.

It was a great thing to behold. Jonah hoped that Alvin, Terrence, and Bobby knew what they had, and always appreciated it.

They were back at the estate around noon on a pleasant but very hot August day. Jonah never got tired of nor accustomed to the Grannison-Morris estate. The gardens were always pristine, and the innumerable trees that surrounded the estate never felt claustrophobic or off-putting. If anything, Jonah thought that it felt like protection. The trees seemed like a barrier to any extraneous forces that dared threaten any Eleventh Percenter here. At this moment, Jonah felt like he was in the safest place in the world, and that was no small feat, given some of the experiences he'd had since he'd discovered the place.

A shriek of delight jarred him from his thoughts, and he was nearly blown over by a blond blur. Someone had just run up and thrown themselves into Bobby's arms. Bobby, who didn't even seem to care about the fresh dirt that was now smeared on the back of his T-shirt, reciprocated the embrace, and lifted the girl off of her feet.

Jonah and Terrence looked at each other and shook their heads. It was Liz Manville; who else would have been so excited to see Bobby?

"Um, we're here, too, Liz," laughed Reena, and Liz detached herself from Bobby. Bright-eyed and chipper as ever, Liz had to be playfully restrained by Reena before she bestowed an earth-laced hug on everyone.

"Oh, right." The smile never left her face as she pulled off the filthy gloves, tossed them aside, and hugged everyone else. "I saw you coming up the drive!" she announced. "I think I trampled some flowers when I dropped them to run up here! Vera and I were collecting carnations for some of my new solutions."

Jonah turned, and realized that Liz's zealous welcome had distracted everyone from the second figure, who'd approached at a more leisurely pace.

Vera was dressed for gardening, and was as dirtied up and sweaty as Liz was. She dispensed with her straw hat and smiled at everyone. Her face flushed somewhat when her smile reached Jonah. As Jonah took in Vera's brown-blonde hair that was pulled back in two haphazard bunches, as well as the barely noticeable scar that ran along the base of her jaw, he felt his own face warm. But he didn't think anything of it. It was a hot, sticky August day, and they were all feeling it. His face was warm because of the sun beating down on it, and Vera's face was flushed with color due to heat and gardening. Yeah, that was it.

"Hey all!" she said.

"Hey, Vera," said Jonah, patting her shoulder. "How goes it?"

"I'm doing a lot better than the last time you saw me," Vera joked, but she indeed looked like the picture of perfect health. The last time Jonah saw her, she'd been convalescing from two sprained wrists, cuts, and first-degree burns that she'd sustained after being taken hostage and having her ethereality abused. Which reminded Jonah of something.

"Vera, how is your training going?" he asked. "Jonathan said that he was going to help you better manage your ethereality."

"Oh, Jonah," said Vera with excitement, which Jonah thought was a rather odd response, because Jonathan made it seem like it'd be strenuous, "it's some of the most fun I've had in years! The spirits and guides that Jonathan put me with are awesome; they're even better than some of *living* teachers I had back in school! Oh, sorry—life never ends...anyway, I'm still a minute early for everything. There isn't anything that can be done about that."

"Ah well," said Jonah, "that sounds like a small price to pay."

His attention shifted to Bobby. "So, are you two official now?"

Liz and Bobby grinned, but neither of them answered. They didn't have to.

"Although," said Terrence shrewdly, "maybe we shouldn't be talking about *them.*"

His gaze slid downward, along with Liz's, Reena's, and Bobby's. Puzzled, Jonah and Vera followed suit. At some point in his conversation with Vera, Jonah's fingers descended from her shoulder and joined hers. Neither of them had noticed that they were freaking *holding hands.* The fact was made more comical by the fact that Vera, unlike Liz, hadn't removed her gardening gloves, so Jonah's bare fingers were entwined with Vera's filthy gloved ones. Embarrassed, they both let go. Everyone snickered, but Jonah noticed that hint of wistfulness in Reena's smile again.

"Let me get my last two bags in here," he said, once again blaming the August weather for the heat in his face. "It's beyond time to get settled in."

Before Jonah and Terrence reached Jonah's room, however, there were more friends to greet. Maxine Pearson waved from a corner, the usual Anime book in her hands. Magdalena Cespedes and Melvin Price broke their conversation and greeted them with hugs and high-fives. Royal Spader had changed his hair, which was no longer long and reddish-orange, but short, spiked, and jet black. He nodded glumly at Jonah and Terrence, and then returned to a game of solitaire. Jonah knew why he was of low spirits; he was no doubt dismayed that

Liz and Bobby were now a couple, and he was doomed to continue his role as unrequited observer.

"And still, he wonders why Lizzie never notices him," he sighed to Terrence. "Yeah, he's smart—exceptionally smart—but he uses that to con and finagle people out of money."

"Jonah, Liz doesn't notice Spader because he is two years younger than her, dresses like a goth bum, and has yet to discover the benefits of a shaving razor," said Terrence. "But he's seventeen; there are plenty of other girls—"

"None like Liz," countered Jonah.

Terrence turned it over in his head. "That's true," he conceded. "For *Spader*, anyway."

They saw Karin Tanke and Grayson Morris, who didn't bother to acknowledge either of them. That didn't matter though, because Jonah wasn't pleased by their presence, either. He had neither the time nor the tolerance for lackeys.

Karin, a tall woman with vividly dyed red hair, and Grayson, a brawny bumpkin who wore a scowl almost as much as he wore clothing, were two friends (if you called sycophantic suck-ups *friends*) of Titus Rivers III, who preferred to be called Trip. Trip's and Jonah's hatred of one another was planted when they met, punctured earth when Jonah accidentally slugged him once in a training, and came into full bloom when Jonah saved his physical life from evil minions. Trip was a superb saxophonist and was a proficient Eleventh Percenter, with a power over sound. But beyond that, Jonah saw no redeeming qualities. Despite his brusque demeanor and sour disposition, he'd attracted cronies and admirers; Karin and Grayson were just two of them. They had no love for Jonah, especially at the present time, because he had been responsible for the revelation of an epic blunder that Trip made. The blunder resulted in heavy disciplinary action for Trip, who took a sabbatical from the estate to visit his mother in Orangeburg.

"So the bastard isn't back, huh?" asked Jonah.

"How should I know?" replied Terrence. "I just got back myself. But I'll take a stab in the dark and say no. They would look less angry if their Lord and Master graced us with his presence."

When they finally reached the stairs, they saw Douglas Chandler, who looked as glum as Spader had. His black hair, which was usually cropped to a neat Caesar, had grown out somewhat and was pressed down in places due to Douglas's fingers.

"Hey, Doug," greeted Jonah. "What's up with you?"

Douglas looked up at Jonah and Terrence so piteously that it wasn't even funny. "No takers for the chess club at LTSU," he answered.

"*That's it?!*" said Terrence without tact. "That ain't a big—"

Jonah whacked him on the shoulder.

"*Ow,* I mean—Doug, that sucks."

Luckily, Douglas hadn't noticed any of the interaction, as he'd buried his head in his hands again. "This is my senior year," he groused. "I founded the club as a freshman, and nobody joined. Sophomore year, the same. A lovely girl joined last year, but she only did it because she needed to be a member of at least one club to be eligible for some cruise. She quit as soon as she got her passport."

Terrence looked at Jonah as though he saw him in a new light. Jonah returned the look, puzzled, but then he realized the reason. He mouthed, "*No!*" to Terrence, but it didn't matter.

"Jonah is at LTSU now, Doug! He can join your club!"

Jonah narrowed his eyes at Terrence, who smirked, but Douglas was completely oblivious. He looked at Jonah with renewed hope.

"R-Really?" he cried. "Jonah, do you play chess?"

"Dude, the closest I've ever come to chess was when I accidentally knocked a pawn into a paint can in high school," said Jonah. "I don't know a thing about the game."

"Doesn't matter!" dismissed Douglas, "You don't even have to play! I promise you that! Just join, please!"

In what he must have thought was a surreptitious gesture, Douglas moved his hand from Jonah's line of sight and crossed his fingers. With another dark look at Terrence, Jonah heard himself say, "All right, Douglas. I'll join your—club. It'd be an honor."

Douglas's smile resembled a child who'd just received candy and crayons. "Thank you," he breathed. "Thank you so much! You won't regret this, Jonah!"

He rose and dashed off.

"He was so happy," commented Terrence. "I thought he was gonna wet his chinos."

"Tell me," grunted Jonah as they went upstairs, "why exactly am I your friend again?"

"Because without me, you'd be socially awkward," replied Terrence, "and you'd lack the proper motivation to do good deeds for people, like Doug!"

Jonah rolled his eyes. "Terrence, I'm going to get Malcolm to make me a ball bat, and then I'll beat you with it."

"Well, if you give me two weeks, I can do that," said a voice.

Malcolm had just exited a bathroom when Jonah and Terrence passed it, where he'd just finished placing a wooden swan over the sink. He had another creation in tow; symmetrical hands joined in prayer atop a marble foundation.

"Like it?" asked Malcolm when he noticed Jonah's and Terrence's eyes on it. "Reverend Abbott's birthday is coming up, so I thought I'd make him a little something."

"Huh," said Terrence. "What is that, the seventh?"

Malcolm smirked. "Yeah, actually," he answered.

Jonah just laughed. Malcolm was a perfectionist. He'd craft and re-craft creations dozens of times before he declared himself pleased.

"Keep it up, Malcolm," said Terrence.

Finally, they reached Jonah's room. That was awesome for Jonah; with all the starts, stops, and socializing, his shoulder and arms began to protest against the travel bag. He dropped it on the floor, flexed his arm, and sat down. He was only mildly surprised when he felt movement near his feet.

"Hey, Bast," he said. "Great to see you, too."

Pleased to be acknowledged, Bast stretched and settled near his feet. "*I hope that your travels were enjoyable, Jonah,*" she intimated. "*And Terrence, how was Maui?*"

"Bast, you have no idea—"

Terrence's words were interrupted by Reena, who slipped into the room and shut the door.

"Alright, Jonah," she said, her face two parts concerned and two parts intractable. "Now, you are going to tell us what had you so rattled back at Terrence's parent's house."

Terrence, initially annoyed by the interruption, now look baffled, but Jonah shook his head. He knew Reena had picked up on his essence. He'd just half-hoped she'd let it go. Nope.

"Wait, what happened at my house?" asked Terrence. "Did Mom and Dad do something?"

"No, Terrence, it had nothing to do with them," said Jonah. His eyes never left Reena, and hers never left him. "Before the cab dropped you off, I saw a man at the stop sign. He vanished when I looked again, so I thought my eyes were just playing tricks on me or something. But then I saw him again when we were all in your bedroom, ragging on Duke. I looked out of the window and saw him again. He was there just a little bit longer that time, but he vanished again."

"There was a man at my house?" demanded Terrence.

"No, Terrence, not exactly," said Jonah. "It was almost like—like he was there for me or something. I don't know."

"What did he look like?" inquired Reena.

"Tall," said Jonah. "Like, really tall; 6'8" or 6'9" or something. He had on a black duster, a dark hooded shirt, black boots, and half of his face was covered, like a cowboy bandit."

Reena's breath caught, and her eyes widened. Terrence looked at her in confusion.

"What does that mean?" he asked, but Reena ignored him. Her eyes were still on Jonah.

"Are you sure?" she asked.

"Yeah, I'm sure," Jonah answered. "What's wrong, Reena?"

For some reason, Bast looked tense as well. She slunk over to Reena, who'd sighed and freed her hair from its clasp. She put her hands to her forehead, like her mind was frontloading information before she could actually process it. This reaction had Jonah quite unnerved at this point.

"Reena," he attempted, "what does that mean? What is the matter?"

"The outfit you described," she said slowly, "it's not good. Jonah, this is not good. You just described the attire of a Spirit Reaper."

Jonah and Terrence looked at each other.

"What?" said Jonah. "Spirit Reaper?"

"And not just any Spirit Reaper," Reena continued. "That's the attire of the Spirit Reapers who followed Creyton."

3

ScarYous

Jonah stared at her.

"Spirit Reaper?"

"Yes," nodded Reena.

"One of Creyton's?"

"Mmm hmm."

Jonah looked over at Terrence, whose shock mirrored his own. He shook his head. "No, Reena, Creyton is gone. Vanquished."

"I didn't say *Creyton*," said Reena impatiently, "I said *followers*. He had a bunch of them, after all."

"He had a bunch of followers?" Jonah demanded. "He used minions! Stupid spirits!"

"Not always, Jonah," said Terrence out of nowhere. "He had other Eleventh Percenters for the longest time. But then…he just stopped. Started using minions. I'm guessing that Creyton planned to recall them at some point, but—then you took him out. Then you took him out a second time."

Jonah looked down at those words. He didn't enjoy thinking about coming across Creyton in disguise. "So I take it that they are probably still around somewhere, angry and confused about being leaderless. But I wonder what this particular guy's thing is. Is he stalking me? Is it a vendetta?"

"Your guess is as good as mine," answered Reena. "But we need to talk to Jonathan, and he can contact the Networkers."

"Networkers?"

"They monitor and police ethereal crimes," explained Reena. "Has anyone told you about the Phasmastis Curaie?"

"I did," mumbled Terrence.

"That's the Spectral High Court," continued Reena. "Ethereal crimes aren't handled by Tenth police, obviously. Spectral Law practitioners do that. Go one step above *their* pay grade, and you have the Networkers."

Jonah gave a shaky laugh. "And Networkers is the best term they could come up with for themselves?"

"Don't joke about them, Jonah," said Terrence in an uncharacteristically serious voice. "The Networkers call themselves that term on account of the vast network they have and need to do their jobs. They are like—the elite of the elite. Dad, Raymond and Sterling are full of praise and respect for them."

"Got it," said Jonah. "So Jonathan can contact them, nab this freak, and we'll all be okay. I won't worry about it. I've spent too much time worried as it is."

Terrence looked convinced, but Reena, even with the dampener around her neck, didn't appear to have taken in one word of Jonah's proclamation. To be honest, neither did Jonah.

Jonah was honest about being tired of worrying, but that didn't stop him from feeling as such. It unnerved him, seeing that weird man standing there, so still that he could have been marble. To see him in a neighborhood of such great people like Terrence's parents almost made Jonah ill, but the he remembered: Anyone who had past dealings with Creyton would be looking to take him out. Terrence's parents could very well be safe, because they weren't the ones who screwed up the evil agenda. That distinction was Jonah's alone.

With that happy thought, he headed for the door. "I'm hungry," he said. "Terrence, let's find food. You can tell me all about Hawaiian cuisine while we eat."

"Jonah, it's okay to be—" Reena began, but Terrence cut her off.

"You know I love to eat," he said. "And Jonah, I'm gonna have a field day recreating some of those dishes."

Reena looked very annoyed as they left the room. Jonah thought he heard her mumble something about "*Pig-headed men*" as she re-tied her hair.

Jonah was glad to resume training, but it wasn't so pleasant once he realized just how out of practice he was. He'd acquired a spiritual endowment from a placid-faced spiritess, and his performance matched her countenance. He got tagged by a strike from Terrence that he probably should have been able to block, and then Grayson, a sly smile on his face, attempted a cheap shot by aiming to hook Jonah's leg with his chain. Jonah realized the trick at the very last moment, and tossed a baton, which hit Grayson full in the face and broke his nose. Bloodied and livid, Grayson charged Jonah, but Jonathan, Alvin, Bobby, and several others quelled the chance for any malicious melee. Jonah didn't know how to feel; annoyed that he'd been prevented from letting off steam, relieved that Grayson hadn't gotten hold of him, or amused that, in the course of breaking them apart, several side scuffles started between some of Trip's other lackeys and Jonah's friends.

Jonathan, who had zero tolerance for internal skirmishes, shouted with an almost feral quality. Everyone involved in the fray, Jonah included, found themselves sprawled on the ground, disoriented and baffled. Jonathan moved to the center of them all, looking something like an angered spider at the core of a fractured web.

"Ladies and gentlemen," he said in a calm but menacing tone, "we will not resolve conflicts this way. The point of these trainings is to hone your skills while endowed and to promote cohesion. We are not here to expend energy with attempts to measure dicks."

He shot a scathing look at Grayson, but a strangely stern one at Jonah, which clearly said, "*You are more mature than this.*"

Jonah was furious. Why the hell should he be rebuked for a reaction? Grayson started the entire mess when he tried to yank Jonah off of his feet with that stupid chain, so he took retaliatory action. Why should he be penalized?? Why should he have to be the mature one? He couldn't get angry when someone attempted to hurt him? He couldn't process natural emotion because he was more mature than this?

"Grayson, cool your heels over there." Jonathan pointed to a large cedar. "And Jonah, over there."

Jonah trudged over to his designated cool off area, which was one of the benches that were present for trainee's rest periods. He still seethed over being treated like a kid. Training recommenced, and he whittled time away wondering whether or not he could hit Grayson from a distance. As he contemplated proper trajectory, a voice broke his concentration.

"Why are you so angry, huh? You did hit him first, after all."

Jonah saw the smug, unshaven face of Spader. What the hell did he want?

"What Jonathan did was necessary," he continued. "You need to cool off, man."

Jonah grimaced. He'd be damned if he'd be Spader's outlet for frustration. It wasn't his fault that Liz chose Bobby, and was barely aware that Spader was in the world.

A retort was at the tip of his tongue, but then he realized that he still possessed an endowment, and had a potential revenge. He edged his hand behind his back, and willed a portion of wind to come into his palm. While Spader flashed that devilish smile, Jonah smiled back, which caught Spader by surprise.

"Spader," he asked, "does that flannel keep you warm?"

Spader raised an eyebrow, taken aback. "What kind of question is that?"

"A simple one," replied Jonah. "Does it, or no?"

"It manages, I guess—what is your game, Jonah?"

"Just wanted you to stay comfortable," said Jonah with a grin, and without any further warning than that, he flung the wind he'd gathered smack into Spader's chest. He staggered directly into the path of Reena's cold-spot trick, which she meant for Magdalena. Spader got the full blast of it, and he collapsed in a shivering heap. Reena glanced over at Jonah, puzzled, but Jonah developed a profound interest in his sneakers. He glanced at her for a half-second, and she stifled a grin.

Not too long after that, training ceased, and everyone trekked back up the path to the estate, while Terrence, Reena, and Jonathan joined Jonah at the bench.

"Raw emotion can prove to be your undoing, Jonah," said Jonathan. "It does not benefit anyone or anything to react blindly."

Jonah took a breath. It was a struggle to keep his annoyance in check. "Jonathan, you aren't going to sit there and chastise me like I started that mess," he spat. "That fool Grayson attempted to take my legs out from under me with that chain—"

"—which means that you would have taken a spill onto soft earth and probably would have sustained negligible injuries," interrupted Jonathan. "I understand that. Your reaction was to pitch a solid steel baton, made even more dangerous by its ethereal properties, at someone's face, where anything from a cracked skull, loss of teeth, or deviated septum could occur. That was unnecessary, and far too excessive."

Jonah closed his eyes. He would never admit it, but Jonathan had just nailed him. When he put it like that, throwing metal, endowed metal, at someone's exposed face was a grisly action. It was too excessive.

"Grayson was wrong as well, do not misunderstand me," continued Jonathan. "But I would prefer it if one of my students not need facial surgery. So that's that. Now, Reena here tells me that you encountered a one of Creyton's Spirit Reapers?"

"Yeah, I did." Jonah told Jonathan about the two brief occurrences where he'd seen the tall man with the hood and face mask. Jonathan was silent for a little bit, and then he ran a finger over his infinity medallion and spoke.

"You didn't glimpse the face at all?"

"Nope," replied Jonah. "Mask covered everything."

"What might this mean, Jonathan?" asked Terrence quickly. "I know it's only one Spirit Reaper, but are my parents a target?"

Jonathan took a deep breath. "It is, as you say, one Spirit Reaper, but trust me, son, one can do a great deal of carnage," he said. "And the ones who followed Creyton…they were a rare breed of evil. I will confer with the Spirit Guides to expand the grids of their watch points to include the Decessio home."

Jonah scratched his chin stubble. "No disrespect, Jonathan, but you never quite explained the whole—um—Spirit hierarchy to me. I get that you're a Protector Guide, and Spirit Guides are above the Protector Guides. Having said that, would the Spirit Guides actually listen to you?"

Terrence widened his eyes, as if he thought Jonathan would be offended. But Jonathan just laughed.

"They would, Jonah," he answered, "without question. Oftentimes, they ask me for advice and insights. It they had any choice in the matter, they'd make me a Spirit Guide, and call it a day."

"Wait," said Reena, "I never knew that you declined to be a Spirit Guide!"

"I did," said Jonathan. "My heart lay here on Earthplane, where I can continue training and protecting the people I've come to love. Being a Spirit Guide makes hands-on influence almost impossible. As a Protector Guide, I can be much more flexible."

Jonathan sounded neither impatient nor annoyed, but he ended the sentence in such a way that let them know that that conversation on the subject was over. Jonah wondered if there might be more to it than just personal freedom. There might be a piece of that story that had touchiness to it. He made a mental note of it, and then returned to the task at hand.

"So what do you want us to do, Jonathan?" he asked.

"Well, for the moment, keep it quiet," said Jonathan. "All of you."

"Say what!" Terrence blurted out. "Jonathan, we need to warn my family! Make the inhabitants of the estate aware—"

"And tell them what, Terrence?" asked Jonathan. "That Jonah saw someone who fit the description of one of Creyton's followers, but you weren't sure? I understand your concern, but I will see to it that no harm will come to your parents. But I think that your family is safe; the Spirit Reaper's focus is likely here. And no Spirit Reaper will cross the threshold of the estate while I am here. I don't like making plans when I don't know all of the facts. So for right now, maintain vigilance and caution, but don't change a thing. Adversity is only successful when it derails the normal course of your life."

Jonah stood and swayed slightly, as he was no longer endowed. That was Jonathan's latest fortune-cookie phrase, which probably made a world of sense to brainy folks like Reena, but may as well have been an ancient language to everyone else. They said their goodbyes to Jonathan, who faded away after their departure, and headed back up to the estate.

"Can one Spirit Reaper cause a sick amount of damage?" asked Jonah.

"Depends on the Spirit Reaper," said Reena. "Eleventh Percenters are just like Tenths in that regard; some people don't make much of a dent, whereas other can cause astronomical discord. Some people are dangerous because they are intelligent, and some people are just as dangerous because they are stupid, and aren't aware of the chaos they cause. It all just depends on the person."

"Well, that's just great," said Terrence. "Leaves us completely confused, no problem! But while he is out and about, we have to be vigilant and cautious. You know, Jonathan's cool, but sometimes I think he's a few sides short of a full meal."

"Jonathan's advice hasn't ever been detrimental to us, Terrence," said Reena sharply. "You know that! If further precaution is needed, you know just as well as I do that he wouldn't hesitate to inform us."

"No, actually," said Terrence. "What you mean to say is that Jonathan wouldn't hesitate to give us enough profound rhetoric to make our brains swim."

Jonah agreed more with Terrence than he did with Reena, but he had no desire to participate in the bickering. When they were back at the estate, he could hear another passionate voice, but this one was excited instead of frustrated. He knew exactly who it was, and sure enough, saw Liz at the kitchen table animatedly explaining some information to several onlookers. Some looked intrigued, some looked doubtful, and some just looked like they came into the onslaught of information because they were in the area for food.

"You're *loco*, Liz," said Magdalena, and Jonah could tell that she was one of the people who happened into the area. "No one could do such a thing."

"I swear on my Aura that it can be done!" gushed Liz. "I've read about occurrences and everything!"

Reena abandoned her debate with Terrence and got a closer look. "What are you talking about, Liz?"

Liz turned to them. Her face nearly glowed with exuberance. "You know how our bodies are basically factories, right?"

"Right..."

"Well, our bodies also work like large computer mainframes as well. And you know that when a computer gets a virus, you can reboot, do a scan, and it's gone. I've discovered that the same thing can be done with the human body!"

Jonah stared at her. "Liz, how would you reboot someone's body?"

"Actually, it's quite simple!" said Liz happily. "Just like a CPU has a shutdown button, so, too, do human beings. If I were to press firmly on this pressure point here—"

She reached for Jonah's torso, but he hopped back.

"I'm good, Liz," he muttered. "That's quite alright."

"Oh, don't be such a square," said Liz, undaunted. She indicated the spot on her own torso. "Pressing down here would cause all bodily functions to cease, and repair themselves. When your body comes back into function, all your faculties are as right as rain!"

Alvin, who was across the room, had dozed off. When he heard that part, though, he straightened. "Wait a second, Elizabeth," he said slowly. "When you shut down a computer, the thing is off. So are you saying that you shut down a person's body, and the person's body is...off? Like, dead?"

There were some apprehensive looks at the query, but Liz simply scoffed.

"You know that life never ends, Alvin," she told him. "Your body wouldn't be *off*. It would be resetting. The same point that shuts you down—" she indicated the area on her torso once more, "—will reactivate you. Your body will be good as new. *Better*, in fact, because all foreign properties will have been wiped."

"And how long would you be, um, *off*, Liz?" said Terrence, who clearly wanted to laugh.

"Thirty seconds, give or take," answered Liz. "Really fun stuff!"

"Did you learn this in college?" asked Jonah, ready to reconsider his admission to a university that touted such bullshit.

"Of course not," said Liz. "No textbook would have that kind of treatment modality. I read about it in a book from the attic called *Inert Healing Arts*. Looked like it'd been there for decades."

"And there was probably a reason why it was called inert," said Terrence in a voice barely above a whisper. "Come on, Jonah, we don't have to eat in here. Let's go to one of my snack stashes."

They left Liz to continue. Reena stayed behind to listen; she appeared genuinely interested.

"Let's leave them to be geniuses together," said Terrence. "I wonder what Bobby would think of his girlfriend trying to shut people down like laptops."

They passed Spader, who was seated in a recliner, disassembling a lock. Jonah didn't want to know where he'd found it. When he overheard Terrence's remark, he made a wry face, gathered the lock components, and left the room.

"Good Lord," said Terrence. "Tough room. Hey, I love that guy!"

He hurried over, and joined Benjamin, Bobby, and several others. They were all watching some show's promotional spot. Suddenly, a man swooped into view. Jonah regarded him. He was a pale-featured man, with platinum blonde hair that was parted with a barber's precision. He looked into the camera with an expression that denoted theatric drama and over-exaggerated importance.

"I have long chronicled my travels, pursuits, and deeds," began the man. Jonah noticed that the guy's tone had a tremulous pitch to it, like his intention was to hook you in just before he dropped a bombshell. "In each instance, I am amazed by the number of secrets the shadows hold. The darkness clutches a book of secrets jealously to her chest, never once exhibiting a desire to reveal them. Well, I reveal them, my friends. As I have proven time and again, the paranormal and the mystical speak to me. And I will share what I've discovered with you. There are new tales this season. Embark with me on journeys that will captivate your mind and tear asunder your disbelief. It is sometimes scary. Yet always serious. It is... *ScarYous.*"

Jonah nearly choked. "*Scarious?*" he repeated. "But—but that's an actual term! Means thin and dry texture, or something!"

"Ahh," said Terrence, who looked just as excited as Liz had been about resetting bodies, "but this isn't *scarious*, Jonah. It's Sca-REE-ous. There is a *Y* in the middle for scary."

Jonah blinked. He felt like he'd been set up for a spectacular fireworks show, but got subjected to a bargain sparkler instead. "That sounds like—like—well, I don't know. I can't think of anything corny enough."

"Don't hate," said Terrence, suddenly serious. "Turk Landry is a master. He's been going around the country for about ten years now, to all the most haunted sites. He has achieved wild notoriety with *ScarYous Tales of the Paranormal*."

"Why, because people buy into that crap?" asked Jonah.

"No," said Bobby, "it's because he has found paranormal activity every place that he's gone."

Jonah felt his eyebrows elevate. "Every place he has ever been?" he asked. "Not a single flop ever?"

"Not one," said Terrence. "Guy's loaded. He's earned every dime of it."

"If there were more Tenths like him, this world would be a lot more exciting!" said some guy nearer to the television Jonah didn't yet know.

"Well, I don't know about the world," said Benjamin, "but it's about to get really exciting around here! Turk Landry is coming to town in about a month!"

"What!" exclaimed Terrence. "He's coming here?"

"Yeah!" said Benjamin excitedly. "According to his website, he's heard about how this area is one of the most actively paranormal sites in North Carolina, so he is devoting a season to Rome! He and his crew are going to be here for months on end! The mayor is pretty psyched; he thinks the publicity will mean great things for the town."

Jonah looked at Benjamin curiously. He shrugged.

"I subscribe to his alerts, and follow him on Twitter," he said. "So what? Who doesn't?"

I don't, thought Jonah. He sat down and allowed his mind to wander while his friends buzzed like kids. He wondered about this new addition that the town of Rome would soon have, but he didn't know how welcoming he'd be.

Ever since Jonah learned about The Eleventh Percent, and that he was an ethereal human, he'd come to respect it very much. The Spectral Sight. The spiritual endowments. And the never-ending facets of life. He'd come to hold it with respect and honor. He appreciated it much like a family heirloom; something that had been entrusted to him for safekeeping. Bearing all that in mind, he found that he didn't really care for this Landry guy. The notion of this man traveling up and down the country, turning spiritual matters and progressions into a side-show spectacle that led to riches and ratings seemed insulting. It felt like an alteration to something natural. Felt like something sacred was being sensationalized for fame and gain.

"Jonah?"

Jonah started, and looked in Terrence's direction. That was who called him. He also noticed that the *ScarYous* conversation hadn't ended. Terrence had detached himself from it.

"You alright?" he asked. "What's on your mind?"

"Oh," replied Jonah. "Just that with that Spirit Reaper, and this *ScarYous* guy, things are about to get really interesting."

4

Haunted

To Jonah's relief, his affirmation proved false. Nothing odd or strange happened for two straight weeks, and that streak showed no end in sight. He spent that time re-familiarizing himself with his training, continued the private lessons with Terrence and Reena (who sometimes included Malcolm, Liz, and Bobby as well), and readied himself for his fall semester. Jonah had faced rogue spirits, villainous shadows, and traveled the Astral Plane, but those things weren't nearly as unnerving as being a student again.

Liz had been more than happy to give Jonah a tour of the campus over the weekend. She happily pointed out landmarks, the registrar, and the quad. But now, Jonah was alone, standing next to his car, with a large stone sign that said *La Tronis State University: The Home of the Hunters* some fifteen feet away.

The university was a smaller one, but still seemed imposing as the afternoon transitioned to evening. To his far right was the Drowdin Building, which Liz told him was the place dedicated to all things science, and her self-proclaimed *third home*. Remembering his own experiences with science, Jonah was thankful that he had no need of that place. Opposite Drowdin was the cafeteria, which Bobby said was affectionately nicknamed The Feeding Grounds because the university nickname was Hunters. Jonah had a fond recollection of frequenting the dining hall in undergrad, where he sometimes settled on three entrees because he couldn't figure out which one he truly wanted. Of course, that wouldn't happen this time around, because he followed Reena's eating plan like a faith. Mostly.

There it was. Jonah spotted his destination—the Britton Building. His class would take place there, on the third floor.

Jonah envied the several students who had evening classes like himself. They were all students, sure, but they strode the grounds with such familiarity. He sighed. As if he didn't already feel like a fish out of water. He closed his eyes, took a deep breath, and willed the curtain to open in his mind. He opened his eyes once his Spectral Sight was activated.

He saw huge blotches of silvery mist all over the place. It was like a layer of cloud had descended across the grounds. Some were bunched together so tightly that they resembled elevated snow, while others spread so thinly that seemed no more than feeble wisps in the wind. Jonah looked around in wonder, but felt no fear or concern about what he saw.

Jonathan had already informed him that in some places, the spiritual count was so vast that it would expend far too much of their essence to separate themselves into specific forms. In those cases, spirits and spiritesses moved about in the form of mist. The mist could sometimes be so rich in ethereality that it could dazzle the eyes like moonlight. Out of all these people, he alone could see this phenomenon.

"Hmm," he mumbled to himself, "that's one thing I have over these kids, if nothing else."

He deactivated the Sight, squared his shoulders, and headed for the Britton Building. Time to be a student again. Almost as important as that, it was time to see what all the fuss was about concerning Kendall Rayne.

Jonah went straight for the elevator. Reena may have thought stairs were a good source of exercise, but whatever.

He emerged on the third floor into a hallway that seemed to have every inch of its walls covered in leaflets, flyers, memos, and crackpot causes that only arose the interest of undergraduates who had no interest in a social life. Laughing to himself, he moved toward the classroom, which was near the end of the hall. He knew he was in the right place when he saw several people slouched against the wall, seated on the floor, or standing inches away from everyone else while playing on their phones.

"Hey there, man," said a guy of about nineteen. He was dressed in all black, but looked more slothful than sinister. "We have to wait for Professor Mavis to get out. Wish I knew that the old bat wasn't going to end his class on time. I would have gotten another—um—snack."

"Uh-huh," said Jonah, who shook his head. The boy was clearly a stoner. He wouldn't have gotten a snack, but he'd have probably *needed* a snack afterwards. He seated himself, and was in the middle of opening his bag when a shadow darkened his line of sight. He looked up.

A woman sized him up as he did the same. She was in her forties unless Jonah was mistaken, and judging by her pantsuit, she had just gotten off work. An indefinable air of superiority radiated off of her. Jonah wondered how he picked that up off of her before the woman had even opened her mouth, but then he remembered, he'd known plenty idiots like that when he was younger. Age didn't always bring maturity.

"Hi there!" Even her voice was annoying. "Are you new here?"

"Ain't we all?" said the stoner as he eyed the woman with distaste. "This is the first day of classes."

The woman regarded him coldly, but turned her attention back to Jonah. "I meant continuing education student," she clarified. "Been out of school a few years, and have returned. Yes?"

"Yep," said Jonah cautiously. He had an idea where this might be going.

"So am I!" said the woman. "My name's Reynolda Langford. I don't even know why I'm taking this course; it's a refresher at best. Writing fulfills me in a way that I truly cannot describe. I've already had things published! How about you?"

Jonah stared, curious about why she would volunteer all of that information before he'd even given his name. The direction of this conversation got just a bit clearer. "I'm Jonah Rowe," he said. "I've written things, but I'm not published yet."

"Ah," said Reynolda. "So do you have an English degree? Creative Writing?"

"Nope," said Jonah with a smile, "I have a Bachelor's and a Master's degree in Accounting. Anything else?"

Reynolda's face fell instantly, and she turned her back on Jonah. His suspicion had been correct: That Reynolda woman was a fish out of water, just like he was. She'd hoped to alleviate her insecurities with the creation of a clique of like-minded gossip folks who were more concerned with sniping behind people's backs than with their education. Pass.

Stoner Guy laughed to himself, but Jonah hardly cared.

"I really don't like that woman," said a voice, and Jonah turned to see another woman seated next to him, using her bag as a cushion. "I saw her around campus today, and she's been accosting everyone who looks older than eighteen. It's quite sad, really."

She was a light-skinned black woman, but Jonah couldn't really see her face, because her hands obscured it; she was massaging her temples as she spoke. "You came too late," he told her. "She was bragging about already being published."

"Yeah, I know," said the woman, unimpressed, and she finally lowered her hands.

Jonah blinked. His new classmate was *really* pretty. Her face was void of all makeup; she probably had a little bit of eye shadow, but that was pretty much it. Her hair was cut short, but the style fit her perfectly. She looked like she was preoccupied with a million thoughts, but Jonah expected that anyone would be on the first day of classes.

Jonah suddenly thought of Vera, and felt a faint twinge of guilt because he was so taken with how attractive his classmate was. A second later, he mentally scolded himself.

Vera and I aren't in a relationship, he thought. *And besides, I just thought this woman was pretty. It's not like I want to marry her.*

"There's more to your new friend's story," continued his classmate. "She is indeed published, which is wonderful. But she seems to think that she is God's gift to writing. She told me this afternoon that she probably knew more than Professor Rayne. No offense, but I've read her stuff, and it *blows*."

Jonah laughed. "Really? Because everyone has a unique style when it comes to writing."

"That's very true," agreed the woman, "but *that* woman's style isn't unique. It's simply bad. She has a style of prose that is unknown to most human beings, let alone writers."

Jonah snorted. He really liked this woman. "I take it you're a writer already?" he asked her.

She shrugged. "I'd rather not blow my own horn, but yes, I am," she replied. "Have a couple of books available on Kindle; they're both mysteries. I love writing. It's always been that way. Classes like this show me that I can always improve, so I always practice. You?"

Jonah took a deep breath. "I've been writing all of my life," he said, "but the thing is, I've dealt with people telling me that my work sucked in the past. I'm ashamed to say that part of me still believes it. I've started several books, but I can't finish them for some reason. It's like my creativity is blunted."

"Really?" said his classmate, intrigued. Her eyes lowered to his bag, where one of his manuscripts had slipped out when he'd moved it. "May I see?"

She extended a hand, but Jonah hesitated. She just laughed.

"With our assignments and presentations, I'm going to see your writing style eventually," she told him.

Jonah made an indistinguishable noise. "Point," he said, and he handed her one of his unfinished works.

The woman glanced over several pages, and her eyes widened with each page she turned. This occurred for several more minutes, and she closed the notebook. "Who in the hell told you that you couldn't write?" she demanded. "They were either blind, jealous, or simply didn't know what they were talking about!"

Jonah exhaled in relief. Coming from an absolute stranger, that was very high praise. "Thank you." he said. "I appreciate that."

"Anytime!" she exclaimed. "I would show you my own work, but I'm quite comfortable on my bag. So you're out of luck."

They laughed over that.

"I just hope that Professor Rayne feels the same way that you do," muttered Jonah.

"Hey," said his classmate, "we all start at the same line. If you write like that, I don't think she can give you any grief."

"You are far too kind," said Jonah. "My name is Jonah, by the way. You are?"

Before she could answer, there was a sound that resembled a stampede, and Professor Mavis's class barreled out of the classroom. Jonah could have cursed. It really was nice conversing with such a competent individual.

"You find a good seat," said his classmate as she maneuvered herself off of her bag. "I'm right behind you."

Jonah navigated the crowd as best he could, and headed for a nice desk near the front with two chairs behind it.

"Hey, you want to park it right th—?" began Jonah, but he looked behind himself and noticed that his new friend wasn't there. He rolled his eyes, annoyed, but then—

"Find seats everybody. Thanks to Mavis, we're on a time crunch."

Jonah wheeled around, and his eyes bulged.

The pretty woman who'd spoken with him, who'd said that if he wrote like he did in his manuscripts, he'd have no problems with his professor…stood near a podium, with her bag slung across a chair. She chuckled freely as she looked around and saw Jonah's expression, which was mirrored on some twenty-two other faces. Reynolda Langford looked seconds away from passing out.

"Yeah, that's right," she said, finally taking her attention from everyone's shock, "I'm Kendall Rayne, your instructor. Mingling with students is a little bit of fun that I do at the beginning of each semester. You never know the things you may learn. Now kindly seat yourselves, and we'll go through this syllabus and head on home."

Forty-five minutes later (the first class had been a meet and greet, and Kendall had to curtail Reynolda, who'd been poised to tell her life story), Jonah left the Britton Building, wondering why he'd had apprehension in the first place. He'd spoken to Kendall (she hated *Professor Rayne*, which irritated Reynolda Langford to no end), before he'd known who she was, and not only had he made a good impression, he had also impressed her with his writing.

That class had to have been the most laid-back, easy-going class he'd ever had. It was such a stark contrast to the hardnosed, prune-faced professors he'd had back in graduate school. Almost everyone (especially the male students) loved Kendall instantly, but one of the people that didn't like her was Reynolda. "I'm being taught by a professor who is younger than me; how can possibly listen to her?" she'd said. "And her teaching style seems a little loose to me. I tend to work better—and am more productive—where there is more structure."

Thankfully, though, no one acknowledged Reynolda's complaints much, and she eventually fell silent. Jonah wasn't the only one who smiled when she shut up.

It was a great first class, and Jonah was actually interested in going to the next one, which was a first. Kendall was cool. She was laid back without being lax, kind-natured without being a pushover, and serious without being a hardass. Maybe being a student again wasn't going to be so bad after all.

Jonah was distracted by a lone figure near the east lot where he'd parked. He sat atop one of the displays for the school. With the lights that illuminated the display from the ground, the person looked to be in an amber spotlight. The person had a dull, dirty face, and clothes so ragged and filthy that he looked like wound on the face of the pristine LTSU sign and the surrounding plants. With a jolt, Jonah realized that the guy couldn't have been more than eighteen or nineteen, if that. This boy made Spader look like a sharp-dressed gentleman.

Under normal circumstances, Jonah would have put distance between himself, locked his doors, and raced out of the parking lot, but something told him not to. He approached with caution.

"What's up?" he asked the boy.

The boy looked up. He hadn't even noticed Jonah's approach, but that was because the lights that lit up the display were quite bright. He dropped down from the display, flattening a row of begonias in the process, and assumed a defensive stance.

Jonah had a brief thought of how his grandmother always bristled when flowers were ruined, but he filed it away.

"Calm down," he said to the boy, lowering his hand into his pocket in a surreptitious fashion. His baton was there in its dormant form, but he could have it ready at once if necessary. "I don't mean you any harm. What's your name?"

The boy didn't answer. He stared at Jonah with rather wild eyes. He looked like he dumped coffee beans down his throat on a regular basis.

Ooo-kay, thought Jonah, still wondering why he was bothering with this. "Do you go to school here?"

The answer to that question was obvious, but Jonah felt that assumptions wouldn't bode well in this situation.

The boy's expression didn't change but he spoke. "No. Homeless."

Despite himself, Jonah lifted his hand out of his pocket, and elevated it to fold his arms.

"You're homeless," he repeated. "Do you have any idea how suspicious you look sitting there? Being on this campus? The female-to-male ratio here is like four to one, most of them eighteen to twenty. It is not cool for you to be roaming around here. Anyone could call the police—"

The boy tensed. "Police? You're going to call them? Where are they?"

"I haven't called any police, boy," said Jonah impatiently. "You've been looking at me the whole time. There are the on-campus police, but..."

Jonah's voice trailed off. Suddenly, he didn't think it was wise to volunteer the information that the university police were borderline worthless. He'd seen them at orientation. Every single one of them was pot-bellied, and seemed to know the layout of Krispy Kreme more than they did the layout of campus. On top of that, the best they could do in regards to subduing someone was shining their flashlights in their faces, and praying that the beam was bright enough to hurt them.

The boy didn't notice Jonah's hesitation, however. He actually seemed a little discomfited. It looked like he realized that coming on this campus might not have been his best idea.

"Why are you here?" asked Jonah. "You're either lost or hungry. Which one?"

The boy's tension relaxed. "Starving," he whispered. "I haven't eaten in—in—I don't know."

Jonah felt so sorry for the boy by this time that any notion to defend himself faded. He reached into his bag and pulled out some trail mix.

"Here," he said, tossing it to the boy. "It's not much, but I think it'll hold you over. And—" Jonah stepped nearer to him (which was tough, because the boy was hygienically challenged), and pressed several bills into his hands. "If you're not lofty, this will cover some meals for you."

The boy stood transfixed, regarding the new items like they were priceless jewels. "Thank you," he whispered. "You showed me kindness...I won't forget it. Thank you."

"It's no problem," said Jonah. "What's your name?"

The boy just nodded. "Showed me kindness—thank you."

He dashed off into the darkness.

"Huh," Jonah mumbled. "Weird. That was just...weird."

After an uneventful drive back to the estate, Jonah was prepared to call it an evening. The day had been great, school was a pleasurable experience, and he was in high spirits. What could go wrong?

"Hey!" said Douglas once Jonah stepped out of his car. "How was your first day?"

"It went well, Doug, thanks," said Jonah with a grin. "How about your own?"

"Pretty well," said Douglas. "I put up a new sheet for the chess club, in any case. I had no problem telling everyone that you were my first member!"

Jonah's smile faded slightly. He'd completely forgotten about his decision to join Doug's chess club. "That's good, Doug," he muttered. "I'm a little hungry, so—"

"Thought you might be," said Terrence's voice from behind them, and Jonah and Douglas turned to see him there with two wrapped bundles in his hands.

"Chili dogs," he explained. "I thought I could get away with a beans-and-franks night, since I hadn't had those since before I went to Hawaii, but Reena had to wreck things. She made damn pasta salad, with rice pasta! She wasn't even willing to have garlic bread with it."

Jonah grabbed a bundle and began to unwrap it. "Thanks, man. Looks like you saved us again."

"Did he?"

Reena was right behind them. Jonah was about to wonder how she had gotten there so fast, but then he remembered her speed ethereality. He cursed under his breath.

"Terrence, Jonah," she said, her expression a fine line between amusement and exasperation, "you are like mischievous third graders who hide their vegetables! And then you corrupt *others*, like Douglas!"

"I don't know what you're talking about!" said Terrence as he tossed the hot dog behind his back. "And I haven't corrupted anyone! Tell her, Doug—"

Terrence froze abruptly. Jonah heard it, too. Reena lost all interest in Terrence's guilty face and tensed, which meant that she heard it, too.

There it was again. It was an unearthly growl that seemed to fill the entire night. It was more pronounced and menacing now that they had stopped speaking.

"What was—?" began Jonah, but at that precise moment, Douglas's eyes bulged so widely that they appeared to be in danger of popping out of their sockets. The three of them turned, and were met with a frightening sight.

Some three feet away from them stood some sort of dog, and Jonah thought that was a loose definition. It was the size of a Great Dane, and looked extremely lithe and muscular. Its fur was the color of dense soot, so dark that the night all around them seemed less prominent by comparison. What really bothered Jonah, however, were its eyes. They were a pulsating scarlet, almost like tiny beacons. And it was then that Jonah realized what angered the thing: When Terrence discarded his hot dog, it ricocheted off the thing's head. There was even chili in its fur. It might have been amusing if the thing didn't look like it was about to tear them apart.

"Holy hell," whispered Reena, horrified. "It's a Haunt."

"A what, now?" asked Jonah, his eyes still on the demon dog.

"A Haunt," Reena repeated, but didn't seem to have the ability speak any further.

Jonah's reached for his pocket, but Reena slowly grabbed his wrist.

"Forget it," she said. "It won't do you any good. Just back away. Slowly, back away. They can't cross the threshold of the estate."

"I wouldn't do that just yet," said a hoarse, grating voice.

A man emerged from the shadows. It took Jonah all of ten seconds to realize that it was the man he'd seen near Terrence's house. He towered over them all, but the Haunt seemed neither perturbed nor alarmed by this new presence.

"Brilliant horde, boy," said the hooded man to the Haunt, "and with Jonah Rowe, no less! Wonderful, wonderful…"

A chilling surge went down Jonah's spine. "You—you know me?"

"Yes, of course," said the figure. "At this point, I feel I know you very well. Allow me to introduce myself."

He lowered his hood to reveal a gaunt, angular face. He looked malnourished, but certainly didn't look weak. Long, greasy hair hung to his shoulders, and his eyes showed no pity, remorse, or, come to think of it, any human emotion at all. As jarring as his face was, Jonah was still at a complete loss as to who he was. The figure picked up on this as well, and responded with a sneer.

"Still stumped, then?" he rasped. "Hold on."

He reached into his coat and pulled out a bunch of twigs, one of which he tossed to his left. When it hit the ground, the dark seemed to shimmer, and a second Haunt appeared. It was just as large and feral-looking as the one at the man's side. Jonah's eyes bulged. Even though he hadn't laid eyes on the guy in a couple months, he knew exactly who he was.

"You," he whispered. "The man with the twigs from the bookstore."

Reena slowly exhaled, Terrence spat a nasty word, and Douglas kept his mouth shut, probably to prevent nausea.

"Indeed." The man smiled, which revealed teeth that matched his pale, ashen face. "But you may call me the 49er."

There was a faint ringing in Jonah's ears, and before he knew it, his batons were in his hands. He flicked the switch at the bottom, so they grew to full size. He wasn't endowed, but he didn't care.

When he pulled out his batons, however, something very odd happened. The second Haunt, the one who'd appeared when the 49er threw down the twig, circled Jonah, Terrence, Reena, and Douglas. The first one growled, and then they tensed simultaneously. Their scarlet eyes gleamed even brighter for a few moments, and they looked at their master, whose eyes flashed with the same scarlet. The 49er smiled.

"Reena Mikil Katoa," he said quietly. "You are correct in your thinking. You are an abomination, a disgrace, and your mother knew it as well. That's why she hated you. Disowning you was a kindness."

Reena looked like someone had slapped her. She grabbed at her heart like it was about to abandon her chest.

"Terrence Wade Aldercy," the 49er continued. "You are about as empty, worthless, and inconsequential as the calories which you consume. Just because the Decessios took you in doesn't make you one of them. Raymond is the daring one, Sterling is the resourceful one, Alvin is the studious one, and Bobby is the athletically gifted one. You, on the other hand, are merely the adopted one."

Terrence looked like he'd deflated. He looked traumatized.

"Douglas Myron Chandler." The 49er sniffed with distaste. "Boy, you don't even matter at all. If I murdered you right now, not even your family would shed a tear. For your own sake, throw a punch at me. That way, at the very least, it can be said that you put up a struggle."

That one did it. One second, Douglas was shivering, and the next, he was violently sick.

"And Jonah James Anderson Rowe." The 49er grinned, and Jonah braced himself. What could he possibly say to hurt him? "Your failures are as numerous as the pages you've covered in ink. But all of them—*all* of them—pale in comparison to Doreen. It is, after all, your fault that she's gone."

Jonah stared at him in open-mouthed horror. The 49er's words to him weren't as long and detailed as the others, but they didn't have to be.

And then, Jonah's body…turned on him. There was no other way to say it. He was drenched in icy sweat within seconds, his head began to swim, and his heart began to bash violently against his ribcage. It felt like the opposite of a spiritual endowment; like an adrenaline rush that had been corrupted or perverted. His legs felt boneless, and he collapsed to his knees, blinking back tears of anger, terror, and despair.

He saw the 49er laughing as he pet one of those demon dogs. "Thank you as always, my dears," he said to both Haunts. "Now if you will exercise just a bit more patience, I will reward you with scraps."

He pulled out what looked to be a sword made of bones. It literally looked like a spine with spiky, jagged bones affixed to it. Jonah couldn't imagine how he crafted such a thing, but his mind couldn't compute much at the moment, anyway.

The 49er looked Jonah over, and shrugged. "You first, I think," he said. "I'm sure your head will come clean off your shoulders."

He swung the sword like a whip, but then one of the Haunts yelped. It was a sound so foreign to the present course of events that Jonah actually jumped.

"You bastard!" the 49er shrieked. "You—!"

Another man barreled Jonah over. He didn't even seem to notice that a person had been in his path. He made a backslapping motion with his left arm, and what resembled a slate-grey shockwave flew at the other Haunt, who leapt at him. It was blasted aside by the wave, which also disintegrated two legs, an ear, and a portion of its tail.

"My pets!" the 49er snarled. "This doesn't concern you, you feculent scum!"

The other man didn't respond, and flung another shockwave, this time at the 49er. He staggered backward, but didn't lose his footing.

"Another time," he spat. He grabbed the maimed Haunt and backed into nothingness. He'd used the *Astralimes* to escape. The man ran forward, grabbed at empty air, and roared in fury.

"SHIT!" he bellowed. "I was so close!"

Despite Jonah's twisted mindset, he noticed more about their savior. It was a black man with a close-cropped, tightly-waved haircut, a pencil-thin beard, and rather focused eyed. He, too, had a hood, but it wasn't on his head. It was bunched at the back of his neck, and attached to a denim jacket.

"You need to get up, boy," he said to Jonah in a rather gruff voice.

He moved toward him, but Jonah scrambled away. What was going on? Why was he so sure that this man was no friend? Why was he so sure that he needed to fear this man? And why wouldn't his heart stop racing?

The man raised his hands in surrender. "I don't mean you any harm!" he promised. "I swear it on all things sacred! Now, get up!"

"NO!" Jonah shouted, still not sure why he was so timid and jumpy. "Keep away!"

"I said *get up,* goddamn it," the man snapped.

He grabbed Jonah by the collar of his shirt. "You're still relatively able-bodied, so walk. You all need to get to the estate."

Now that Jonah was upright and facing the opposite direction, he remembered his friends. Terrence rocked back and forth. Reena had propped herself up against a tree and stared at the ground, her face still frozen in horror. Douglas lay supine on the ground. He'd fainted.

"Wake that one, you." The man looked at Reena when he made his command. "You, boy—get up from there."

Like Jonah, Terrence and Reena weren't keen on following this man's orders. They seemed equally as afraid of him.

"Why should we do anything for you?" asked Reena in a voice unlike her own. "Why are you here?"

"Yeah!" piped up Terrence. "Why should we go anywhere with you? You'll probably kill us!"

"I'm not the one trying to kill you!" the man shot back. "*He* just used the *Astralimes* to get away with his crippled pet!"

Jonah didn't get it. The man frightened the hell out of him. Everything about this situation frightened him. Why was that?

"I know you're scared," said the man, "but you need to focus as best you can. I'm trying to help you."

"Why?" persisted Reena.

The man swallowed, as though he didn't have much patience left, but when he spoke, it was in a calm tone. "Because you've been Haunted, and the effects will be dire if left unchecked. Now, move!"

5

The Happy(?) Leader

Jonah wasn't sure what motivated him to move, but he shuffled forward like the man asked. Terrence did the same. Reena didn't wake up Douglas, because she never took her eyes off of the stranger, so the guy lifted him off of the ground in a fireman's carry and hauled him with no trouble.

Now Jonah could relate to Douglas's nausea. His own stomach churned, and it took all his remaining strength to prevent a game of show and tell with his lunch. He didn't know what was going on. His bodily functions and emotions were all out of whack. That man—the 49er or whatever his name was (didn't that name have something to do with gold?)—really messed him up. He'd voiced Jonah's inner torments...and he had no way of knowing them. Did it have something to do with the glowing dog's eyes? If so, how the hell did that work? And he'd said Doreen.

He'd known Nana's name...

The steps of the estate were under his feet before he knew it. Thank God he hadn't tripped and face-planted, because his body was screwed up enough already. The door opened, and Jonah stared into the face of the absolute *last* person he wanted to see him this way: Vera.

"I was wondering where you guys had gotten off to," she said. "I thought you were avoiding Reena's pasta salad—"

Her voice trailed off when she got a good look at Jonah's face.

"Jonah? Jonah, what is it?"

He shook his head. "I—I don't know. We've been Haunted, or something."

"Liz!" called Vera. "Come quick!"

Vera's call not only summoned Liz, but Bobby, Malcolm, Magdalena, Spader, and several others. Liz regarded Jonah with concern.

"What is it?" she demanded. "And who are *you?*"

The man entered the door carefully, as he had Douglas on his shoulders. Terrence balanced himself against a wall, and Vera and Malcolm tried to get Jonah and Reena seated. The stranger shook his head.

"They need to go into the kitchen," he said in a firm tone.

"Who the hell are you?" repeated Liz a little waspishly. "They look fevered. If I can do a proper inspection, I can figure out—"

"Little girl, your healing won't achieve jack shit," said the stranger flat-out. "You're a Green Aura, I'm guessing? Well, a different skill set is needed here."

"Hold it, dude." Bobby got in the man's path, and despite a height difference of almost eight inches, he didn't back down. "Watch how you speak to Liz. And put Doug down! What've you done to him?"

Despite his mental disarray, Jonah couldn't help but feel a grudging respect for the stranger who saved them. He was surrounded by Eleventh Percenters who didn't view him kindly at the moment, yet he was unafraid and undaunted.

"Where's Jonathan?" the man asked the group at large.

"He's Off-plane, not that it's your business," said Malcolm in his quiet tone, which still carried impressively. "How do you know him?"

The man didn't answer. "I know the heralds are still around," he said. "He still uses them, right?"

"Yes, of course—"

"Then get one to summon him," interrupted the stranger. "If I remember correctly, Bast is the most efficient."

His familiarity with Jonathan and Bast baffled the group, and Jonah saw Liz approach the man herself. Her jade eyes were piercing.

"Sir, you are a trespasser on protected grounds," she said. "I ask you again—"

"Liz," said the stranger in that calm, forced voice, "isn't that what that woman at the door called you? I am not hostile. You have my word. If you are a Green Aura, you understand the importance of treatment. You see the condition in which your friends are? It will get a whole hell of a lot worse if you don't allow me to help them. I'm adhering to the rules of a first responder, after all!"

Something about those words softened Liz. She nodded shortly, and stood aside. They all entered the kitchen, but the stranger only paid attention to Jonah, Terrence, Reena, and Douglas.

"Sit," he ordered the three of them while he deposited Douglas into a chair, "and someone rouse him."

He went to the pantry and began to fumble through it like he did it on a daily basis. He reached for wines of all things, but placed each one back with a scowl. Finally, he closed the pantry and headed over to the glasses cabinet, where he pulled out four glasses. He placed them in front of Jonah, Terrence, Reena, and the recently-awakened Douglas, completely oblivious to the curious audience he now had. Bobby broke the silence.

"Why are they like this?" he asked.

"They've been Haunted," mumbled the man without looking at Bobby. He dug into his pocket and pulled out a dark brown bottle, which he slapped on the table. Jonah stared at it.

"That's Distinguished Vintage," he commented hoarsely. "That's hard liquor. It's like, ninety-proof."

"I know." The man cleared his throat. "I want each of you to take a shot of it."

Terrence lifted his sweaty visage to regard the man. "Are you a drunk?"

The man's eyes narrowed. "I am an alcoholic," he confessed, "but I haven't had a drink in seven years."

"But why do you keep—"

"Not your concern," the man snapped. "Now take a shot."

Reena, as unnerved as she was, glared at the man. "I don't drink."

The man was unmoved. "You will tonight."

"You expect me to drink hard liquor?" whispered Reena.

"Yes."

"*Why* do we have to—?"

The man was in Reena's personal space so quickly that it seemed like an attack was imminent, but he paused a few feet shy. "For the fourth time, you have been *Haunted,* woman," he snapped. "Your body is rebelling against normal functions. You know how your heart is racing right now? If you don't drink the Vintage, your heart will *burst.*"

That last part hit home for Jonah. Terrence blinked. Reena just stared at the stranger, open-mouthed. Douglas looked to be near tears. The man must have realized they were now willing to comply, because he poured them all shots. Jonah drank, and tightened his eyes. The liquor set his insides ablaze, but to his amazement, it also burned away his jumpiness, anxiety, and inexplicable fear. His heart rate even returned to normal. He could tell that his friends were experiencing the same sensations. The stranger noticed it as well, and he nodded with satisfaction on his face.

"This is good," he said. "The ethanol takes the toxic edge off of the shock, centers your nerves, and levels out your heart."

"I'll be damned," said Jonah, "I feel like myself again. Still don't care for this Vintage, though."

Reena's usual demeanor was back in place, and she eyed the man about as scornfully as Bobby, who was still seething over how the man had spoken to Liz. Jonah wasn't too keen on the guy himself, but he did just save them. That was much more appealing than a busted heart. So he decided to intercept.

"Appreciate you saving us," he muttered. "Now will you tell us who you are? And how do you know so much about Jonathan and Bast and everything?"

The man put the cork back into the Distinguished Vintage, and pocketed it. It seemed now that all the danger had passed, he was now aware of all the eyes on him. *Now* he looked disconcerted. "My name's Felix Duscere," he told them all. "And I know Jonathan because—"

Malcolm snorted, and Felix looked his way.

"What?" he asked.

"Your name is Felix Duscere?" he asked.

"Yes," said Felix slowly. "So?"

Malcolm snickered again. This mirth was so far removed from his usual nature that Jonah was a little puzzled. "Those are Latin terms," he revealed. "In Latin, your name means *Happy Leader.* Tell me you knew that."

Judging by the look on Felix's face, he was *not* privy to that information, and he was the furthest thing from happy at the moment. Luckily though, everyone was distracted by the sound of hurried footsteps beyond the kitchen door. It flew open to reveal Liz, with Bast at her side, and Jonathan at the rear. Jonah knew that Liz had filled Jonathan to the best of her ability, but when Jonathan saw their visitor, his eyes narrowed. Felix met his gaze, and Jonah thought he saw an understanding pass between them. Weird.

"Evening, Felix," said Jonathan. "Seeing as it's you, am I to assume that the Spirit Reaper roaming around is the 49er?"

"Yes, sir," said Felix.

"Did he have Haunts with him?" asked Jonathan.

"Yes, sir."

Jonathan swore softly, but the exclamation was followed by a silence that spiraled so badly that Jonah had to break it.

"Um, I'm sorry," he said as he rose from his chair. He was tired of being confused, and also glad that that disproportionate fear was gone. He might not have had the courage to be so forthright otherwise. "But Jonathan, you know who the 49er is. You know this Felix guy, too. What does all this mean?"

Jonathan glanced at Reena's half-finished shot of liquor like he wanted a drink of it himself. "It means everyone needs to head out to the courtyard," he said with his eyes closed. "There are things you all need to know."

* * *

Twenty minutes later, every resident present at the estate congregated themselves in the estate courtyard, which was a spacious expanse of land steadily tended by Liz and her friends. Because he preferred the gazebo, Jonah had only been in this courtyard once.

And just like that last time he'd been here, the feel of it was tense, alert, and wary.

He sat down at the front of the amphitheater that was set up there. His recent experiences with fear were now replaced with curiosity. Jonah was probably more thankful than Terrence, Reena, and Douglas that his nerves had been centered and heart had leveled out, but he couldn't shake the residual guilt and anger that lingered in the wake of the confrontation with the 49er. *All of your failures pale in comparison to Doreen. It is, after all, your fault that she's gone.*

How had he known about the guilt that Jonah had about his grandmother's passing? He had never spoken to anyone about it. He wasn't close with the family members he'd had, and he hadn't even told Nelson, Terrence, or Reena. He'd buried it deep and tried to never think about it. So to be reminded of it by a stranger, and then have his emotions and body feel like they were turned inside out, was beyond jarring.

He refocused when Terrence and Reena joined him. Terrence was still seething over his humiliation, and his fists were tightly clenched. When Reena sat down, Jonah caught a whiff of peppermint. She must have rinsed out her mouth with the nonalcoholic mouthwash that Ben-Israel made for the estate. She also had a bag of chopped strawberries, which she ate while they waited on everyone to get settled.

Jonathan placed himself at the center of the crowd, whereas Felix, who looked awkward, stood to the side to allow all of the focus to be on Jonathan.

"Eleventh Percenters," said Jonathan to the group, "I've gathered you all here to give you warning and notice. There is a particularly dangerous Spirit Reaper on the loose, who goes by the name of the 49er. He was one of Creyton's most loyal followers."

Some folks looked at each other, alarmed. Terrence, who still looked combative, snapped, "I've heard that name from Dad, but I don't know his story. What makes him so dangerous?"

Jonathan and Felix looked at each other. Jonah didn't appreciate that. It let him know that everyone else was in the dark, plus it made the situation seem graver.

"You must understand, Terrence, that Creyton chose his followers much like a jewel collector," said Jonathan. "Each one was valuable to his cause, and while they weren't quite as dangerous as he was, they were all terrible and vicious in their own right. They were also an…erratic bunch. Without Creyton in the mix to corral them…"

Jonathan looked as though he didn't really know how to finish that, so he simply let it hang there. Bobby piped up.

"Since there is no more Creyton," he threw an appreciative glance Jonah's way, "is it possible that his followers are, like, guns for hire?"

"No," said Jonathan flatly. "The Spirit Reapers who pledged themselves to Creyton adhered to no other master. Now that he is gone, the ones that weren't apprehended or killed by Networkers slunk back amongst Tenth citizenry. If they act, it is purely of their own volition. Creyton was the only one they'd follow."

"Not trying to be rude, Jonathan," said Magdalena, "but who the hell is this guy?"

She pointed at Felix, who took a deep breath.

"Felix Duscere's the name," he said, and Jonah was surprised to hear his voice so serene and level. He looked at Terrence, whose eyes narrowed, and Reena, whose postured straightened. They'd known Felix to be brusque, abrasive, and irritable in the past two hours alone, so this serenity was a bit off-putting. Jonathan spoke once more.

"Felix is a dear friend of mine," he explained. "He even lived here at the Grannison-Morris estate on occasion during his teens."

"What do you do, Felix?" asked Liz, who was over her initial dislike of him.

"I'm a—bounty hunter, I suppose you'd call it," responded Felix. "I've been tracking the 49er for a while now. But he uses those Haunts for misdirection."

Jonah felt a chill run down his spine. "What are those...things?"

"I can answer that." Reena rose and cleared her throat. "Haunts are manifestations of negative emotions that are given form and sentience from the darker aspects of the Astral Plane. They are pure negativity and adversity that take the canine shape because they are the natural enemies of the heralds."

Jonah got that. The Haunts took the form of dogs because they were the natural enemies of the heralds, which were cats. *That* part of this made sense.

"That's correct, Reena," said Felix. "Haunts are vile, emotion-perverting fiends. The 49er has a unique bond with them, and uses them to weaken enemies."

"By doing what?" said Terrence. "Mind-reading?"

"Not exactly," replied Felix. "It's more like—baggage reading. It tends to work a whole lot easier for them when the individual they are Haunting wears their heart on their sleeves."

He glanced at Jonah. The icy surge in him was warmed by a prickle of anger. Where did the guy get off judging him?

"Because Haunts are an amalgamation of negativity, they thrive on what is like them," continued Felix. "Regret, guilt, anger, and the most potent, fear, are their primary weapons."

"How do they...do what they do?" asked Douglas, who sounded as though he'd forgotten how to use his voice.

"They smell the emotions," answered Felix. "You ever heard the old saying that dogs smell fear? Well Haunts exhibit that same trait, although they are not true canines. They smell your fears, guilt, regrets, your ugliest thoughts, and then they transfer them to the 49er through a psychic link. He then uses the emotions to make psychological bile, which attacks your internal organs and emotions. This is what it means to be Haunted, and if it's left unchecked, it will kill you."

"Wait," said Maxine, unnerved, "did you say psychic link?"

"Yeah, I did," said Felix.

"Let me ask you something," said Grayson, his voice contemptuous, "Blue Man Rowe there carries two ethereal steel batons that have allowed him to slip out of many a tight space. Why didn't he just brain the bastards?"

Jonah rose, furious, but Felix held out a hand. He eyed Grayson with irritation. Reena, Jonah could tell, sensed the shift in essence, and stood. It was clear by her expression that she had no interest in further testosterone-filled displays.

"Don't you know *anything*, Grayson?" she asked in a cool tone. "Jonah didn't attack the Haunt because I warned him against it. Jonah, were you afraid?"

Jonah frowned at the question. Yeah, he'd been afraid, but was it necessary to break him down in front of everyone?

Reena noticed his hesitation, and scowled.

"Were you afraid, like all of us were?" she rephrased.

Jonah sighed. "Yeah, I was."

"Thought so," said Reena. "Grayson, you just heard Felix say that fear was the Haunt's most potent weapon. That wasn't propaganda. Fear is a Haunt's primary weapon because as long as you are afraid of them, as long as that fear of them has a hold over you, they're invulnerable. Haunts can only be wounded or vanquished if you've mastered your fear."

Douglas hung his head, as if he knew beyond a shadow of a doubt that he'd never kill one.

"But Felix killed one, and maimed another," said Terrence. "How—?"

"I'm not afraid of Haunts, boy," said Felix. "I've been dealing with the 49er for years."

Terrence fell silent with a frown. Jonah had trouble with the information as well. A creature that was invincible unless you weren't scared of it? If that was what it took, he hoped that he never saw one again. Its powers alone were frightening, let alone everything else.

"In any case," said Felix, "it would have been unwise for Jonah to have attempted to attack one of those Haunts. If someone managed to survive their psychological weapons, then they would have to deal with their teeth and claws, both of which are made of ethereal steel."

A shudder went around the group. Even Grayson, Karin, Markus, and the rest of Trip's friends were rattled.

"Forgive me," said Maxine quietly, "but let's go back to the 49er using psychic links for a minute. What kind of Eleventh Percenter is psychic?"

Felix exchanged glances with Jonathan, and then sighed. "49er is not an Eleventh Percenter," he said. "At least, he's not anymore."

The confusion in the group was obvious.

"49er is no longer an Eleventh Percenter?" asked Liz.

"No," said Felix. "He calls himself the 49er because he is a miner. A miner of blood. His psychic links are almost inconsequential in comparison to his strength and desire for blood."

Liz made a little squeak, Maxine gasped, and several other people tensed. It was like they understood what these things meant. The silence could be felt, like everyone knew something. Jonah was completely lost, or he hoped that he was. Something was on the edge of his mind, but it couldn't be...that was just ridiculous. Vera looked confused, too, but Liz whispered something in her ear, and she paled. What the hell did Liz just tell her?

"Hold on one second, Felix," he said slowly. "You said that the 49er wasn't an Eleventh Percenter anymore. Then you mentioned psychic links, strength, and the desire for blood..." Jonah's voice trailed off. He was hesitant to voice his idea. He had only heard those characteristics concerning one subject, but it couldn't be...it was stupid. "Surely, you aren't talking about vampires, are you?"

He felt many incredulous eyes on him. Reena buried her face in her hand, while Terrence gave him a look of pity.

Felix frowned at Jonah. "You're kidding, right?"

Jonah sighed with relief, and lowered himself down.

"Of course I'm talking about vampires."

Jonah missed his seat, and hit the ground.

6

Let the ScarYous Games Begin

It had been a week or so since the revelation of the existence of vampires rocked Jonah to his core, and he still had trouble fitting it into his mind. It was almost as jarring as when he discovered that he was an Eleventh Percenter, but that information was simple (enough) to digest, because it explained some of the weirdness of his life. But *vampires*?

Despite the time that had elapsed, Jonah remembered, with perfect clarity, the exchanges that he had with Felix, Terrence, Reena, and Vera the night he'd discovered vampires were real.

* * *

"You're serious, Felix?" he said once he'd righted himself after his fall. "We deal with the ethereal world, and that's spiritual. Spirits, essences, Eleventh Percenters…that kind of thing. Vampires don't fit that mold!"

Felix shook his head at Jonah like he was a simple-minded child. "Do you know what a vampire is, Jonah?" he asked. "The true textbook definition? They are a race of beings who subsist on blood and essences of other creatures. They are described as *undead*, but since life never ends, that term rings hollow. In actuality, vampires are creatures that exist between the physical and the ethereal world, because they are corporeal as well as spiritual. It's what vampire hunters like myself refer to as a life limbo. For this reason, they are a danger to physically living beings *and* spiritually living beings. If that doesn't fit an ethereal mold, I don't know what does."

The meeting ended shortly after that. Jonah glared daggers through Terrence and Reena.

"You knew vampires were real?"

"Of course I knew vampires were real," said Reena with that usual air of obviousness. "I even encountered a couple before I hooked up with Jonathan. If it weren't for my speed ethereality, they'd have drained me."

Terrence looked more understanding, but he, too, treated it like information that was commonly known. "Never met one myself," he said, "but Dad told us all kinds of stories about 'em. I might have been a teenager when I heard those stories, but they were a whole lot more effective than a stupid boogeyman. Believe that."

The only one that understood Jonah's mindset was Vera, who, like him, spent her childhood among Tenth Percenters, where vampires only existed in stories. If Jonah judged her by the way she'd paled when Liz whispered in her ear, the information had been just as earth-shattering for her as it had been for him.

"Can't believe that!" she exclaimed. "Makes my Time Item powers seem downright normal, huh?"

* * *

A little more than a week had passed since all that occurred. Since that time, Felix had returned to the estate ready for business. That was obvious by his vehicle.

It was a 1994 charcoal Jeep Grand Cherokee, but had been fully restored, fortified, and appeared to have more bells and whistles than most modern cars. Felix was tight-lipped about the details of his Jeep, and only said that he was "transient," and liked being fully supplied. Jonah thought the damned thing looked like a Decepticon, and Terrence nicknamed it the *mobile bunker*. Felix also got Jonathan's permission to bring the residents up to speed on vampires, which he informally referred to as *Vampires 101*.

"Vampires aren't complicated creatures," he told everybody, "but the lore surrounding them is. So I'll tell you what's true, and what isn't true. First of all, vampires don't dress like Elizabethan era stiffs. That is purely Hollywood myth. So is the whole sleeping in coffins thing. They are revolting scavengers who live on the outer fringes of humanity, and stick to the shadows. Second of all, crosses don't do shit. Vampires predate Christianity, so it would be illogical to assume that the Christian symbol would hurt them. You may have also heard that vampires' hearts don't beat, and they have no pulse. That's bullshit, too. Their hearts do beat, but barely. Their pulses, though negligent, are present as well. But the vulnerability to sunlight, garlic, and silver—that's all legit. Vampires occasionally move around in sunlight, but they have to be hooded, and buried under layers of clothing. Another thing that you may not have heard of is lavender. It, like rose water and garlic, is an apotropaic—"

"Huh?" said Jonah and Terrence at the same time.

"Symbols and objects that ward off evil entities," said Reena. "Don't you guys read?"

After the brief vampire education sessions, Felix disappeared again, and returned with a huge tank strapped to his back. He looked like some kind of badass exterminator.

"It's a solution of my own creation which consists of rose water, bleach, lavender, and garlic," he explained to all the curious onlookers. "Bleach is the most invaluable component because it desensitizes the sinuses and dulls the sense of smell, so it will make it harder for the 49er and his Haunts to smell blood. Now leave me alone. I need to focus."

Felix sprayed the solution in a wide ring around the estate grounds, which Jonah thought would be challenging because of its sheer size and the number of trees. But Felix did it without a word. He barely even broke a sweat. Jonah noticed that the man didn't take too many breaks, yet he didn't fatigue quickly. The tank on his back was huge, but Felix wasn't freakishly muscular or anything. Truth be told, he was more or less the same build as Terrence, though he looked a bit harder. That was about it. Jonah also noticed that despite Felix's claims of being a bounty/vampire hunter and his willingness to kick someone's ass, he wasn't grizzled or scarred. With the manicured beard, three sixty-wave haircut, and handsome features, he looked—and there was no other way to say it—*privileged.* Reena noticed this as well, but she was at a total loss herself.

"There is a story in his eyes, but I can't gauge him," she revealed to Jonah and Terrence. "Maybe he's got that good genes thing going on. But I don't really trust him."

"Why not?" asked Jonah.

"I can't read his essence."

Terrence scoffed. "Wait a second, Reena," he said. "You are a mysterious woman, and are hard to read. But when you meet other people like that, you don't trust them?"

"That's right," said Reena without hesitation. "It's served me well, too."

One night, Felix even joined in the evening trainings. He took an endowment, picked up some weapons, and marveled at the slate-gray color of his aura. When he noticed eyes on him, he sniffed.

"As a vampire hunter, I don't usually deal with villains that are human, which means my weapons are usually silver or wooden, not ethereal steel," he explained. "So I don't see the color of my aura much. But I don't need the weapons."

He tossed them aside. Everyone looked stunned. He looked at all of them with raised eyebrows.

"Are we going to train or what?"

With a shrug, Malcolm aimed a strike at him. Felix blocked it and pushed him on his back with one hand. Bobby and Alvin attempted to double-team him, but he smoothly stepped aside and shoved Bobby full force into Alvin. Terrence tried a double-leg takedown, but Felix steeled himself, elbowed Terrence in the back, lifted him off of his feet, and unceremoniously dumped him on the ground. Benjamin, Ben-Israel, and Magdalena all tried ethereal attacks, but were dispatched. Reena used her speed attack to try to knock Felix down, but Felix whipped into her direction and stopped her in her tracks. She attempted a strike to a vulnerable area, but Felix parried it almost slothfully. Reena roared in frustration and kicked Felix in the gut as he'd raised his hands to block her strike, then she tried to follow it with her cold-spot trick. Felix, quicker than anyone's eyes could see, caught her hands at the wrists, spread them apart so they wouldn't connect, and flung her to the ground.

Jonah almost laughed when he saw Reena get humbled, but he endeavored to take Felix by surprise. He willed the current from a nearby light to his palm, which he flung at Felix's back. Felix whipped around, yanking a silver object from his belt as he did so. He held the object up so as to absorb Jonah's current, and then threw it at him. Jonah didn't expect that to happen, and got blasted off his feet by his own power. Felix looked around at all of them, and shook his head.

"You people's attacks are all emotion-based," he murmured, "and you all rely on your ethereality far too much."

"Now Felix," said Jonathan with narrowed eyes, "not everyone has the same background as you. Kindly keep the judgments to yourself."

Felix rolled his hands to stretch them. "I'm not judging, sir," he replied. "Just making an observation. But please carry on. I think I'll call it an evening."

He headed up the path from the Glade, leaving silence in his wake. Jonah stared after him, irritated and nettled, but it was nothing compared to the look Reena gave him. She clearly didn't appreciate being one-upped by a man.

The initial concerns over the 49er's presence faded somewhat as excitement began to build. Turk Landry and his *ScarYous* crew were coming into town.

"This is going to be crazy!" said Terrence after he, Jonah, and Bobby finished a weight training session. "I heard that Landry's staying at the Milverton Inn and Suites while they film this season!"

Jonah whistled. He'd been in Rome long enough to have familiarized himself with most locations. Many of the motels and inns were old and derelict, and put Jonah in mind of those lodging areas where naïve groups of spring breakers came to grief in the horror movies. But the Milverton was an exception. Terrence had taken Jonah there, and even though they'd only seen the lobby, it had been more than enough. The floors were so glossy and sleek that Jonah had to remind himself that it was indeed a floor and not still, dark water. The ceiling was Victorian style, with a beautiful ivory sheen. All the furniture looked plush and comfortable, and the widescreen in the lobby was almost otherworldly. And the cost of a room was two hundred and sixty bucks a night.

"You're remembering how much it cost," said Terrence, which brought Jonah back to the present. "Remember, everything is complimentary."

"Oh, please." Jonah rolled his eyes. "Everything is always complimentary until you see the bill."

Terrence laughed.

"Can you tell me why such a swanky place isn't in a more populated area?" asked Jonah.

"It's the oldest trick in the book," said Bobby. "Those city folks get really sick of those populated areas, and they come in droves to quiet areas for weeks on end. It's never slow at the Milverton, so I heard. This may be the country, but that place earns *city* money."

Terrence returned there on the day Landry was due to arrive in town, and Jonah came with him just to avoid the supplication that was sure to occur. When they got there, there were a bunch of folks already there, like this was some kind of red carpet event. Since the dude was a celebrity, Jonah didn't find it surprising. But he was surprised to see Spader there as well, exchanging pleasantries with some woman. He was quite a sight, because not only had he shaven, his hair was all the same color.

"The hell is Spader doing here?" asked Jonah.

Terrence snickered. "I'm not supposed to know this, but Doug filled me in. When something really big is about to happen, like high school trips, proms, weddings, reunions, or whatever, Spader gets cleaned up. There is a casino here, see. Small time, of course, but solvent. Spader comes in, masquerades as a friendly gambler just having fun. He racks up."

"How does he do that?" asked Jonah, awestruck.

"You're asking the wrong one, man," said Terrence. "Latent power, luck...I'd get caught the second I opened my mouth."

They heard louder sounds, and Terrence's eyes widened.

"I think it's him!" he exclaimed. "Landry!"

He dashed into the crowd of people almost before Jonah could follow. Jonah found it hilarious to see how his best friend's excitement made him regress to a prepubescent mark. But it wasn't like Terrence was alone. There were dozens of people around the hotel who were just as ecstatic.

A velvety blue tour bus pulled in front of the hotel. As it moved closer to Jonah's line of vision, he noticed that the velvet blue was merely a backdrop. The entirety of the bus was designed with misty fog on the sides, and the side that faced Jonah displayed a large depiction of Landry's eyes, complete with spiritual apparitions reflected in them. The bus came to a halt, the doors opened, and several people stepped out, with the man of the hour at the rear. Landry descended the steps in a truly dramatic fashion while his bodyguards made a path through the people. Jonah saw that the black T-shirt that Landry wore said *ScarYous Tales of the Paranormal* on its front, and *Illusions Torn Asunder* on the back. Now that he noticed, Landry's entire outfit was black, which made his pale features stand out rather starkly.

"Dear Lord," Jonah said to Terrence. "The man is eating this up!"

"He's earned the right!" replied Terrence. "He has never, ever been wrong! He's been put to the test a million times by skeptics, debunkers, agnostics, scientists, and magicians, and he's embarrassed every one of them. I'd eat it up, too!"

Despite what Terrence had just said, Jonah just couldn't get excited about this guy. He decided to close his eyes, breathe deeply, and will the curtain to open and the actors to perform in his mind.

Now that he was in Spectral Sight, he could see the huge concentrations of vapory mists again. He hadn't expected anything less, though, because this crowd was far too big. Jonah moved his eyes to Turk Landry. There was no mist around him whatsoever. His eyes narrowed at that fact as a similar experience at his old bookstore job crossed his mind. But then Jonah analyzed Landry's smug face, obvious swagger, and devil-may-care attitude, and came to the conclusion that maybe Landry was good at handling loss. He probably filed it away like so many things on his daily itinerary. No harm done, and no big deal there.

Jonah exhaled, relieved. *Maybe I* am *overreacting,* he thought as Terrence muscled himself nearer. *Maybe he really is just a paranormal expert.*

There was a brown-haired woman nearer to the doors of the hotel, with a cute little girl of about eight or nine who could only be her daughter. They both looked as though they had to speak to Turk. They acted as though it were a dire need. The mist near them elongated smoothly, almost lovingly, and formed into an elderly spiritess. The spiritess moved to the woman, and placed her hand on the little girl's shoulder. The girl contemplated her shoulder curiously, like she'd felt a cool breeze or a slight nudge there.

Jonah understood. The spiritess was the little girl's grandmother, and the woman's mom. By the vividness of her red dress and sharpness of her slight form, she had only recently passed into Spirit. That meant that all the emotions were still fresh, and still raw.

Jonah was sharply reminded of his own need for closure that he so needed when his Nana passed away. He'd never gotten that closure. When he'd discovered that he was an Eleventh Percenter, he'd also discovered that he couldn't see his grandmother, because Elevenths couldn't see the spirits of those they were close to. He'd only gotten the mild solace that his grandmother had crossed to the Other Side and was okay. But he still wished that he could have had closure…

He suddenly wanted Turk Landry to see the woman and her daughter. He wanted the paranormal expert to give them the peace that they so desperately needed.

"Notice them," he said aloud; who in this crowd was going to hear him? "Notice the brown-haired family, spirit celebrity boy, notice them, please.…"

Jonah got his wish. Turk's crew was busy with keeping the masses at bay, but he raised a hand to a stern-looking bodyguard on the right, who was the one that was all set to barrel across the girl and her mother. He then raised his hands to silence the crowd, who assumed silence almost at once.

"Please, you two," said Landry in a welcoming tone. "Come forward."

Slowly, the young girl and her mother shuffled toward him, free of interference from his entourage and crew. Jonah saw that the spiritess stayed with them. Her hand was on her daughter's shoulder now.

"You recently experienced a loss, didn't you?" asked Landry.

They both nodded.

Landry raised a pensive forefinger to his slightly unshaven chin. "I feel an elderly presence, very sweet demeanor," he announced. "She went to the next life at the age of eighty-four, yes?"

The little girl nodded enthusiastically, but her mother began to blink rapidly so as to fight tears.

"I'm getting a very strong impression of the name Marlena in my mind," said Turk. "Was that her name?"

The mother, still fighting tears, nodded. Jonah began to hear sniffles throughout the crowd.

"She's right here with you." The assurance in Turk's voice would have swayed anyone. He stepped forward and took the little girl's left hand and the mother's right. "She never left you. Actually, she is next to you, ma'am. I can almost see her form—white hair, and a very pretty red dress."

The little girl smiled, and the mother brought her free hand to her mouth as tears spilled out of her eyes and onto her fingers.

"She was buried in her favorite red dress," she managed after she'd pulled herself together somewhat.

Jonah's eyes widened. That was impressive!

"Ma'am." Turk smiled at the both of them. "Marlena is okay. She is great, actually. She doesn't want you to worry about her anymore. There is no need to. She is pain-free, happy, and she desires more than anything that you understand that she is on a new path. She is not on that path to leave you behind, but to continue on with her own journey."

The mother somehow curtailed her sobs, and managed a watery smile. Her daughter abandoned all pretenses and wrapped her tiny arms around Landry's waist. With a smile, he knelt so as to embrace her properly.

At that, weeping and applause broke out amongst the masses. Jonah clapped right along with them.

"Told you so!" yelled Terrence over the noise.

"Shut up!" said Jonah, but he laughed as he said it.

So Turk Landry was the real deal. Sure, his approach was a little too dramatic for Jonah's taste, but it didn't matter. Anyone in that same situation would have taken in every detail, no matter the approach. In a world of dark ethereality, evil people, and apparently, vampires, Jonah hadn't ever been so happy to be wrong about someone than he was right now.

He was just about to give his eyes a rest and de-activate the Spectral Sight when something caught his attention. The elderly spiritess looked Landry straight in the eye. Landry stared right back at her. The smile slipped off of Jonah's face as curiosity took over.

The gaze with which the spiritess had fixed Landry was desperate, longing, and pleading. Clearly, she was in the act of some wordless begging of some kind. It looked like whatever she desired was as dire a need as her family's need for validation that she was okay…

Landry held her gaze for several moments, and then he nodded and winked. The actions were so smooth and subtle that no one noticed.

Jonah frowned. Huh?

The spiritess broke out in tears of bliss. Landry's nod, that simple nod, was apparently the thing she longed for most…

And then the spiritess closed her eyes, reverted back to mist, and dissipated. She literally dissipated, like film off of a windshield when the defrost got turned on. She was gone. She was even absent from Jonah's Spectral Sight. There was no trace of her whatsoever.

Flummoxed, Jonah snapped his eyes back to Landry, but he'd already entered the lobby with his crew.

"What the HELL?" said Jonah, but no one heard him. At that same moment, Terrence turned to him, glee on his face.

"Did you say something?" he asked.

The excitement that Terrence exhibited forced Jonah to smooth out his features. This wasn't the time or the place.

"No," he murmured. "No. I didn't say anything."

When he and Terrence returned to the estate, Jonah left Terrence at the kitchen, where he was free to tell Benjamin and Bobby everything. He barely missed a step as he descended the stairs, passed the fitness area, and entered Reena's art studio. He took the paint brush out of her hand, grabbed her arm, and pulled her into the armory. She looked curious and annoyed at the interruption, but Jonah launched into the story about the town's temporary paranormal impresario.

Her annoyance diminished with each word, and at the end, she looked just as puzzled as Jonah felt.

"She was gone, Reena," concluded Jonah. "Not a single trace of her essence was left."

Reena pulled her hair free. "She wasn't even visible by Spectral Sight?" she asked.

"No," said Jonah. "The mist that comprised the other spirits and spiritesses remained, but *her* essence wasn't there. It was almost like it had been wiped clean."

"And what was it that you said happened beforehand?" asked Reena. "They shared and exchange and he nodded?"

"Yeah!" answered Jonah. "Well, no, actually. I mean, no words were exchanged. They just looked at each other for a bit, and then he nodded. It was like they'd had a previous agreement and he was making good on it."

"Did you tell Terrence this?" asked Reena.

Jonah fixed Reena with that *Isn't it obvious?* look that Reena usually reserved for all of them. "No, of course I didn't. Terrence is a huge fan, and I didn't want to ruin that. I'm not made that way."

"Huh." Reena looked pensive. "Are you going to let it go?"

"Hell no, I'm not going to let it go." Jonah's answer was instant. "I'm going to keep an eye on that man. Shouldn't be hard; he wants everyone's eyes to be on him, anyway. I'll have plenty of chances, seeing as how he'll be filming his whole season here in Rome. Want to help me check him out?"

Reena smiled in a mischievous way. "Research is what I do. It's not even invasion of privacy; the man's a celebrity. But what are we looking for? If he communicated with the spiritess, then he is clearly not a fraud or a charlatan."

"That's true." Jonah put a finger to his chin and gave it some thought. "We can find out where he's been, and what he's done. The media are piranhas, and always manage to let something slip. Maybe there are some unsavory bits of his past that his beloved website skated over."

Reena fingered her dampener, and gave Jonah an intense look. "Why are you so passionate about this, Jonah?"

Jonah took a deep breath. "I'm not cool with someone sensationalizing the Spirit World. Reena, you should have seen his frickin' bus! I've seen mediums before, so I know they come a dime a dozen. But this man—it was like he was a rock star going on a world tour. The way those people just groveled like mice at his feet. He ate it up. Then he made that woman cry, and then her little girl looked up at him and hugged him like he was the greatest thing since sliced bread—"

"Which is not great, trust me," mumbled Reena.

Jonah shook his head. Reena's disdain for unhealthy food was legendary, but this wasn't the time to dignify it. "It seemed like he made a deal with that spiritess, and then she vanished like a minion or something. It was just—off. As an Eleventh Percenter, it just felt off. Aren't you a little miffed? Aren't you proud of the things we do?"

Reena's eyes never left Jonah's face, but her expression was unclear. She took a deep breath, and allowed the silence to spiral before she answered him. "Of course I'm proud of what we do. Why would you even ask that question?"

Jonah raised an eyebrow, unmoved. "Why did you hesitate, Reena? Is everything alright?"

Reena paused for the faintest trace of a second, and then nodded. "Everything is fine, Jonah. I guess I'm still annoyed at Felix is all. I'd better get upstairs to make sure Terrence doesn't try another beans-and-franks night. See you in a bit."

She left the room.

Jonah stared after her. Reena might be the smart one, but he wasn't an idiot. Either Reena was hiding something, or something was troubling her. Add that to the list of things in his mind.

He lifted a staff and looked it over. His brain was on autopilot.

With 49er, his demon Haunts, school, Terrence's hero worship, and now something up with Reena, wasn't his own life *ScarYous* enough without the arrival of Turk Landry?

7

Three's Company, Too

The one place where life still made sense was school. That fact was a rather odd change to what Jonah had known in the past, back when home had been the escape from school. But his class was a refreshing haven for him, and he hoped that the last fifteen minutes of Kendall's class would pass as slowly as possible.

"The thing about creativity, whether it's writing, painting, dancing, or whatever, is that it cannot be manufactured," she said as she leaned against her desk. "It cannot be taught to you."

There was an unmistakable scoff, and Jonah heard Reynolda Langford mutter to a neighboring student, "If that's the case, then what is the point of this class?"

Jonah felt his fists tighten. He was *so* damn sick of this woman's antagonizing. But it turned out that he needn't have worried. Kendall had it under control.

"The point, Reynolda, is to understand that talent is not given, but *cultivated*," she told her without missing a beat. "Say I told you to write me a book on peanut butter using articles from the FDA. You could write it swiftly, sure, but not a single iota of creativity went into it. But if I told you to craft me a work on peanut butter using only your mind, and you've spent no time at all cultivating your creative talents, your ideas probably wouldn't cover a sticky note, let alone an entire page of paper."

Reynolda blushed such a vivid scarlet that it looked like someone had filled her face with red ink. The stoner guy, whom Jonah discovered was named Chancer Davies, laughed openly along with several others. Jonah himself had to stifle a snicker.

"Writing is conveying soulless data," continued Kendall. "But *creative* writing is where the message is felt. Where it's seen. It's what makes you think, or makes you react. Which brings us to this assignment, which I expect in three weeks."

She grabbed the hat that she had had on at the start of class and held it up.

"Inside this hat are subjects of every kind," she announced. "I want you all to pick one at random and write about it—"

Jonah noticed how many people relaxed. Some even laughed. They all thought this assignment would be a freebie; a throwaway. But Jonah had a strong feeling that Kendall hadn't yet dropped the hammer on them.

"—with absolutely no point of reference," she finished.

There it was. It was when Jonah saw the smiles fade off of so many faces that he felt a smile light his own.

"No research, no reference, no secondhand information whatsoever," said Kendall. "Only your own thoughts, your own opinions, and your own mind. It may be a challenge, but creativity is like exercise. It's not supposed to be easy. Only by surmounting challenges do your skills get stronger and better."

Jonah got the hat first, as he was the one nearest to her. He pulled out a folded piece of paper and looked at it. His jaw dropped somewhat.

Ghosts and/or Celestial Beings

Jonah stared at it. How exactly had he been able to pick such a familiar subject at random? He had to write about a subject that was not only easy, but one that personified his very life?

Wait.

His smile faded somewhat. Kendall said that no secondhand information could be included. He could only craft his work with his own thoughts and opinions. All of it had to be him and him alone.

Suddenly, this dream assignment wasn't so appealing.

Only by surmounting challenges do your skills get stronger and better, Kendall had said.

Truer words had never been spoken.

It was clear that some of his classmates thought along same lines as he did as they looked over their own pieces of paper with worry, confusion, and in Reynolda's case, disdain. By some odd coincidence, she'd picked the piece of paper with Peanut Butter written on it. The irony of that was enough to make

Jonah ignore his own misgivings and chortle along with Chancer and some others.

"Well folks, I think that makes it a night," said Kendall. "Goodnight!"

Students began to leave, and Reynolda shot Kendall a look of disgust before departing. It didn't go unnoticed by Kendall, who responded with a sweet smile. Jonah approached her.

"You really handle that woman well," he observed. "I'd have probably told her off using every curse word that I know."

Kendall laughed as she placed several papers into her satchel. "There is no need for me to do that, Jonah. I get that all the time."

"What?" Jonah looked at her in surprise. "From where?"

"How old are you, Jonah?" Kendall completed packing her satchel and looked him in the eye. "Twenty-four? Twenty-five? Well, I'm twenty-nine. A young twenty-nine at that; just had my birthday. I got this job right out of grad school because my favorite professor was retiring and put in a good word. The old dust that's left in this department fear change of any kind, and they were very cool on the idea. *Frigid,* to be honest."

"Ahhh...." Jonah got it. "You're a threat to the established order they've got in the department. Why is that, though? Just because you're new?"

Kendall half-smiled. "Because I'm new, I'm fifteen years younger than the woman that *was* the youngest in the department, and I'm great at my job without adhering to their tried and true methods. They don't get me. I'm not some moldable piece of clay, and they can't deal with it."

Jonah nodded, impressed.

"It's all women in this department, and they also weren't too keen on a twenty-something woman succeeding like I have, because it means they can't coast like they used to," continued Kendall. "I earn the respect I get. So after the things I've dealt with, a few steely looks from a woman who can barely write her own name doesn't faze me."

Jonah let that sink in. Kendall had just gone up several notches in his mind. After all that, Reynolda really wasn't worth thinking about. It also reminded Jonah of what Felix had said some time back about wearing emotions on one's sleeve. He couldn't help but feel just a bit of annoyance at that.

"I wanted to thank you, Jonah," said Kendall out of the blue.

"Huh? What for?"

"Have you noticed how your male counterparts have suddenly started dressing sharper, trying to impress me?" Kendall asked.

Jonah thought on it, and sure enough, he had noticed the other guys had begun to pay more attention to their wardrobes in the couple of classes they'd had. Some guys that were flat-out slumming that first night now wore button-downs and slacks, while others had dispensed with cracked, dirty sneakers and sported loafers instead. Even Chancer the Pothead had added a belt and cut his hair. It didn't seem like much, but given how scraggly and disheveled he'd been in the first couple of classes, it was a marked change.

Kendall allowed him his thoughts before she continued. "Well, you didn't do that," she said.

Jonah frowned, and surveyed himself in the window's reflection. His khakis weren't all that wrinkled, his navy blue polo shirt was decent, and his cross-trainers weren't cracked. He'd never be on any runway, but he didn't look terrible.

"You didn't do that, and it let me know that you actually cared about this class," said Kendall. "You take my class seriously, and you pay attention to my lessons, not my body. It's so refreshing! You have no idea how much I appreciate it."

At those words, Jonah wasn't so self-conscious. Kendall praised him for doing what he was supposed to do? He was suddenly glad that he hadn't tried a dressy casual look. It just wasn't him.

He bade Kendall goodnight and went to his car, thankful that that teenage bum wasn't present tonight. He'd had his fill of weird people.

Well, people weirder than *he* was, anyway.

The trip to the estate was uneventful, but Jonah noticed that Felix's mobile bunker vehicle was still present on the grounds. He noticed Liz and Bobby on a stroll; the grounds were vast enough to make their walk a full date. Jonah grinned at them. He was so distracted that he almost forgot to do his paranoid scan of the area. The spot where they'd laid eyes on the Haunt stuck out to him now, but thankfully it was empty. There was just him…

Then Bast appeared out of nowhere, walked across the grounds like she owned the place, and stood in front of him.

"What's up, Bast?" said Jonah.

Bast stretched, and then looked him in the eye. Words splashed across his mind: "*Hello, Jonah. Is school still going well?*"

Jonah laughed. "Pretty well, thanks."

"*Good. And Jonah, you needn't worry about the vampire Spirit Reaper or the canine companions. Between us heralds, Jonathan, and Felix, they are no longer a threat here.*"

Jonah blinked. "Well, thanks for that, Bast. I'm glad to hear it."

The herald inclined her head, and scampered away. Jonah went inside the estate, and was met with a sight that puzzled him: Terrence, Alvin, Benjamin, Spader, and a bunch of others had bunched up chairs and taken up the floor. Bowls of popcorn were as plentiful as people. Jonah raised an eyebrow at them.

"Pull up a seat, Jonah!" invited Alvin. "*ScarYous* is about to come on!"

"What?" frowned Jonah. "But the dude is here to film his season. The entire season. He won't be done for months!"

"Too true," said Terrence, "but because he was so thankful to Rome for allowing him to film his whole season here, he has decided to treat the town, and the country, with a *ScarYous* live special!"

With an inhale, Jonah made a split-second decision. He dropped his backpack. "I'd love to."

He grabbed a handful of popcorn from Alvin's bowl and sat next to Terrence.

"I meant to ask you, because I didn't get the chance to the other day, with the Haunts and the vamp and all," said Terrence. "Were Alvin and Bobby right about that Rayne lady?"

Jonah smiled, momentarily forgetting his displeasure with Turk Landry. "Oh yeah. She is gorgeous, but she is also a fantastic teacher."

"Uh-huh, yeah." Terrence punched Jonah's shoulder. "Okay."

Jonah smirked and returned his eyes to the television, where Landry came into view. He and his crew stood in front of an extremely aged house that looked older than the ground on which it stood.

"Wow!" Maxine was very excited. "That's the old St. Christopher house the next town over!"

Landry looked into the camera and began his tale in his usual dramatic fashion. "We are now at the former home of Creswell St. Christopher, an oil tycoon who amassed his wealth throughout the forties and fifties. His net worth, at its peak, nearly rivaled that of Warren Buffett at that time. His meteoric rags-to-riches story is matched only by his cataclysmic fall from grace in the early seventies, when a mysterious illness forced him to sign over his power of attorney to the only relative he had that could stomach his behaviors, his accountant Cremo Winfield."

Jonah had to concede one thing. Landry could tell a story. He could hook people. He had that quality that made even Jonah hang on to his every word.

"Winfield was a superb accountant in the prime of his career, but by 1972, shady dealings, alcoholism, and a tarnished reputation left him a broken shell of his former self, with a soiled brand. That brand extended to Creswell within weeks of Winfield taking over his fortune. Within four years, St. Christopher's immense fortune was a mere several thousand."

Jonah's eyes bulged. "Dude's cousin blew that much money?"

"Yep," said Terrence. "Dad was just a kid at the time, but he told us all about it. That man pissed away nine hundred million dollars on dumb shit and crappy investments. I remember Dad saying that he would have loved to have had an eighth of that guy's net worth."

Jonah agreed, but returned his eyes to Landry.

"St. Christopher made a miraculous recovery from his disease, only to discover a new nightmare," continued Landry. "His name was worthless, and his fortune was all but squandered. He confronted his cousin in a drunken rage at this very house." Landry spread his hands wide, which made Jonah think of a game show valet presenting crap that they viewed as fabulous prizes. "No one knows what words were exchanged in that confrontation," whispered Landry. "But the outcome was a torrent of blood and whiskey, and a hail of bullets. The aftermath spoke louder than any words could have. The citizenry of this town have avoided this land ever since; some even claim to hear the arguments and the shots in the stillness of the night. My team and I hope to bring you, our audience, concrete proof that spirits walk among us. It is now time for things to get... *ScarYous*."

Jonah's friends all sat forward with interest. Jonah narrowed his eyes. What was Mr. ScarYous' game?

The entire episode was a clinic in spectral activity. It was crazy from the second Landry and his crew set foot in the house. Glass shattered, long-forgotten items got upended, and at least one voice repeatedly shouted, "*GET OUT!*" Jonah attempted Spectral Sight while watching the live special, but unfortunately, it didn't work through the television. Talk about disappointing.

The wild adventure ended on a truly frightening note when one of Landry's cameramen, who'd already been yelled at twice by the unseen spirit, got concussed by an ancient vase, which, on live television, whipped across the room and shattered across the back of his head. It was one of the nastiest hits Jonah had ever seen. The poor man crumpled instantly.

"My God!" shrieked Magdalena. "Why would they keep that in there?"

"It's *live*, Magdalena," answered Spader, unperturbed. "Remember? And besides, that's market value!"

The chatter almost drowned out Landry's final words. "We have what we came for, my friends," he declared. "This dwelling remains troubled, and ridden with strife. In the wake of the grisly ordeal that occurred here, we are left with as many questions as answers. Will these spirits ever find the peace that they so rightly deserve? At the current time, it is impossible to know. I am Turk Landry, and this has been *ScarYous Tales of the Paranormal*. Good night."

After much excited conversation about the live special, the group dispersed, and soon, Jonah and Terrence were alone. Some of the excitement left Terrence's face, and was replaced by something Jonah couldn't place.

"Jonah, I need to ask you something."

Apprehensive, Jonah braced himself. Was there something weird going on with Reena *and* Terrence? "What's that?"

"Remember when we went to the Milverton Inn and Suites to see Landry come into town?" asked Terrence.

"Duh."

"Well, something weird happened."

Jonah raised an eyebrow. "Yeah?"

"When Turk told that lady those things about her mother, there was some kind of exchange between him and the spiritess, and then she disappeared from Spectral Sight."

Jonah was so relieved that he didn't know what to do. So Terrence had seen that as well.

"You saw that, didn't you?" Terrence asked him.

"Yeah, I did, Terrence. I saw the whole thing. Reena knows, too."

Terrence looked alarmed, as if he'd heard something that he didn't want to hear. "You two are looking into his history, ain't you?"

Jonah felt a twinge of guilt again. He hadn't wanted to keep Terrence out of the loop, so he chose a different tack. "Terrence, I understand that you're a huge fan of the guy, but what if we are? Why does it matter to you?"

Terrence squared his shoulders. "Jonah, I don't believe in a lot of things. After my idiot parents, and then my idiot *adopted* parents, I suppose I got kinda jaded and cynical. I'm thankful that Bobby and Alvin found me, and that the Decessios took me in, but that didn't undo my first thirteen years of living. I guess I developed a hatred of people letting me down, you know? And I like being an Eleventh Percenter, but it ain't something we're shouting from the highest mountain. But Landry…" Terrence paused for a second. "He is good at what he does. And he gets spirit stories out there, at least in his own way. The spirits, the paranormal stuff…he gets it out there for the people to see. They've tried to discredit him, and he's shut them all down. I'd just really hate for all of that…for all of it to be a lie. Like, some sleight of hand or some crap."

Jonah stared. Terrence was rarely ever serious, unless of course the subject was food. But he was adamant about this matter. It made Jonah just a little afraid. If Turk Landry wasn't on the level…if he was a fraud…something might break within Terrence. It would be a huge blow. "Well, we know it isn't sleight of hand," he told Terrence in a reassuring voice. "Else he never would have interacted with the spiritess. He even divined her name."

Terrence looked slightly appeased. "Right. Yeah. So are you guys looking him up, then? What have you found out?"

"Nothing at all." Jonah was happy to say that. For now at least. "But I'll need to speak to Reena again. I'm sure she's bent over backwards checking things out."

They headed to Reena's art studio, and she didn't even have to ask why they came.

"First of all, Turk was born on the twenty-second of August in 1973," she said promptly.

"Wait." Jonah thought that over. "Twenty-second of August. Like, Twenty-two August? That sounds—"

"British," supplied Reena as she spun a paintbrush between her fingers. "He was born in London, but he was only there about five seconds before his parent relocated to Escondido, California. I wouldn't be surprised if he has no memory of England at all."

"Huh." Jonah shrugged that information off. "Anything else?"

A slightly puzzled look crossed Reena's face at the question. "This man has a tight—and I do mean tight—lid on his personal life. He's a celebrity, so it's understandable. But this…it's almost like no one knows anything about him at all away from *ScarYous Tales* and all that. But I did discover that he has had forty-seven jobs since he left college. Paranormal investigator was the forty-eighth, and obviously the one that struck gold."

"Forty-seven jobs." Terrence looked amazed. "Talk about persistence! I'm glad he created *ScarYous Tales*, though. It's obviously his calling."

But Jonah met Reena's eyes and knew their thoughts matched. This man was only slightly past forty, and had been employed in forty-seven places. Jonah had never heard of such job-hopping. A guy that had had that many jobs was either an aimless fool, lacked guidance, or had something to hide. And Jonah hoped, for Terrence's sake, that the answer was one of the first two options. Hell; he'd even take a combination of the two.

Because the third would only serve to screw things up for all of them.

8

Lifeblood

Luckily, none of the three of them had much time for mulling over Turk Landry, as Jonah, Terrence, and Reena had their own responsibilities keeping them busy. Terrence was tucked back into his job at the high school, and jokingly told them that the students found a janitor who vacationed in Hawaii very interesting. Reena's clerical job made her quite irritable. She'd confided in Jonah that after her boss made her draw up another form one day because the first one looked like it had "frayed edges," she'd contemplated clapping once to freeze him. Jonah spent his own time collecting his thoughts and working on Kendall's assignment.

It truly was a tough one, made so by the fact that his opinion was so limited. This whole thing had to come from his mind? Even when he'd written editorials for the *Daily Rap*, he could use references, but Kendall really gave them a difficult task. For several moments one day, while he tried to overcome the hump of the introductory paragraph, he'd wished he'd traded places with Reynolda Langford so he could write about some damn peanut butter.

What could he say about ghosts and ethereal beings that came from his own mind? That spirits never actually tried to haunt people; they had as much right to walk Earthplane as physical being did? Nope. The world wasn't ready for that, let alone his creative writing class. Was there anything that he could fudge, make it seem as though he conjured it from his imagination, but in reality were simple facts about the Eleventh Percent?

Jonah felt a shiver of inspiration. What if he wrote about the Eleventh Percent through purely fictitious accounts? That would be a great deal better than Landry, a psychic Tenth Percenter with potential skeletons in his closet (forty-seven skeletons in fact, which constituted a graveyard). Jonah actually *was* an Eleventh Percenter—he had firsthand knowledge of the Spirit World. With a grin, he put pen to paper and wrote:

> *The spirit world, ethereal world, or whatever one's personal interpretation labels it, is one that has been described, deciphered (allegedly), and understood as the proof needed that there is a life beyond this one.*

> *But what would someone say if they had no book, no opinion, no extraneous "two cents" to influence their own thoughts? My own belief, I would say, is that the beings in Spirit, if they are indeed there—*

Jonah frowned slightly when he wrote that last part. It was slightly annoying to have to write about something doubtfully when he knew it to be true.

> *—are not to be contested, nor are they to be doubted, debunked, challenged, or dismissed. Just accepted. The common truth, I feel, is that the Spirit World, and its inhabitants, or ghosts, do not live independently of us. I believe they live interchangeably. Not in a different world, per se, but an extension of this world, like their world is but the epidermis of our own.*

Jonah straightened, flexed his neck muscles, and read over his writing. "Good stuff!" he muttered to himself. It was always a marvel how the creative mind worked when allowed to wander. Kendall was right after all—the fruits of creativity could not be manufactured.

Movement beyond his window caught his eye. He saw Reena and Liz conversing at the base of the woods. The subject must have been important because Reena hadn't bothered to change from her work clothes. They both seemed very passionate about the conversation. Jonah had never seen Reena that cheerful. She held up a plant with blue petals for Liz to see, but Liz shook her head, happily picking a red plant out of her basket and pointing to it. Reena then asked another question, and Liz indicated a place on her torso.

"Oh," mumbled Jonah to himself. Their conversation was about that physical body reset thing. Jonah knew that Liz was a naturally gifted healer and Green Aura, but he didn't see the allure of a body reboot. So Reena was interested in it. She was the smart one, after all, and she loved expanding her knowledge. That was cool. But what did the plants have to do with it?

Reena was more focused than Jonah had ever seen her that night during their evening training. Jonah wasn't put off by it at all. After he saw her so troubled a few days ago, it was nice to see her game face back in place. But her intensity was off the chart. Jonathan noticed this, too, and after Reena sent Terrence and Douglas sprawling and freezing Alvin on three different occasions, he called a quick break.

"Reena, what's up?" said Jonah as he and Terrence sat with her near a cedar tree with their water. "You're out there like you've been eating red meat!"

Reena gave him a sidelong glance, and then sipped at her water. "You know the answer to that question," she muttered. "I'm—working on something. Something that might change everything for me. Change everything I've ever known."

Terrence's eyes gleamed. "A painting, then?" he asked. "You're finally going to market your stuff?"

Reena's closed her eyes. "It is indeed a work of art, Terrence," she said. "I don't think I've ever tried anything like it. But if I'm successful, my God..."

Jonah thought of that skyline painting that she hadn't yet completed, and while it looked very good (better than good), he could think of at least fifteen other pieces she had already finished that could change everything. "Why wait, Reena?" he asked. "You have treasures upon treasures down there—"

"You know my stance on that, Jonah," said Reena, and her eyes snapped open to show a stern gleam. "This is different. I just know," she added, when Jonah was about to make further inquiries. "I can't tell you how I know. I just do."

After another forty minutes or so (which included Jonah taking a few rounds with Reena, and a blessedly uneventful round with Karin), training ended, and everyone scattered. Jonah saw Liz and Bobby join hands and disappear into the night, saw Jonathan voice instructions to three heralds, Bast included, and saw Malcolm present Felix with an assortment of what looked like jagged, wooden lightning bolts.

"Stakes," said Terrence, who followed Jonah's puzzled gaze.

"Really?" Jonah frowned at the crude form. "And Malcolm, the perfect artist, made them that way?"

"I know," said Terrence. "But apparently, Felix asked for them to be made jaggedly. Something about them not coming out of a vampire's heart if they tried to yank it out or whatever."

He shrugged, and led the way back to the estate, where many of their friends had already congregated around the widescreen for a live special of *ScarYous*. Landry and his crew would investigate a farmhouse somewhere in the tri-county area. Jonah, who had no opinion or interest, headed toward the stairs, with a vague thought about writing in his journal. But then, the front door banged open, and Liz and Bobby spilled into the room. Everyone looked at them, confused.

"Liz, what's wrong?" asked Reena, who'd stopped short of the kitchen when they'd entered the room.

"Your fun night is over," declared Liz.

"Why?" asked Terrence, who rose from his seat.

"Trip's coming," answered Bobby, who looked as if his nerves were on end, "and for some reason, he is pissed!"

Jonathan had emerged from the kitchen. Jonah presumed he had finished his conference with the heralds, but he seemed resigned about something. Liz's gaze turned to him immediately.

"Jonathan, sir—" she began, but Jonathan shook his head.

"I know Titus is on his way, dear," he said calmly, and Jonah immediately knew that that was the reason for his resigned expression. "I know he's livid as well. Don't worry—I'll handle it."

Jonah imagined Trip must've been really angry, because Liz looked at Jonathan with doubt after he said that.

Thundering footsteps reached their ears, and seconds later, the front door was just about bashed off its hinges. Trip was there, and wasted no time slamming his bag to the ground. He must have lifted religiously during his time in South Carolina. He wasn't larger, but he was a great deal leaner and more cut. The muscles in his arms were prominently featured because his fists were balled. He looked like he'd explode if he didn't strike something soon.

"Where is he?" he whispered frostily. "Where is he, Jonathan, and why is he here?"

Jonathan hadn't flinched or blinked when Trip stormed into the room. He appeared to be as bored as he was before, almost as if he had seen episodes like this one in the past. "He is here, Titus," he said calmly, "because the one that *should* make you angry is back, and active once more."

Whatever that meant, Trip chose to ignore it. Jonah noticed that his anger hadn't abated in the slightest. "I want him out of here. I don't give a—"

"He is as welcome at this estate as you are, Titus," said Jonathan, whose voice now carried a hint of anger. "This was once his home, after all—"

"AS IF I NEEDED REMINDING!" bellowed Trip. "FELIX DUSCERE WILL LEAVE HERE NOW, OR I SWEAR ON MY SPIRIT—"

"Titus." Jonathan's voice was dangerously quiet. Jonah and everyone else present had been snapping their heads back and forth between the two of them like it was a tennis match. But now, all eyes were on Jonathan, who radiated power and emotion. "I understand that feelings on your side are still raw, but you will *not* speak to me that way. You will not raise your voice when we are perfectly capable of carrying on this conversation rationally, and at a respectable tone of voice. And lastly, you will not threaten anyone under this roof. Do you understand?"

Jonathan's voice hadn't elevated a single decibel. He sounded professional. Tactful, even. But every single syllable was laced with such authority that Jonah was almost compelled to comply, even though he hadn't done anything.

Trip's expression remained the same, but even *he* wouldn't test Jonathan at this point. "Whatever."

At that very moment, Felix came through the kitchen door with a plastic kit of some kind in his hands and a troubled look on his face. "Jonathan, we've got a problem—"

He froze. His expression became one of ice and stone, and he allowed the plastic kit to fall from his hands as they balled into fists. "Trip."

Jonah noticed Reena place her ethereal dampener directly on her skin, and guessed that the volatile emotions had to be taxing to her essence reading.

Trip's jaw worked for a small amount of time before he spoke in a deliberate tone. "This will be my first and last time telling you this, Duscere," he whispered. "Stay the *fuck* away from me. You've been warned, and I won't do so again."

He yanked up his bag from the floor and went upstairs, leaving behind a tension so palpable it was almost electric in his wake.

"Um—shall we return to *ScarYous,* anyone?" said Spader, hoping to cool things down.

"No," said Jonathan. "It's my understanding that the paranormal specialist will be here many months to film his season. It would be no loss to miss one of the live specials."

Spader turned off the television without hesitation. Jonathan turned to Felix.

"Now I believe you were going to say something important before the interruption, Felix?" he said.

But Felix remained silent. It seemed to be a challenge for him to regain his composure. It wasn't possible for him to ball his fists any tighter, and a vein worked in his temple.

"Felix, breathe," said Jonathan, who looked concerned. "In through your nose, and out through your mouth. Just like I taught you years ago. You're stronger than this..."

Felix closed his eyes and implemented the breathing exercises. Liz stood and mouthed, *"Does he need help?"* to Jonathan, but Jonathan shook his head and held up a finger. After several seconds, Felix looked more relaxed.

"Right," he said. "So Trip hasn't changed. Whatever. But I'm glad that so many of you are here right now."

He bent down and retrieved his plastic kit while everyone looked at him in wonder. Jonah wasn't too thrilled with his own location in the room now. Since his plan had been to leave when *ScarYous* came on, he was positioned closely to Felix. After he'd seen him struggle with anger over Trip, Jonah didn't want to be near him. So he took two subtle steps back. Felix didn't even notice.

"I'll trust you guys to carry this information to the residents not present at the moment," Felix carried on. "Jonathan, I've discovered what the 49er is after."

Jonathan drew himself up to his fullest height. "Yes?"

Felix tightened his grip on the kit so much that the plastic cracked in protest. "He's after lifeblood, sir."

Jonathan pursed his lips. Jonah was confused as hell, but he was happy to see that he wasn't alone. Even Reena looked puzzled.

"What does that mean?" he decided to ask. "He takes your life by taking your blood?"

Felix rolled his eyes. "No. I mean lifeblood. Jonathan, would you be so kind?"

Jonathan nodded. "You have been endowed."

Felix shuddered for just a moment after the sudden invigoration, but was all business seconds later. He extracted a knife and a mirror from the left pocket of his cargo pants. Then he laid the mirror down on his kit and ran the knife blade across his palm.

"What are you *doing*?" demanded Liz.

"Calm down, Lizzie," said Felix, eyes still on the cut he'd just created. "I consider it a great day if wounds such as this are the only ones I receive in the field. Now watch closely, everybody."

Jonah looked on with everyone else as Felix squeezed his fist, which caused blood to drip onto the mirror. The small puddle of blood lay stationary for several seconds, and then something very strange happened.

The blood rose independently from the mirror, leaving no traces on the surface. What seemed like vapory red mist freed itself from the hovering mass, and elevated even higher. What was left behind darkened, curdled, and fell back onto the mirror. It had the consistency of half-dried school glue.

Jonah heard small gasps from his friends, but his own eyes never left the vibrantly red mist still hovering in the air. Felix pulled a vial from his plastic kit and ran it across the vapor, much like a kid attempting to catch a firefly. When he'd contained it all, he held it out for all to see.

"This is lifeblood," he announced. Jonah noticed that even though it had the appearance of vapor, it moved about like liquid in the vial. "Haunts love this because it allows them to traverse Earthplane, even though they are Astral creatures. And vampires crave it because drinking it makes them indefinitely sated, and damn near untouchable."

"Disregard what the cinema and the lore have told you about vampires drinking blood," Jonathan chimed in. "They do indeed consume blood—" he pointed at the curdled mass on the mirror, "but that is only because it's included with what they truly desire, which is lifeblood." He pointed at red vapory liquid in Felix's vial.

Malcolm regarded the curdled blood on the mirror. "Huh. Like the fat that you trim off of meat?"

"Exactly," said Felix and Jonathan at the same time.

"Wait a second," said Reena. "Vampires drain people dry. I've seen pictures, and even had the unfortunate experience of witnessing it a few months before I moved here. But you're saying that they don't care for blood?"

"Again," said Felix with a trace of impatience, "they will drink both types, but it's the lifeblood they crave. Lifeblood exists in everyone's blood, though it's more potent in Elevenths than it is in Tenths. Lifeblood is also why vampires are so dangerous."

Jonah tried hard to follow and connect the dots. He really did. But he had nothing but blank on this one. "What are you saying? We already know that they're dangerous to Tenths and Elevenths."

"Very true, Jonah," said Jonathan. "But they are also dangerous to *spirits*. Like Felix said, lifeblood exists in everyone's blood, but when a person passes into Spirit and dispenses with a physical body, lifeblood is what courses through their veins."

"Whoa, whoa, whoa," said Terrence. "There ain't no way. Spirits and spiritesses *bleed*??"

"Yes, boy," said Felix. "They are still living beings, as you know. If a being is still alive, then it has to have something in its veins. Vampires are a danger because of the life limbo I told you about some time back. It allows them to extract blood from physical and spiritual beings."

Jonah felt like his head was about to explode. Why did every new thing have to suck in the worst possible way? "So what does he need it for? Fun? Power? Insatiable thirst?"

"That's the problem." Felix bound the wound on his hand. He treated it like an afterthought. "He doesn't seem to be drinking it. I think he is storing it. It seems that he's been getting samples from all over the place."

Jonathan gave Felix a sharp look. "Is that what you've found? A body trail?"

Felix sighed. "Yes sir," he confessed. "I've found some Tenths, and several Elevenths as well, in places along the state line. They weren't fully drained, but they were hanging by the smallest of threads."

"Hold on." Douglas swallowed. "Does that mean that you had to put them down?"

Once again, Felix looked discomfited. "It was necessary. Either the Haunts would have tortured them until they passed into Spirit, or they would have turned, and began hunting themselves. Trust me; you do *not* want vampires, as in plural. The carnage would be catastrophic."

"This is why Creyton allowed the 49er into the fold," explained Jonathan. "49er would collect lifeblood, hoard it for Creyton, and be allowed a portion himself. It was a perfect arrangement. Creyton would use it to bribe other vampires, and I have no doubts that he probably did countless experiments on the substance himself. If it was something he could control, he would use it. Guaranteed."

"But Creyton isn't here anymore," said Reena. "And Felix just said that the 49er isn't consuming the lifeblood; just storing it. So what is the point?"

Jonathan fingered his infinity medallion, which made Jonah's gut jolt. Jonathan only did that when he knew something sucky. "It's impossible to say at the moment," he said. "But it only makes it more imperative that he be stopped. He is the miner of blood, after all. It just happens to be lifeblood. God only knows what he's up to if he's storing it."

"So that's it? Creyton's gone, so the 49er's on some free agent tip? Is he storing all that lifeblood up so that he can drink it and become some vampiric supersoldier?"

Terrence's triple-barreled questions weighed on Jonah's mind as he, Terrence, and Reena sat in the art studio. He hadn't ever heard of anything so alarming in his life, and that was after discovering the existence of vampires.

Now one of them (who used to work for Creyton, no less) was murdering people left and right so as to store some mystical potion in their blood. It sounded like some sick kind of steroid or something.

Reena sat cross-legged on the floor, fingers at her temples. She hadn't yet contributed to the conversation, but that might have been because Terrence didn't let either of them get a word in edgewise.

"Maybe the 49er doesn't plan to drink it all," he continued. "Maybe he plans to turn some folks into vamps and make them drink it, so he'll have some super-vampire army."

"No." Reena didn't lift her head, but her voice was firm. "He wouldn't build an army."

Jonah looked down at her. "And how do you know that?"

"According to my research, vampires are elitists," answered Reena. "A dominant hierarchy, if you will. A vampire will turn someone when if there is something in the act for them, but that's rare, because many of them view turning as diluting their ranks. Think of those corporate jobs that everyone wants, but they don't ever hire anyone new. They've got who they want, and don't want to change up the regime. They might turn an Eleventh now and then, but they would never turn a Tenth on principle. Besides all that," she finally lifted her head, "if the 49er's aim was to build a vampire army, then he wouldn't have left the trail of bodies that Felix found."

"Okay," said Jonah. "The 49er is out for himself. Got that. And he is storing samples. I might sound a little superstitious, but I think he is aiming for some magic number."

"Huh." Terrence looked as if he wanted to wrap his mind around that one. "It kinda makes sense. But what magic number, do you think—?

"Fifty," said Reena without hesitation.

Jonah and Terrence stared. Reena noticed their expressions and sighed.

"He is a miner of blood who refers to himself as the 49er," she said, like it was plain as day. "He is also a vampire who used to be an Eleventh Percenter, so his blood is already ethereal. He would need forty-nine more samples to get up to scratch. It was a simple enough theory to form."

Jonah glanced at Terrence. That theory was *not* simple in any way, shape, or form. How Reena pulled that out was beyond either of them.

But for some strange reason, it made sense. Fifty samples of lifeblood sounded like a nice round number that would appeal to a superstitious person.

"But you know what?" said Terrence, hope in his voice, "maybe it won't even matter. Maybe we can leave it to Felix and Jonathan. Felix is the vampire bounty hunter, and Jonathan...is Jonathan. Maybe together they can squash the 49er's ass."

"While we're on the subject of Felix," said Jonah, keen on a subject change, "I wonder what the hell is up between him and Trip. I thought they were going to rip each other's heads off! I mean, Trip hates everyone, but it seemed like Felix made him go supernova or something."

Reena contemplated her fingers again. "I just hope that they can keep their tempers in check. No telling what damage can be done if they don't watch themselves."

Jonah raised an eyebrow. "That's obvious in regards to Trip, but how do you know that about Felix? I thought you said you couldn't read him."

"I can't," replied Reena. "But just think of his fighting skills. Look at what he has done in the Glade. Have you seen the weapons that he has in that rolling bunker of his? I just—I just think that if you add anger to that mix, you can have a frightening individual."

Terrence shook his head. "Vampires...lifeblood...crazy ethereal dogs...makes you wish you were just a Tenth, doesn't it?"

"You've no idea." Reena had such longing in her voice that Jonah and Terrence frowned.

"I was kidding, Reena," said Terrence.

"So was I, Terrence." Reena seemed neither caught off guard nor awkward.

But Jonah knew that that was a lie. He didn't know how it was so clear to him, but it was. Reena's expression and voice tone hadn't changed. She looked as level as ever.

But something told Jonah that all wasn't well with his other best friend.

9

Extra Credit

The 49er's quest of hoarding lifeblood put every inhabitant of the Grannison-Morris estate of alert. Jonathan nixed the idea of indefinite spiritual endowments though, explaining that they would only make residents more attractive, and therefore more vulnerable, to 49er and his Haunts. Jonathan told them that the enemy could be avoided with a combination of common sense and the prowess that he trained them to hone each night.

"That is not to say that you need to refuse a spiritual endowment should the need arise," Jonathan hastily added. "But unless it is necessary, please refrain from maintaining it for longer than three-and-a-half to four hours at a time. Remember the fatigue that occurs when you relinquish them. In this situation, that may very well make you a sitting duck."

Felix, who received the green light from Jonathan, requested (it was more like a demand in Jonah's eyes) that everyone carry his personally made "kits." The things puzzled Jonah, because not only were there plenty for everyone, they also contained some interesting things.

"It's necessary to have everything in there," insisted Felix when Jonah questioned him about the inclusion of salt, rubbing alcohol, and pouches of rice. "Lifeblood can survive for up to ninety-six hours outside of our bodies, because we are Eleventh Percenters. That means that 49er and his mutts can still sniff it out and hoard it. It's not like a Tenth's blood, which holds no value once it hits open air. Thus the ingredients you see. The salt will dry out the lifeblood. In the event of no salt, pour the rubbing alcohol over any spilled blood and set it ablaze. If neither of them are available, throw the rice, which will soak up the moisture of anything, including lifeblood."

"You know," said Jonah with a laugh, "I read somewhere a while back that if you carried a pocketful of rice and a vampire tried to attack, you could throw it at them and they'd be compelled to count every single grain."

Felix gave Jonah a look that was so stony that it wiped all the mirth from his face. "That is Tenth garbage. If you were to chuck rice at a pursuing vampire, you'd simply piss it off more."

Felix packed up the mobile bunker with kits to take to Reverend Abbott's infirmary at the Faith Haven. Jonah sneered at the back of him.

"I was just making a damn joke," he said to Terrence and Reena. "That dude takes things too seriously."

"Yeah," said Terrence. "He certainly ain't warm and fuzzy. He is such a—"

"I concur," interrupted Reena, whose eyes were still on the dust trail the mobile bunker made on its way down the drive. "His fuse is either short, or simply non-existent."

"You always put things nicer than I would, Reena." Terrence shook his head and reached into his pocket. "Anyway, take these."

He handed them pocket-sized mirrors. Reena nodded and thanked him without comment, but Jonah surveyed it questionably.

"What good is a mirror?" he asked. "I saw on T.V. that vampires don't cast reflections."

"That's actually Tenth bullshit, too—" began Terrence, but Jonah threw up his hands.

"For the love of—is *everything* a lie? Or a myth? Are you going to tell me that they don't actually have fangs next?"

"Of course they have fangs!" Terrence didn't register much of the sarcasm in Jonah's words. "The mirrors are a nifty little trick that Dad told us about after Bobby told him about the whole 49er business."

"Okay." Jonah prepared himself. "What purpose do they serve?"

"Ever hear that old saying 'The one place that you can't lie to yourself is the mirror?' asked Terrence. "It's usually something that people tell folks who have rounder bellies than they'd like to. But it's actually steeped in ethereal lore. If you see a vampire in a mirror, you will see their true form. The one that he or she conceals with that human façade."

Jonah pocketed the mirror. Once again, Terrence blitzed him with brilliance that he usually kept to himself.

Hours later, Felix returned, with what he referred to as the final piece of the kits: Superglue.

"If you sustain cuts, it would function like blood in the water. Easily traceable by Haunts and vampires, so the glue would come in handy during those times."

"But that's damn near a biohazard!" said Liz with indignation. "Do you know what's in glue? And you expect us to introduce it to our nerve endings and bloodstream?"

"Don't be such a prude, Lizzie," said Spader, whom Jonah knew was only playing devil's advocate to get Liz's attention. "When I left a couple foster homes, I used superglue many a time to seal up wounds."

Liz fixed a frosty gaze onto him. "Huh. That explains why you're an immature thieving bum who needs adult supervision in any room where things aren't nailed down."

Spader froze. The Twizzler he'd been nibbling on fell from his hand.

"Good thing that he is a thief," muttered Bobby to Jonah. "Maybe he can steal himself some dignity."

Of course, there were some people that had little to no interest in Felix's additional protection.

Trip and his buddies defiantly refused the kits and the precautionary briefings, and none of them took part in the watches that were set. As Trip had his fair share of supporters, his indifference to their plight put a reasonable dent in potential manpower for the watches. The fact that most residents of the estate didn't care for Trip and his inner circle softened that blow, though. Whenever Felix was around, Trip either vacated the room or visibly restrained himself from attacking him. Felix ignored it for the most part, but Jonah noticed that he employed the breathing techniques that he'd seen him do the night Trip returned. Jonah also noticed that Felix kept weapons on his person when Trip was near.

"Jonathan," said Jonah one evening after a training session, "I have to know. What is the deal with Trip and Felix?"

"Ah." Jonathan looked pensive as he lowered himself to a wooden stump. "Titus has lived here for almost twenty-five years, Jonah, and the first few of those were divided between here and his mother's. When he first moved here, or started spending time here, I should say, Felix resided here as well. His mother sent him here for training, because his father was gone a lot and wasn't able to do it."

Jonah nodded, waiting for more.

"Felix was about two years older than Titus, but age can be immaterial at times. Titus was a bundle of skills, but lacked guidance, so Felix took him under his wing."

Jonah looked at Jonathan, stunned. He couldn't imagine Trip forging such a positive bond with anyone.

"Felix treated Titus like a younger brother, which was a dynamic that was intriguing to both boys, as neither of them had many friends. Several years passed that way, but then an unfortunate incident occurred concerning their fathers—"

A meow jarred them both, and Jonathan turned to see a tabby near them, presumably with a report.

"We'll resume this story later, Jonah," said Jonathan, and Jonah couldn't help but notice that the Protector Guide seemed thankful for the interruption. "You had best get some rest, no? You have class tomorrow, don't you?"

"Yeah, I do," Jonah replied, but instead of heading to his room, he went straight to Terrence and Reena and told them what he'd found out from Jonathan.

"Really." Terrence looked incredulous. "Trip had a best friend? Trip *Rivers*?"

"And that best friend was Felix?" added Reena, who looked about as skeptical as Jonah felt. "The guy whom he looks like he's three steps from murdering every time he sees him?"

"Yeah, I know." Jonah couldn't believe it either. "Apparently, something went down with their dads, so I'm assuming that's why they hate each other now."

"I wondered what that could have been," said Reena.

"You don't know anything about them?" asked Jonah, his eyes on the both of his friends.

"I've been here since I was fourteen," said Reena, "but I'd never heard of Felix before, and I'm willing to swear that the name Duscere is rare. It's quite possibly unique to Felix's family. As for Trip...it isn't like he volunteers any information, since he hates everyone. And I never had any inclination to look into his back story. He has done great things as an Eleventh Percenter, though."

"Like what?" Jonah's skepticism bled into the question. "Did he say good morning to someone during breakfast once?"

Terrence laughed. "I don't know many specifics, but Jonathan is complimentary of him, even though he puts him in his place at times."

Jonah looked over at the kit he'd gotten from Felix. Trip was a lost cause. That was obvious. But Felix...

"I'm trying to figure Felix out." It was almost like Terrence pulled it out of Jonah's mind. "He is usually so calm and informative, and then he gets cold...and then he goes out of his way to make these kits for us, with a bunch to spare for Reverend Abbott. He is a tough one to read."

Automatically, Jonah and Terrence looked at Reena, who shook her head.

"It's just odd." She shook her head again. "But I just can't read him. It's like his essence is enveloped or something."

Jonah was instantly wary. "You mean like he's hiding something?"

"No no, it's nothing like that," said Reena slowly, "It's more like his essence is—barred. Locked. It's like he is trying to get a feel for everyone around him while offering nothing in return."

Jonah thought on that. The man was definitely mysterious, and it was more than likely that he had a secret or two, but he had helped them so much recently. Terrence was right. He was a tough one to read.

"Well, he needn't bother getting a feel for Trip," he told them as he grabbed his kit. "I can tell him exactly what Trip and his buddies are thinking, and I don't even need Turk Landry's gift for it."

Kendall's classes were probably the most fun Jonah would have all week. He had done steady work on Kendall's assignment, but it was still far from completion. He had nothing but gratitude about the week that he had left before it was due. He had no trouble whatsoever with Kendall's task for tonight, though. It entailed writing a composition on how personal experiences had shaped them creatively throughout the years. Jonah blazed through the assignment. He could have written a short story on the matter, but he resisted the urge to do so and complied with Kendall's wish to keep it between three and four pages. When they shared portions, Jonah had no problem recounting tales from his past concerning people who told him that writing wasn't for him. When he got to the part about his middle school English teacher dismissing his writing as "overblown tall tales," several classmates had looks of incredulity. He couldn't help but think *Where were you guys when I was a kid??* It was baffling to him to be surrounded by competent and intelligent people. Why couldn't that have happened back in Radner? Where were the intelligent people then?

Jonah had a very hard time maintaining tact and professionalism later on in the class, when it was Reynolda's turn.

She began tolerably enough, but, true to form, she deviated and became absurdly tangential. The focus on her suffered accordingly.

"It was painfully obvious, at least in my eyes, that the subject conveyed was meant to depict my discovery of the intellectual nature of my soul—"

"Reynolda." Kendall tried and very nearly failed to maintain her patience. "I only asked how old you were when you wrote the poem, not the reasoning behind it."

Reynolda's eyes flashed, but (praise God) she fell silent.

"How dare she be offended?" whispered Lola Barnhart, a classmate who shared a table with Jonah. "Kendall only asked one simple question, and the woman broke off into a damn soliloquy!"

"It's obvious, isn't it?" whispered Jonah. "She can't comprehend that no one gives a crap about hearing her voice but her."

"Well, this has been a very interesting class," said Kendall a short time later. Several classmates, Jonah included, agreed, but Reynolda had already packed and now impatiently shifted her weight from one side of her seat to the other. Kendall barely acknowledged her presence. "I wanted to tell you guys one more thing, and then you're free to go. It's my belief that to be successful in creative writing, you must have a healthy respect for other art forms as well. If you're like me, sometimes you just might find inspiration for one aspect of creativity while perusing another. So let's put that theory to the test, shall we? Tomorrow night, there will be an art exhibit in the Menthe ballroom." She held up a campus map from her desk and indicated the location for the people who didn't know it. "Be there; seven-thirty. Your attendance will generate beneficial credit to your mid-term grade."

Kendall's last statement proved to be the balm that renewed the attention spans on Jonah's classmates. He smirked at Kendall. She knew exactly what she was doing when she threw that cherry on top, but he'd have gone anyway. It would be a welcome change from looking in Trip's face or seeing the marathon of *ScarYous Tales* reruns.

"You coming?" asked Lola as she slung her purse on her shoulder.

"Oh yeah," said Jonah. "I even know a couple of people who might want to come with me."

"It'll be fun, trust me," Jonah promised Terrence and Reena over dinner. "Just think Reena; you'll get to see some different perspectives from your own, and Terrence—well, it wouldn't kill you to miss an episode of *ScarYous.* Besides, it will be you guys' first break from the estate since it's become Little Transylvania. Would one night of not sniffing garlic on the air be so bad?"

"Will there be food?" Terrence asked in a way that let Jonah know that might be a deal breaker.

"Of course there will be food, man." Jonah snorted. "Why would I drag you to an event where there was nothing to munch on?"

Terrence laughed, and nodded assent. Reena rolled her eyes.

Jonah didn't bother dressing up. To his relief, Terrence didn't either. Reena's loathing for dressy wear ran deep, but she compromised with a neat pair of olive khakis and a polo shirt. Jonah knew that a bun was out of the question, but Reena looked just fine with her hair pulled back as usual.

The Menthe ballroom was a semi-circular setting that had been rounded and squared at the west end. Jonah imagined if he had an aerial view of the place, it might resemble a circle that was halfway complete, and then abandoned. Over a hundred people comfortably strode about the place, weaving in and out of paintings, sculptures, and pottery. Jonah passed what looked like an earthen pitcher that would have been entirely unremarkable if not for the fact that it was shaded with every color of the spectrum on one side, and a pure, immaculate white on the other side.

"What do you think this is supposed to mean?" he asked Terrence and Reena.

"Isn't it obvious?" said Reena.

"Yeah," said Terrence through a mouthful of pepperoni, "the painter ran out of paints halfway through."

Jonah and Reena both snorted, but while Jonah did so in amusement, Reena did so in scathing impatience.

"It means that the person's soul was a blank slate at one time," she snapped. "To combat that, they tried every tactic in existence to mesh with the world; the multiple colors represent that fact. The two sides created a contrast. The object is but a metaphor, meant to illustrate that the soul, when pushed to the brink, can be easily broken, like this pot. It's hilariously obvious."

Reena turned to someone else's work, and Jonah looked at Terrence. He was relieved that he hadn't gotten the meaning of the white and multicolored pot, either.

"Well, how about this—" began Terrence, but his path was barred by a rotund man with a bushy moustache in a burgundy smoking jacket with a fedora to match.

"Don't walk here!" he barked, aghast. "You will not besmirch a captivating masterpiece!"

Terrence looked as confused as Jonah felt. Thankfully, Reena hadn't caught on, either.

"We, um, we're just walking, man," said Terrence. "How does that hurt this art?"

The man pointed a thick finger straight down. Jonah, Terrence, and Reena followed the finger, and Jonah saw it.

Where Terrence nearly stepped was not the floor, but a painting that looked like it. Every detail was in place; it was as if someone took a photograph, enlarged it, and plastered it to the floor. Now that Jonah paid attention though, he noticed that there were subtle differences. The paint was darker, and the illustration was just a bit more richly detailed, which made it look like someone had cut out a piece of the ballroom's well-trodden carpet and inserted a clean, brand new portion.

"Sir, if you don't mind my saying, and I truly mean no harm," said Jonah, "but why do you have this here? Shouldn't this area be roped off or something?"

"Ah." The man had the air of a mad scientist about to explain an intricate experiment. "My boy, that was my plan all along! Why rope it off when there is so much fun in maintain the illusion? I find it entertaining to correct people who don't know that art lay beneath their feet."

"Uh-huh." That was all Jonah needed. "We'll be going now."

They spent the next half-hour or so looking at the other works. Some of them were impressive. While Jonah saw no more multicolored pottery, he did see an armless sculpture, a bust of what looked like the mythical Minotaur, several paintings that showed a range of things from people to animals, and an abstract violin.

Jonah also noticed that the experience was far more enjoyable when he simply looked at the paintings and didn't try to understand them. Too many things already vied for space in his head, so there was no need for him to extend it further. Besides, it was entertaining for him to just listen to Terrence and Reena debate over different works. It was hilarious to hear Reena decipher complex meanings where Terrence (and, if he was honest, Jonah himself) saw none. When the three of them came across a rather risqué painting of a woman, Reena got so incensed at Terrence's unabashed ogling that Jonah was surprised that she didn't start to emit sparks.

"When you're thinking of painting, do you honestly think of something like this?" she asked, jabbing a finger at the woman in the risqué portrait.

Jonah didn't dare respond, but Terrence, who hadn't even taken his eyes from it, cried, "Yeah!"

"Well it's not!" snarled Reena, who snapped her fingers in Terrence's face to get his attention. "This is not painting! It doesn't come from the heart, it doesn't tell an emotional story—its sole purpose is to invoke a reaction! Most of this crap has no value as all; you saw Lord of the Floors over there. This is not painting. It's meretricious. Hell, it isn't even art. It's visual noise."

Terrence, whose eyes had edged back to the painting, looked at Reena in confusion. "Uh...did you just say something about Merry Christmas? Because that's a ways off. It's late September."

"Kendall!" said Jonah loudly when he spotted his professor. He was so thankful that she'd come into view. It gave him a golden opportunity to diffuse the situation. The look on Reena's face was homicidal, and Jonah didn't care too much for one of his best friends to rip the head off of his other best friend.

Kendall turned, and her face broke into delight. "Jonah! Oh thank God!" she exclaimed as she walked over to him.

"Huh?" Jonah was confused at such an exuberant greeting. "What was that—? Oh."

He saw why Kendall was so pleased to see him. She'd been in a conversation with Reynolda and Professor Mavis. So how about that. She'd rescued him, and he'd rescued her, too. The very thought made him laugh.

"Are you going to introduce me to your friends?" she asked.

"Of course! These are my pals Terrence Aldercy and Reena Katoa."

Kendall smiled warmly and offered her hand to both of them in turn. Jonah noticed that Terrence gawked at the portrait no longer; his eyes were on the woman that just shook his hand.

"Meet—wait, I mean nice to meet you," he sputtered.

Reena looked at him, clearly still annoyed. She then emptied her expression and smiled at Kendall. "Jonah has told us all about, ma'am"

"Oh, please God don't call me that." Kendall looked appalled. "That's Mavis over there."

They looked over at the ancient professor, who, like Reynolda, cast contemptuous looks at the people around them. Jonah sighed. It looked like Reynolda had finally found her friend.

"Let me guess," Jonah shook his head, "did they have long, backwards interpretations of this art?"

"Backwards is an understatement," muttered Kendall, and Jonah laughed. "I don't know who they think they're fooling. I'm a little disappointed. Most of this stuff is crap. Empty of meaning."

"Funny you say that," piped up Terrence, who'd been silent up that point, "because Reena thought—*Ow!*"

Reena thumped Terrence hard on the shoulder, and he shot a look at her. Jonah did as well, but Reena said nothing.

Before Kendall said anything further, she got hailed by a man who appeared to be Mavis's age, but far more cheerful. She gave Jonah a quick nod and walked away. Jonah turned back to his friends, with half a mind on getting a plate of hors d' oeuvres, but then he noticed that Reena was leering at him. Her arms were folded across her chest.

"I'm mad at you, Jonah."

"Huh? Jonah was bewildered. "Why? It'd better not have anything to do with those paintings, because if it does—"

"*That's* your professor?" demanded Reena. "That's Kendall Rayne?"

"Uh, yeah." Jonah still didn't get Reena's reaction.

"You never told me how gorgeous she was!" snapped Reena.

"Yeah!" Terrence looked here and there in an attempt to glimpse her again. "She looks as good as that painting! You've been holding out!"

"Now hold on!" Jonah wanted to take offense, but he couldn't stifle his smirk. "Terrence, it isn't my fault that Alvin and Bobby didn't tell you that Professor Rayne was beautiful. Reena, well…" he was at a true loss, because he couldn't see why it would matter to her. Now that he'd seen Reena's annoyance, though, something dawned on him. He thought about it for a few seconds, and realized that when Kendall conversed with them, Reena's demeanor changed. Her critical, aggravated side vanished entirely in Kendall's presence. And (could it be?) Reena looked down at her polo and khakis as if she wished she'd worn something else.

How was Jonah supposed to know that Reena would be attracted to his professor?

Jonah realized that he hadn't actually finished his sentence, but it didn't matter.

"That woman is the only work of art in this entire ballroom," Reena muttered, and then she left for the refreshments table.

Jonah heard it. Reena had had that wistfulness in her voice again. But Terrence missed the whole thing.

"I don't know why she went over there for food," he told Jonah, "because the only thing over there she'd be willing to consume is water."

Jonah silently agreed, but had a suspicion that snack hunting wasn't the true reason Reena wanted to get away from them.

The rest of the evening passed without incident. Jonah gave Reena privacy, and she nodded her thanks when he'd suggested that he and Terrence look over the collages made of glass and stone. Thankfully, Terrence had picked up on the odd vibe by this time, and when they were among the glass and stone collages, he accosted Jonah.

"Bring me up to speed. What's up with Reena?"

Jonah sighed. "You've known Reena longer than me."

"True," shrugged Terrence, "but we weren't bosom buddies when we were teenagers."

"Did you ever know about Julia Gallagher?"

"Oh hell yeah." Terrence scoffed. "Reena fell hard for that girl. But she went to college up north, and Reena ain't seen her since."

"That much is true, but now there is more to it." And Jonah told Terrence about his and Reena's conversation at nelson and Tamara's wedding. He even told him about the ring that Julia returned to her.

Terrence looked at Reena from across the room, his brow furrowed. "So Reena never got over that Julia girl. She's carryin' that around like a chain on her neck?"

"Mmm hmm," mumbled Jonah. "Something like that."

"Well, damn..." Terrence's voice trailed off, but Jonah was fine with that. What else could they say?

"Go keep her company, man," said Jonah. "I need to speak with Kendall and then we can head on home."

Terrence walked off, and Jonah found Kendall.

"Exhibit's almost over, and I didn't give you this." Jonah gave her the ticket stub that confirmed his presence there so he could earn his extra credit.

"Thanks for this, and thanks for coming, Jonah," said Kendall, pushing his stub into the stack she had. Jonah noticed that his was now beneath Chancer's and Lola Barnhart's. "Tell me something. Did you think these paintings and works of art were sensationalized crap as well?"

Jonah almost responded with "Huh?" but checked it just in time. "Some of it, yeah."

"Thought so," said Kendall. "If it's any consolation, I did, too."

"Really? Then why come? And why assign us to come?"

Kendall lowered the stack of stub into a bag. "I meant it when I said other art forms inspire me. But on the whole, this is for appearance's sake only. We teachers all have these obligatory affairs where it is necessary to show our faces. So I figured if I had to suffer, you guys would share my damn burden, provided I add an incentive. That way, I get my 'brownie points' for being here and you all get extra credit for being with me."

"Considerate," laughed Jonah.

"See you next class, Kendall." It was Chancer. He'd spoken in a phony lower register that made Jonah roll his eyes.

He wasn't alone, either; several of Jonah's male classmates were with him, and they were all prim and proper. Chancer was the sharpest of all in a white dress shirt, pinstriped slacks, and loafers. He also noticed that the boy looked over Jonah's outfit with a smirk. Jonah didn't even get angry. It was more amusing to wonder how much money Chancer took out of his marijuana fund to buy those clothes. If he only knew that Kendall wasn't impressed by such gestures.

"They are trying so hard for you to notice them," said Jonah. "Maybe they hope you'll cave one day."

Kendall found that very amusing. "They ought to expend those energies on their studies. They aren't my type."

Just that quick, Jonah was annoyed. He heard that from women more times than he could count, but he never really understood it. What the hell were types anyway? "Kendall, I've heard that in the past." He tried to keep the irritation out of his voice. "If you don't mind, what exactly do women mean when they say that a certain man isn't their type?"

Kendall grinned at him. "I don't know what other women mean when they say it, Jonah, but what I mean when *I* say it is that I have zero interest in these college boys."

10

Hodgepodge

Jonah's brain hadn't ever been so chocked full of thoughts in his life. It seemed like the estate, the college, and Rome were the only places on the planet. He wondered whether or not there was some forgotten bit of ethereality that allowed people to delete certain thoughts from their minds without erasing their entire memories.

The assignment that Kendall had given them three weeks to do was complete. He received an A, one of five students the class to do so. He couldn't help but grin. It was no small feat.

Reynolda glared at her B minus with the utmost revulsion, and descended upon his table and looked at his grade without an invite. "Good job, Rowe. I must admit that I didn't think *you'd* be one of the ones to make an A."

"And what is that supposed to mean?" demanded Jonah.

"Oh well, you know," replied Reynolda with a sweet smile, but then she returned to her seat without another word.

Jonah counted backwards from ten, but it was unhelpful. He had been pleased with himself, which didn't happen often as it was, and then that bitch had to mar the moment.

Don't pay her any mind, Jonah," said Chancer later. "That turd woman was pointing out the high points of her paper. Or what she thought were high points, anyway. And she, in her infinite wisdom, misspelled the word 'peanut' in her conclusion! When Lola pointed it out, she had the audacity to say that her spell-check must have been broken! Can you believe that?"

Jonah laughed. He felt better after that.

100

Events at school notwithstanding, Jonah couldn't help but feel just a bit awkward around Reena now. She was attracted to his *professor.* Kendall might be a cool teacher, but Jonah didn't know her well enough to tell her that his best friend wanted her, and it wasn't the one that was a man. He also didn't want Reena to get hurt. Then again, Reena was smart. She had to know that Kendall wouldn't go for that. But he didn't know how to tell her to let it go. After her experiences with Julia years back, he just didn't know how to approach the situation.

Jonah ran his concerns by Terrence first, but was met with another problem.

"Reena needs to catch a clue," he said. "She's gonna get her heart broken again. How can she like a woman who doesn't like women? Besides, I've decided that *I'm* gonna ask Kendall out."

"Huh?" Jonah gaped at him. "What?"

"I'm gonna ask Kendall out," Terrence repeated.

"Um, Terrence, I don't think that's a good idea—"

"Why?" Terrence's eyes narrowed. "You don't think I'm good enough or something?"

"What? It's not like that! Don't try to twist shit, man. It's just…Reena likes her. Reena ought to know better, but it is what it is. So if *you* try to ask her out, don't you think that would be just a little bit awkward?"

Terrence shrugged. "I don't know. Things will just work themselves out. Like I said, Reena needs to catch a clue. I love her like family, but she ought to know that she'll just get her feelings hurt. I'm gonna go watch *ScarYous Tales* on Netflix."

So that made it clear that Jonah had no assistance from Terrence. He decided to try to clear his head through training. That didn't turn out so well, either, because he got paired up with Felix. At the end of it, he felt as though he'd been brutalized. Felix wasn't a barrel-chested or burly man, but he had the strength of one. Jonah felt like his skill set as an Eleventh Percenter was growing, but Felix made him feel like he did the first few nights he was at the estate. With the exception of a stiff kick to Felix's side, Jonah got in no offense whatsoever. He confided this to Terrence and Reena at the end of the training (it was a blessing that they had something else to speak on besides Kendall), and Terrence was in full agreement with him.

"I know what you mean," he said. "I've practiced against him a few times. It was like his bones were made of stone or something. I wish he could be training against Trip out here."

"Nah," said Reena, "that might end with physical lives being lost. Whose physical life might be lost, though, is a mystery to me."

"Felix is probably just in superb physical condition, being a bounty hunter and all," said Reena. Jonathan told you how he got training here in his teens, plus whatever experiences he's picked up during his travels. He's free to travel wherever he wants, so who knows what he's seen and done?"

Jonah noticed something strange in Reena's voice. He couldn't place it. It was something like...longing. Not wistful or anything, just...just like she desired something. He hoped that it wasn't what he thought it was.

"Are you okay, Reena?" he asked. "Is something up?"

Almost reflexively, Reena fingered her dampener. "Yeah, something is up, but it's nothing you guys can help me with. I've got a lot on my mind. I'll be fine soon, I promise you that. It's just that—some things have to happen first. Night."

Jonah and Terrence stared at her as she walked away.

"What the hell was that about?" Jonah asked Terrence. "What things need to happen first?"

Terrence shrugged. "If you ask me, I think all that rabbit food is starting to affect her brain."

Since training nearly rendered Jonah disabled, he tried to quiet his mind by learning chess under Douglas's tutelage. He always enjoyed learning new things, he figured that it couldn't hurt.

He couldn't have been more wrong.

Chess was one of the most complicated things he'd ever attempted, and that included all the ethereality. It may as well have been learning a foreign language. Jonah couldn't understand the reasoning for half of it; if he strategized one way, Douglas had ten counters for it. If he managed to counter Douglas, than Douglas had an additional ten counters for that. Accounting hadn't been this complicated.

What was worse was that Douglas was unabashedly smug about it. He wasn't particularly sharp with ethereality, but chess was second nature to him. He delighted in slaughtering Jonah again and again. Jonah gave him credit for his assistance, but it just became more and more confusing after the first few questions.

"What about this move?" mumbled Jonah as he moved a pawn diagonally.

Douglas tightened his features to keep himself from smiling. "No offense, Jonah, but that's a ridiculous move. See my knight there?"

"Oh." Jonah looked at the board, unable to see exactly why it was a ridiculous move, but he took Douglas's word for it. "Right."

"But since you *made* the move—" Douglas put Jonah's king in check and Jonah had no idea how to rectify it. "Checkmate."

Douglas grabbed the king's piece, and they watched the board and the pieces turn silver, which was the color of Douglas's aura. The board and all of its pieces were made of ethereal steel, so playing the game while spiritually endowed made it so much more interesting. But beyond the board's vacillating between Douglas's silver and Jonah's blue, Jonah found no more fun. He saw now why no one joined Douglas's chess club for three quarters of his undergraduate years.

"God, you stink to high heaven," commented Spader several minutes later as people congregated around the widescreen for *ScarYous* reruns. "Have you ever seen a game of chess?"

"Look, boy." Jonah's eyes narrowed. "I don't need reminding, because I was sitting right there when I lost over and over. And what would you know about it? It's not like one of your card games."

"I happen to know a great deal." Spader's expression was as smug as Douglas's had been earlier. "If you can play poker, you can play chess. I also know how stupid it was for you to have sacrificed your queen in that first game. And in that last one, you might have captured his man and avoided checkmate, seeing as your own knight was right there."

Jonah's eyes widened maliciously. "You're telling me this *now*? You were standing right there! Why didn't you tell me?"

"Where's the fun in that?" shrugged Spader, and then he ran off before Jonah could strangle him.

The outer bands of the hurricanes that thrashed the coastline made the last couple weeks of September very wet and nasty, but by mid-October, the residents of the Grannison-Morris estate were elated the changes that early autumn made on the grounds. Not only had the earth dried out, but the trees became a perfect spectrum. The cedars that arched the gravel driveway dispensed their green, the birches near the courtyard were now vibrant orange, and the maples around the gazebo smoothly transitioned from their usual dark green to a vivid red. When the sunlight hit them, it resembled red fire.

The colorful landscape made Jonah's excursions to the gazebo that much more enjoyable. He camped there on most days because it was a great place to either tackle Kendall's assignments or pass the time writing random thoughts or prose.

One of Kendall's assignments had him stumped one afternoon as he lounged in the gazebo. The class had been given the task of fleshing out a story premise using what they saw in their dreams. It was almost as challenging as his attempts to write books. But the more that Jonah thought on it, the more he realized that it might not be his old mental blocks that hampered him this time. It might be the dream that he'd chosen.

He'd had the dream a few nights after the art exhibit. He was on the Astral Plane, but there wasn't any fog or haze this time. His consciousness had created very unique depictions, but the landscape remained a purplish prairie. He was surrounded by people who wore crowns on their heads, and had heavy jewels at their wrists and throats. Despite such dazzling possessions, they detached, hardened, and weary. It was almost like the only things they owned were the jewels that adorned their heads and necks.

When Kendall first assigned the project, Jonah had jumped on it. Dreams could be metaphorical for anything. But right now, several weeks removed from the initial inspiration, he found himself at a loss. Why did he choose this dream again?

He lowered his pen and notebook, and massaged his eyelids.

At that very moment, a very pleasant fragrance gently entered his nostrils. He turned, and saw that Vera was standing behind him.

His eyes widened. She'd approached him so quietly that he assumed that she used the *Astralimes* to get there. She saw his expression and raised her hands.

"Didn't mean to startle you." She mistook his surprise. "I just came to check on you. We haven't had a good conversation in a while, and you've been out here for hours."

"Oh no, you didn't scare me at all," said Jonah, who rose. His lower body was thankful for the blood flow; he'd been seated for a long time. "What are you wearing?"

Vera raised her eyebrows. "Do you think I'm overdressed?"

She thought he meant her outfit, which consisted of black jeans, a baby-blue top, and high heels.

"Not the clothes," he said, "the perfume. Is that rose oil?"

Vera's eyes widened. "Wow. How did you know that?"

"Nana swore by begonias, impatiens, and white roses," Jonah explained. "She had them in her garden for as long as I can remember. The roses always had that scent."

"Huh." Vera looked impressed. "Well, you're right. It's rose oil."

"Why are you—? Wait." A random thought crossed Jonah's mind. "Does this have anything to do with the vampires? The whole vampires and wild roses thing?"

Vera grinned. "No, actually. Felix assured Liz and me that that was a myth. I'm wearing it for my date."

Jonah blinked. "Huh?"

"My date, Jonah," repeated Vera. "I'm double-dating with Liz and Bobby. We're going to that new movie theater two counties over."

"When did you meet a guy?" asked Jonah, who tried so hard to sound casual that he almost sounded accusatory instead.

For some reason, Vera's skin flushed. "I haven't actually met him yet. He's one of Bobby's teammates, and he is also in Liz's chemistry classes. They're thinking that he and I will hit it off."

She snorted. Jonah didn't. He'd known several student-athletes in undergrad and now at LTSU, and on the whole, they weren't the brightest individuals. Idiots, if one preferred to call a spade a spade.

"I don't normally do blind dates." Vera still looked on the fence about it. "I'm hoping that this one isn't a bad idea."

"I'm sure it'll be fine." Jonah's response was automatic, but he did manage just enough emotion to make a passable attempt at encouragement. "I hope that you have fun."

"I'm not leaving just yet," said Vera hastily. She joined him on the bench, where he'd resumed his seat. "You look frazzled. What's up?"

Jonah was so distracted that he'd almost forgotten his homework. He told Vera all about Kendall's assignment, the dream he'd chosen, and the corner that he'd backed into by choosing said dream.

"I have no idea where to go with it," he finished. "It's my own mental block curse come back to mess with me."

Vera looked thoughtful. "I don't think so, Jonah. It all depends on how you look at things."

"That's the thing," said Jonah. "I've got too much on my mind. I'm having trouble shifting perspective."

Vera took Jonah's notebook out of his hands and dropped it on the bench. "There is this thing I learned when I started doing plays," she told him. "One of our instructors called it Jump. It meant our personal shit didn't matter when we were on that stage. When it came time to be your character, you needed to *jump* into it. Jump into that frame of mind. Jump into that emotional state. The point was to put yourself above whatever issues or emotions would prevent you from performing. It took a lot of practice, but I got it. And I'm sure you can, too. Right here, right now. You're going to do it with me."

She grabbed his notebook and held it in his face. "People on the Astral Plane, standing in a huge field. That's their perspective; their frame of mind. They don't know anything beyond what their eyes are showing them, but they don't think. So all they see is the field, but none of the opportunities that it might yield. Now, Jonah, close your eyes and *jump* into the frame of mind of these people."

Jonah blinked, but closed his eyes. "Um...um...they're wearing crowns and jewels, but they look broken..." His eyes shot open. "Wait. I think I got something. They look down and out despite the jewels...because they're placing the most worth on the wrong things!"

Vera nodded slowly. "Go on."

"Alright, alright..." Jonah couldn't believe it. Had Vera's Jump thing yielded benefit that quickly? "So they place value on the wrong stuff. While they pine away for the things that they believe will make them happy, they neglect themselves!"

"Exactly," said Vera with a grin. "Because material riches are the only things that they consider valuable. If they'd bother to remove the blinders, they wouldn't simply see field. They'd see things of true value around them."

"That's my premise." Jonah couldn't get it out of his brain fast enough. "People who are blind to the true value in their lives because they're focused on this happy illusion. Yes!"

He punched the air as fully formed ideas took hold of his brain. He scribbled vigorously, and then looked at Vera. He knew his grin looked idiotic, but he didn't care. He saw the formation of yet another A in his class. And Reynolda would *not* screw this one up.

"Vera, your technique was amazing!" he exclaimed. "But still, how did you do that? The filling in the blanks and all that?"

"I'm an actress, Jonah," Vera replied. "Just because I haven't been on the stage in a long while doesn't mean I've forgotten my tricks."

Jonah opened his mouth to say something else, but Vera glanced at her watch. Her eyes widened, and she shot up.

"Damn! I'm holding everyone up! Bobby should be back with his friend by now! See you, Jonah! Wish me luck!"

Vera descended the steps with surprising grace for high heels, took the path, and hurried away. Jonah stared behind her, with an inexplicable feeling of disappointment. He gathered up his homework, and decided to call it an evening. There was no way he could concentrate when he still smelled the scent of roses.

* * *

"You can get up now. The temperature is mild again."

Reena laughed as Jonah helped Terrence and Spader from the ground. They'd been damn near flash-frozen by Reena's cold-spot trick. Despite the thermal top beneath his long-sleeved T-shirt, his skin still rebelled against the arctic temperatures that Reena had only recently rectified.

"It ain't all that mild." Terrence rubbed his arms. "We're on the wrong end of October. It's getting colder."

Jonah rubbed his own arms, but Reena reached out and stopped him.

"Focus your warmth on your heart. You want the excess blood there to re-disperse to your extremities."

Jonah frowned at her. She was inordinately sunny-tempered and chipper. It was an odd change to the moodiness she'd had in recent weeks.

"I thought you were supposed to be trying new tactics," complained Spader. "Didn't Felix say we all relied too much on ethereality?"

"You should cherish the nights that Felix doesn't train with us." Reena's smile didn't even fade. "Because if he had been out here tonight, *he'd* be the one making fools of you instead of me. Later!"

She hurried off to convene with Jonathan. Jonah looked at Terrence and Spader.

"Is Reena ever this cheerful?"

Terrence must have been comfortable by this point, because he lowered his hands from his arms. "Nope. Reena hasn't ever been a downer or anything, but she hasn't ever grinned so much. It's odd, ain't it? Because she was brooding before. What do you think is going on?"

"I'll tell you what's going on." Spader smoothed out his flannel, which was a lost cause. "Your girl is up to something."

"What? Nah." Jonah shook his head. "If she were up to something, she'd be looking guilty. But she isn't; nowadays she's acting she just won a dozen lotteries."

Spader was unmoved. "You don't get it. Guilt is how you feel when you've done something wrong. But you don't feel anything like that when things are going right."

"What makes you say that?" asked Terrence. "What makes you think she's feeling successful?"

"Because I had that same mirth on my face when I left the Milverton Inn and Suites the other night," replied Spader. "Those folks were dropping Franklins like candy, and I took advantage at the casino."

"Really, Spader?" said Jonah. "Tricking people into thinking that you work at the casino and skimming money doesn't make you feel guilty?"

"Not at all," said Spader indifferently. "Those people have money hanging out the butt. If they didn't, they wouldn't throw it around so liberally. If they're going to be so charitable, why should I feel guilt about partaking?"

"Um, is there a point in there somewhere?" asked Terrence. "What were you saying about Reena?"

Spader picked up his switchblade, which flashed with the brass-shaded color of his aura. He put it in his top pocket and cracked his neck muscles before he answered. "I said all that to say that Reena is up to something, and it's either *going* well or has *gone* well. Just wait. Her happiness will continue."

Indeed, Jonah hadn't seen Reena so happy in the couple years he'd known her. As October bowed out for November, she was jocular when she described holiday preparations, patiently explained complicated meanings in situations where she'd usually be exasperated, and did four new paintings in a week. But the strangest thing happened one Saturday afternoon before he went to the gazebo to do some writing.

"I told Reena that I refused to have vegetable juice for breakfast, and I wanted wheat toast, fried eggs, Canadian bacon, and sausage," said Terrence.

"So what?" said Jonah. "You and Reena debate over breakfast almost every morning."

"Exactly!" said Terrence. "But that didn't happen this time, Jonah. She didn't disapprove. *She helped me make the breakfast.* Fried eggs, sausage, bacon, and wheat toast. With nary a criticism or guilty jab. She just told me that an extra round of cardio would 'clear my indiscretions right up!'"

Jonah gaped at Terrence. "Reena helped you fry pork and eggs?" he demanded. "Reena Katoa??"

"I know," said Terrence, "I'm scared too. But I need to go grocery shopping before some other strange things happen."

Another weird thing was the fact that Reena used ethereality less and less. Sometimes, she was even reluctant to take a spiritual endowment. Jonah would have attributed this to Felix's criticisms of them all, but it wasn't like Reena trained new modalities. Five trainings passed where she just supervised.

Jonah and Terrence couldn't take it anymore. They cornered her in the art studio one evening, where they discovered that she'd begun a fifth painting. It had such detail and style that Jonah fought the urge to ask her whether or not she would get paid for this one. Their questions made her laugh. It was as though she thought their suspicions were absurd.

"Can't I turn over a new leaf?" she asked them. "Can't I be more positive about things?"

"I don't see why not," said Terrence slowly, "but Reena, over the course of a bunch of weeks, you went from Miss Stern to Miss Bubbles and Sunshine. That's not a new leaf; that's a personality glitch."

Reena's eyes flashed, and the smile snapped off of her face. She lowered her paintbrush slowly and deliberately, as though she prepared herself for an attack. "So I'm supposed to be serious all of the time? "I'm in a good mood, looking forward to days without a scowl, and that's a glitch? So something has to be wrong, because everything's only right when I'm a bitch perfectionist, telling people off, reading people's essences, and lecturing them on how to eat. Is that what I'm hearing?"

Jonah saw Terrence glance at him awkwardly. Jonah was so reluctant to get in Reena's warpath that he took a step back. She had changed so quickly. She'd taken offense to this. It was confusing; she and Terrence had had exchanges worse than this in the past.

"That isn't what I said." Terrence was taken aback as well. "I-I didn't even mean—"

"Then what did you mean?" snapped Reena.

"Um—well, see—"

"Just get out of my damn way," Reena snarled. She pushed past the both of them, and stalked up the stairs.

Jonah and Terrence looked at each other in complete shock.

"What the hell was that?" demanded Terrence. "I make an observation, and she goes from zero to b—"

"Yeah," said Jonah slowly. You really pissed her off. But why did she get so angry? She was so bubbly not even two minutes beforehand!"

"You think Spader is right, then?" asked Terrence. "You think she is up to something? Hell, you think she might be smoking something?"

Jonah didn't answer. That last thing Terrence said? Doubtful. But in regards to Spader's suspicion…he couldn't see Reena doing any dirt. But her behaviors had to have a foundation somewhere.

Jonah still hadn't gotten the whole thing out of his mind halfway through Kendall's class later that night. His mind just wasn't on the current activities, and Lola Barnhart had to snap her fingers in his face.

"Jonah! Jonah, are you in there?"

"Yeah." Jonah gave himself a mental shake. "I just zoned out."

"You're damn right you zoned out!" Lola cried. "You just volunteered to partner up with Reynolda for our next assignment!"

"What! I just did *what*?!"

Jonah hadn't meant for his voice to be so loud, but several people stared. With a jolt, he realized that half the class wasn't even there, and Reynolda stared at him with something like puzzled defiance.

"Where is everybody, Lola?"

Now Lola looked concerned. "Jonah, Kendall called for a break a couple minutes ago. I'm guessing some folks went out for a smoke break, or just to stretch. You didn't realize that? Are you alright?"

Jonah ignored both questions. "When did I volunteer to do an assignment with Reynolda?"

Lola looked at him with even further alarm now. "Jonah, Kendall was telling us about an improvisational writing experiment that she'd be assigning after Thanksgiving," she said. "We all sat here and paired up. Everyone went silent when it came to Reynolda, and Kendall asked if anyone was willing, and you said, 'Yeah, fine.' Are you sick?"

Jonah racked his brains, and realized that on the outer rim of his mind, he kind of remembered agreeing to something, but he was so far removed from tonight's class that he'd had no earthly idea what he was agreeing *to*. He swore softly.

"Jonah, was your mind wandering that far?" asked Lola.

"Yeah, it was," groused Jonah. "I didn't realize what I was saying. You know if I'd been fully aware, I wouldn't have volunteered to do anything with Reynolda. You know that."

Lola's concerned face morphed to pity. "Man, that's bad news, Jonah," she said. "You're stuck with her, because we're all paired up now."

Jonah would have roared in frustration if the class hadn't filed back in at that moment. With a final look of suspicion at him, Reynolda returned her attention to the front of the class.

Jonah tried hard, but he couldn't engage in the last half of Kendall's class. He spent the whole time trying to figure out some way to undo his blind volunteer. He even wondered if he could do the assignment solo. But when Kendall further explained the assignment, he discovered that there was no way: one partner wrote a passage, and the other had to do an improvisational follow-up. He couldn't get out of who his partner was, and solo was not an option. He ground his teeth.

Mercifully, class ended shortly thereafter (Jonah never thought he'd say that in Kendall's class, but at least it had nothing to do with her personally). Kendall passed a previous assignment back to them on the way out, and Jonah got a thrill of pleasure when he saw the A minus atop the paper, but grimaced when he saw the sticky note next to it where Kendall wrote: *Partnering with Lunsford? Did you desire a challenge in life?*

He passed Reynolda without a word. He didn't trust himself to be civil tonight.

The trek to his car would have been automatic, but he'd deviated from his usual parking spot so as to avoid the meter. He'd parked behind one of the university buildings currently closed for renovations. Chancer had warned Jonah that the earlier he left the spaces, the better, because "shady things" happened there after a certain hour due to the building's temporary closure. At this moment, though, Jonah didn't care.

So Reynolda was his partner for this assignment. A woman who had no respect for Kendall, didn't feel life was complete unless she gave her opinion, and allegedly couldn't spell the word "peanut." Oh, this was going to be marvelous...

"Thanks a lot, Reena," he muttered, but then he caught himself.

It wasn't Reena's fault that he'd agreed when Kendall asked who'd partner up with Reynolda. But she was the one who'd been on his mind at the time, so maybe, just maybe, a scant amount of the blame was hers.

But what was Reena's deal? She'd been moody, then sunny, then snappish. On top of that, Terrence's fascination with that Turk Landry guy was at an all-time high. Jonah hadn't asked Reena is she'd discovered anything else lately; she was too radioactive.

And for some strange reason, Jonah didn't much care for the way Vera acted lately. Apparently, she and her blind date boy hit it off pretty well, and they'd made plans for a couple more dates. He didn't know why it mattered so much to him, though. He felt a little guilty for wishing that the first blind date had fallen flat.

It was *way* too much going on. Way too much. Jonah paused several feet from his car and closed his eyes. He had to file things away, or else he couldn't properly focus on the road.

"Get a grip, Jonah," he muttered to himself. "You've got enough on your plate as it is."

He opened his eyes and took a step toward his car, and froze.

He was surrounded.

There were four men, three women. They stood so still; they were like figures cast in bronze or stone. But their eyes ruined the illusion. Every single one of them glared at him with grayish, crescent-shaped, and fierce eyes.

As if they weren't bad enough, the 49er appeared in front of him, and tossed a twig down. Jonah stepped back, but one of the men behind him raised a hand and rasped, "Don't."

"I must say that it's about time." The 49er crunched the twig underneath his foot. "My apprentices here wanted to go on campus and get you. I told them that too many Tenth deaths in a concentrated area would only complicate things. But you wandered out here so willingly, so far away from everyone else..."

Jonah had no idea what to do. He saw no way out of this, and his batons lay ineffectually in his pocket. Didn't matter much, anyway; he had no spiritual endowment. Perhaps if he raised his voice, someone might hear—

The 49er shook his head, as if he knew Jonah's thoughts. "I imagine that you're thinking of getting someone's attention. It won't do you any good. I know the layout of this campus like the back of my hand. The fat campus police officer has already been around here once with his flashlight. Even if he bothered to return, he'd become nothing more than a snack for my friends here."

Jonah knew that 49er's powers were fear-based or something, so he did everything in his power to curtail the icy surge that threatened to engulf him. "What are you doing here?" he demanded. "And who are these people?"

The 49er tilted his head. "The first question is obvious," he answered. "And the second—"

He pointed downward, and Jonah looked down. He nearly recoiled, and the cold fear finally gripped him.

He stood near a puddle of water that wasn't large or deep enough to cause an issue. But it was substantial enough to cast a reflection. As such, Jonah could make out all the reflections of the people around him. It turned out that Terrence had been right, but Jonah couldn't think about anyone but himself at the moment.

The figures around him were creepy enough, but the reflections in the water were even worse: They all had translucent skin that was pulled back against their skulls like tightly applied masks. Their eyes were upturned and bestial (more bestial than their human facades), and their fangs were elongated well past their parched lips. It was a scene straight from Jonah's worst nightmare, but Jonah tore his gaze from it. The reflection couldn't hurt him.

The sources of the reflections, however, were a different matter.

Confusion compounded Jonah's fear. "But you were one of Creyton's followers. They told me that vampires didn't make armies."

"What can I say?" The 49er half-shrugged. "I desired the company of like-minded individuals. Spirits and their lifeblood are wonderful, but you Eleventh Percenters? Much more fun."

Jonah dropped his backpack, pulled out his batons, and flicked the witches to make them full sized. "I ain't going down without a fight."

"Yes you are," yawned the 49er. "Now, what was your qualm again?"

He reached into his coat, pulled out another twig, and tossed it on the ground. A Haunt emerged, saliva at its smoking maw. Its scarlet eyes flashed.

"Ah yes." The 49er smiled crookedly. "Doreen. Your biggest failure. Well, you needn't worry. You'll see the bitch again soon enough. Within minutes, actually."

Jonah shouted through clenched teeth. There is was for the second time. He couldn't hold himself upright. His body turned on him again. His heart started hammering with such ferocity that he feared it'd puncture itself as it thrashed against his ribs.

"Many thanks." The 49er smiled in the direction of the Haunt. "You may have the scraps when we're done."

Jonah dropped the batons and grabbed his head, which seemed to have emotional poison and bile sloshing around within it. It felt like acid had engulfed his sinuses, eyes, and spine. He had just enough focus left to hear the 49er's next words.

"Like I showed you before, full drainage of blood, or he won't die. I want him to be a corpse. He is the Blue Aura, so his lifeblood will keep us strong for weeks, maybe months."

One of the vampires moved forward, fangs at the ready.

"WRONG!"

A voice shouted the word out of nowhere, and Jonah saw a figure barrel into the vampire that had been near his throat. The vampire cried out in surprise as he flew through the air and came to a painful landing on a pile of cinderblocks.

Jonah's vision cleared enough to see that it was the homeless boy he'd given cash to his first night at L.T.S.U. He still had on the same outfit that Jonah had seen in August, and he smelled even more rank than he had then. But he stood in front of Jonah in defensive mode, with two Mason jars full of milky liquid.

"Get away from here, boy!" shrilled Jonah. The toxic fear that currently manhandled his insides now stretched to fear for this boy's well-being. "They'll kill you, too!"

"No, friend!" The boy sounded confident and determined. "They won't like this!"

He slammed the bottles at their feet, and a bubbly mess spilled from them. Jonah recognized the rancid smell at once. It was that garlic bleach solution that Felix had had. How did this homeless kid know how to repel vampires?

The crew of vampires hissed and jumped back. The boy grabbed Jonah and walked him to the center of the spill zone.

"If you wanna snack, you're gonna have to brave the garlic bleach!" he shouted." You got the balls for it?"

The 49er fixed a cold glare on the homeless kid. "Another one?" he demanded. "*Another* one? In this backwater town?"

Jonah had no idea what the 49er meant, but it didn't matter. The other vampires decided to throw caution to the wind and tried to approach him and the boy. Apparently two meals were worth more than their safety. The Haunt, who had no aversion to garlic, sprang at them. He leapt so high that he cleared the vampires' heads. The homeless boy aimed a kick at the thing's head, which knocked it several feet away. Jonah figured that the boy must have been afraid of the Haunt (*he* certainly was), because it rose, completely unscathed.

"The two of you cannot stand there until dawn, you filth," the 49er snapped at the boy. "We are in no hurry."

Another pang of terror stabbed Jonah at those words. He didn't know how much longer he'd last; he needed help because of the Haunting. He looked at his "savior," but the boy looked as though the thought of the 49er's willingness to wait them out hadn't occurred to him. Jonah wished more than anything that he could think and fight, but it wasn't possible. His heart, brain, and nerves had other plans.

The Haunt advanced again, and the boy kicked it away once more. It was on its feet more quickly this time around, and looked further pissed than before. The 49er lifted a hand, and it ceased its advance at once.

"As I said, we are in no hurry," said the 49er, who crossed his arms. "It will be quite amusing to see how you will try to escape now."

Jonah saw the boy look at the 49er and the other vampires. He looked at the soot-black Haunt, and then down at the ground. He must have been in deep thought.

"I'm sorry, friend," he said to Jonah. "I don't know what else to do."

Jonah took that to mean that they boy was out of options, but that wasn't what he meant. He pulled out an outdated squirt gun and sprayed garlic bleach all over Jonah's clothes. The smell was thick up close, and Jonah gagged. He then sprayed himself. The boy already had a less than delightful odor, and the smell of garlic and bleach did nothing to help.

The vampires hissed in rage, and the 49er looked angry enough to chew bricks.

"You feculent bastard," he growled.

The boy ignored him. He looked at Jonah, but Jonah didn't meet his eyes. He was trying hard to remain conscious, and he didn't think his body could take too much more of this.

"They won't touch us now, friend," the boy told him. "And you don't look so good."

"Ha-ha-have to g-get h-h-home—" Jonah's breath came out in painful spurts.

"Where is home?" asked the boy.

"Gra-Gra-Grannison M-Morris—"

"Oh!" The boy's eyes widened. "That real big house up the interstate? I know the way there!"

The boy grabbed Jonah's bag, lifted the keys out of his pocket, and marched him to his car.

"Wh-what are you d—?" attempted Jonah, but the boy shook his head.

"They can't take our blood now, friend," he explained. "So now, they're pissed. They can't touch us, but they'll probably wanna kill us now out of spite."

"But—"

One of the vampires, so incensed that she'd been denied lifeblood, flung something at them. The boy swore and knocked it aside, but Jonah couldn't take it anymore. The last thought he had before he blacked out was whether or not he could get home in time to get help for the Haunting, because he didn't want the last moments of his physical life to be spent on the run from eight vengeful vampires while in the arms of an impulsive, reeking minor.

11

Green-Handed, Red-Handed

Jonah awoke to find himself uncomfortably bunched up in the back seat of his own car. His heartbeat was at a fever pitch, and his fear hadn't abated. What was going on? If he was in the back seat, then who was at his wheel?

"Exit 81," said the driver with bated breath. "Come on, come on, come on."

Jonah nearly passed out again. He was still with that crazy boy. The boy was driving his car.

"Wh-wh-what is going on?"

The boy snapped his attention to Jonah before returning his eyes to the road. "Them vampires are chasing us, friend," he said. "I knew they would. I made 'em too mad when I cost 'em a snack. These are faster than the ones I've met in the past."

"H-how do y-you know about vampires?" It was troublesome for Jonah to gather enough air to speak.

"I been running from them things for years," said the boy. "They always worked so close with the bad people who hurt spirits and whatnot."

That shocking revelation threw Jonah for a loop. This homeless boy knew about vampires *and* Spirit Reapers? He knew how they manipulated spirits and spiritesses?

He faded out of consciousness, but got awakened when something rocked the car.

"GET AWAY!" shouted the boy, and violently swerved the car. Jonah loosed a curse word, and the boy glanced back in horror.

"No! You're too hysterical! Your heart'll give out!" A regretful look came across the boy's face. "I'm sorry about this. Super sorry."

Jonah saw a filthy, scabbed fist hurtle toward his nose, and everything blacked out again.

* * *

Jonah achieved consciousness again, but he kept his eyes closed. He didn't know what he'd see, and he damn sure didn't want to get punched again.

Strangely enough, his nose, which had exploded with pain before the boy knocked him out, was just fine now. It simply felt very warm. Weird.

He took a quick inventory of himself, but still didn't open his eyes. His body felt straight and comfortable, so he wasn't bunched up in his own back seat anymore. He also didn't smell disgusting and sour anymore, and his clothes were dry.

With a jolt, he remembered. He'd gotten Haunted. His heart had been about to burst out of his chest and his nerves had gone haywire. Had he received aid in time? What if this was—?

He shot his eyes open, and regretted it instantly, because a bright light overhead wrought havoc on his eyes, which hadn't yet been trained to them. He was distracted from the discomfort, however, when a familiar voice spoke.

"Thank God!" Liz sounded so relieved. How long had he been out? "I thought I was going to have to reset you!"

Jonah's eyes adjusted, and he realized that Liz wasn't the only one present. There was a crowd around him. Bobby, Ben-Israel, Alvin, Malcolm, Benjamin, Spader, and Douglas were there. Maxine, Magdalena, and Melvin all breathed sighs of relief. Vera, whose worried expression hadn't quite left her face, put a hand to her head and gave a shaky laugh. But to his right, and closer than the rest of them, were Terrence and Reena, both of looked tired. Liz was on the left. She tightly clutched the side of the infirmary bed.

"Thank God," she repeated. "You woke up. You woke up. I thought..."

"It's alright, Liz." Reena circled Jonah and placed a reassuring hand on Liz's shoulder. "We were scared, too."

Liz still looked pale, but her breathing was much steadier. Bobby gently pulled her away from Jonah's bedside.

"How long was I out?" he asked the room at large.

"A day." Terrence spoke in a voice that was so overcome with relief that it almost sounded like he was about to laugh. "You didn't even move. Liz thought, like she said, that she might have to do her little reset thing. But thankfully, that wasn't necessary."

Very slowly, Jonah sat up. He didn't want any lights to dance in his head. "What happened?"

"Just wait, Jonah." Reena tried to hide her still-trembling hands. "What happened to you?"

Jonah sighed. He guessed that was fair. He took a sip of water that ultimately became the full glass, and then told the group everything from blindly volunteering to partner up with Reynolda to being punched in the face by the boy.

"The last thing you remember is that boy knocking you out?" asked Terrence.

"Yeah," answered Jonah, still angry about it. "He said I was hysterical, or something. Felt like he broke my damn nose."

"He had," said Reena. She sounded much calmer now that she knew Jonah was safe. "In three places. I set it, and Liz threw some bone solidification solution on it."

Jonah looked over at Liz, who sat against Bobby's knees. She managed a faint smile, and waved a vile of jade-green liquid the same shade as her eyes.

"Your nose is going to feel oddly warm for a little while," she told him. "But that'll wear off, I promise. I thought you ought to know, Jonah—the boy did you a favor when he broke your nose."

"What favor was that?" demanded Jonah. "Damaging my nose so I couldn't properly decipher how bad I smelled?"

That earned a few snickers from the crowd, but they were quelled by Douglas of all people.

"Being out cold meant that your heart wasn't working as hard," he said. "This boy saved your physical life in more ways than one, whoever he was."

"Yeah, okay." Jonah was still on the fence on the subject. Douglas, after all, didn't get his nose broken by a rescuer. "Did that boy get me back here? When we were on the road, he said something about the vampires chasing the car."

"Well," piped up Bobby, "I was outside practicing sprints up the drive when your car came rolling up, horn blaring. I was wondering why you were laying into your horn like that, but then I realized that it wasn't you driving. Not only were the 49er and the other neckbiters behind your car, but there were also about five Haunts."

Jonah's eyes widened, but he noticed that this story was new to only himself. "Five Haunts, eight vampires, and you were out there alone, Bobby?"

"I was ready to fight," recounted Bobby, "but then Jonathan showed up. I thought he'd need Felix, but he was a soldier all by his damn self."

"A bunch of us were outside by then," said Spader. "That boy kept blowing the horn. Jonathan was shooting something at those demon dogs and the vampires straight from his hands. It looked like golden fireworks."

Jonah frowned. "Golden fireworks?"

"Yep," said Terrence. "I have never seen nothing like it. Those golden sparklers came straight from his hands. He destroyed all the Haunts, and hurt the vampires pretty bad, too. Had them things putting boots to ground faster than a prairie fire."

"And that boy?" asked Jonah. "Where was he when all this was going on?"

Reena frowned at the question. "He stopped blowing your horn, and then got out of the car and bolted. Jonathan couldn't do anything about it; he was too busy disposing of enemies to give chase. The vampires didn't even stop him. They parted like the Red Sea."

"Of course they did." A trace of humor found its way into Jonah's mind. "He used a squirt gun to spray garlic bleach on the both of us, remember me saying that? That was his brilliant plan to prevent the vampires from touching us. He couldn't hurt the Haunt, though."

Malcolm raised an eyebrow. "This kid knew about garlic bleach? *And* vampires?"

"Yeah," replied Jonah. "I wondered about that, too. He said he'd known about them for years and years. He knew about Spirit Reapers, too."

Jonah thought he saw Reena look away for a second, and then refocus her attention on him. Odd.

"I'm glad that I didn't have to reset you," said Liz. "But I would have if it were necessary."

Jonah was inwardly thankful that Liz hadn't done that damn reset thing on him, but he gave her a smile. "Would it really have worked, Liz?"

"Oh, I'm absolutely sure of it." Liz's answer was instant. "Being reset forces all negative afflictions away. It had the potential to even right issues you were born with."

Alvin sniffed. "Well, if that's the measure necessary to fix things, I'd rather not, thank you very much."

Everyone laughed, and Liz rolled her eyes. Bobby, who tried not to laugh out of respect for her, patted her shoulder in support.

Jonah was alone for the first time about five hours later. Terrence and Reena left to eat and shower, so he figured that he had a bit of time left before they returned. He stretched out on the infirmary bed deep in thought, but not sure which thoughts to dedicate his mind to.

He had royally screwed up by parking so far from civilization after his class. He walked into a damn trap. If it hadn't been for that boy saving him—however nasty and unorthodox his methods—Jonah wouldn't be healing right now.

The 49er had Jonah's number, and he knew it. He had his damn Haunts delve into Jonah's mind more deeply than any surgical tool, and turn every emotion inside out. He had been Haunted twice now, and it was twice too many. He was angry to have such vulnerability. The 49er, courtesy of those Haunts, had thrown his guilt concerning his grandmother's passing into his face more than once, and it broke him. He thought to be the Blue Aura meant that he had some strength he was unaware of. He thought there would be something that would give him an edge against these idiots. But he had as many imperfections as the next guy. And because he was the Blue Aura, his imperfections would be the ones most likely noticed and acknowledged. It was almost like being in elementary, middle, and high school again, where his stupid peers fixated on the shortcomings of one person because it was such satisfactory misdirection from their own.

Terrence and Reena reappeared, which prompted Jonah to file those thoughts away. Although they no longer looked concerned, they still seemed to regard Jonah with apprehension when they approached him. It was like they were afraid he couldn't take another attack or something. That notion only heightened his doubt of his capabilities.

"Dinner was quiet," said Terrence as he settled into a nearby chair. "Of course, Trip and his merry band were like 'no big deal' when Jonathan talked about what happened to you. I swear to God, if Trip, Karin, Grayson, Markus—any of them came across a Haunt, I don't think I'd be satisfied with just a Haunting. I'd rather they just got their heads torn off."

Reena grinned mulishly, but Jonah was intrigued because something in his memory got stirred.

"How was a I brought down from the Haunting?" he asked. "It wasn't like I could drink any more Vintage when I was out."

"Well, your heart slowed a lot on its own because you were unconscious," said Reena. "It was still erratic, but it slowed. Liz had this brilliant idea to take a syringe and inject red wine through a vein in your neck. I thought a nice sweet snack would also benefit you now."

She handed him some honey-flavored granola. Jonah bit into it. It was some good stuff.

"Got something else here, man." Terrence gave him a paper cup of red wine, which he sipped with gratitude. He wasn't big on alcohol and never had been, but the wine went down a lot smoother than the Vintage.

"I'm glad you guys are my friends," murmured Jonah. "And Reena, I've also noticed that you're wearing your dampener almost daily now. Is the essence around the estate crazy or something?"

"No." Reena's voice was idle. "No crazier than usual, anyway. I just have no interest in infringing on people's essences anymore. Keeps me in a sunnier mood."

Jonah glanced at Terrence. They made a silent agreement not to even touch that subject.

"Jonah, I need to know something," said Reena suddenly. "You said that the 49er said that you failed concerning your grandmother. I remembered that he said something similar that night when he Haunted the three of us and Douglas. What did he mean? What did the Haunt show him?"

Jonah hung his head, ashamed and a little annoyed. He wasn't annoyed with Reena for posing the question. She had every right to be curious. He was annoyed by the fact that the question had to do with his lingering feelings of weakness.

"Does it cut a little too deep?" asked Terrence. "Because if it does—"

"Nah, I'm good." Jonah sighed. "The night that Nana passed into Spirit, she'd been feeling off the entire day. She'd had trouble breathing, she'd slept a little too long at some points during the day…something was just a little off the whole day long. I kept asking her if she wanted me to call the doctor, but she shot it down each time. She maintained that she was alright. So, despite my misgivings, I listened to her. And later that night, she passed into Spirit. The one time I failed Nana. The one time I didn't go with my gut—she paid for it. I should have defied her. I should have been stubborn; I should have ignored what she told me. I could have even called that nurse that sat with her every day, but Nana said as hard as she worked, she deserved rest. I should have done one, or *all* of those things. But I didn't. And because I didn't, now Nana is gone."

Jonah tightened his fists, grateful for the anger and frustration that went down to his very core. As long as it was present, Terrence and Reena would never see a tear. Not a single one.

Terrence sat forward. "You've never told anybody that stuff before, have you?" he asked.

"Nope," responded Jonah. "Like I told you before, I didn't have many friends before I found out I was an Eleventh Percenter, and what family I did have weren't worth my time. I didn't even tell Nelson that stuff."

Reena nodded slowly, like she expected Jonah to say something like that. "Jonah, may I speak freely?"

Jonah braced himself. "Would it stop you if I said no?"

"No, actually," admitted Reena.

Terrence snorted, and Jonah sighed.

"Go on."

Reena ran a finger over her ex-girlfriend's ring, which was now on right ring finger. "Did it ever occur to you that your grandmother's passing wasn't your fault? You said she was in her nineties; did you ever think that she deserved the rest?"

Jonah frowned. "So…what? You think she was tired of physical life? Tired of being there for me? Tired of being there for everyone that loved her?"

"Pretty much." Terrence took his chance to join the conversation. "All of the above. If Ms. Doreen was in her nineties, then she was tired, man. I don't mean tired of you; she was tired of a long physical life of work. Think about it. Your grandma lived through childhood, teen years, and early adulthood, which can't have been paradise in that fart of a town, Radner. She got married, and became somebody's mama. Then after decades of marriage, she buried her husband. Then your own mom turned out to be a sorry sack of shit, so your grandmother raised *you*. So yeah, she was tired of physical life. She buried her husband, and played a parent role twice. Wouldn't you say she earned the break?"

Despite himself, Jonah felt the anger ebb away. Terrence actually had a point. Jocular, comic relief Terrence actually made perfect sense.

His gaze lingered on Terrence just a little too long, which prompted Terrence to raise his hands in a questioning manner.

"What?" he asked. "I thought was pretty good!"

"Oh, it was," said Jonah hastily. "It's just...I hear you, man. I hear you both. I just never gave myself the chance to process it and move on. Like I said, I've never talked about it."

Jonah said the words with that finality thing with his voice that Jonathan had down to a science. He knew that they meant well, and he appreciated it, but he felt like it was time to put those feelings and memories back in the box. He thought after all these years, he would be better at dealing with it, but he hadn't progressed as far as he'd thought.

Reena sat back and exhaled. "So that's the hold the Haunts have over you. The 49er's link with them gives him power, because he can turn your guilt against you with the dark ethereality of the Hauntings."

Jonah rolled his eyes. So the conversation was going to continue. Swell. "Yeah. I'd imagine so."

He knew the next thing they'd say. That didn't mean he wanted to hear it, though.

"Felix might be able to help you fight them," said Terrence.

Jonah nodded. "I'm way ahead of you. I'm gonna ask him tomorrow. I had already been thinking about it."

Terrence and Reena flashed looks of relief at each other, which made Jonah understand why they seemed so wary when they walked in. They must have expected refusals, stubbornness, and resistance. They had probably also prepared themselves to argue Jonah down until he saw reason. In all honesty, that may very well have happened, but Jonah knew that it'd be just too damn tiring.

"Well, that's that!" Terrence didn't even bother to hide his relief. "How about some dinner for you?"

* * *

Liz wasn't able to give Jonah the focus she usually would have, due to her exams. She spent many nights studying hard, and even had Vera giving her impromptu reviews. Because she was indisposed, she left the supervision of Jonah's recovery to another Green Aura, Ben-Israel. It wasn't fun to say the least.

Jonah got along well enough with Ben-Israel; he was a pretty decent guy. Although he wasn't quite as talented as Liz, he was solid and intelligent. But he lacked Liz's sunny disposition, and was annoyingly by-the-book. Whereas Liz was light-hearted and put people at ease, Ben-Israel was all business when it came to healing. His approach made the infirmary get old really quick to Jonah, and he was glad to be free of it a couple days later.

Friday was upon them again, which meant that many residents of the Grannison Morris estate would scatter to visit family members, road trip, or do whatever else they did to make the weekend fun. But Jonathan made an announcement that afternoon that stopped everyone in their tracks.

"In light of recent events, it is my desire that no one leave the estate this weekend," he told them.

Unsurprisingly, people protested, and Jonah couldn't blame them. People were more than ready to de-stress and put the tense week behind them in a pleasurable fashion. But Jonathan raised two fingers to silence them. His face was intractable.

"I understand that this has been a long, unforgiving week for all of you. Some more so than others." Thankfully, he didn't look at Jonah when he said it. "But my priority is the safety of everyone here. The 49er's activities have now changed a great many things. He is building a cabal of vampires. This poses a threat to the entire community in Rome—Tenths, Elevenths, as well as the spirits and spiritesses. I want to spend this weekend doing a border and exterior patrol around these grounds. While we hold the fort down here, Felix will scour the town, the heralds will investigate the tri-county area, and I will confer with other Protector Guides to check for the presence of vampires on the Astral Plane."

Jonah shook his head. He'd almost forgotten that vampires could harm spirits as well.

"The first patrol begins at ten o'clock tonight," continued Jonathan. "After the brazen breach of our grounds, I want this place tightly protected, while Felix, the heralds, and we Protector Guides make our rounds. You will need to make the necessary preparations for a long night, my friends. Carry on."

The minute there was movement, Jonah felt a hand on his shoulder, and heard a sharp clearing of someone's throat. It was Ben-Israel.

"Oh, it's you." Jonah didn't want anything to do with the guy at the moment, but he put on a pleasant face. "What is it?"

"I really don't think that you should take part in the patrols, Jonah." Ben-Israel sounded like a dad dashing someone's night. Half of that was true. "You need to rebuild your strength."

"Uh-huh," said Jonah. "Thanks for thinking that. Now if you'll excuse me."

Ben-Israel didn't move. "I've got to insist on it, Jonah. You aren't back up to scratch. That last Haunting you suffered lasted almost three hours. You just left the infirmary. You need to relax."

"I'm good, Ben-Israel," muttered Jonah. "Now leave me alone."

"It's a Green Deal," said Ben-Israel.

"Green Day, you mean?" said Jonah. "Not a fan. Not sure why you even brought them up. Goodbye—"

"I said Green *Deal*, Jonah," said Ben-Israel. "It means that you have been prohibited from doing ethereality by a Green Aura. The spirits will not endow you, and defiance will result in consequences that can be taken all the way up to the Phasmastis Curaie."

Jonah blinked. Seriously? "Ben-Israel, I'm fine. I've been through worse. Physically, anyway. I don't need to sit somewhere convalescing because you think I can't handle—"

"Yeah, you do, Jonah." As annoying as it was, Jonah didn't see smugness or pettiness in Ben-Israel's features. He truly looked concerned about Jonah's welfare. "I can bring you back to one hundred percent. I can do just as good a job as Liz, but you have to let me."

Jonah's eyes widened. "Is that what this is about?" he demanded. "You're trying to prove that you can hang with Liz's healing by using me as your test subject?"

Ben-Israel's eyes narrowed. "You've been Green Dealt, Jonah. End of discussion."

Jonah breathed through his nostrils. "Fine," was what he said as he pushed past the guy and went up to his room, where Terrence and Reena were waiting.

"We were wondering what was keeping you," said Terrence. "Did you get to speak to Felix?"

"No," grumbled Jonah, "I was talking to Ben-Israel. He's banned me from going on the grounds patrol tonight. I've been Green Dealt or something."

Reena looked pensive. "I thought you might be. And I agree."

"What! Why?"

"That's a good question, Reena," said Terrence. "Why would you agree with that guy?"

"You know the procedures, Terrence," said Reena calmly. "The Green Auras are our medics for a reason. You don't have to agree with them, but they do have a job to do. And we can't go around bucking their orders if we're injured—or recently recovered. You need to rebuild your strength, Jonah. Now excuse me. I have to prepare for tonight."

With a quick nod, she left. Jonah glared after her.

"Is she friends with Ben-Israel?" he asked Terrence.

"Not really," said Terrence, still displeased. "Reena is probably just on that you-don't-need-to-take-unnecessary-risks tip. Ben-Israel annoys the crap out of me. He is too fixated on following rules to the letter. When I'm, around him, I have to be careful not to trip over the pole up his ass."

Jonah plopped down in his computer chair. "Why did Liz leave me in his care?" he demanded. "There are about twenty Green Auras here. She could have put me with Sherman, Kendra, Ryan, Akshara—anybody! But I got Stumpy McDwarfington. What was Liz thinking?"

"I get it, dude," said Terrence. "Liz just picked him at random, I guess. But Ben-Israel...hmm. He Green Dealt Bobby once back when they were in the tenth grade. It was right before a high school playoff game, too."

Jonah whistled. "Why did he do that? What happened to Bobby?"

"We were training in the Glade one night," recalled Terrence. "Bobby got a little overzealous with Derek Hass—he's an Eleventh who used to hang around here—and suffered some mild damage to his sternum. It was a throwaway injury; may as well have been a hangnail. But Ben-Israel Green Dealt him, and told Mama that she needed to pull Bobby from the game. As overprotective as she is, she complied with the Green Deal, and told his coach that he had an injury. He didn't play, and they lost by one point. He's hasn't been cool with Ben-Israel since."

"How do you feel about him?"

"If he took the pole out of his ass, he might actually be a decent person," Terrence replied. "Why?"

"Because I have no intention of staying in here tonight."

Very slowly, Terrence turned to Jonah. "That ain't a good idea, man."

"Why not?" said Jonah. "What if something happens out there tonight?"

"But what if something doesn't?" countered Terrence. "You want to take that risk? Plus, we will all have spiritual endowments. You're the Blue Aura...the only one, in case you forgot that. If you have to use your batons, Ben-Israel will see blue, and he'll make sure there will be hell to pay."

Jonah didn't skip a beat. "I had a feeling everyone would have spiritual endowments, but I've thought it through. I'm not going to have one. The spirits wouldn't endow me anyway, seeing as how Ben-Israel dropped the hammer on me."

Concern went across Terrence's face. "You're willing to be vulnerable like that? With the vamps and the Haunts and everything else?"

"I'm not worried," shrugged Jonah. "There will be damn near eighty people on the grounds tonight. Jonathan will be back after he looks on the Astral plane with his Protector Guide friends. I can say, in all sincerity, that I'd feel safe in the middle of a force like that."

Terrence looked impressed. "Well, when you put it like that…but Jonah, I gotta ask you something."

"What?"

"I'll help you out either way tonight, but can you do me one favor in return?"

"Duh." Jonah snorted. "What do you need?"

"Turk Landry is doing spirit readings at the civic center Monday night. Spader scored me several tickets for free."

"How did Spader—?"

"Don't know, didn't ask," interrupted Terrence. "I probably don't want to know."

Jonah thought for a moment. He had paid little to no attention to Landry and *ScarYous* since his last Haunting. First there were all the damn live specials. Now the guy planned to show off his stuff in front of the townies. He remembered how he and Reena hadn't found much on Landry, and he wanted very much to know what the guy's deal was. He wasn't a charlatan; his track record spoke for itself, plus Jonah had a firsthand account of what he could do. But something about Landry was off. Something was amiss.

The event at the civic center would be an opportune time to look for more clues to how Mr. Paranormal did his thing.

"Yeah, Terrence. That'll be cool."

Terrence had left Jonah him in his room, and the other residents took spots outside for evening patrol. Jonah had given any last minute stragglers fifteen minutes to get on outside, and then he exited the estate himself via a side entrance that no one ever used or paid attention to.

He wore one of Terrence's oversized hoodies, which wasn't suspicious at all. Thanksgiving was two weeks out, and the evening air carried a very nippy chill. Most everyone had light jackets, windbreakers, or hoodies of their own, so Jonah didn't worry about anyone giving him a second look. He had his batons, full-size, in his jeans pocket, but he hoped he wouldn't need them. That would definitely bring the attention that he wanted to avoid tonight. He checked his left and his right, and then headed for the grounds spot where Terrence said he and Reena would be.

He walked by several groups of people. Some were alert and watchful, other were a little fearful, and others spent time shooting the breeze and conversing. Liz playfully restrained Bobby, who somehow managed to keep equal portions of his attention on his girlfriend and his task. No surprise there. Malcolm went from group to group and passed out wooden skewers that Felix left for them (Felix preferred the term *skewers* because he felt that *stakes* was overused and cliché). Jonah had to figure out how to snag one of them for himself.

Maxine was with a group near a collection of birch trees, which none of them seemed pleased about. Douglas and Magdalena killed time playing chess on a regular, non-ethereal board, while Alvin looked on.

Jonah finally spotted Terrence and Reena, and sped up just a bit, but froze shortly thereafter. The smell of roses caught his attention.

Vera was a few feet away, in a conversation with Felix of all people. That was odd; shouldn't he be out scouring the town of Rome? Eyes narrowed in concentration, Jonah moved closer so that he could eavesdrop.

"That rose oil that you're wearing," said Felix with a note of mirth in his voice that Jonah hadn't ever heard before, "is it from white roses or blue roses? The differences are subtle, but still distinctive."

Vera straightened. "It's from white roses, man. But why would you ask about blue roses? They aren't even real. Liz knows a lot about plants because she uses them for healing, and she told me all about how blue roses don't exist in nature. Something about limitations being imposed upon variances in nature. I think that's what she said, anyway."

Felix chuckled. "That's cute. They exist, Vera. You won't find any in North Carolina, though. Granted, they're exceedingly rare, but the same can be said for anything, if you don't know where to locate it. My hunts have taken me all over, and I've seen a bunch."

"You're serious?" Vera looked intrigued. "Roses are about the only flowers I like. Can you tell me about blue roses, and where to find them?"

Jonah didn't like the way Felix's eyes took the scenic route as they rose to Vera's face. But he stood up from the back of his mobile bunker.

"Sure, why not? We've got time."

Jonah walked toward Terrence's and Reena's location with such an annoyed haste that he almost walked smack into Trip, who paused and leered at him.

"Watch where you're going, boy," he snapped, which was a relief. If Trip had known that it was Jonah under that hood, he'd have called him something a lot worse than "boy."

"Sorry," said Jonah in a flat tone, and he hurried off to his friends, both of whom knelt on the ground.

"What's up?" he said in mock bright tone.

His sudden appearance took Terrence by surprise, but he recovered. Reena spun on her knees, her eyes wide with alarm.

"Jonah? What are you doing out here?"

"Not being sick and shut-in, that's what," replied Jonah as he knelt down with them.

"You've been Green Dealt, Jonah," Reena reminded him in a terse whisper. "If Ben-Israel sees you—it *Trip* sees you—"

"I've already seen Trip, and he didn't give me a second look," said Jonah. "I'm not worried about Ben-Israel. He's only going to notice people that are eye-level. I'm batting a thousand here, Reena."

"Well let's hope it stays that way." Reena tried hard, but her angered faded. "I'm glad you're here."

"Everything will be cool." Terrence didn't look worried about a thing. "Let's bring you up to speed, man."

He told Jonah what they'd heard while he was inside waiting out the stragglers. No Haunts had breached the grounds, but Jonathan had appeared long enough to announce that several spirits and spiritesses had been attacked off-plane. He said that that particular matter wasn't difficult to contain, but it was possible that it was misdirection, so he vanished again. Reena revealed that many spirits and spiritesses chose to stay near the Eleventh Percenters for safety, so Jonah went into Spectral Sight to check it out. She was right. They were frightened out of their minds.

He was about to deactivate when he noticed the spirit of a young boy near him. He wore the unkempt, disheveled clothing of a farmhand, and simply stood some feet away from Jonah, with a look of amusement and interest on his face. Terrence and Reena, who were also in Spectral Sight, eyed him with curiosity.

He lifted his hand a pointed at Jonah. "You shouldn't be here."

Jonah frowned. "What makes you say that?"

The young spirit smiled. "Your fingertips are green. You got Green Dealt, but you didn't listen."

Jonah looked down at his hands, and his eyes widened. His fingertips, which had been completely unremarkable before, were now green. The sheen pulsated somewhat, like a weakened glow-stick. He swore under his breath and place his hands palms down, but then the backs of his hands began to shine green, too! He looked at his friends, both of which looked full of anxiety.

"How did I forget?" said Reena, banging her head with her palm. "Green Dealt patients are marked if the cross the threshold without permission!"

Terrence looked here and there to make sure no one paid attention, and then plunged his hands in his jacket. He threw a light bundle at Jonah.

"Here!" he hissed. "I've got football gloves just like Bobby's. Put them on!"

Jonah buried his hands in the gloves as quickly as possible. His hands glowed so brightly that it almost looked he actually had an endowment. But the gloves concealed all traces of the incriminating florescence.

The boy laughed openly. "I knew. I didn't tell, but I knew. I wanted to help you before you got in trouble."

"I appreciate it, spirit." Jonah made sure the green didn't show through the gloves, but he needn't have worried. "Thank you. Now run along, or whatever you wanna do, just—bye now!"

With a smile, the boy vanished.

Jonah closed his eyes and willed the actors to cease and the curtain to lower in his mind. "That is bullshit," he snapped. "I thought when Ben-Israel said Green Deal, he was just making a proclamation. I didn't know he was tagging me!"

"Well, there was always a risk with you sneaking out here," said Reena, who looked over the gloves to make sure no green showed. "But if I'd remembered, I swear that I would have told you."

"That was way too close," said Terrence. "I swear, sometimes I'm jealous of Tenth Percenters. Things like that don't happen to them!"

"Lucky," grumbled Jonah, but then he noticed that Reena had said it at the same time. He and Terrence stared at her. Jonah remembered that that wasn't the first time that Reena voiced such sentiments.

She shrugged at their bewilderment. "I mean, who wants to be marked when they've done wrong?" she asked. "Where is the fun in that?"

Jonah held eye contact with her for a few moments, and then let it drop.

"I wonder where Felix got off to," said Terrence.

Jonah fastened on to that quicker than breathing. "If Felix scoured the town, then it must not have taken him long," he told them. "He's over there—" he pointed westward, "—regaling Vera with tales of blue roses."

"Blue roses?" repeated Terrence. "Is that a song?"

Reena sighed. "Blue roses are very rare flowers, Terrence. You won't see them—"

"—in the state of North Carolina," finished Jonah in a bored voice. "You won't find them in the bordering states, either. I heard it all from Felix over there. Apparently, Vera is quite impressed."

"That's odd," said Terrence. "Didn't she hit it off with that blind date guy she met a couple weeks back?"

"Didn't you hear?" said Reena. "That fizzled out. The guy revealed himself to be a neurotic idiot, so Vera dropped him flat. Sorry-ass men."

"You mean *man*, Reena," said Terrence. "You said sorry ass men."

Reena scratched her temple. "Maybe I misspoke, and maybe I didn't."

But Jonah paid no attention to their banter. He was more curious about how Mr. Tough-as-Nails Vampire Hunter knew so much about roses.

Several hours later, the evening was much quieter. The groups around the grounds decided to sleep in shifts, and Jonah, Terrence, and Reena were no different. Reena took the first watch because she didn't want Jonah to doze off and aggravate the gloves. She roused him at two in the morning, and now Jonah was on watch, along with several other residents across the grounds who took their shift.

The quiet of the night, particularly rural nights, always left Jonah just a little discomfited. Now that he knew what the night held, he was even less keen on it. But this was actually serene. This was alright. It wasn't like back in Radner, where it was him and his grandmother in the old farmhouse. Here, he was surrounded by friends. Surrounded by people he trusted, save a few. All was peaceful.

Then Jonah looked to his left and almost swore out loud.

Walking in his direction were three people he did not want to see at the moment: Ben-Israel, Trip, and Jonathan.

"Terrence!"

Terrence opened his eyes with difficulty. "Wh-what? It can't be four in the morning yet—"

"Jonathan, Trip, and Ben-Israel are coming this way!" hissed Jonah. "Get up and take watch, or we'll all be in trouble!"

Instantly, all the drowsiness faded from Terrence's face. He scrambled to a sitting position next to Reena's sleeping form as Jonah darted behind a nearby cedar tree. He peeked around it, and listened with almost the same sharpness as the night creatures he didn't wish to see.

"I haven't seen anything, sir," Ben-Israel said to Jonathan.

"And you, Titus?" said Jonathan. "Anything amiss from an auditory standpoint?"

"No, sir," said Trip. "No derangements or disturbances in the sound waves. And I haven't detected any physical presences, either."

Jonah heard Jonathan's sigh of relief.

"But what is the big idea?" said Ben-Israel. "I thought that vampires viewed themselves as the elite. Why would the 49er buck tradition and start building an army?"

"I truly cannot say, Ben-Israel," said Jonathan. "As the 49er is acting unpredictably, none of my suspicions have firm foundation."

Jonah didn't buy that. Jonathan always knew more than he let on. But what did he know this time?

"You know, Jonathan," said Trip in his usual voice, "I have mentioned—"

"Yes you did, Titus." Jonathan sounded bored, and just a bit annoyed. "You've spoken your piece, and I have spoken my own."

"Be that as it may," said Trip a bit mulishly, "I still can't find it in me to believe that these events are coincidental. It shouldn't just be the vampires. You need to investigate the sa—"

"Titus," said Jonathan in a stern voice, "we are at risk from no one other than the 49er, his cabal of vampires, and his Haunts. Besides that, what you speak of isn't logical. They are natural enemies. Why would natural enemies be in accord?"

Trip shrugged, his expression sardonic. "You were the one talking about people behaving unpredictably," he said. "I'm merely following your train of thought."

With a nod, he strode off into the dark. Ben-Israel looked up at Jonathan with unhidden confusion, but Jonathan stopped him before he could ask any questions.

"Please return to your duties, son."

Ben-Israel nodded without a word, and walked across the grounds himself. Jonathan sighed, and disappeared.

Jonah left his hiding place and looked at Terrence, who shrugged. Reena, who was still asleep, missed everything. But Jonah wasn't thinking about that.

Truth be told, it was the first time all night that he had his mind on something besides his green-glowing hands.

The entirety of the weekend passed without incident. People were relieved because there were no attacks, yet concerned because 49er and his group of cronies escaped once again.

Jonah and Terrence didn't get around to telling Reena what they'd heard because she was in an inexplicable mood. Any questions yielded nothing, and Terrence was all for giving her space.

"She is overworking herself, man," he told Jonah as they sat in two comfortable chairs at the civic center Monday evening. "I ain't gonna worry myself about it. When she wants to talk to us again, she will. She'll probably just paint her stress away or something."

Jonah snorted.

Pretty soon, the seats filled up and the place buzzed with excitement. Turk Landry walked onto the makeshift stage in his usual dramatic fashion, and people applauded him like he was the Second Coming. Even though he maintained a calm face, Jonah could tell that he loved every second of this. He had a sneaking suspicion that Landry had deliberately delayed coming on stage just to make the people salivate more. It made it even more of a struggle to fight the sneer that tugged at his lip.

"My friends, my debunkers, and my fellow followers on the paranormal path," he began in that usual overselling voice, "I am not here to disprove, to co-sign, or to show off. I am here to serve as a vessel to the Spirit World, as I always have."

The audience hung on Landry's every word. It was the effect he desired, after all. As a storyteller, Jonah could respect the gift of captivation. There were supporters, naysayers, and other practitioners who hoped to glean something.

Whether they loved him or hated him, they paid to see him. Fish in a net. A very lucrative net.

Jonah hadn't been completely honest with Terrence about why he accompanied him. Did he want to investigate Turk Landry further? Sure. But ever since his second Haunting, he wondered if Landry could contact Nana. It was impossible for Eleventh Percenters to see spirits they were close to, as well as the spirits of other Eleventh Percenters. But what about a Tenth medium with a flawless track record? Could Landry's gift reach the Other Side?

Landry went to work. Jonah was in Spectral Sight the whole time. Each spirit or spiritess was there; Landry was on the money each time. Jonah was sold after about the seventh of eighth spiritual message. He even forgot that there was something strange about the guy.

Jonah raised his hand. Turk picked him out.

"Yes, my friend?"

Could Landry do it? Could he contact Nana? Could Landry be the key (or vessel, whichever he preferred) to Jonah finally quelling the very tools 49er and his Haunts used against him?

"Thanks, Mr. Landry. I wanted to ask—"

Jonah paused. Several people in the audience noticed it, too. Landry's eyes widened, and then narrowed. Terrence looked on, just as confused as everyone else.

"Um, is something wrong?" Jonah asked Landry.

"Your vibrations are tainted, boy," said Landry quietly.

"What?"

"Your vibrations are laced with doubts, disbelief, and scorn." Landry's voice was very matter-of-fact. "I see we have yet another skeptic in our midst."

Many of the puzzled faces hardened. Jonah felt a prickle of anger. This man had no idea! What the hell did he mean when said "vibrations were tainted?"

Landry completely ignored Jonah for the rest of the event. He picked people next to him, in front of him, and even the guy directly behind him. This bastard had made him Public Enemy #1 in this room. It pissed him off. Terrence was the only one who hadn't cast evil, cold looks on Jonah. He simply looked at him with a befuddled expression and mouthed, *"Tainted vibrations?"*

Two hours later, the thing was over. It jarred Jonah from his thoughts, because he hadn't taken in anything else past Landry's snub.

"Thank you all, my friends," said Landry. "I hope that you have had to chance to be fulfilled, to be enlightened, and put at peace. I bid you good night."

"I'm really sorry about what happened, Jonah," said Terrence. "Who would have guessed that?"

"Whatever," grumbled Jonah. "It isn't like you were the one who made me look like a fool."

"Here are the keys, dude." Terrence tossed them to Jonah. "I gotta go to the can, and I won't subject you to waiting for me around these people."

Grateful, Jonah took them, and Terrence faded in the throng.

Jonah shook his head. Not only was he angry, he was disappointed. He thought he might have received a message from Nana, but that idiot wrote him off due to "tainted vibrations..."

He threw a look of disgust at Landry, but paused.

Landry moved several paces from everyone, nearer to the shadows of the stage. He looked like he had trouble breathing. But that couldn't be right. So why was he—?

No. NO! It couldn't be!

Praying that he was wrong, Jonah mirrored Landry's actions. With an icy jolt, he realized that his prayers wouldn't be answered.

An almost debilitating dislike arose in him. It was so near to hatred that it wasn't even funny.

So that was Landry's game. That was how he became a multi-millionaire, had all the tours, and had changed all those lives. Jonah caught him red-handed.

He hadn't had trouble breathing. He had deactivated Spectral Sight.

Turk Landry was an Eleventh Percenter.

12

The Mind Cage

"You're serious?"

"Yes, I'm serious."

"Are you sure you weren't mistaken?"

"Hell no, I wasn't mistaken!" Jonah fought the urge to grab Reena by the shoulders and shake her. The thing that prevented him from picking something up and throwing it was the fact that they were in Reena's art studio. Yeah, he was riled, but he wasn't stupid. "Turk Landry is an Eleventh Percenter, Reena! I saw him deactivating Spectral Sight! That was why he pulled that 'tainted vibrations' vibrations crap out of his ass. He didn't see any spirits around me!"

Reena shook her head.

"What?" demanded Jonah. "You still don't believe me?"

"No, it isn't that," said Reena. "It just makes some things clear now."

"Like what?"

"Like the reason why Landry had so many jobs after he graduated college," Reena told him. "Like why he is so adamant about keeping such a tight lid on his personal life. And there is brilliance in that; can't you see? To the untrained eye, he keeps himself to himself because he is a celebrity who wants his privacy respected."

"Uh-huh," said Jonah. "And it also explains why no skeptic, scientist, or de-bunker ever topped him. He goes into every situation with an upper hand. A *spectral* upper hand. It's like going into a fight with weighted gloves."

"Wow." Reena placed her fingers to her temples. "This changes everything. I expected him to be some elaborate fraud or something—"

"Reena, he *is* a fraud!" snapped Jonah. "Or he may as well be! He has used the Eleventh Percent to become a millionaire! He isn't a spiritual medium; he's exploiting these people! And Terrence idolizes the guy..."

Reena's hands dropped from her head. "Terrence," she whispered. "Did you tell him?"

"Do you really think I'm that cold?" asked Jonah. "No, I didn't tell him. It'd break him."

"I understand that, Jonah," said Reena. "I really do. But this time, we just might have to bite the bullet. It's not like Terrence is a kid, waiting on Santa."

Jonah hung his head. "You're right, Reena. But Terrence told me how he hates when people let him down because it happened so often when he was younger. This blows. I almost wish Landry *was* a charlatan. At least then it would be a simple truth. But what does this mean? Do you think he might be a Spirit Reaper?"

"Impossible." Reena had absolute certainty in her voice. "If he were usurping, spirits, they wouldn't be pleased. You told me that that spiritess that vanished at the hotel was in complete bliss. No spirit would be blissful if their essence was at stake."

Jonah let that settle in. Reena made a lot of sense. Turk Landry wasn't a Spirit Reaper. But it still didn't take away from the fact that he was a low specimen of humanity.

"I support your not telling Terrence, at least right now," said Reena. "Maybe you can hold off until after the holidays."

"Really? Why is that?"

"You'll need all your wits about you when you ask Felix for his help with the Haunts."

Jonah grimaced. His recent discovery had almost driven Felix from his mind. "I still don't get that guy," he admitted. "I don't even know how he'd go about helping me."

Reena grabbed a paintbrush and twirled it between her fingers. "I don't get him, either. Not really. But he has one redeeming quality."

"What's that?" asked Jonah. "The fact that he is good at killing vampires and Haunts?"

"Nope." Reena grinned. "Trip hates him. And anyone that Trip hates can't be all bad, right?"

Jonah snorted. "Nah, I guess not."

As it turned out, Terrence wasn't really complimentary of Turk Landry after he'd slighted Jonah the way he did. This made Jonah's life a great deal easier; remaining mum about Landry's ethereality would have been much more of a challenge if Terrence kept singing his praises.

"I've been at this estate for a while now," said Terrence one morning after he, Jonah, Bobby, and Benjamin finished a workout, "and I ain't ever heard anyone say anything about tainted vibrations. I swear he made that up."

"Oh, I'm almost certain he did," replied Jonah, but he stopped there.

"But it doesn't even matter," said Terrence with a gleam in his eye. "I've got his number."

"What do you mean?" asked Jonah absently as he toweled off his face.

"What I mean is that I know why he did that crackpot cover-up when you were about to ask your questions," answered Terrence.

Jonah nearly dropped the towel. "Y-you do?"

"'Course I do," said Terrence impatiently. "Don't tell me you haven't figured it out."

Jonah didn't know how to play this. When had Terrence figured out that Turk Landry was one of them? He had been in the bathroom when the man deactivated him Spectral Sight.

"So?" Terrence raised his eyebrows. "You figured it out, right?"

"Yeah," confessed Jonah, "yeah, I did."

"Good." Terrence looked relieved. "Then you know that that sly dog was trying to spend more time impressing the women!"

"What?"

"Come on, Jonah." Terrence shook his head. "You said you'd figured it out. Turk was more interested in showing off for the women in the crowd than he was spending time on the rest of us. If you watch *ScarYous Tales,* you would see that most of the people he meets are women. He had no interest in delving further with you, so he conjured up some fake complication, and then went right back to the ladies. It was obvious. Very screwed up, but obvious."

"Ahhh." Jonah breathed a sigh of... what? Relief that Terrence hadn't actually figured out the truth? Annoyance that he hadn't actually figured out the truth? Amusement at such a bullshit conclusion? "Right, man. You're absolutely right."

"Of course I am!" said Terrence. "Now, do you have any idea what you're gonna say to Felix?"

A great time to approach Felix revealed itself that evening after training in the Glade. Felix took part, and once again decimated damn near everyone before he declared himself tired. Jonah relinquished his spiritual endowment, rested a few minutes, and then found Felix sharpening a wooden skewer at the back of his mobile bunker.

"Jonah." Felix hadn't actually lifted his head when he said Jonah's name. Had he sensed him, or something? "Something I can help with?"

Jonah regarded the tip of that skewer. It was wickedly sharp. That thing looked like it might pierce iron. Why did keep sharpening it? "Um, yeah, actually. I've got a dilemma, and I don't want you to take this the wrong way."

Felix lifted his eyes from the stake. "Then be careful with your words so as to make sure that I don't."

Jonah blinked. "Alright, fine, here goes. I feel pretty screwed right now."

Felix lowered the knife and placed the stake across his lap. "May I ask why?"

Jonah shrugged. "The first time I got Haunted...the way 49er and those stupid devil dogs picked in my brain and got my body to turn on me like that...that was one of the worst things I've ever felt in my life."

Felix nodded. "I don't doubt it."

"Then the second time that it happened, no one was around to do what you did," continued Jonah, now aggravated because of his self-consciousness and apprehension. "That boy saved me and I'm grateful, but the one thing that I remember is feeling everything wrong in my body and mind. I was...scared that I wouldn't get help in time, and my heart would give out."

Jonah gritted his teeth. Felix raised his eyebrows, inviting him to continue.

"I remembered that you said you'd been dealing with 49er and his Haunts for years," Jonah went on. "You know how to fight them. You know how to keep them from screwing with your mind and body. I want you to show me how to do it. Teach me how to get over the Haunt barrier and shield myself from the 49er's mind games."

Felix tilted his head to the side, and looked Jonah over. Jonah had to admit that that confused him somewhat. If it were a mental thing, how could Felix gauge him with this physical assessment?

"I'm not Jonathan, Jonah," he warned. "I'm not full of sage stories and anecdotes. You might not be up to the way I do things."

Jonah breathed in and out through his nostrils. "I don't have a choice, man. The 49er and those dogs have me at a disadvantage, and I hate everything about it."

Felix raised an eyebrow. "You got a substance to you; I will grant you that. Fine. I'll give you a shot. There is a free room in the basement, near the gym. It's nice and wide. Be there a week from tomorrow. I'll be on the road during the Thanksgiving holidays."

"Really?" asked Jonah curiously. "You have family to see?"

"No," replied Felix. "I just don't observe Thanksgiving. The history books really dropped the ball on that one. I thought I'd find beautiful Vera an early Christmas present of blue roses."

Something hot worked its way through Jonah's insides, but he kept his voice level. "How is that going to work? Where will you find rare roses in late November?"

"Don't worry about that, Jonah." Felix grinned. "If there is something you want, then there is a way to obtain it. It's that simple."

Jonah frowned. "Huh. Okay. Last question: How do you know about that free room in the basement?"

Felix returned to sharpening the skewer. "It was my room when I lived here."

The man said nothing else, so Jonah turned his back on him and headed back to the estate. He took a few things away from the brief conversation.

The first thing was that Felix Duscere was the most mysterious man on Earth. Jonah that *Jonathan* was bad.

The second thing was that, despite his mysteriousness, he'd still managed to make Jonah jealous of him.

The third thing was that he was about to receive Haunt defense lessons from him. Jonah was about to receive defense lessons from a man who annoyed and confused him. At the same time.

This was going to be one very interesting holiday season.

A week later, it was Thanksgiving. Jonah even invited Kendall, who was an instant hit among his friends. She and Reena got along fabulously. Jonah knew that Reena hadn't gotten over her crush, and he hoped that she wouldn't make things awkward.

Many residents went to join their families, but just as many stayed at the estate, and invited their families to eat with them there. Jonah had always marveled at how the Grannison-Morris estate always managed to accommodate so many people. He wondered if it could be attributed to the sheer vastness of the place, or maybe something more. It was a matter for a different day. The only thing that mattered on Thanksgiving was the food that weighed down the tables.

Thanksgiving with Nana was always a simple affair, as it was just the two of them. But this was nothing short of amazing. Terrence, Reena, Magdalena, Mrs. Decessio, and Douglas's grandmother handled all of the cooking. And they didn't disappoint: there were at least a dozen turkeys, bulk mashed potatoes, macaroni and cheese, French bread, cranberry sauce, Cornish hens, salad, candied yams, and several green bean casseroles. Several types of stuffing had been made as well, but Jonah (and several other people) only had eyes for Terrence's and Mrs. Decessio's sausage stuffing. Reena had prepared corn and herb stuffing as a nutritious alternative to the sausage ones, but a lot of people acted as though they weren't even there. Liz, Maxine, Alvin, and Magdalena took generous helpings out of respect.

"You people are incorrigible," said Reena as she prepared her own plate. "Do you know what most of this food will do to you if you eat too much of it?"

"Never learned," said Terrence, "and don't plan on doing it today! Hey, pass that ham, Spader!"

"Don't even mind them, Reena," said Kendall reverently. "Your stuffing is the best in the house!"

The frustration left Reena's face, and she beamed. Jonah, on the other hand, beckoned to Kendall, and they went away from everyone.

"Kendall, I invited you here to eat good food, make new friends, and enjoy yourself, not offend the women competing for the best stuffing!"

Kendall realized her mistake too late, and her eyes widened as Terrence joined them. He, too, looked nervous about Kendall's proclamation.

"Oh, damn," she muttered. "How could I forget dueling cooks in the holiday season? How do I make it right?"

"Easy," said Terrence. "Grab a portion of each one."

Kendall looked horrified.

"Not to eat!" said Terrence hastily. "Just to make amends! When you get to the table, pass them off to Bobby, Alvin, Kendra, Dad…hell, I'll even take some. Just don't say stuff like that anymore!"

"Thanks, Terrence." Kendall looked relieved that she had a way out. "You're a wise, man."

Terrence gave her a sly smile. "I'm full of wisdom. I'd love to converse more if that's alright with you."

Kendall's smile faded somewhat. "Let me think about that."

"It doesn't even matter," said Douglas loudly, "because Grandma's onion and celery stuffing tops all, anyway!"

He looked at his grandmother hopefully, but she simply glared at him and returned to her food. Douglas's face fell.

"Um, Douglas, what was that all about?" asked Jonah. He settled next to him with a fourth helping of green bean casserole and sausage stuffing.

Douglas grunted as he picked at his mac and cheese. "Grandma is angry with me right now. All because of an offhand comment I made yesterday."

"What about?" said Terrence through a mouthful of Cornish hen.

Douglas reached into his vest pocket, pulled out a picture, and showed it to Jonah and Terrence. It was a beaming couple who held a sleeping baby between them. "The man is my Uncle Silas."

Jonah and Terrence stared. Uncle? The guy looked maybe ten minutes older than Douglas.

"I know, I know." Douglas correctly interpreted their confusion. "He's not much older than I am. He's my dad's baby brother, and Grandma's youngest child. He and Aunt Evangeline there just had their son on the ninth."

"Well, that's good, right?" asked Terrence.

"Eh," shrugged Douglas.

"I don't get it," said Jonah. "How does their having a baby match up with your grandmother being mad at you?"

Douglas rolled his eyes. "It's all because of something I said yesterday. Grandma's been talking about that little doo-doo machine like she's a new grandparent. There are five of us! Well, *six* now, counting the baby. Anyway, Grandma was wondering aloud yesterday about what to do for Christmas. She said, 'How about I buy a nice little something for my new grandson?' and I said, 'How about buy a nice little something for your *old* grandson?' She got all mad."

"Well, Doug," laughed Terrence, "didn't you think that that the timing of that response was just a little off?"

"It's never the right time with that woman!" snapped Douglas. "There is no pleasing her, ever! Consider yourselves lucky you don't have grandmothers who live close by. You aren't always having to prove yourself to someone."

"You need to look on the bright side, Doug," said Jonah, suddenly annoyed. "You *have* a grandmother to prove yourself to."

Douglas opened his mouth to counter, but then realized what he'd said. His eyes widened in horror.

"Oh no, man, I'm sorry," he yelped. "I didn't mean it like—"

"Shut up, it's fine," mumbled Jonah, who had no desire to stomach any rambling. "You just need to be thankful for what you've got. That's the point of the holiday, after all."

"Yeah, of course," said Douglas hastily. "Of course."

"Hey Jonah," said Terrence out of nowhere, "why don't you sample Mom's pumpkin pie? Goes great with whip cream!"

Appreciative of the distraction, Jonah gave a terse nod, and rose from the table. He hadn't meant to get so aggravated with Douglas, but he would have given anything he had to have his grandmother there.

On a brighter note, Terrence hadn't lied; the pumpkin pie was amazing. Jonah wondered how Mrs. Decessio got all the textures and spices in the proper proportions like that. He couldn't have asked for a more flavorful slice.

"That's some great stuff, isn't it?" said a voice behind him, and Jonah turned to see Vera. "I've already had two slices of it."

"I don't know if I'll stop at two," grinned Jonah. "Say, Vera…you don't have any family to visit for Thanksgiving?"

Vera shook her head with a halfhearted smile. Jonah managed to quell his curiosity. It was a good day, and he certainly wouldn't be the one to screw that up.

"Don't you even worry about it," he consoled. "You have Liz, Reena, Maxine, Magdalena—all of your friends."

"*You're* included in that number, too, Jonah," Vera informed him.

Jonah was about to smile like a fool after that statement, but he got distracted by Malcolm, who snorted as he passed them, pecan pie in tow. Jonah and Vera glanced down. They'd locked fingers during conversation again. How the hell had that happened a second time?

Mightily embarrassed, they parted and turned in opposite directions. Jonah ran into Terrence, who invited him to the den to watch football, and Vera ran into Liz, who promised that she'd reset Vera in the event that she ate too much pie and experienced "postprandial somnolence."

After football, dessert, video games, and more dessert, Jonah settled in the computer chair in his bedroom. With a laugh, he thought about how Reena had gone out of her way to converse with Kendall, and Terrence had gone out of his way to avoid his mother's invitation to wash the fleet of dishes. He planned to write in his journal when Terrence knocked on his door and entered.

"Did your mom leave any dishes for you?" Jonah chortled.

"Don't even speak that into existence," hissed Terrence. "She might follow me up here. Alvin got trapped doing dishes with her; he never was good at saying 'not it' in time. I snagged some more stuffing. It's just as good when it's cold, trust me."

Jonah forgot his plan, and grabbed the wrapped portion that Terrence brought him. That sausage stuffing was some great stuff.

"Are the holidays always full-throttle like this?" he asked.

"Usually," nodded Terrence. "Dad and Mom come here every year; Reverend Abbott does, too. Doug always manages to tick off his grandma one way or another. It never fails. But you know he didn't mean anything by what he said, right?"

"Yeah, I did," said Jonah. He'd felt justified at the time, but now he felt a little ashamed about snapping at Douglas. "I'll smooth things over with him tomorrow. I'll humor him with a game of speed chess or something."

Terrence stared at him. "Speed chess? He'll destroy you!"

"Yeah, I know," said Jonah. "That's the point. Tell me something. What the hell is postprandial somnolence?"

"Something the both of you will experience in about twenty minutes," said Reena as she entered Jonah's room. Though her voice was stern, there was also laughter in it. "Here."

She gave them bottled waters, both of which fizzed with some type of effervescent ingredient.

"Alka-Seltzer," guessed Jonah.

"Yep," said Reena. "You'll need it."

She sat on Jonah's bed. She tried for exasperation, but it just didn't work. Jonah noticed this, and raised an eyebrow at her.

"You got to see Kendall off, huh?"

"That I did," replied Reena. "She had to get going, so that she could check in on her own family tomorrow. I invited her to sleep a few hours in one of the spare rooms, but that woman's a trooper."

Reena closed her eyes. Jonah glanced at Terrence, and shook his head. Reena needed to let her attraction go. He didn't want her to get hurt again. But how could he breach the subject? On top of that, he noticed that Terrence looked less than joyous concerning Kendall. His pride must have been wounded after her snub. Jonah was hardly an authority on the matter, so he chose to not even bring it up.

"Reena." Jonah needed a subject change. "That thing you said we'd get in a couple minutes—?"

"Yeah, tell us," Terrence jumped in. "What is postbrandy insomnia?"

Jonah snorted at the mispronunciation. Reena sighed.

"*Postprandial somnolence* is that feeling of lassitude and lethargy you experience after consuming an enormous meal—"

"Oh, *that* feeling." Terrence waved a dismissive hand. "The kids at the high school where I clean have an easier phrase for that. Food coma. Can we just say that?"

Reena flung a pillow at him.

"I'm glad I know that that's what it is," said Jonah, "because now I can tell Vera to run away from Liz if she ever has it. Liz promised to reset her if she experienced it."

The three of them laughed. There had been so much joy and fun throughout the day. It made the subtle feelings of familiarity take hold in Jonah. As much as Jonah liked that, a part of him wanted to fight it. The last time he had comfort and stability like this, it got taken away. Completely. He didn't want that to happen again. But his mind and heart had other ideas. Such was life. Some of his laughter faded.

"Are we always gonna be bickering ad joking like this?" asked Terrence when his laughter subsided.

"Who knows, you know?" said Reena. "Life can change on a dime."

Jonah noticed that some of her mirth faded as well. What the hell did she mean by that? It carried such an ominous air. Just for that moment, Jonah wished that he possessed Reena's gift of essence reading. She hadn't used it a long while now, so it wasn't like she'd miss it.

Jonah tried his damndest to push all stressful thoughts to the back of his mind as he descended the stairs to the empty room on the basement level at Felix's requested time. Thoughts of Landry, his assignment with Reynolda Langford, and whatever was up with Reena would have to wait. No matter how prevalent they were.

Felix was already there. He absentmindedly flicked a lighter on and off. The lighter looked interesting. It was polished silver, with an intricate fleur-di-lis on each side.

Felix noticed Jonah's interest. He ignited it one last time before pocketing it. "Like the lighter, huh? It's a family heirloom, I guess you could say."

"Really?" Jonah didn't hide his curiosity. "Did your father pass it down to you?"

Felix's face darkened. "No. I managed to procure it after his physical life was ended."

Jonah frowned. Why did Felix react that way? And what did he mean when he said his father's "physical life was ended?" Did he get killed or something?

"But we aren't down here to take trips down memory lane." Felix implemented breathing techniques again, and appeared back in control. "I'm here to teach you how to successfully fight Haunts, thereby breaking the hold that they and the 49er have over you. What I'm going to teach you isn't practiced by everyday Eleventh Percenters. It's powerful ethereality that's usually practiced by the Networkers."

Jonah stiffened. "Networkers? You're one of those people?"

"No."

"Y-You're not?" Jonah was confused. "Then how do you know it?"

"I just do." Felix narrowed his eyes. "Do you want to learn or not?"

Jonah felt a ripple of irritation. For the thousandth time, what was this guy's deal? "Of course I want to learn!"

"Good." Felix began to pace left and right, presumably to loosen his muscles. "The ethereality that I am going to teach you is called the Mentis Cavea."

"Hold on," said Jonah. "Let me think—Malcolm's been helping me become better with Latin—does that mean Mind Cage?"

Felix paused in his pacing and looked at Jonah with newfound interest. "Yes. An oversimplification, but yes."

"Um, not trying to be combative, bit will a Mentis…a Mind Cage help me?"

Felix nodded, like that was a fair question. "The link that the 49er has with his Haunts allows him to delve into your guilt, desires, and fears," he explained. "Mastering a Mentis Cavea will spectrally cage the emotions that would make your body turn against you, like it does when you get Haunted."

"Wait," said Jonah, leery, "Spectrally cage my mind? You mean like those ethereal chains I've seen on spirits and spiritesses?"

Jonah remembered those things well, and he wanted them nowhere near his brain. But to his relief, Felix shook his head.

"Not at all," he said. "The Mentis Cavea works along the same lines as Spectral Sight in many ways. You clear your mind to see spirits. In this case, you're caging it."

Jonah still had trouble understanding, and he knew Felix was aware of that. "How do a do a Mentis—a Mind Cage?"

Felix frowned at Jonah's simpler terminology. It must have irked him like it irked some people to hear improper English. Jonah didn't care. He was going to stick to Mind Cage. Mentis Cavea sounded like some type of upscale entrée.

"The Haunts utilized regret, guilt, and fear to pervert your bodily functions," said Felix. "But the Mentis Cavea employs the one emotion that trumps all of those."

"What's that?" asked Jonah. "Happiness?"

"Dear God, no." Felix scoffed. "Anger, Jonah. When in the hell has happiness ever benefitted anyone in a fight?"

Jonah was more confused than ever. There was no other way to put it. "Anger is the weapon? Are you serious right now? You told us that unresolved anger could be used against us."

"Correct," agreed Felix, who removed the lighter from his pocket once more. "*Unresolved* anger. It's very different if you have unresolved anger, because that isn't natural. but just plain old anger, which is to say, the natural emotion that all humans experience from time to time? That can be used as a weapon that you can guide toward the Haunts."

Jonah slowly started to wonder why he didn't ask Jonathan for help. At least his riddles made sense. Eventually.

"Everyone has anger, Jonah," continued Felix. "Some people allow it to eat the up from the inside. Some people try to numb it. Some people try to bury it, not realizing what's buried can still grow. Those that have mastered the Mentis Cavea, however, do not spurn their anger. They use it."

Felix took two steps away from Jonah, which gave him more room. "Much like using the *Astralimes*, the Mentis Cavea is a two-step process. The first step involves spectrally caging your mind. The second step is using the weapon of expression that it forms."

"Huh?" said Jonah quizzically.

Felix concentrated for a moment, and closed his eyes. Several moments later, he opened them. "I've achieved the cage; that's the first part," he announced. "Now, the second part—"

He drew back and whacked open space. It looked like he backslapped the air. A wave of essence, slate-grey in color, whisked past Jonah and made contact with the wall behind him.

"That's what I mean when I say weapon of expression," said Felix. "After your mind is fortified by a successfully executed Mentis Cavea, it grants you a weapon of expression to combat the Haunts. And to a certain extent, the vampires, too. Each one is unique to the ethereality of the Eleventh Percenter, and is the color of that Eleventh's aura. As you saw, mine is something like a grey shockwave. Jonathan's looks like a golden fireworks show."

Jonah remembered his first encounter with Felix, and how he'd thrown that grey sonic wave-thing at the Haunts. He also remembered that he'd been told about how Jonathan leveled the 49er's motley crew of Haunts and vampires with, as it had been described, "golden fireworks."

"Some weapons of expression are only powerful enough to subdue a Haunt, in which case you follow it up with a spiritually endowed weapon. Other expressions, like mine, can flat out destroy them. Now, we get to work."

Felix placed that bottle of Distinguished Vintage on a camp table nearby. He must have brought it with him; the room was otherwise empty. Then he closed the distance between himself and Jonah.

"Sorry about this," he murmured.

"Sorry for wha—?" began Jonah in confusion, but he needn't have bothered. He discovered it instantly.

Felix gave him a vicious, open-handed slap across the face.

"What the *HELL!*" Jonah brought a hand up to his stinging face. "What was that for?!"

"Your emotions have to be raw and surface-level for this to work," said Felix calmly. "It isn't like you can practice on an actual Haunt. Brace yourself!"

Felix gave Jonah a matching swat on the other side of his face.

"Damn you!" Jonah threw a wild punch, which Felix blocked with a lazy raise of his hand.

"Whoa there, heavyweight," he warned. "Remember why you're here."

But Jonah had immense difficulty focusing on the point of this meet. He was seething from the two slaps, not to mention the pain that accompanied them.

Felix took a deep breath. It looked like he had to steel himself for something.

"What was your grandmother's name? Nadine?"

"Doreen," growled Jonah.

"Right," said Felix. "Was she a weak woman?"

"No."

"Did she have strong belief systems? Strong faith?"

"Yes, she did."

"Was she well respected in her community?" asked Felix.

"Everybody loved Nana," hissed Jonah. He didn't see how this line of questioning would assist with mastery of a Mind Cage.

"Was she faithful to your grandfather?"

Jonah straightened. "And what the hell kind of question is that?"

Felix shrugged. "There is no way for such an upstanding woman to meet such an abrupt end like that. Her kindness, strength, and faith failed her all at the same time. She failed in there somewhere."

Jonah was about to tear Felix's head off. "YOU DON'T KNOW A DAMN THING ABOUT—!"

Then it happened. Jonah's blood ran as cold as ice water. His heart shot off with rapid and violent beats. His body turned on him once more.

"Here we go," said Felix, his voice tense. "Now Jonah, you need to envision your mind being caged. It's tough as all hell, but not impossible. Do that now."

Jonah heard Felix's instructions somewhere in his head. His heart was going to give out. He was sure of it. His blood was cold, just like the sweat he felt on his head and back. If he focused, he could see a cage around his brain. That part was simple.

But there was a problem. He couldn't envision the door of the cage closing.

Jonah tried to will it shut, but it didn't happen. It felt like Jonah was on the losing side of a tug-of war.

He lost his mental grasp entirely and fell to the floor. Felix moved to him instantly, and yanked him into a sitting position.

"Here." He handed him a small glass of Vintage. "Do not sip. Gulp it down."

Jonah had to quell his harsh, ragged breathing before he could do as he was told. The liquor burned uncomfortably, and he hated it. But the feelings brought about by the Haunting ebbed away. The strain on his heart faded.

He glared at Felix once all his faculties were fully restored. "How did you Haunt me? You have access to those dog things? Are you a vampire, too?"

Felix's eyes flashed. "I did not Haunt you. The taint is already in you; I just had to get it to rear its head. And by the way, never call me a vampire. I'd just as soon have you call me a Spirit Reaper."

Jonah ignored the last part entirely. The beginning took precedence. "Taint? I swear, if it's not Turk Landry talking about B.S. tainted vibrations, it's you saying that I have a taint *in* me. Do you mean that I can be Haunted again if someone pushed the right buttons?"

Felix nodded. "That's why Spirit Reapers and vampires love having Haunts as allies. The dangers they pose linger."

"Can it be purged?"

"Of course it can be purged," said Felix impatiently. "Mastering the Mentis Cavea purges it from you."

Jonah's eyes widened as realization hit him. "Wait—that means that Reena, Terrence, and Douglas—"

Felix nodded slowly. "Yes. Your friends will eventually have to master the Mentis Cavea as well."

That made Jonah think. Terrence was a maybe. Reena…hell, Reena might probably started teaching people how to do it within a couple days. But Douglas…Jonah hoped his chess games never became too stressful.

"Back to the task at hand," said Felix. "I didn't expect you to get it the first time you tried. Beginner's luck is a myth, particularly with this."

Jonah still clutched the glass even though the liquid it contained had long since been consumed. He put it back on the table.

"I'm sorry about those things I said." Felix didn't sound mechanical. He actually sounded apologetic. "I just have to choose avenues that would ignite your anguish, because that's where the Haunt's taint is. But your grief is too unresolved for that. I am sorry."

Jonah looked at him, confused. This guy was callous and scathing minutes ago. Now he showed actual decency?

Jonah was ready to give up on reading Felix. The man vacillated between moods too much.

"Why didn't you warn me that you were going to rile me?"

"The reactions have to be real, Jonah," replied Felix. "You will need to be able to just drop into a mental defensive mode when the need arises. You can't be forewarned, and it can't be planned."

Jonah nodded curtly. "I guess I can understand that. I could see a cage in my mind. The door needed to be closed. But when I attempted to mentally close it, there was resistance. A lot of resistance."

"I don't doubt it," said Felix. "You're accustomed to being a victim of your anger, not using it as a tool or a weapon. Clearly, you have allowed unresolved anger to fester in your life for years. But you aren't alone in that. You just need to learn to mentally cultivate the necessary reins to control it."

Jonah closed his eyes. It was true that he had spent years ignoring negative emotions. He hadn't really learned to master them. He learned very early on that ranting or speaking problems out only got one branded as an attention-seeker or a whiner. There hadn't ever been a need for a happy medium.

Until now.

Jonah gritted his teeth. "Let me try it again."

Felix shrugged. "Alright then."

"No more talking about Nana, okay?"

"I can respect that," said Felix with a nod.

Jonah attempted to brace himself. "Will you need to hit me again?"

"Nope," said Felix. "Your emotions are close enough to the surface now. Now, I'm going to need another emotional avenue. Let's see...were you bullied as a kid?"

Jonah's jaw clenched. Was rehashing old bad memories the only way to master this Mind Cage thing?

Although Felix was oblivious to Jonah's inner war, he noticed the muscles working in his face. He nodded. Jonan's silence was confirmation that he had his new avenue.

"Why did you let them get away with it, Jonah?" he asked quietly. "Why didn't you ever fight back?"

Jonah's eyes narrowed. "I didn't have anyone on my side."

Felix shook his head. "You had *you* on your side. That would have been sufficient."

"Are you serious right now?" demanded Jonah. "What kind of logic would that have been for a child?"

"Plenty of kids stand up to bullies," said Felix. "Why couldn't you have been one of them?"

Jonah felt his eye begin to twitch. That was never a good sign. "You have no idea what it was like," he whispered. "Imagine kids who only ran their mouths only when their group was six or seven deep—"

"Been there, done that," dismissed Felix.

"Imagine the teachers being useless," continued Jonah like there hadn't been an interruption. "Female teachers said, 'Ignore them,' and the male teachers put me down even more and said I needed to toughen up."

"Oh, so now the blame is on your teachers?" said Felix. "*They* were the reason that you didn't take up for yourself."

"You have no idea!" snarled Jonah. He tried very hard not to shout again, because that was when the Haunting resurfaced last time. But Felix's feet were very near the line with this. "These weren't isolated incidents, Felix. This went on for years. There was no help to be had. Nana tried, but she could only do so much. The authority figures were useless. So the idiots I grew up with pretty much had free rein to mess with my self-esteem every single day."

Jonah had to catch his breath. He hadn't spoken on his childhood in a long while. But he managed to not raise his voice. That was a win, right?

Then Felix did something peculiar. He laughed.

"Why are you laughing?" demanded Jonah.

Felix covered his mouth. "You said they messed with your self-esteem, Jonah," he cackled. "It's called *self*-esteem! How could *they* mess up how you felt about *you*, huh?"

Jonah almost upended the camp table, but then the Haunting took over once more. He clamped the table; he now needed the support of the object he was just about to overturn.

"Knew it was coming," said Felix. "Now Jonah, concentrate. Focus. Don't linger on my verbal jabs; they were just means to an end. Now, look in your mind! Close that cage!"

Jonah's system was completely out of whack, but he had enough of his mind to know that Felix was insane if he thought that Jonah could just forget what he'd just said. He tried to concentrate on closing that mental cage door. Just like before, that resistance fought him. Jonah's own unresolved emotions, the ones he'd buried, had strength that he couldn't imagine. He needed to close the cage. He imagined pulling the door, kicking it—anything that might assuage his violent heartbeat and the frigid cold in his veins. In his mind, the cage door shifted a few inches. As the door shifted, so too did his bodily condition. His heart slowed somewhat, and his skin didn't feel quite as cold.

Unfortunately, the second that Jonah paused to marvel at the small achievement, it all fell apart. He collapsed once more.

Felix put a fresh glass of Vintage in his face. He snatched it, and reluctantly downed the contents.

"I did something there," said Jonah as his mind and body regulated themselves. "The door I pictured in my head...it moved. The effect on my body changed a little bit, too."

Felix nodded. "It's a start. It's time that your anger worked for you for a change."

Jonah regarded Felix. "And you're—pleased that you're bringing emotions to the surface like that? There is no other way to teach me the Mind Cage?"

Felix re-corked the bottle of Vintage and put it in his pocket. "Anger is the fuel for the weapon, like I told you. The only way to use your anger is to master it. Taking control of your emotions closes that cage in your mind, thereby giving you mastery of the Mentis Cavea. I offer no apologies for how I teach it; I told you I wasn't Jonathan. Hollywood actors channel their emotions on a daily basis. Why can't normal people do the same?"

Now it was Jonah's turn to laugh. "What part of any of this normal?"

"True." Felix half-smiled. "Let's call it a night, Jonah. Be here, same time, next week. Do yourself a favor and gargle in mouthwash. And oh yeah—"

He handed Jonah a small container.

"What is this?" he asked.

"It'll help with swelling," said Felix. "You don't want to go out into the world with a red face, do you?"

13

Holiday Heat

Jonah had no trouble with sleep the night of his first Mind Cage training. Sleep wasn't even the problem. It was what occurred after sleep took hold that was the problem.

His dreams were rife with rehashing of past memories, Felix's scathing words (it didn't matter that they were a "means to an end;" they still cut like an acid-laced blade), and the occasional sounds of a Haunt's snarls. Or were they the 49er's? That angular, calculating face was present in Jonah's head as well.

"You look like hell," commented Terrence the next morning at the kitchen table. "Was Haunt defense that hard?"

"Short answer, yes," replied Jonah. "First, Felix said I needed to use my anger. Then he slapped me—"

"He slapped you?"

"Yeah, he slapped me. I was that close to tagging him back, but he blocked it and told me that my emotions needed to be on edge. I was forced to turn the other cheek. Literally."

"That is just absurd," said Reena. "I've never known a situation where bashing someone in the face was beneficial. I'm glad and thankful that we aren't taking those lessons with you, Jonah. Just saying."

"I'm cool with that." Jonah drained his coffee mug. "Because someday soon, you will."

He told them about the Haunt's lingering taint in someone's system until they mastered the Mind Cage. Terrence frowned darkly; Reena's eyes may as well have sparked.

"Yeah, I know," muttered Jonah. "But Douglas is in this, too. Imagine what he'll say."

"I know one thing's for sure," said Terrence, his tone serious. "You need to learn it, Jonah. And learn it fast."

"Why?" said Jonah.

"Because you're the one's that's gonna teach us," answered Terrence.

"What? Why me?"

"Simple." Terrence dumped more sugar into his coffee. "If Felix comes near my face with a slap, I'm going across his with my steel knuckles."

The residents of the estate began to buzz with excitement all over again. With Thanksgiving done, it was officially Christmas season.

The estate was much too large to adorn with garland and lights, but the living room, courtyard, and den were all fair game. Liz, Bobby, Benjamin, Magdalena, and Alvin soon turned the banisters and halls into hideaways of green, red, and gold. Jonah hadn't ever seen so many garlands in his life. Liz even had some educational fun, coaxing Bobby and Alvin to aid her in fashioning the garland like DNA helixes in the den. Bobby barely contained his laughter, and assisted her without complaint. Alvin scoffed at his younger brother, wondering how he could be so taken with such a geek.

The most fascinating thing about the Christmas decorations was the tree. Jonah, Terrence, Reena, and Malcolm chopped wood with ethereal steel axes (which meant that the process took about twenty minutes) and returned to find a beautiful tree in the left hand corner of the living room. It bathed the whole room with the smell of fresh cedar. It was easily fifteen feet tall, and took up the entire corner. Jonah knew for certain that it hadn't been there when they left to chop the wood. But it was there, decorated with holly, a complex interconnection of lights that blinked every color imaginable, and enough candy canes to induce a toothache just by staring at them. The awe-inspiring scene was made complete when Jonah looked at the top and saw an awesomely-detailed wooden North Star. No doubt Malcolm made that. Which meant that there probably nine to ten "flawed" North Stars in his woodshop.

"Nice, Jonathan!" beamed Terrence. "Malcolm even had a North Star ready! You are really good at that!"

Jonathan looked flattered by the compliment. Jonah had to give him a double take; he hadn't been there before, either. "Many thanks, son," he said. "Christmas time has always been my favorite time of the year. It's only right that I put my best foot forward."

"And that you did, sir!" Reena regarded the tree with a grin. "You even beat your time for last year! What was it? Thirty-six minutes?"

"Forty-six," corrected Jonathan. "Don't know why it took so long. Maybe I was distracted or something."

Jonah looked at everyone. No one asked the obvious question. Reena correctly interpreted his puzzlement, and placed a still-gloved hand on his shoulder.

"You're probably wondering how Jonathan did all this in that amount of time, right?" she asked.

"Wow, you guessed." Jonah couldn't help the sarcasm.

"Well, you're going to be disappointed." Reena snorted. "We wonder the same thing every year."

Jonah frowned, and looked for Jonathan. He'd vanished again. He wasn't too sad by that, because it gave him privacy to speak with his friends.

"He hasn't ever told you?"

Terrence shook his head. "It's the million-dollar question, man."

"I was fourteen when I had my first Christmas here," recalled Reena. "We went to bed on a Monday, and Tuesday morning, this tree was here. It was a tiny bit shorter then, but it was the same tree. I've asked Jonathan again and again how he does it, but he keeps saying the same thing."

"Which is?" asked Jonah.

"'*Christmas spirit is a wonderful thing,*'" recited Terrence and Reena in unison.

Jonah stared at them, and then all three of them laughed. All of their friends had come down to admire the tree as well. Jonah had a sneaking suspicion that Jonathan's disappearance was no coincidence. He probably wanted to grant them all the pleasure of enjoying the tree and not mar it with another round of Twenty Questions.

"But where does he store it, though?" Jonah had to ask. "That's the same tree from when you were fourteen, Reena? That isn't possible. For it to be this green and lustrous for that long a time—"

"That's the beauty of it!" Liz grinned and approached the tree. "The tree doesn't need storing! It's still alive!"

Jonah looked at the girl, and wondered if her over-studying for exams had finally taken its toll. "Um, Liz, darling? That can't be a live tree—"

"She's right, Jonah," said Terrence. "The tree is still alive. See for yourself."

He pointed to its base, and Jonah stared. There was no foundation in place to keep the tree upright. It didn't need it. There was no tree skirt. There wasn't even evidence that the tree had been cut. It had no actual end; it almost seemed like the floorboards decided to sprout an imposing wonder.

"It looks like it just shot up out of the floor," he said.

"I know!" exclaimed Liz. "It's like nature extends a gift every single year!"

"What?" said Jonah blankly. "You make it sound like it goes back outside when the holidays are over or something."

Liz continued to beam. Reena managed a half-smile, and Terrence looked smug. He relished the rare opportunity when he wasn't the one that was two steps behind.

"Look at it, Jonah," he said to him. "You know this tree. You write next to it all the time."

Jonah looked the tree over once more in pure shock. "The cedar next to the gazebo?" he marveled. "It can't be. I just saw that tree yesterday. Its leaves were red and some of them were this nasty brown—"

"—and now it's green and big and taking up residence in the estate," interrupted Terrence. "Just like every year. And when Christmas is over, it goes back to its original place and just keeps on living, waiting for the next holiday season."

They were all entertained by Jonah's surprise. He gave the tree another once over, and then did the most logical thing.

He grabbed a cherry candy cane off one of the lower limbs and crunched into it.

Jonah wished that the holiday greatness would continue to sustain him as he walked in the on-site university coffeehouse to meet Reynolda. The assignment that Kendall gave them almost a month prior was near its deadline. Jonah and Reynolda had an ingenious method.

They didn't speak to one another.

Reynolda wrote out her section (the subject was Maintaining creativity in spite of rigid everyday life), and then emailed them to Jonah as an attachment. He would pick up her cue, write his piece, and send it back. Some of Reynolda's musings were maddeningly questionable, and Jonah was certain that his contributions irritated her in return. But that was only because his contributions made sense to normal human beings.

Somehow, though, they managed to make the arrangement plod along well enough.

Until now, that was.

Unfortunately, the conclusion had to be done together. And that required the one thing that neither of them wanted…communication.

"Ah, Rowe." Her upper lip curled when she saw him. "You are so late. I contemplated leaving and hashing the conclusion out myself."

"As this is a dual effort, you know that isn't possible." Jonah was neither moved nor intimidated by her words. "If it were, I'd have done the entire assignment alone. And I'm not late. I'm ten minutes early."

"I sent you a text message clearly explaining—"

"—that you were already here," interrupted Jonah. "You sent it to me as I was en route. I disregarded it."

"It boggles the mind how so many young men are so inconsiderate these days—" began Reynolda icily, but Jonah had had enough.

"Look here, woman." Jonah's voice was as heated as Reynolda's was cold. "Don't you dare call me inconsiderate when you were the one who rescheduled your son's afterschool calculus tutoring so as to hurry me out of your schedule. I don't want to be here anymore than you do. Believe me."

Reynolda's eyes registered nothing but shock behind her thick glasses.

"That's right, don't say anything. I know all about that. So you thought that you would re-shuffle your kid's tutoring to an earlier time so that I'd cater to your schedule? No. Hell no, actually."

Jonah couldn't help but feel triumphant. Reynolda's son went to the high school where Terrence was one of the janitors. He'd heard Reynolda's B.S. plan because he'd been sweeping while she was in the calculus class with the teacher, and brought Jonah up to speed.

But that wasn't any of Reynolda's business.

She stared at him. It was clear she was hard at work for a comeback. She must have come up dry, because she scratched her left eyebrow with a finger that was a not-so-subtle rude gesture to Jonah, and then spat, "Let's just work."

There had been a reason they hadn't had much personal contact during the assignment. It was a nightmare. Their "bouncing ideas" off of each other disintegrated into a debate so heated that Jonah feared that the taint of the Haunting would take over again. But by the time the manager shuffled them out, they'd actually managed to complete the assignment. It was a blessing to Jonah. It almost felt like the air was cleaner now that the project was done.

"Rest assured that we will never be partners again," snapped Reynolda as she threw her belongings in her car.

"Oh man, do you promise?" said Jonah. "Can I get it in writing?"

She sped off. Great. Now Jonah could do what he wanted to do.

He looked around to make sure no one had eyes on him. He went to a cluster of trees not far from the coffeehouse, closed his eyes, and took a deep breath. As the stage curtain lifted in his mind, he opened his eyes and couldn't help but feel relief.

He knew that going into Spectral Sight was a gamble, because he didn't know if any spirits or spiritesses would be around due to the presence of vampires and Haunts. But he struck gold. There was one spiritess nearby. He smiled and approached her.

"Hello, spiritess," he said kindly. "I was wondering if you were willing to assist me with an important matter."

The spiritess's eyes narrowed somewhat, but it was more out of intrigue than suspicion. "What do you need, Eleventh Percenter?"

"Well, I'm about to head to a mall two counties over, see," explained Jonah. "Present buying. 'Tis the season, you know?"

The spiritess nodded slowly.

"And it's um…it's for a woman. It's not the only present I'm buying or any-thing—I've got a bunch of friends. I just wanted to make a great choice is all."

The spiritess nodded again, but something was different about it this time. "I noticed you before you activated Spectral Sight to see me, Eleventh Percenter," she revealed. "You seemed full of anger. Then I saw the woman you were with inside. Is this present for her?"

"For Rey—oh hell no," said Jonah without thinking, then he scolded himself. "I mean, no ma'am. I wouldn't buy that woman day-old buffalo wings."

The spiritess looked amused. "I understand now. You want a clear mind when you go shopping for the woman you have in mind. But the woman who just left here muddled your thoughts with frustration and irritation. Is that about right?"

"Yes, ma'am," said Jonah. "That is about right."

Now the spiritess smiled hugely. It was like nothing would make her happier than assisting Jonah. "Good luck with your purchases, young man. You have been endowed."

As the spiritess's endowment surged through Jonah, he knew that he couldn't have chosen a better spirit for that counsel. Her endowment filled him with renewed energy that extinguished the heat that he'd built concerning Reynolda.

Most importantly, though, it gave him clarity. He could have laughed out loud.

He knew the perfect Christmas present for Vera.

Three hours later, Jonah was back at the estate, where he placed Vera's present underneath Jonathan's behemoth tree. He felt particularly proud of himself not only because he'd found the perfect present, but also because he'd gotten it done in wrapping of immaculate white, which was the color of Vera's aura. When he rose and stretched, he saw Douglas exit the kitchen. He had a sour expression on his face as he deposited a small box in close proximity to Jonah's underneath the tree. Jonah had to hide his grin, because he knew exactly what it was all about.

"So I take it that present is for your new cousin?" he asked.

"Mmm." Douglas rose, and straightened out some creases in his chinos. "It was mandated by Grandma. Little brat isn't even old enough to appreciate it."

Jonah shook his head, patted Douglas on the back, and went to find Terrence and Reena, both of whom he knew would be in Terrence's room wrapping presents of their own.

Reena acknowledged him with a nod, but Terrence raised an eyebrow when he saw how sunny Jonah was.

"How are you are you happy right now?" he asked. "I thought you'd be chewing bricks when you left that Langford lady."

"That's over and done with," said Jonah with a wave of his hand. "I went to the mall two counties over and got some presents."

"*Present,* you mean to say." Reena gave Jonah a shrewd look, and then laughed.

Jonah cast a wary eye at Reena's neck, but saw that her dampener was there. He shouldn't have been surprised. It had been a fixture on Reena's neck for almost three months now; he wondered if she showered with the damn thing. His quick inspection did pick up a noteworthy absence on Reena's person: Julia's Gallagher's ring. Reena didn't have it on her finger anymore.

That actually gave Jonah pause. Had Reena finally let it go? That was just one of the questions that popped into his head. But he filed them away. Matters for a different day.

"Terrence, when did you have time to buy all these presents?" Jonah asked. There was a quite a pile atop Terrence's bed.

"Oh, all year," said Terrence with pride in his voice. "Holiday sales are a joke, so I buy Christmas presents all through the year before the price gouging. We have a lot of friends, and I'm cheap as hell, so I have to have some tricks up my sleeve. Year-round shopping is one of them. Want to help us?"

"Yeah, sure."

Jonah sat down next to Reena, who passed him an already wrapped present.

"It only needs a bow," she explained.

Jonah looked the present over. The wrapping was an awesome blue. "Great color. Matches my aura."

"As well it should, Jonah," grinned Reena. "It's your present."

Jonah snorted. "It better not be a calorie counter."

Reena gave him a look of mock scorn. "Like I'd really get you something that I know beyond a shadow of a doubt that you won't use? No. That is much more practical."

Jonah and Terrence looked at one another. Reena was such a staunch advocate of health and vitality, so there weren't too many other things that the present could be. Jonah just hoped that he wouldn't be forced to pack it away at the bottom of his foot locker.

Suddenly, the Christmas tree wasn't the only wonder in the family room. The boxes underneath also dazzled everyone who passed.

Jonah noticed that almost all of the gifts had name tags, but there were several that didn't. Many people took a page out of Reena's book and just put Jonah's gifts in blue-wrapped boxes. Since he was the only Blue Aura, no one felt the need to put his name on his presents. He didn't know how he felt about that. He certainly didn't want to stick out like that; it felt very isolating. But after he gave the matter some thought, Jonah decided to content himself in the knowledge that it wasn't a negative gesture. His friends thought enough about him to put presents for him under the tree. It was the thought that counted during this season after all. Supposedly.

Jonah's last class with Kendall before they started the second half of it in the New Year was truly fun. He'd gotten a stack of cards for the people he liked, and received many cards in return. Lola Barnhart made a big deal out of the card Jonah gave her, which he didn't really understand. He gave the same card to Chancer, Elliston, Regina, and Evan. When Kendall noticed Lola's glee, she smirked and shook her head, as did Regina and Chancer. It was only then that Jonah realized what he'd missed. Lola had a crush on him. Swell.

There wasn't much time to dwell on it, though, because Kendall announced the grades for that semester. Jonah and Reynolda received an A-minus on the project, the third-best grade behind Elaine Frett and Matt Herrin, who got an A-plus, and the Booker twins, who received an A. Jonah was elated! He was ready to frame that A-minus for the whole world to see. But Reynolda looked at the grade with contempt. Whatever. An A was an A. Regardless of whether or not it was a minus behind it.

Reynolda and her ladies-in-waiting were easy to ignore. The mood was light, and morale was high due to everyone's receiving great marks. Jonah waited for class to adjourn before he approached Kendall to give her the Christmas card.

"Thank you so much, Jonah," she said. "I have newfound respect for you for dealing with Reynolda for the entirety of the project. I should have given you extra credit for not killing her."

"It crossed my mind, muttered Jonah, who caught Reynolda's final glare before she left the classroom. "She's is probably going to declare holy war on you for that A-minus."

Kendall shrugged. "I need to stay as far away from that woman as possible. I'm allergic to bitch, see."

Jonah laughed. If he'd had teachers like Kendall when he was a kid, he might not have hated school so much. "What are *your* holiday plans, Kendall?"

"Kendall clasped her satchel and brought it to her shoulder. "I'll be with my parents and my sister on Christmas Day. Afterward, it's me time. A college professor is nothing if not always busy, so rest is always treasured."

"Amen to that," nodded Jonah. "Well, see you in January, Kendall. I hope that your holiday is a pleasurable one!"

"Oh, it will be, Jonah. It will be."

There was something about how Kendall said those words that made Jonah smirk. Sounded like her "me time" wasn't going to be alone. She must have a man in her life.

"Have your fun, Kendall," he said under his breath as he exited the classroom. "Have your fun."

* * *

A not-so-great surprise occurred on a Tuesday evening about a week before Christmas.

The unpleasantness began with Mind Cage training right after Jonah chopped more wood with Terrence. Thankfully, Felix did not resort to slaps, but he continued pushing Jonah's buttons with his past. He had discovered a vein of gold when he stumbled on Jonah's experiences with bullies when he was young, and he didn't let up. It wasn't total failure for Jonah; he'd actually pushed the mental cage door a bit further than he did before, but progress remained slow.

"I can't believe you've made it this far in life without clearing all that muck out of your mind," said Felix, who handed him a glass of Vintage. "It sucks, doesn't it? Your past is the one enemy you can't fight with those damned batons."

"Dude, cut me some slack, alright?" grumbled Jonah as he tossed the empty glass on the table. "I haven't addressed many of these things in years. I did move the cage door a little bit more."

"Uh-huh." Felix pocketed the bottle. "A little bit. Amazing, Jonah. Let's end this now. Jonathan said he wanted—"

"—to meet with everyone before they dispersed for Christmas," finished Jonah in a curt tone. "I already know. But let me wash my damn mouth out first."

Jonah followed the Vintage with several glasses of water, and then he and Felix rejoined the group in the family room, which bustled with activity. Terrence and his fellow marks were deep in holiday reruns of *ScarYous* (Jonah bit his tongue so hard that he was surprised that he didn't taste blood), Spader alternated between showing off card tricks to a small group of residents and stealing candy canes off of the tree, Reena and Liz were deep in conversation, and Douglas and Malcolm played speed chess on an ethereal chessboard.

But Jonah saw someone in the corner of the room that he hadn't expected to see in a zillion lifetimes: Trip.

The "official" reason for Trip's prolonged absence was because his jazz band had a number of seasonal gigs all over North Carolina. But Jonah had his number. Trip's sudden upswing in gigs coincided with Felix's presence. For some reason, they hated each other. There were mortal enemies. And as far as Jonah was concerned, the enemy of his enemy was… an inscrutable guy who slapped him across the face, chided him for being a wimp as a child, and then made him wash it all down with hard liquor.

Jonah filed that thought away.

Jonathan appeared at the center of all the activity of the family room, and everyone ceased all actions at once.

"As I know so many of you have plans, this will not take long," he said. "I just wanted to say to the people who will be with their families to have a wonderful Christmas and a blissful New Year. And please, remain vigilant and wary, and keep the kits that Felix gave you at the end of summer. The 49er is still on the loose. And remember that he has a small group of vampires around him now, not to mention the Haunts."

Jonah shuddered, almost by reflex. He was angry with himself for his fear of them.

"Jonathan," said Trip without lifting his head from the saxophone he was polishing, "you keep warning everybody about the vampires and the Haunts. I believe that they should also know about another menace out there known as sazers."

Jonah frowned, confused, but the term elicited some very strange responses from the other residents. Jonathan's eyes flashed, like he wanted to swat Trip. Reena looked at Trip in horror, as did Terrence. Felix shook his head.

It was Ben-Israel who asked the question that burned in Jonah's mind. "Sazers? What are they?"

Trip rose. Karin and Markus followed suit. "Simply put, Ben-Israel? They're mistakes. Just thought you ought to be aware that bloodsucker and devil dogs aren't the only things that prowl in the night. But please continue with your little yuletide plans."

He and his crew left the living room in complete silence. Jonathan fingered his infinity medallion. Felix just shook his head again and grumbled, "Jackass." Ben-Israel, on the other hand, looked as baffled as ever.

"Mistakes? What does that mean? I-I don't—"

"Reena," said Jonathan. "Please explain to everyone what sazers are. I trust that you recall our conversations about them when you arrived here. And Felix, I am glad to see that you and Jonah are done. I would like to discuss our defenses over the holidays."

Felix followed Jonathan without another word to Jonah. But he didn't care; all eyes were on Reena. She had anxiety in her face that Jonah couldn't understand. Reena never looked like that.

"First of all, Ben-Israel, sazers aren't mistakes," she said. "They are...hybrids of vampires and Eleventh Percenters."

Alvin stiffened. "What? Half-neckbiter, half Eleventh?"

"I only call them hybrids for lack of a better term," said Reena. "It isn't true duality. They possess many traits of Elevenths, like auras, access to spiritual endowments, and Spectral Sight. But they also have vampiric traits as well."

"So what, then, asked Jonah. "Super-strength, speed, increased mobility and dexterity at night, and a thirst for blood?"

"Very close, Jonah." Reena ran a finger across her dampener. Sazers do have strength, speed, and nocturnal instincts, but not in the same way as vampires. It's...blunted, I guess you could say. And they don't thirst for blood. That's the tricky part."

Jonah's mouth twisted. This was just great. It was bad enough to have to worry about Haunts and vampires, but now there was a fringe group of beings that may as well have been vampiric stepchildren?

"No thirst for blood?" asked Spader. "I thought you said they were half-v—"

"I never said they were half anything, Spader," said Reena tersely. "That's what I'm trying to tell you! They're mostly Eleventh Percenter; the vampiric aspect makes up about twenty, twenty-five percent tops. There is no taste for blood, because they aren't true vampires."

"That's good, right?" said Maxine in a voice full of hope. "We don't have two groups of bloodsuckers."

Some people nodded in agreement, but the look on Reena's face told him that they all hadn't heard the worst part.

"Sazers don't drink blood," she said in a careful tone, "but they're still dangerous. Their impulsive tendencies compensate for the absence of thirst through the alternative aspects of their personalities. As such, they can have intense anger issues, compulsive behaviors, and the tendency to become addicts."

"Ooo-kay," muttered Bobby, who cracked his knuckles. "So they are kinda strong, kinda fast pothead basket cases. Sounds like some kind of nut job missing link business."

"Wait." Terrence stood up. "Dad told us about sazers, Bobby. Don't you remember? You too, Alvin! He told us when Creyton would use vampires like freelancers or something, the Networkers would sometimes find common ground with sazers to help out. He said sometimes Spectral Law practitioners would have been up the creek without a paddle had it not been for sazer's help."

"Hold on," said Alvin, "I remember now. Dad told us something else, too, Terrence. He said that sazers and vampires were natural enemies, and when they came across each other, innocent spirits, Tenths, and Elevenths got caught in the crossfire."

"Oh yeah!" Bobby snapped his fingers. "Dad *did* tell us about those things! Oppositional tendencies, impulsiveness, and—what was it, Terrence, Alvin? Red Rage?

Jonah snorted. "Red Rage? That's sounds like a video game."

It's not a joke, Jonah." Reena reclaimed control over the conversation. "If sazers provoked too strongly, they can succumb to a bestial, unadulterated anger that's called Red Rage. It's named as such because their eyes flash red before they succumb to it. When they get that angry, they are capable of horrible things. It's like a vampire in blood frenzy."

Jonah looked at Terrence, and then at Reena. "How do you know all this, Reena? Jonathan said you guys have had conversations about these sazers. Why?"

Reena closed her eyes. "Because I almost got killed by one," she revealed. "It was right after my uncle passed into Spirit, and I was alone. I came across one who wanted to kill me because she wanted my clothes. She was homeless and almost naked, and she wanted my clothes. Jonathan saved me. That's how I wound up here."

"Whoa." Terrence frowned. "I never knew that, Reena."

Reena contemplated the wall. "I don't like to talk about it."

Several minutes of silence followed all the words that had been spoken. Magdalena broke it.

"I don't say this disregard what you guys have said, but am I the only one who wants to know why Trip brought up sazers in the first place? Seemed kind of random, don't you think?"

Jonah looked at his friends. Not even Reena had an answer to that one. It was a heavy matter, but Magdalena was right. Trip bringing them up like that was random. No disrespect to Reena, but he wished that Jonathan and Felix hadn't left. They could have explained it all just fine.

"Maybe it wasn't random," said Terrence. "Maybe it was just Trip being Trip. Can't allow folk to get too happy, can he?"

Christmas Day was an overcast day complete with a stinging breeze and a slight dusting of snow on the estate grounds. Jonah awoke due to Bast's insistent scratching at his door. He couldn't really complain, because it didn't leave him jarred or disgruntled. That wouldn't have been a great way to start Christmas at all.

In short order, the family room was a mess of noise, paper, and people. Everyone rummaged through their presents like children. Terrence proudly wore Jonah's gift to him (Duke Blue Devils athletic gloves) despite the fact that there was no need to in the warm, toasty living room. Jonah laughed at that, and sat down to his blue pile.

In a short amount of time, he was the owner of a cobalt blue journal from Liz, a set of dumbbells (Bobby), a new grip cover for his steering wheel from Terrence, two cerulean blue fountain pens from Reena, and an English to-Latin dictionary complete with a polished wooden bookcase from Malcolm. Spader had gotten him casino-style playing cards, and Douglas got him his own chess set that was made of glass, not ethereal steel. Reena nimbly navigated through the sea of paper, ribbon, and limbs to reach him, with a wide smile on her face.

"This is awesome, Jonah," she exclaimed. "I've never had a paint kit from Bob Ross!"

"I'm glad you like it, Reena," smiled Jonah, "and I cannot wait to see what you create with it."

Jonah looked under the tree, and noticed that Vera's present was obscured under a pile of garland. She hadn't seen it yet.

"Excuse me, Reena."

He grabbed it and approached Vera, who chatted with Liz on the sofa. Liz happily showcased her new sterling silver necklace, which included a charm in the form of a periodic table. Jonah smiled. Bobby did pay attention to something other than sports.

"Merry Christmas, Jonah!" Vera clapped him on the arm. "I've got your gift right here! I didn't want it to be lost in the mess of paper over there."

Jonah took it and opened it. It was a cool collection of thought-provoking games, puzzles, and activities that required snap decisions and quick thought.

"Brain stimulation," she explained. "I thought activities such as those would sharpen your mind for writing. Maybe even help you conquer that mental block."

It was a considerate present, and Jonah loved it. He hadn't done brain games and puzzles in a while, and looked forward to it. "Thanks Vera. I appreciate you doing that for me. I have something for you, too."

"Funny," said a familiar voice. "I do, too."

Felix was there, with a large wooden box in his hands. He moved to the opposite side of the sofa, and seated himself next to Vera.

"But I won't be rude or overbearing." Felix lowered the box to the floor. "Go on with your present, Jonah."

Vera looked a bit awkward between the two of them. She wasn't blind to the display of manhood. This was obviously something that didn't happen to her often.

Jonah narrowed his eyes. Why did Felix have to show up now? He had no love for Thanksgiving, but he was Santa Claus, Jr. on Christmas? Couldn't he have waited ten extra minutes? Or even until the next day? "No, Felix. You go. I'll wait."

Jonah had no issue waiting. Felix could give Vera those stupid roses. They'd wither and fade in a couple weeks anyway.

Felix shrugged, unclasped the box, and pulled out a magnificently crafted vase full of shining blue roses.

Vera's jaw dropped. She reached for the vase but pulled back, as though she feared damaging it in some way. "Felix, the vase…is that—?"

"Yeah, it's sapphire." Clearly, Felix relished her shock. "That's your birthstone, if I'm not mistaken."

Jonah blinked. He didn't even know Vera's birthday, let alone her birth*stone*. It never occurred to him to ask. How did Felix find out?

Liz gaped at the gift, along with Maxine, Magdalena, and several other women. Even Reena looked off-balance. But Vera finally managed to pull her attention off of the vase and look at the shiny roses.

"What's their story?" she asked.

"Ah." Felix milked the moment. "They would have wilted shortly after the New Year. So I had them preserved in crystal. The color, consistency, and composition will never fade. You are now the owner of twelve blue roses that will never die. Life never ends anyway, so I thought it was fitting."

Jonah heard the collective sighs of the women and the collective groans of the guys. He was quite thankful that he wasn't one of those sazers, because he'd probably have gone into that Red Rage thing and smashed the entire set.

"Felix, this is beautiful." Vera shook her head in amazement. "Beyond beautiful. Thank you. Thank you so much."

"You're more than welcome." Felix smiled, and then his gaze lifted to Jonah. There was no mistaking the vibe. *Top that, Blue Man.*

Vera turned to Jonah. "There's still your present, Jonah. May I have it, please?"

The eyes of all the people around burned Jonah as he extended the white box, which seemed so insignificant in comparison to that wooden contraption and vase. Out of the corner of his eye, he saw Terrence shake his head. It did nothing to help his mood.

Vera opened the box, and her eyes widened. "Merchandise from *Wicked*!"

She pulled out a T-shirt that displayed the famous witches. Jonah tried hard to ignore Felix, who buried his face in his hands.

"Yes," he said loudly. "I remembered that you said you loved *Wicked,* and that it was your lifelong dream to star in it someday. So I got you the T-shirt, the hooded sweatshirt, the mug, and of course, a poster of Elphaba."

Vera looked touched. Sincerely so. She even pulled the T-shirt over her tank top. But Jonah didn't need Reena's intellect to know that her reaction wasn't in the same ballpark as what it had been when Felix presented those damned roses. Hell, it wasn't even in the same universe.

Why did he let Felix go first? He almost wished a Haunt would show up to ruin the moment. No, perish the thought.

His jealousy of Felix, already high, shot through the roof.

"That was an unfair advantage, Jonah," insisted Terrence over Christmas lunch later in the day. "Your gift appealed to Vera's dream. Felix dug deep in his pockets for that gaudy monstrosity."

"Uh-huh," grunted Jonah, who speared a piece of glazed ham so viciously that the fork clanged the pate underneath. "A sapphire vase? Roses preserved in crystal? Who does that?"

"Well, actually—", began Reena in that knowledgeable tone, but Jonah and Terrence threw murderous looks her way.

"Please keep it to yourself, Reena," said Terrence.

"Fine," conceded Reena. "I'm cool with that."

Damn. Reena actually conceded? It was truly a rare moment, and Jonah couldn't even appreciate it the way he should have.

"Tell you what, Jonah," she said instead, "why don't you and Terrence follow me in your cars to look at Christmas decorations around Rome? It always clears my mind."

That actually sounded appealing, but Jonah looked at her, curious. "Why don't we all just go together?"

"Because I'm not coming back here," Reena explained. "I go check out people's decorations, and then find a room somewhere to just be by myself for a few days. The rates are amazing, and I like a few days of quiet. It's my after-Christmas ritual."

Jonah nodded. It sounded like a welcome distraction from the morning, so he rose from the table to get his coat and keys. At the same moment, one of Spader's cards flew through the air and hit Reena's cup of water, which tipped over, and wet several inches of Christmas linen.

"Damn you, Spader!" shouted Reena. "What the hell is wrong with you? Do you have any sense under that scruff?"

"You take that back!" exclaimed Spader. "It wasn't even me! Douglas did it!"

Douglas looked down at the cards in front of him, but before he could say anything, Reena was out of her seat, eyes still on Spader.

"Nice try, boy," she snarled, "but I saw you throw the deck at Douglas before you lied."

Spader looked sheepish. "Oh, you noticed that?"

Bobby, Terrence, and several others laughed at his idiocy. Jonah patted Reena on the shoulder.

"I'll get your keys, Reena," he muttered. "You're better off handling this yourself."

"Thank you, Jonah. They're on the dresser. Can you bring my travel bag, too?" Reena took a paper towel to the stain. "Insipid child. No wonder Liz treats him like he's invisible."

Laughing, Jonah went upstairs to Reena's room. He hadn't ever been there before, so he looked around the place.

Everything she owned was neat and organized; there weren't stray clothes like his and Terrence's rooms. With a smirk, he noticed that Reena had tied her cross trainers to the straps of her travel bag. She refused to take a break from running. Her dresser had all of her school achievements, which included trophies, medals, and the like. She smiled at him from several pictures, but the smiles didn't reach her eyes in any of them. Not a single one. She may have been happy when she won the awards, but every smiled seemed forced.

Jonah noticed a flash of silver, and saw a ring near a picture that had been placed face-down.

It was Julia's ring. So the picture must be—

He knew that he shouldn't. But he couldn't file away his curiosity. He lifted the picture and took a look.

Reena was younger in the picture, but she didn't look too different, apart from her hair. She was with a pretty blonde girl who looked like there wasn't any other place in the world she'd rather be than in that cramped photo booth with Reena.

So that was Julia Gallagher. Jonah could tell that Reena's smile in that picture was the only one that was genuine.

So why was it facedown, then?

Jonah gave himself a mental shake. This wasn't his business. He was up here to get Reena's car keys and travel bag. He placed picture back in a facedown position and grabbed the keys. He planned to ignore anything else that might grab his attention.

Unfortunately, his rapid gesture tilted over a corked vial, which rolled toward the edge of the dresser. Jonah didn't pause to think as he trapped it with his hand. That was a relief. Hopefully no more spills would happen today.

Jonah made to put it back in its proper place when something about the vial caught his attention. Damn.

The vial was unremarkable; Liz had dozens just like it. The liquid within was red, but smelled strongly of citrus. But none of that was what caught his attention.

It was the label. Or more accurate, a word in the label.

Curse.

Jonah lifted it to his face (which was necessary, because he'd left his reading glasses downstairs), and made out: *My joy. The end to this curse.*

"Jonah, what's taking so long? My stuff is in plain sight—"

Reena froze in her tracks when saw what Jonah had in his hands.

Great. Not only was Jonah confused about what he'd just read, he'd gotten caught. He felt like a kid who got caught stealing from his mother's wallet.

Reena's gaze froze over. It matched the temperature outside. "What the hell are you doing with that?" she whispered.

"What the hell is it?" Jonah shot back. "Since when are you cursed?"

"Jonah, you don't have the right to ask me about my things!" spat Reena. "How dare you go through my—?"

"I didn't go through anything!" Jonah jumped to his own defense. "It almost rolled off of the dresser when I grabbed your keys!"

Reena's frosty looked warmed somewhat. "You saved it from breaking?"

"Yeah, I saved it. I was putting it back when the word 'curse' caught my eye. I didn't have my reading glasses, but I caught that word. What is this, Reena?"

It was Reena's turn to look awkward. She swallowed hard.

"I'm your best friend," prodded Jonah.

She sighed, and closed her bedroom door. "You read it, Jonah. It's my joy. The end to my curse."

Jonah raised his eyebrows, and nudged her to go on.

"I've been combining plant solutions with Liz's healing tonics," revealed Reena, her eyes on the floor. "She helped me research some, and I created other ones myself. I've been at it for months. After several failures, repeats, and distractions, I finally succeeded in creating a solution that will suppress my ethereal nature."

"What?" Jonah's voice was hollow. "For how long?"

Finally, Reena looked him in the eye. "Permanently."

Jonah felt weird. It felt like part incredulity, part numbness. It all made sense now. Reena's moods, her resistance to being challenged, her sudden desire to display her art... it all fit. She had even helped Terrence cook high-fat, high-caloric food. Spader called it. He'd been on the money. "*Something is either going right, or has gone right.*"

Jonah half-hoped that the solution wouldn't work, but his more intelligent side knew better. If Reena set her mind to something, then there was no way in hell it would flop.

"Liz actually helped you make this?"

"No, of course not," said Reena. "She only assisted me in discerning which plants and solutions had the most powerful neutralizing effects. She is amazing at solutions, as you already know. But I can usually improvise good solutions myself when I have a decent foundation."

Jonah didn't doubt that either. Then something occurred to him. "Does this mean you would lose your speed?"

Reena nodded.

"The cold-spot tricks? The endowments? The essence reading?"

Another nod for that.

Jonah took a deep breath. "Will it take away your mental acuity? Make you less intelligent? Would it affect your aptitude for the arts?"

It was below the belt, and Jonah knew it. But it achieved the desired effect. Reena winced when he mentioned those things. She adored her intelligence and her ability to draw and paint. But after a few minutes, she shrugged.

"It's a small price to pay to be normal."

"Normal, Reena?" cried Jonah. "Normal? Have you lost your damn mind?"

"I've never been clearer, Jonah!" Reena's dull, resigned voice was suddenly strong. "You mentioned things that I'd leave behind, but you left out the other side of it. You failed to mention all the non-desirable qualities that I can finally kiss goodbye, like the mental snags, the creative blocks, having to deal with Spirit Reapers, having to keep myself in check for endowments, and that damn sensitivity to people's essences!"

She reached into her shirt and pulled out the dampener. "Do you remember what happened last spring?"

Jonah swallowed. "I-I try not to think about it."

"Woo-hoo for you, Jonah!" said Reena in a cold voice. "I never forgot that. It's tough enough having to wear the thing to keep people's essence out of my consciousness, but then I took your emotions in, and *that* happened. Coming across that sazer as a teenager and what happened last spring are two things that I never quite got over. And then that Haunting." Reena looked away for a second. "Those other two things were frightening, but that? That was the final straw. That let me know that this life was no longer for me."

"No longer for you?" Jonah couldn't believe that Reena couldn't see the flaws in this plan! "Reena, you were born an Eleventh Percenter! It's not like you can cure it like a disease!"

"Numerous people have been born into undesired situations and fixed them—"

"Oh Reena, just stop!" He didn't know the label to put on his emotions. Fear? Anger? A determination to stop this at any cost? "Not being susceptible to ethereality doesn't stop it from happening! It's not like our world would just disappear because you swallowed that miracle juice. You wouldn't become a Tenth; you'd be like a—like a lapsed Eleventh or something! This is not logical. You can't do this!"

"DON'T TELL ME WHAT I CAN AND CAN'T DO, JONAH ROWE!" shouted Reena. "It's so typical of you men to impose limits on women who can think for themselves! I have no more desire to be a temperature-altering, clairsentient sponge! All things occur for a reason, right? Well I don't know why I was born an ethereal human on top of everything else. But I have the mental faculty to do something about it. I will control my own life, my own decisions, and my own love. And I will do so without the Eleventh Percent."

Jonah stopped registering words after love. He wasn't Sherlock Holmes, but something fired in his mind. He glanced at Julia's ring, which lay next to the facedown picture. Then he returned his eyes to Reena. "You've got a new girl-friend, don't you?" he asked. "You aren't going to be alone when you reach your hotel room...wherever."

Reena looked over at Julia's ring. "Yes, Jonah. I do."

"Who is she? Someone we know?"

"You know her very well by now, Jonah. It's Kendall."

Jonah did a double take. "What? My professor?"

"Do you know another Kendall, Jonah?"

Jonah gave a sort of stunned laugh. "Wow."

Reena's eyes narrowed. "Does that shock you?"

"No, not really—it's just—back at that art exhibit, all the guys from class were all dressed up, trying to impress her. She said they weren't her type. I took that to mean that she didn't like *boys*. As in, college boys."

"Well, you were right about that." Reena smirked. "She doesn't like boys."

"How long have you been dating?"

"Since before Thanksgiving, give or take a day or two."

"What?" said Jonah. "Really? When did you guys speak? How did you hook up?"

"We spoke at the art exhibit," replied Reena. "There was something between us then. When you got Haunted that second time, I used your phone to call her and make up some excuse for you missing one of her next class. We wound up talking for hours about a bunch of other things. We arranged a couple meet-ups, and just hit it off."

"Huh." Jonah knew that they were off-topic, but the distraction was a powerful one. "So you two were already dating when I invited her for Thanksgiving…why did you keep it a secret?"

"It wasn't a secret, Jonah," scoffed Reena. "Why would I do that? It's a new relationship. You never want everyone in your business when you're just starting out."

Jonah looked away again. So Reena was dating his professor. That wasn't a big deal—wait. He refocused on the matter at hand. "Reena, are you doing taking that stuff for Kendall?"

"No, Jonah." Reena sounded firm. "It's for me. Only me. It's been on my mind for a while now. Kendall just happened in the midst of it all. But I'm grateful for her."

"So you're over Julia? Seriously?"

Reena's eyes hardened. "Jonah, there is something that I didn't tell you at your friend's wedding about Julia. Remember when I said that she wrote that she'd found love in the traditional way? That was only a small part of it. She referred to what we shared as an aspect of her former life, Jonah. She hasn't even told her husband about her past!"

"Are you kidding me?" said Jonah in disbelief.

"I would never kid about that, Jonah!" Reena pointed to the ring on her dresser. "That ring was saturated with her essence! You know what else? She is a damned liar. She has buried who she is. She still thinks about women. But she has chosen to play a character up there in Princeton, with her husband and baby."

Jonah shook his head. This revelation made something else make sense. "So that's why you've been wearing your dampener all the time. You've been wearing it since then. After that, you didn't want to read anybody's essence ever again."

"Yeah," answered Reena. "Pretty much. That tore me up, Jonah. But Kendall…Kendall dissolved the crap that Julia left in me. I'm grateful for her. I'm in love, and I'll be damned if it gets screwed up again. When this mess with the 49er is over, I'm drinking that solution, and purging myself of my ethereality."

Jonah looked at her hopelessly. Reena's goal was to be who she wanted to be by purging the person that she actually was. He had only been involved in ethereality for a short while compared to her. He wasn't in her mind, so he didn't know how she could be so resolute about this. But Jonah knew that he couldn't imagine abandoning the Eleventh Percent, even after all the odd and scary things that had happened. Just the thought of returning to the way things were before he discovered the Eleventh Percent would be tantamount to, dare he think it, a living death.

"Reena, please." Jonah didn't even try to mute the desperation in his voice. "You have to think about this. There is no coming back from—from purging yourself. I can kind of see how you feel. I imagine it's perfectly normal to—"

Reena raised a hand to silence him. "I don't want to discuss it any further, Jonah. I've made my choice, and I'm following through with it. Besides," she frowned at him, "what could you possibly tell me about something being perfectly normal? Weren't you just heckling me about the decision to become normal?"

"You guys have been up here for a wh—"

Terrence opened the door as he spoke, but the tension in the room shut him up. Jonah and Reena stared at each other. Neither acknowledged Terrence's presence.

"Am I missing something here?" he murmured.

Reena grabbed her bag and pulled her car keys from Jonah's hand. He hadn't even realized that they were still in his grasp.

"Merry Christmas, Jonah," she said, "and thank you again for your present."

She paused long enough to say the same thing to Terrence, and then exited the room.

14

Lifeblood on the Gridiron

Never before in Jonah's life had he ever experienced a stranger beginning to the New Year. It was supposed to mark new beginnings, but all he could think of was the stuff he'd dragged into the new cycle. Felix had outshone him on Christmas, yet he couldn't avoid him due to the Mind Cage training. The 49er and the Haunts were still a threat, not to mention the little cadre of vampires that 49er had created over the course of the months.

But as huge as those things were, they paled in comparison to Reena's plan to purge her ethereality and become a Tenth Percenter.

And there wasn't a damned thing he could do about it.

Jonah hoped that Reena hadn't hoped to keep it from Terrence, because he told him the first chance he got. Surprisingly, though, Terrence latched on the wrong piece.

"I can't believe it! Kendall is into women? Damn! I never had a chance at all!"

Jonah looked at his friend in disbelief. "*That* is what you took from what I just said to you, Terrence? I'm going to need you to let that go! Reena is about to make herself a Tenth Percenter!"

Terrence muttered under his breath about Kendall for a few more moments (Jonah rolled his eyes in exasperation), but then he finally got on board. "She is going to purge herself of the Eleventh Percent? Has she lost her mind?"

"She says she has never been clearer," answered Jonah. "She said she never got over the sazer incident from her teens, and that she hasn't forgotten the dampener thing. But she said experiencing the Haunting was the last straw."

Terrence stared. "That can't have been all there was to it. We go through crazy stuff all of the time!"

"You're right, man," said Jonah. "She also said that she was tired of being a 'spectral sponge' or something. Evidently, she is really burnt out on the essence reading ability she has." Jonah didn't mention the part that Julia played in that. It wasn't Terrence's business, and the only reason he knew was because Reena got worked up and spilled her guts. "She also said that she was ready to handle her own life and her own love and what have you."

Terrence's expression showed that he'd fixated on the same piece as Jonah did himself. "Her own love, huh? So Julia played some piece in this. Is that right?"

Jonah rolled his eyes. Damn. Despite his mentality from time to time, Terrence was no fool. "Yeah," was all he said to that particular question, "but I'm sure that Reena had moved on. She said being with Kendall dissolved a lot of the crap she harbored all these years."

"That's it, then." Terrence hadn't ever sounded more certain of anything in all the time Jonah knew him. "She's doing it for Kendall."

"She insisted that it was her choice, Terrence," said Jonah. "She told me that it had been on her mind for a while now."

"Uh-huh." Terrence was unmoved. "She might have convinced herself of that, too. It's bullshit, Jonah. You know it, and I know it. That is such a shame."

Jonah was about to agree with Terrence, but then he realized what he meant. "It is *not* a shame that Kendall likes Reena and doesn't like you, Terrence. That part isn't the issue here. It's the whole purging thing that I can't agree with."

"Yeah, okay," said Terrence heavily. "You're right. And she is gonna go through with it after we've dealt with the 49er?"

"So she says."

Terrence looked at the ground. "Is it wrong that I want the 49er to be a problem for a little while longer now?"

Reena returned to the estate on the fourth, which was the same day that Jonathan's Christmas tree resumed its original place outside the gazebo. It also resumed its original bare state because of the winter. Jonah thought that was apt for the situation.

He and Reena came to a silent agreement to put their argument behind them, and pretty soon, they were back in the swing of things along with Terrence. Endowment training resumed, debates over healthy food vs. unhealthy food, speculating over the 49er's plans…things were back to normal. Or some semblance of it.

The subject wasn't breached again until right before Jonah's next Mind Cage lesson, which occurred halfway through the month.

"How are you faring with that, Jonah?" she asked after she'd returned from a run.

"I can get the mental cage door up to halfway closed now," replied Jonah. "I can even feel the action level out my body somewhat. But the Haunting taint took over again, and I still haven't created a weapon of expression yet."

"I forgot about that lingering taint," muttered Terrence. "I'm not kidding, Jonah. You have to learn that thing so that you can teach us! Well, me. I almost envy you, Reena. When you're a Tenth, the taint will be null and void in you. At this particular moment, I'd love to have a chance!"

Reena swallowed, but didn't reply. Terrence considered her in resigned kind of way, but Jonah didn't have time to think about it. He just went to meet Felix in their usual spot.

There was a marked change in Jonah's ability to fight the toxic effect that the Haunting had on his system. Nonetheless, that cage door in his mind would still only close halfway. That pissed Jonah off. He was angry with himself about it, and he did *not* want the taint in his system anymore. What would happen if he came across the 49er and those dogs again?

"You might not want to hear it," said Felix as he handed Jonah a small portion of Vintage, "but you're right on schedule. You have enough control to attack to knock a Haunt off-balance and run for help now. That is much better than collapsing on the ground and being easy pickings."

Jonah made a face as he chased down the liquor with a whole bottle of water. "That cage door is getting on my nerves. I'm sick of reaching halfway and not being able to go any further. It burns me."

"Apply that frustration to your efforts, and you'll have it before you know it," said Felix. "And once you master the Mentis Cavea, you can do it at anytime, regardless of the circumstance."

Jonah allowed himself to be minutely placated by Felix's words, but then he remembered his ostentatious gift to Vera. Maybe he could apply *that* frustration to the Mind Cage as well. "Right," he heard himself say.

Felix caught the subtle change in Jonah's demeanor, and sat on a metal chair with an inquisitive look. "I tried a different tack that time when I spoke about your parents. Did you get along with them?"

Jonah looked at him. So Mr. Roses was curious about that, too? "I never knew my parents."

Felix looked surprised. "You don't know them? Your grandmother never talked about them?"

Jonah rolled his eyes. How many times in his life had he told this story? "My mother was Nana's daughter. Her name is—or *was,* I don't know if she is still physically alive—Sylvia. By all accounts, she wasn't fit to be anyone's mother, and Nana said that I was better off."

"Huh." Felix frowned. "Harsh words to say of one's own daughter."

"Not if it's true," grunted Jonah.

Felix nodded. "I'll give you that. And your dad?"

That one was easy. "Took off after he knocked up my mom. Never knew his name, don't know where he is or what he looks like. All I know is that he was almost twenty years older than my mother. Nana never said much about him. She passed into Spirit hating him."

Felix cast pensive eyes on Jonah. "Coming to terms with that animosity may assist with mastering the Mentis Cavea, Jonah."

Jonah inhaled and exhaled through his nostrils. What the hell did Felix know about it? "I don't *have* any animosity, Felix. Both of my parents were worthless pieces of trash. Nana was my mother, so Sylvia doesn't matter. And that man who knocked her up? He is a non-entity."

Felix shook his head before Jonah even finished speaking. "Not true, Jonah. You might believe the part about Sylvia not mattering, because you had a strong mother figure in her stead. But your dad isn't a non-entity. I bet the lion's share of your unresolved emotions concern him. It's untamed because it's not actually malice, but anger and confusion. You haven't had the chance to deal with it because, unlike the situation with your mother, you never had a name, face, or person to attach your emotions to in your father's case."

Jonah kept his face down so as not to betray how he felt. How could Felix know all those things? How could he know that Jonah held a lifelong grudge against a person he'd never seen?

This whole Haunting and Mind Cage business...sucked. It sucked. Jonah felt like a container of liquid. The top of the liquid was clear enough because all of the crap in it had settled to the bottom. But these experiences disturbed the container. It made all the crap that had settled at bottom swirl about once again.

"Whatever," he managed.

Felix smirked, corked the Vintage, and pocketed. It was Jonah's turn, since Felix wanted to be so chatty.

"Felix, why do you keep alcohol?" he asked. "I remember that you said you were a recovering alcoholic and have been sober for seven years. Why keep the temptation near you like that?"

Felix cut his eyes at Jonah, but Jonah didn't feel threatened. Felix appeared to be weighing words in his mind. When he spoke, his tone was so calm that it was almost robotic. "I've been dealing with vampires, Haunts, and Spirit Reapers for years now. When I was a kid, Creyton had a bunch of followers, but the 49er was always the one that gave me the most hell."

"Why?"

Felix didn't answer. "My way of dealing with the stressors of that time was liquor. My alcoholism also coincided with when I lost my dad. Mama followed him in Spirit three years later." His face darkened, but his voice remained steady. "Eventually I hit rock bottom; every addict hits bottom. But I clawed my way back up. The bottle reminds me of where I could end up if I don't stay on the straight and narrow."

A memory flashed in Jonah's mind. "You've been dealing with vampires, Reapers, and Haunts. What about those people Trip mentioned? Sazers?"

Felix nodded. "I've worked closely with sazers in the past. As the natural enemies of vampires, they can be invaluable allies."

"Are they dangerous?"

"They are just like the rest of the population," said Felix. "Some are alright, and some you don't need to mess with. Can't paint them all with one brush."

Jonah nodded. That made sense. "I got to ask something else. Do you have any idea why Trip brought them up before Christmas? My friends and I agreed that it was kind of random."

Felix rolled his eyes. "Trip considers the day wasted if he hasn't blessed someone with his discord. But if I had to stab in the dark, I imagine that he wanted to plant seeds of doubt into everyone's mind about the kid who rescued you when you got Haunted at LTSU."

Jonah straightened. "You know about that?"

"Yes. Jonathan filled me in when we fortified defenses. Remember that night you got Green Dealt and all the residents created a watch on the estate grounds?"

"Oh yeah, I—" Jonah stopped short. He couldn't very well reveal that he had been out there with that night. Besides, he didn't care very much for remembering the illuminated hands and hearing Felix regale Vera with tales of rare flora. "Yeah. I remember."

Felix raised an eyebrow at Jonah's response, but continued. "That was in response to your attack. The boy who rescued you exhibited characteristics of a sazer."

"But Trip sounded accusatory," recalled Jonah. "Why would he be like that if they guy helped someone out?"

"Jonah, in the time you've known Trip, have you ever known him to be positive about anything?" asked Felix. "But it just so happens that Trip has a history with sazers that poisoned him against them eternally."

"What happened?"

Felix took out his father's lighter, casually lit it, and let it go out. "Can't help you there, Jonah. Ask Jonathan. He understands it better."

Jonah didn't miss Felix's tone. It made him wonder if Felix actually believed that, or if he simply had no willingness to reveal what he knew. But he chose to respect him. With a nod, he rose to leave.

"One more thing about sazers, Jonah." Felix lit the lighter again. "It's always a wise policy not to judge people before you actually know what they're about. Nothing that Trip says is the gospel. Believe that."

Jonah didn't have it in him to tell Felix that it actually *hadn't* been Trip who said the unsavory things about sazers, but he took one thing to heart. Just like with Felix himself, if Trip hated them, they couldn't be all bad. He nodded in acknowledgement and left Felix, who stared at the lighter's flame in an almost meditative silence.

"What the hell does Felix know about Trip?"

Terrence's question hit, Jonah, and Reena like low-lying fog as they relaxed in Jonah's room. Jonah was just as confused as Terrence.

"I wish I knew, man. I don't mean to make him sound like he was hiding something. He didn't get standoffish or anything. He just said that Jonathan would know more. Which is a laugh, because you know just as well as I do that Jonathan will just speak in riddles."

"Riddles which always unwind and make perfect sense in the end," Reena reminded him. "But here is the thing. Trip hates everyone, but he hates sazers especially. Makes me wonder why they get the preferential treatment."

"I still maintain that they aren't the monsters they're made out to be," insisted Terrence. "Yeah, Mom and Dad told us about the Red Rage and the impulse control problems and whatnot, but anybody could have those issues. And they have been so helpful to Elevenths in the past, particularly with vampires. Spirit Reapers hate them almost as much as the vampires do."

"Apparently, Felix agrees with you," muttered Jonah. "He says that he has worked with them in the past, and it wouldn't be intelligent to judge them just based off what Trip said."

They both looked at Reena, who correctly interpreted their expressions and sighed.

"I won't deny anything you guys have said," she granted, "but I *will* point out that sazers can be brutal when they dispense anti-vampire justice. Maybe Trip was attacked by one, like me. I don't know. But he's got strong feelings about them, which is saying something."

Jonah nodded in agreement. "Felix told me that he thinks that the kid that saved me at LTSU is a sazer, and that Trip didn't want anyone to regard him a heroic or anything."

Terrence looked surprised, but to Jonah's surprise, Reena looked skeptical.

"What's on your mind?" he asked her. "You think that Felix is lying?"

"Not really," said Reena slowly, "but to plant seeds in that way seems very elaborate, even for Trip. If Felix is right and that boy *is* a sazer, I hope he's taking care of himself."

"I don't doubt his safety," said Jonah. "Not at all. If anyone comes within three feet of his body odor, they'll run from *him*."

* * *

Jonah had no idea what this New Year might bring, but it was still fun to watch his friend's routines. It was just as entertaining as writing and gaming to him, and was a healthy distraction from his crazy mind.

Football season was over, but Bobby still trained like he had a game every week. Liz told him over and over that his body wasn't meant to be taxed like that, but he wouldn't listen. It was only after she "accidentally" tweaked something in his calf muscle during a massage that he calmed down and took a break. Bobby insisted that Liz didn't do it on purpose, but Spader, Alvin, and Terrence believed that the boy must be truly blinded by his affections to believe that Liz just *happened* to jar a nerve in his calf that prevented him from doing exploder sprints and Hindu squats. Jonah agreed with them.

Douglas spent so much time with online chess that Jonah wondered if he could stand and walk after so many hours in that chair. He'd told Jonah that the new semester looked "promising" in regards to the chess club, because he'd coordinated events so as to round up new members. While he applauded his efforts, Jonah had a hard time believing that anyone would be interested in joining a club that included a nerd square and a guy who could barely play the damn game in the first place.

Jonah also noticed that Vera included her *Wicked* mug into her daily routine, but he hadn't seen her wear her T-shirt or sweatshirt since Christmas morning. When he inquired about this, she looked at him like he'd grown an extra head.

"Jonah, are you out of your mind?" she exclaimed. "I can't wear them; they're sacred!"

"Sacred?" repeated Jonah, flabbergasted. "I thought you might sleep in them or something."

Vera looked aghast. She actually paused in the act of running her hand through her hair. "*Sleep* in them? Jonah, you have no idea. That's clothing from *Wicked*, not some bargain crap you got from the Dollar Den."

Jonah was about to respond when he noticed Vera's arm. When she ran her hand through her hair the loose sleeve of her shirt fell back, and revealed a jagged scar on the underside of her arm. Vera caught where his eyes had gone, and she shook the sleeve back down.

"Vera, are you ever going to tell me how you got those scars?" he asked.

"I got them the same time I got *this* one, Jonah," she said, and pointed to the one at the base of her jaw.

Jonah didn't understand why the scars made her so self-conscious. As far as he was concerned, they weren't even there. "Vera, your scars don't matter. You're beautiful regardless."

Vera snorted, but Jonah thought she blushed. Yeah, she blushed.

"You're far too kind, Jonah," she said before hastily changing the subject.

In a very interesting turn of events, Jonah and Terrence spent a lot of time in the gym with Alvin. It was a much less hellish experience with Bobby out of commission. To Jonah's surprise, Terrence introduced Douglas to weightlifting, which amused the taciturn Malcolm.

"A-Are you sure about this?" Douglas was nervous, and looked so awkward in athletic pants and a cutoff T-shirt. Jonah was so accustomed to seeing him in the chinos and golf shirts that he barely believed he owned anything else.

"Of course I am," said Terrence without hesitation. "You pushed Jonah out of his comfort zone with chess, didn't you? Lighten up. Who knows? If you get cut up, maybe some women at LTSU might join your little club."

Douglas actually gave Terrence a sharp eye after that comment. "I've been told that women prefer men with something upstairs."

Malcolm chuckled. "That may very well be true, but in my experience, women also prefer a good-looking staircase."

When they were done with Douglas, the poor guy could hardly move. Jonah could relate. He remembered how his every fiber screamed with disagreement when he began working out with Bobby, Terrence, and Alvin. The smile never left his face as they assisted him to the infirmary, where Ben-Israel scolded them for pushing him too hard.

"Day 1 is always torture, Ben-Israel," Terrence told him.

"All the more reason to be delicate with an uncoordinated novice!" snapped Ben-Israel. Chandler only has capacity for intellectual stimulation; hitting him with this physicality is not logical! Look at him!"

"Geez, Ben-Israel." Irritation permeated Douglas's already pained gaze. "What do you say about me when I'm *not* here?"

"Let's leave them to it," said Terrence with a laugh.

When they left, they could still hear Ben-Israel scathing rebukes, and Douglas's halfhearted attempts at defiance.

Jonah didn't know what to think about Reena. Beyond the conversations they'd had about the 49er early in the New Year, she'd been pretty reticent. Many residents attributed to a desire to remain tightlipped about her new relationship. But Jonah knew that it was far more than that. He had a suspicion that Reena wanted to detach herself from everyone because of her plan to purge her ethereality. Jonah wished she didn't feel the need to be detached from people. She'd dealt with that her entire life. But he had to be honest. He wished that he hadn't ever discovered her plan. It unnerved him. Reena was one of the first people to welcome him to the estate, and one of his best friends. It was hard to fathom that one day soon, she would be a Tenth Percenter, and no longer in their circle.

He tried to treat things like they hadn't changed, but that was a bust. The subject was the elephant in the room, which made the tension all the more unbearable. There had to be a way to make it work, because if they carried on like this, the taint of the Haunting might return in one of them.

Jonah approached Reena one evening while everyone crowded around the television for Turk Landry's spot on Rome's nightly news for *ScarYous* (Jonah hadn't forgotten that fraudulent Eleventh, but other matters put him in the back of his mind). She had retreated to a corner in the family room, and didn't pay attention to anyone as she thumbed through yellowed papers on her lap and made checkmarks on a notepad.

"Can I join you?" he asked.

"Me too?"

Both Jonah and Reena looked up in surprise. Terrence was there. He actually turned his back on the show that featured his idol?

Reena hesitated, and then nodded. She made room for them both, and they joined her there.

"What are these, Reena?" Jonah indicated the yellowed pages.

"Clippings from awards I won when I was a kid," said Reena, who extended one for him to see.

Jonah put on his reading glasses and looked it over. "These are from when you were in Hawaii, right? Is that one of the places you'll go when you leave here? Visit your family?"

"My family is in *Virginia*, remember?" said Reena. "I'm trying to familiarize myself with these places again because I want to retrace them without my mother's influence."

"Did you guys live in Maui?" asked Terrence almost the second Reena mentioned her mother. Because I'm sure my brother Lloyd can help you get used to things again."

Reena looked touched, but shook her head. "Thanks for that, Terrence, but my family lived in Kauai. Waimea, to be exact." She sighed. "There might be people who remember my mother, though. She knew *everyone*. Maybe I should go to Kahoolawe. No one would know me there."

Terrence laughed, Jonah didn't. When they looked at him in puzzlement, he shrugged.

"What? Was there a joke in there?"

"*Yes*, Jonah," said Terrence. "Kahoolawe's uninhabited because ain't any freshwater. Lloyd told me all about it when I visited him."

"Oh," was all Jonah said. Didn't mean anything to him, after all.

Jonathan appeared in the family room seconds later. People looked at him with interest, and Alvin muted the television.

"Good evening, Eleventh Percenters," he said, "I hope that you all are having a peaceful evening. Tomorrow is Saturday, and I would like to make a request of you all."

"Oh no," said Spader. "Are we stuck here again?"

"Quite the contrary, Royal," said Jonathan. "I would like for all of you to disperse and engage in leisurely pursuits away from the estate."

Everyone stared at him.

"Why, Jonathan?" Reena pushed the clippings away. "Has the 49er been spotted?"

"Yes, he has," said Jonathan. "He and his cabal of Haunts and vampires have created enough havoc on the Astral Plane that they can no longer hide in the shadows. The Phasmastis Curaie has been closing in, surprisingly."

Jonathan grimaced, which surprised Jonah. Was he not pleased with the way the Curiae's way of handling the 49er? Jonathan hadn't ever shown disdain for his superiors, so something had to be up. It sent a chill down his spine.

"Pardon me." Jonathan smoothed out his face and continued. "As I was saying, the 49er is not a rash being. While I don't expect *him* to do anything yet, his group of vampires…"

Jonathan closed his eyes, and let his silence do the work for him. Jonah didn't like that at all. He had gotten used to the idea that Jonathan could solve any issue that threatened the estate. But in this particular situation, he seemed to be at a disadvantage. It was as if he were especially hampered by his inability to interfere directly. It was in that moment that Jonah figured out all he needed to know about Jonathan's displeasure with the Phasmastis Curaie.

"While you all are out and about, I will be fortifying the estate's defenses with the help of two specialists."

"Who will that be, sir?" asked Benjamin. "Some of the Protector Guides? Or is the Curaie sending some practitioners of Spectral Law?"

"Or even two Networkers?" suggested Magdalena.

"None of those," answered Jonathan quietly. "Felix and Titus."

There were so many simultaneous gasps that Jonah was surprised the family room hadn't lost its air supply. He neither started nor exclaimed, but fixed his mentor with a pronounced look of alarm. What the hell?

"A-Are you sure that's a good idea, sir?" he asked.

"It's a great idea, actually," said Jonathan in a calm voice. "Felix is proficient with vampiric defense, and Titus's auditory expertise will aid in alerting us of Ghost Waves and the usage of twig portals."

"That is all fine, sir," said Jonah anxiously, "but expecting them to cooperate would require a miracle on the level of loaves and fish."

That got some snickers, but Jonathan remained calm. "Felix and Titus are adults. I am certain they can see past the petty asides that splinter them in favor of preventing further physical and spectral lifebloodshed. They will understand. And if they don't, then I will *make* them understand."

There was that dangerously calm voice. Jonah still had doubts, but maybe Trip and Felix could co-exist if Jonathan used *that* voice on them.

Jonathan vanished, and everyone erupted into conversation. Before Jonah could say anything to Terrence or Reena, he got accosted by Bobby.

"Hey, Jonah, I wanted to invite you, Terrence, Benjamin, Al—hell, *all* of you to come up to LTSU tomorrow for a scrimmage football game."

Jonah frowned. "That's an oddly random, request Bobby. Were you planning on doing that *before* Jonathan asked us to disperse?"

"Well, no, actually, "Bobby admitted, "but it's a golden opportunity to keep in shape, you know? The estate doesn't have the same equipment as the school."

Reena moved her notepad. "Bobby, I understand the guys, but why do you want *me* there? Wouldn't you rather take Liz in the event of—"

"*No!*" hissed Bobby, but then he realized his mistake.

Reena laughed. "So *that's* it. You want to bring me along because I can perform medic duties. Why are you trying to give Liz the slip?"

Bobby gave Reena an innocent look that wouldn't have fooled a child. "I-I just thought Lizzie would like to have a day of fun without me was all."

Reena's eyes flashed. "Are you going up there to see another girl?"

"Oh God, no!" Bobby looked scandalized.

Reena rolled her eyes. "Level with me, or I'm ripping off the dampener."

"Alright! Fine!" Bobby looked behind them. "Vera is taking Liz to a play in Raleigh. That much was going to happen before Jonathan's announcement. I wanted to use the time to stretch out this leg she put on ice."

"Put on i—wait." Reena snickered. "Did Liz aggravate a pressure point in your leg to make you slow down?"

"It was an accident," insisted Bobby. "It just coincided with what Liz requested of me. She's too sweet to have done that on purpose."

Reena gave Jonah a quick glance, which he responded to with a nod that meant, "*Yeah. He bought that.*"

Reena sighed, but it was clear that she enjoyed Bobby's dilemma. "Fine. I'll go along and watch you men kill yourselves. You owe me, Robert Decessio. But after your game, you're on your own. I've got plans with Kendall."

Bobby punched the air. Jonah and Terrence smirked at each other. That had been an *epic* crash and burn, but at least Bobby made it work in the end.

Jonah left them and headed for the kitchen. It was an "every man for himself" night, which meant that no one cooked and they were on their own if they wanted to eat. But a quick look outside showed him that Jonathan hadn't gone off plane or anything. He was in the middle of the heralds, with Bast at the forefront. Apparently, the cats had jobs in this fortification as well. He was struck with sudden inspiration.

He went outside (it was cold as hell, but Jonathan could have been who-knew where by the time Jonah got his jacket) and got to Jonathan right when the heralds separated. Bast paused long enough to nuzzle his leg, and then raced off into the darkness.

"Hello again, Jonah!" said Jonathan. "What's on your mind?"

"Two things, sir," said Jonah. "First off, do Trip and Felix know they're working together?"

"Ah," said Jonathan shrewdly. "Cooperating with one another doesn't mean that they have to *see* one another, if you understand me."

Jonah laughed. So they'd be working the same job at different times. Jonah knew that Jonathan wouldn't put them face to face. "Awesome plan. I wanted to ask you something else about those two men."

"Oh?"

"Well, I was doing a Mind Cage lesson with Felix—"

"'Mind Cage?' You mean Mentis Cavea?"

"Yes sir, that too. Anyway, I asked Felix about why Trip brought up sazers before Christmas, and he said two things about it. The first thing was that Trip might have said it to imply that that boy who saved me a while back was one—"

"He is," said Jonathan. "I'm certain of it."

"Huh," said Jonah. "Cool. Anyway, the second thing he said was that Trip experienced something with sazers that brought this hatred. He said I should ask you about it because you would know more about it than him."

Jonathan's expression darkened, much like Felix's had the other night. But when it changed, Jonah was surprised to see that it was neither elusive nor awkward. It was pained. He looked on the verge of tears. "I wish that Felix hadn't whetted your interest, Jonah, because I won't discuss Titus's business."

Jonah's frustration mounted almost instantly. "I'm sorry, but what the hell are you hiding, Jonathan? This could be some serious stuff! Why can't you tell me?"

"Because it would be just like cutting skin that's already been scarred, Jonah. I'm not willing to do that."

Don't get me started on scars, thought Jonah, who thought briefly of Vera. He filed that away. "I'll respect your wishes, Jonathan, but I hope to God that you know what you're doing?"

Jonathan looked at him. "What do you mean, Jonah?"

Jonah tried very hard to keep his voice level. "What I mean is that Felix and Trip are both in the same place, and they're both powder kegs. It only takes one powder keg to go off to make everything go with it. But *two*..." he shook his head. "A lot of people are here, Jonathan. And those people can go up in smoke if both kegs are going off at once."

Saturday morning crept up on them all. The sun was bright in the sky, yet it provided no warmth. Jonah couldn't help but reconsider his decision as he walked onto the crunchy football field with everyone. But once they started moving about, the cold wasn't much of an issue. Bobby had even gathered some of his teammates and classmates, and they were a cool, fun bunch. The experience was a lot more fun than Jonah expected. He never thought that football would be enjoyable. He'd had sports forced down his throat as a kid, particularly football, and developed an intense dislike for the sport. But none of the old irritants were present on this wintry Saturday afternoon. No guilt trips, no obligations or expectations. Just a bunch of guys having fun while a few women watched in the bleachers.

About two and a half hours into it, Jonah fancied himself a wide receiver and ran as hard as his non-athletic legs would carry him after one of Bobby's buddies lobbed a pass his way. For a shining moment, it seemed that the pass would connect, but then he got blindsided by another of Bobby's friends. When the freight-train of a guy collided with Jonah, all thoughts of catching the touch-down evaporated as every bit of oxygen he thought he owned got knocked out of him. Whatever was left got knocked out when they hit the ground.

Even though Jonah only registered stunned shock, everything still seemed to work. All his muscles were intact, all the bones were still connected, and as he took in a deep breath, he got rewarded with the discovery that *not* all the air in his body was gone.

"Sorry man," said Jonah's tackler. "Didn't mean to hit you that hard."

Jonah managed enough breath to mutter, "Forget it," when the guy looked down and winced.

Jonah sat up, curious, and realized the issue.

The back of his right hand was bleeding rather badly. The guy had tackled him at a place where the field met the track that oval-ringed the field. The back of Jonah's hand must have hit the hard surface and created a gash across his knuckles.

Of course the sting kicked in once Jonah saw the cut, but it wasn't too bad. He'd had worse than this.

Bobby and Terrence helped him to a standing position, and Bobby looked it over.

"Nothing a wrap-up won't fix," he told him, and then in an undertone, "This is why Liz and Reena are godsends. I could never bring Ben-Israel out here. He'd say the wrong thing and get punched in the face.

Jonah sat out the last few minutes of the makeshift game with a wad of toilet paper on his hand. Once the game was over, Bobby's friends all piled into a van and left. His caveman pal issued one final apology before they left. Bobby and Alvin headed home to spend time with Mr. and Mrs. Decessio. Terrence promised that he'd join them later on in the day, which left him, Jonah, and Reena alone.

Reena grabbed his hand and inspected it. He wished he wouldn't. It wasn't a big deal.

"I know you're trying to be a badass," she told him, "but this gash isn't pretty. It's dirty, and I don't want it to get infected before I put balm on it. Your new semester resumes in a few days, and you don't want issues with your writing hand, correct?"

That hadn't occurred to Jonah. Why did Reena always have to appeal to his rational half?

With a scowl, he stopped trying to wrest his hand from her grasp.

"Thank you," she snapped. "Now I might not have anything for this, but I can improvise something. That'll take your aid, Terrence."

"I don't know the first thing about healing salves!" said Terrence.

"You can follow instructions, right?" said Reena.

"Oh yeah...."

Reena shook her head. "I will *not* miss that when I move out of the estate."

Terrence made a mocking face, and then turned to Jonah. "Jonah, go run your hand under some cold water. The locker room is right over there," he pointed. "You can't miss it. I'll go with this woman and help her with this damn salve."

"You two play nice," grinned Jonah as he headed for the locker room. Terrence's directions were pretty straightforward, and he found the locker room in minutes.

For a second, he thought that it'd be locked, but the door was ajar. He wondered why that would be, but then he remembered Bobby's buddies. They could have easily opened things up when Jonah and his friends were on the way. They might have come in here to fill water bottles, relieve themselves, whatever. But they didn't lock it back. He sighed. Football jocks weren't a bright bunch.

Jonah pushed the door open, walked inside, and took an all encompassing glance around so as to familiarize himself with his surroundings. It was nothing spectacular; just three rows of lockers facing the crimson and white wall. He looked around some more, but saw no sinks. Jonah had to walk to the very back of the locker room to find the bathroom.

Then Jonah realized that he'd made a bit of a mess. He had trailed droplets of blood behind him as he moved through the lockers. The toilet paper on his hand must have shifted with his movements.

"Well, damn," he muttered. He'd have to clean that up, but it would have to wait. One thing at a time.

He reached the sink and simultaneously turned on that faucet. As it was cold, it took a minute for the water's temperature to elevate.

There was a footfall behind him, but he didn't turn around.

"I was wondering when you guys would quit bickering," he said, eyes on the water. "Want to hand your homemade salve over? I need to clean the flo—"

"Please don't dilute your lifeblood like that."

Jonah froze. That voice wasn't Terrence's or Reena's. He saw a reflection in the mirror that made him go as cold as the water that stubbornly refused to warm.

For the second time in months, a reflection betrayed the true image of evil: translucent skin, maniacal eyes, and elongated fangs—

Jonah whipped around. The vampire grinned, which accentuated his fangs.

"Thank you," he said. "There is nothing worse than diluted blood."

Jonah was appalled to see that the blood droplets that had fallen on the floor now stained the vampire's fingertips. And it wasn't "vampire." It was *vampires*.

Two more slunk out of the shadows, and both of them had Jonah's blood on their fingers. Or lifeblood, whatever. He didn't see the 49er or any Haunts, which was good. At that moment, mastering a Mind Cage was the furthest thing from his mind.

Wait…what the hell was he thinking? Nothing in this situation was good. The three pairs of murderous dark eyes told him that much.

"Haven't fed in weeks and weeks," said the first one. "The spirits flee, the humans hide, and our Master gave us up. But then you wandered right into our midst, dripping glorious bits of Lifeblood as you came. The lifeblood of the Blue Aura, no less. Come, my friends, we will dine like kings!"

15

The Snitch

Jonah didn't paralyze himself with analysis. Maybe the night that he almost lost his physical life to the vampire and Haunt double act was eternally embedded in his consciousness. Maybe he didn't want the taint of the Haunting to overtake him again.

Or maybe he just hated vampires.

Jonah went against everything he'd ever been taught in his trainings at the Glade, and made the first move in a fight. Before the first vampire could do anything, Jonah rushed him and swept his legs out from underneath him. He didn't even wait for the beast to hit the ground before he darted back to the sink, dunked his injured hand in the water, and threw and handful at the second one's feet. That vampire (who'd moved forward to intercept Jonah) slipped so sharply that he almost made a full-circle in midair, but that feat was prevented by his head, which slammed against the concrete like broken eggs. The resulting crack was sickening, but Jonah didn't have time to be nauseous. If everything that Felix said was true, the injuries that the vampires just sustained would heal very soon.

Jonah didn't even pause to wonder why the third vampire was off to the side, and strangely detached from the skirmish. He lunged for the backpack that contained his change of clothes and grabbed his batons. Since they'd all taken spiritual endowments the previous night on Jonathan's orders, the batons cackled with blue essence. But then Jonah noticed something else in his bag that almost made him drop a baton. It was that silly anti-vampire kit that Felix gave everyone several months before. Jonah hadn't given it another thought. Until now.

He grabbed the garlic bottle and threw some at the third vampire, who yelped and backed away, but not before a small portion hit his forearm. Jonah hadn't ever seen the banes of vampires outside of movies, so it was quite a nasty shock when he saw the flesh on the vampire's forearm steam, bubble, and burst.

"Aaaagghhh!" he shouted. "Keep it—!"

Jonah swatted him in the head. Although he'd hit his mark, he'd wasted too much time, and paid for it with a whack across his back with a freakishly strong arm. Jonah landed hard on the floor, and just barely avoided breaking the hand that betrayed him in the first place. As the gash on the back of his hand wasn't bad enough, warmness on the back of his neck let him know that his lifeblood had yet another exit route.

"You just had to make this difficult," snarled the vampire who'd skull had just cracked. "But it did you no good. Your lifeblood is ours—"

The abrupt silence prompted Jonah to focus past the bright spots in his eyes and look upward.

The vampire's eyes were wide, like he'd experienced a sudden shock. Then a truly unnerving event occurred. The vampire's skin became even paler, as though what little lifeblood he had was now gone. His eyes, almost catlike in brilliance, eroded to white. Stranger still, his body withered and sunk in until he resembled nothing more than a hollowed out husk.

The remains fell to the floor. A jagged wooden stake was lodged in the back. Behind the body, mystified and rather repulsed, stood Terrence.

Jonah barely even registered the second vampire's shriek as Reena used her ethereal speed to charge him into the wall so viciously that it cracked. While he was off-balance, Reena dumped her entire bottle of garlic in the thing's face. The vampire brought his hands to his face and screamed, but seconds later, the sounds ceased and his body underwent the same decomposition as the other one.

Reena glanced at Jonah's bag, noticed the kit, and nodded.

"We kept ours, too," she explained. "I didn't actually believe I'd ever need it!"

Terrence's eyes hadn't left the hollowed corpse at his feet. "I've never vanquished a vampire," he whispered. "I didn't know what happened after you staked them."

Jonah didn't even care about what they said. He was just thankful to see them. "How did you know what was happening in here?" he asked. "How did you know to bring the kits?"

Terrence finally got his eyes off of the vampire's body and looked at Jonah. "I got bored while Reena was concocting that salve for your hand, so I decided to go into Spectral Sight. There weren't any spirits around, which wasn't surprising since most of them are hiding from the 49er and whatnot. But Reena saw one spiritess outside. Just one."

"And she'd been bitten," said Reena. "Completely drained of lifeblood, I guess. So we ascertained that there were drifters around here somewhere, got our kits, and came looking for you."

"You found a drained spiritess?" asked Jonah. "But the vampire Terrence vanquished said that they hadn't fed in weeks."

"Must have lied," grumbled Terrence. "I wouldn't put it past 'em."

Reena checked out Jonah's hand, but he answered the question before she asked.

"Yeah, my hand betrayed me," he told her. "They were after my lifeblood. But I held my own—for a little while, anyway."

Jonah hadn't thought about Felix's advice for so long that he'd nearly forgotten it. Vampire's existed in a life-limbo, not truly physical beings, and not truly spirits. It made them two-tiered threats, much like the Haunts.

"Is that spiritess alright, Reena?" he asked.

Reena shrugged. "I didn't know what to do. I've never treated a spiritual being. I called Felix to come help."

"Great job, Jonah!" said Terrence suddenly. "You held off two vampires alone!"

"No, there was actually another one—"

The minute Jonah said it, he tensed. He'd almost forgotten that last one. He picked up his other baton and readied himself for a fight. Terrence and Reena were quick on the uptake themselves, and readied for another skirmish.

But the last vampire made no move to fight. He actually knelt and raised his hands.

"Stake me!" he snapped, but there was supplication in the words as opposed to anger. "I'm right here! Kill me!"

Jonah glanced at his friends, who clearly didn't know what to think. "What are you talking about?" he asked the thing.

"I'm talking about killing me!" the vampire snarled. "I'm sick of it! I'm sick of starving!"

"You're tired of starving?" repeated Reena. "What about that spiritess out there, huh?"

The vampire lowered his hands, which made Jonah, Terrence, and Reena even more suspicious. But the vampire looked like he had no will to do anything violent. Truth be told, he didn't look like much of a threat on his knees. "We hadn't had lifeblood for over a month," he murmured. "The two you just vanquished hogged that spiritess; I didn't get a drop. We broke in here to get away from the sun. As for why I didn't attack you…I didn't want to. I'm tired of this. I figured you'd want revenge. Aren't you still angry, Jonah?"

Jonah blinked. "How do you know my name?"

"Don't you remember me?" asked the vampire. "That night that you were ambushed in the university parking lot, when your putrid friend doused you in garlic and bleach?"

Jonah's eyes widened. He remembered the vampire. On that night, though, he was a zealous, hungry, feral beast, nothing at all like the defeated heap that knelt before them now. "So that's why you didn't fight," he said slowly. "You wanted me to destroy you in a fit of rage."

The vampire nodded. Terrence piped up.

"Um, excuse me, Mr. Neckbiter? Why are you so eager to get vanquished? Why haven't you run back to the 49er?"

The vampire flinched at the question, which confounded Jonah. He wanted to be vanquished, but he was afraid of the 49er?

"If you help us," said Reena, who made her voice provocative, "we can discuss granting you the release you desire."

A look of longing crossed the vampire's face. "The 49er abandoned the three of us," he revealed. "We chased you and the sazer when you drove off, but then you got to that mansion and the Protector Guide started picking us off. Those two and I—" he jerked his chin at the two hollowed corpses, "—fled the scene. That Guide was crazed and angry; we didn't stand a chance. We managed to get back to the 49er, but he called us cowards and left us to the Haunts. So then, we had to escape him too, and we've been scrounging for lifeblood ever since. We couldn't even find spirits, because the Astral Protectors—"

"The Spectral Law practitioners," corrected Reena.

"—have tightened things on plane and Off-plane. We had to sustain ourselves on random spirits and spiritesses we were lucky enough to find, but the one this morning should have been a blessing—"

"That was *not* a blessing, you parasitic pariah!" snarled Reena, who had to be restrained by Jonah. "You had no right to attack an innocent spiritess!"

The vampire shrugged, and Reena doubled her efforts to get to him. Jonah figured out his scheme. He wanted to piss them off to them point that they'd vanquish him out of spite.

"Reena, he's trying to rile us," he said, eyeing the beast with disgust. "He's trying to get you to expedite your promise."

"I'll do it, then," said Terrence coldly, and he raised the stake.

"No!" snapped Jonah. "Stop! This little bastard will spill his guts before we do anything for him."

Terrence struggled with himself for a moment, but lowered the stake. Reena stopped struggling against Jonah, and made no further attempts to attack.

"Now, listen to me." Jonah narrowed his eyes at the vampire. "You will cease the provocations. We are your only ticket to oblivion. Talk, and you'll get what you want. Deal?"

The vampire shrugged again, but it was in resignation this time. "Fine."

Jonah still didn't lower his batons. It was the principle of the thing. "Alright. How long were you around the 49er before you got canned?"

"Six, seven weeks," answered the vampire.

"Do you know what he is planning?" asked Jonah. "Why he went quiet, on Earthplane at least?"

The vampire scoffed. "Don't you know anything about us? Vampires lure prey into a false sense of security. Have you Elevenths been neglecting the protection at the estate?"

Jonah didn't answer the question.

"As I said, I've been hiding from him for about a month, so my details may be out of date," the vampire continued when Jonah didn't say anything. "What I do know is that he replaced us, and has a full cabal now. And of course, he has the Haunts. Many of them."

Jonah swallowed and closed his eyes. He didn't know what he hated more; the Haunts, or his fear of them. But it didn't matter right now. "Why does he need a full cabal? Is he still stockpiling lifeblood?"

The vampire raised his eyebrows at Jonah. "The lifeblood is only the tip of the iceberg, Rowe. You truly don't get it, do you?"

Jonah opened his mouth to ask what that meant, but Terrence interrupted him.

"Why should we trust your information, bloodsucker?" he demanded. "I mean, you're snitching so easily; you're singing like a little birdie! I know that you want to be vanquished, but even with that in mind, you're a little too co-operative."

"The 49er left me to the wolves," grumbled the vampire. "Or the Haunts, I should say. I will gladly face death if I know that the 49er follows right behind me."

"You know that death isn't—"

"Never mind that," said Reena. "Look, scum, finish what you were saying, and you will have your vanquishing."

The vampire opened his mouth to speak, but just then, what looked like a silver nail pierced his shoulder. He bellowed, and keeled over in agony. A sharp wind swept through the locker room, and then Felix was there, a crossbow in his hands. It had several more lethal-looking silver nails armed and ready to go.

"Felix?" Jonah stared at him in alarm. "How did you shoot him before you got through the *Astralimes?*"

"What in hell's name are you doing?" Felix roared. "Why haven't you vanquished this piece of trash?"

"Felix, what about the spiritess out there?" asked Reena tersely. "That's what I called you for! To help her!"

"Wasn't anything that could be done for her," snapped Felix. "I had to put her out of her misery, and vanquish her to the Other Side."

"What! But you—"

"Shut up and stop trying to change the subject, Reena!" Felix looked angry enough to chew bricks. "Why haven't you finished him? I see that you killed the other two!"

"He was answering questions for us—"

Felix gave Jonah a murderous glare that made the rest of the words fail in his throat. He lifted the vampire like a sack of potatoes and headed for the door.

"NO, FELIX!" shrieked Jonah. "WAIT!"

Felix ignored him, banged the locker room door open with his foot, and flung the vampire outside. He exploded the second the afternoon sunlight hit his skin. The remaining embers flickered and faded as they flew away on the wintry breeze.

"Damn it, Felix!" Jonah flung a baton against the wall in frustration, where it ricocheted and cracked the mirror above the sink. "Why did you do that?"

Felix looked defiant. "I did the three of you a favor."

"Like hell you did!" Reena was just as angry as Jonah. "The 49er deserted him! He was about to give us information to help fight him!"

"Forget it," said Felix.

"What?"

"Forget it," repeated Felix as he disassembled the crossbow. "Forget every word he said. You cannot trust the words of a vampire. Vampires are addicts, and just like with all addicts, what comes out of their mouths is not the truth. I should know; I've had experiences with vampires and addicts both. Now get out of here. I need to sanitize the scene."

Jonah turned his back on Felix without another word. Terrence and Reena followed him.

He didn't give a damn about Felix's experiences. They were immaterial. All he knew was that that vampire hadn't been lying. He knew it.

He also knew that valuable information that may have helped the entire town of Rome had just gone up in smoke and sparks.

16

The Truth-Laced Liar

Felix may have said to forget it, but that didn't happen. What that vampire said swirled about Jonah's head like a sandstorm. And the few answers he got only had the infuriating effect of creating more questions.

Vampires lure prey into a false sense of security...

The 49er hadn't done anything on Earthplane for a bit. Offplane attacks were one thing, but there hadn't been any mysterious murders on Earthplane for a little while. Was that supposedly a false sense of security?

The 49er now has a full cabal of vampires...

That was the most disturbing piece of information. Obviously, a cabal of vampires didn't have to be large to be dangerous. And they'd be doubly dangerous if they were all hocked up on lifeblood.

The Lifeblood is only the tip of the iceberg, Rowe. You truly don't get it, do you?

That was exactly it. He didn't get it. And now, there was no way to know. Felix and his overdeveloped throwing arms saw to that.

In a strange way, the experience had a silver lining. The awkwardness between Jonah, Terrence, and Reena was gone. There was just no room for it after the vampire sparked their curiosity and nerves. But Jonah was fully aware that they needed to bounce ideas off of each other while they still had the chance, because once Reena was a Tenth, those days would be over.

"I just wish I understood what the 49er was doing," snapped Reena one Saturday after Jonah's second semester in Kendall's class had started. "He has trashed every rule that vampires hold dear! They're hemocentric—"

"They're what, now?" asked Terrence.

"Hemocentric," repeated Reena impatiently. "They think their blood is superior. They feed, and they kill, but they don't ever turn other physically living beings. It only happens in special circumstances, or so I've read."

"If they consider themselves so exclusive, then why do they spend so much time gorging on the lifeblood of those supposedly below them?" questioned Jonah.

Terrence raised his eyebrows, as if to say that Jonah had a point. But Reena quelled them with a scoff.

"Come on, you two. It's not like they're the first group in history to be hypocritical."

Jonah let that settle into his consciousness. "Reena, I've got to ask you. Vampires sound quite unstable. It seems like they'd go on a rampage with the proper amount of lifeblood around. Why would Creyton have ever worked with them?"

"You just said it, Jonah." Reena twirled a paintbrush between her fingers, like she always did when her mind went a mile a minute. "Their instability was a priceless gem for anyone who wanted to cause chaos. They're like expendable soldiers; point them in a certain direction, and then watch them cause crazy amounts of carnage until someone manages to put them down. Just like sazers, actually."

Jonah waved that last part aside. "And the 49er was Creyton's right hand?"

"Probably not," said Reena. "But he was definitely in his inner circle. One thing is for sure, though: If Creyton were still here, abusing the Eleventh Percent and all that, there is no way he would allow the 49er to behave this cavalierly. I just can't find it in me to believe that."

"Good thing Creyton isn't here, then," drawled Terrence. "Things would probably be worse than this."

Jonah agreed, and looked to Reena once again. "I still don't understand something. If the vampires are so elite, then how did so many get loose into the world?"

"I'm guessing inexperience," said Reena. "Vampires could get lifeblood from spirits and spiritesses, but that wasn't an issue for them, because spirits don't turn. But I'm sure a bunch of them didn't properly drain some of the Tenths and Elevenths they attacked. Full drainage constitutes a kill. If there wasn't full drainage, well... you can figure it out."

"Wait a second," said Jonah. "I get what happens to physical beings, but what about spirits and spiritesses? They are just doomed to be drained over and over for as long as the vampires need them? It's not like they can pass into Spirit again."

"No," said Terrence. It looked like something occurred to him. "Spirits can't pass again, true. But they can still be adversely affected by attacks. When spirits get drained, they become psychic vampires."

Reena frowned. "No, Terrence. Spirits can't turn."

"You're wrong, Reena." Terrence sat down. He looked as if his mind was at a faster pace than he enjoyed. "I remember something. It's been years, so I kinda forgot it. But I got it again. Spirits cannot turn into fanged fiends and steal lifeblood, but they can become psychic vampires."

"What does that mean?" asked Jonah.

Terrence looked like he had a headache. "Psychic vampires can use your emotions to damage your body. It's a—what's the word—*devolving* situation. Psychic vampires just lower and lower into a primal, feral, rabid state, and they become—"

"Haunts." Jonah felt cold so all-consuming that Reena might have used her cold spot trick. "People that get attacked by vampires become vampires themselves, and spirits that get attacked eventually become Haunts. My God."

Reena had to sit down herself. "Terrence, I just learned something new. Why didn't you tell us that before?"

"I told you, I forgot it!" said Terrence. "I heard that forever ago! It didn't apply to anything at the time, so I never thought about it! When the 49er showed up and Haunted us that night, I knew there was something I should remember, but I didn't 'til now."

"It makes sense," said Jonah. "You said it last year, Reena. '*Haunts are manifestations of negative emotions, given form and sentience from the darker aspects of the Astral Plane.*' The Haunts were once spirits and spiritesses. Terrence, where did find this out?"

"Sterling—he's another one of my brothers," said Terrence when he saw Jonah's puzzlement at the name. "He's Mom and Dad's second son, about eight years older than Alvin. He's an Eleventh historian by trade. Knows almost as much as Dad. I did already tell that when stuff goes in here—" he pointed to his head, "—I have no idea when it'll come back out."

"That isn't even the issue here," said Jonah, his voice hollow. "The 49er has been running wild attacking spirits on the Astral Plane. Jonathan said as much."

"But he also said the Curaie cracked down on them," said Reena. "They must be destroying the Haunts that have been created. But that vampire said that the 49er still had many Haunts. The 49er can't have been dumb enough to think that turning vampires and creating Haunts wouldn't get noticed. So how is he using all this to his advantage?"

Once again, they were all silent. After the several minutes of firing on all cylinders, Jonah found the return to the unknown rather jarring.

"Jonah, we don't know what's about to happen with 49er," said Terrence, "but you'd better not get wound up too tight about it."

"What are you talking about?" said Jonah.

"You've got a Mind Cage lesson with Felix, right?"

Jonah felt his face harden. "I don't want to go anywhere near that guy. We could have had so many answers if he hadn't ruined the ride and barbecued the snitch."

Reena stood, lowered the paintbrush, and placed a hand on Jonah's shoulder. "That's very true. But in light of what we've just figured out about Haunts, it's that much more necessary for you to learn how to fight them."

"You're running behind, Jonah."

"Oops. My mistake." Felix's greeting grated on Jonah's nerves, and he didn't make any attempts to mask it.

Felix wasn't fooled in the least. "Still pissed at me, are you? Well, I'm not sorry, Jonah. What that vampire fed you was bona fide bullshit. I am sure of it. I saved you from a wild goose chase."

Jonah decided that if Felix wanted to do this, fine. "And how do you figure that, exactly?"

Felix smirked. "Jonah, that lifeblood looter was cornered, outnumbered, and famished. He would have said anything to get euthanized. A blind, deaf, and dumb person could have understood that."

"Oh really?" said Jonah. "Well I have trouble believing that, seeing as how the 49er threw him out like old trash. He wished him a sound defeat, just like us."

"You are surprisingly naïve, Jonah," said Felix. "Tell me, do you think that's a trait that Altie would find enjoyable?"

Jonah frowned. "Who the hell is Altie?"

"Vera told me that her given name is Altivera," said Felix in a smooth voice. "I thought it would make a cute nickname, no?"

That did it. Jonah was already angry at Felix, and that one pushed into taint territory.

He grabbed his head as a debilitating pressure began behind his eyes and cascaded downward.

Felix abandoned the smooth voice; he was businesslike once more. "Thought that would achieve it," he said. "I hate that I had to do that. Now focus, Jonah."

Jonah didn't hear Felix's words. He didn't need the motivation. He was more determined than ever to master the Mind Cage. He centered every fiber of his being on closing that mental cage door. It became much simpler to move with each lesson. And just like with the previous lessons, the more that Jonah moved the cage door in his mind, the weaker the Haunting got. The cage door moved several inches further, and the tension in Jonah eased enough for him to crack his eyes open.

Felix stood a few feet away. He had already poured Vintage into a glass. Just the sight of it—a visible indication that Felix expected failure again—filled Jonah with a fury that didn't impede his efforts at all. It fueled them. He didn't close his eyes as he continued to move the mental door to its destination.

The door was inches from closure when the floor began to shake. It had enough force to upend the chairs and a camp table. Felix's eyes bulged. He had an expression that looked like...fear?

"Stop!" he cried. "Jonah, STOP!"

The shrill distraction made Jonah lose concentration, and the Haunting claimed him. He collapsed, but Felix almost bowled him over as he thrust the glass into his hands.

"W-W-Why did you stop me?" Jonah's tone might have been rougher if he hadn't stammered. "I had it! I was gonna do it!"

Felix still looked nervous. "I know, Jonah. I know. It was great. Superb. You don't even need that much Vintage. You see there are only a couple of swallows in there."

Jonah wasn't appeased by the praise. "You deliberately stopped me from closing the mental cage door, man! What's superb about that? Do something to piss me off. I'm doing it again."

"No!" Felix spat. "You can't!"

Jonah narrowed his eyes in confusion. What was wrong with this guy?

Felix regained his composure. The restoration to his usual demeanor was so abrupt that Jonah began to feel nervous himself.

"The lessons are no longer necessary, Jonah," he said.

"What?"

"I think you've got it," said Felix. "I'm sure of it, actually."

"But I didn't even—"

"Trust me, you've got it!" interrupted Felix. "If you come across the 49er and his Haunts, you will know what to do."

* * *

No one had changed over the holidays in Jonah's class. Part of him was even pleased to see Reynolda again. In a world of vampires, Haunts, and confusion, the notion of a middle-aged bitch who liked the sound of her own voice was refreshing.

"Evening, everyone!" said Kendall in her usual attention-grabbing way. "I hope that you have had a great New Year so far!"

"How was yours, Kendall?" Chancer blurted out.

Jonah stifled a snort. Chancer's inquiry was innocent enough, but he craved any tidbit he could get about Kendall's personal life. It was his usual practice. And as usual, Kendall disappointed him.

"Wonderful" was the only word she said on the matter, and then she passed the semester's syllabus.

Jonah had to hand it to Kendall. She wasn't like many other people who were in new relationships. She wasn't overly chipper, giggly, or goofy; she was just as informal and fun as ever. But Jonah knew by now that since Kendall was such an easygoing person to start with, there wouldn't be an overhaul in her personality anyway.

Their first class back was a smooth one that included reviewing of expectations, as well as what assignments carried more weight than others. Midway into it, Lola Barnhart "accidentally" pushed a heavy book into his lap. Jonah grunted with pain, and then she methodically removed it and made a point to pat him on the knee as she said, "Oh, Jonah, I am so sorry."

Jonah approached Kendall right before he left. She grinned at him.

"What's up, Jonah?" she asked. "I hope you had a great holiday."

"I know *you* did," he told her. "Why didn't you tell me that my best friend was your girlfriend?"

"With all due respect, Jonah, it wasn't any of your business," said Kendall as she grabbed her satchel. "I'm in a relationship with Reena, not you. Got me?"

Jonah could respect that. "Got you. You think Reynolda is going to be a hassle this semester?"

Jonah was extra wary and vigilant when he headed out to his car. He'd had two dangerous encounters on this campus, so he'd do anything he could to avoid a third one. He experienced no disquiet, but there was an old, lumpy piece of paper clamped under his windshield. Curious, Jonah pulled it free, and a cloudy, spherical stone fell into his hand. The paper was aged and slightly dirty. It wasn't even blank; the front advertised some car wash event from the previous year. An untidy message was scribbled on the back:

> *Hey Frind,*
>
> *Herd about what happened in that lokker room.*
>
> *Sory that I won't there to help you this time.*
>
> *But Im glad that you made it out in one pece.*
>
> *Anyway, I thought you culd use this as good luk charm. Least I could do after the kindness you shoed me. I don't never forget kindness.*
>
> *Hope its good luk for you too*
>
> *Oh yeah: Sory that I punched you in the face. I had to calm you down.*

Jonah smiled. The gesture itself was a decent one, even if the page was filthy and the boy's handle on the English language was questionable. There wasn't anything remarkable about the stone, though. It looked like large, misty marble.

Jonah wasn't worried. He didn't have to know what it was. He knew someone who did.

"Liz." Jonah found her in the kitchen munching on a Pop Tart, with her head in a biology book. "You know all about healing and stones and all that. Would you please tell me something about this one that I don't know?"

"Absolutely, Jonah!" Liz took the stone from him, inspected it, and smiled. "Oh! This is apatite."

"Appetite?" said Jonah. "Hunger is not a stone."

"Huh? Oh." Liz giggled. ""I don't mean that. A-P-A-T-I-T-E. It's supposedly a good luck charm. There is an easier term for it, though. Cat's eye."

Jonah raised an eyebrow. "Huh. A good luck charm against what?"

"Anything that threatens you, basically," said Liz. "It's purely superstitious, but it's said that a cat's eye is helpful against vampires, because they hate cats and everything to do with them. Kind of poetic, given the present climate."

Jonah could have laughed. So that alleged sazer boy actually knew what he was talking about. "Thanks, Liz. You're the best. Happy studying."

"Always, Jonah!" Liz kissed him on the cheek buried, and her head back into her book.

Jonah went upstairs and found Terrence and Reena.

"Will you guys look at this, please?" He extended the stone. Reena frowned.

"A grubby note and a piece of apatite?" she murmured.

"Apatite?" repeated Terrence.

"Cat's eye," said Jonah hastily. "Just call it that. I know I will. It's from that supposed sazer boy. He wanted to look out for me, and thought this good luck charm would help."

Terrence didn't make the connection, but Reena did.

"Ward against vampires, huh? The boy *must* be a sazer. How was your class?"

Jonah looked at her, not fooled at all. "Fine. We just went over the syllabus and the meatiest assignments. Girl named Lola dropped a book in my lap just so she could move it and apologize. And oh yeah." He decided to humor Reena. "Kendall was her usual self. Beautiful as ever."

Reena smiled to herself while Terrence did his usual grimace whenever the subject came up.

"Didn't really want to distract her while she got back into the swing of things," Reena explained. "I won't see her again until the weekend."

"Well that's all very interesting," said Terrence, "but Jonah, I was wondering whether or not you wanted to break in your casino cards? I think Spader can round up some folks for Hold 'Em."

Soon, everyone was back into their routines. Reena's desire to strangle her boss re-emerged right on schedule, while Terrence wanted to strangle nasty children and adults at the school where he worked. Spader resumed his fortuitous but questionable enterprises (he returned home pleased with himself every night, but he refused to upgrade his wardrobe). Douglas began to confer with members of his family about his next step. He was mere months away from finishing undergrad, but didn't yet feel ready for the workforce.

"I've decided to go to graduate school," he told Jonah one Saturday morning after an obligatory visit to his grandmother's. "I'd be a professional student if I could."

"That would be fun, Doug, I'm sure," laughed Jonah, "but I don't think your grandmother would care very much for that decision."

Douglas waved a hand. "She has six sons, and several other grandchildren to impose her will on. I'm applying tomorrow."

Vera had turned Liz on to theater, and they spent as many weekends out of town watching shows as Liz's homework would allow. Even though Bobby tried to distract himself as much as possible with sports, weights, and PS4, he was still woebegone when Liz wasn't around. Alvin and Terrence enjoyed giving him a hard time about that.

"If Dad, Ray, and Sterling could see what you've become," laughed Alvin, "they'd take you to a bar and get you strung out on wings and ribs."

"Ray would probably stretch him with some Greco-Roman holds," said Terrence. "See if Lizzie was on his mind then."

"Leave him alone," said Reena sternly, which prompted Bobby to look up at her in surprise.

"Oh, bring it down a million, Reena," said Terrence. "We're all just having some fun."

"You aren't having fun," said Reena flatly. "You're ragging on Bobby because he takes pride in enjoying the company of his girlfriend, and that's threatening to you?"

"Threatening?" scoffed Alvin. "I'm fine, truly."

Reena smiled coldly. "Let me translate that for you. You are just another man who is afraid of displaying his inadequacies around women. So instead of confronting that, you attempt to bruise the ego of a man who outstrips you with his own wonderful relationship."

That wiped the grins off many a male face in the room. Jonah, who hadn't actually taken part in the conversation, fought against laughing at the looks on so many faces.

"Oh, but please keep laughing," said Reena in a sweet voice. She clapped Bobby on the shoulder, and turned to leave. Jonah fell in step with her.

"Is this the part where you roll your eyes and grumble about men?" he asked.

"Nope!" Reena sounded gleeful. "That was just plain old fun! You men are so easy to manipulate!"

Jonah scowled, and Reena sobered.

"Let me rephrase that," she said. "Ninety-nine percent of men are easy to manipulate."

February was a blur. Kendall's class remained fun, but she still kept their noses to the grindstone. Jonah's mind hadn't gotten these kinds of workouts since Felix stopped the Mind Cage lessons. He didn't even think this hard when he tried to write those novels. But he wondered that maybe Kendall's assignments would stimulate his mind enough to actually complete a novel. Or several. That was a great thought. An even greater thing occurred in one class where Reynolda openly criticized his prose as clumsy during a group assignment. Jonah smiled, and kindly informed her that she'd attempted the same style, and when it became clear that she couldn't get it right, she wrote it off as clumsy. Reynolda knew she'd been busted, so she loudly changed the subject.

Valentine's Day came and went, and Jonah was glad of it. What happened on Christmas Day still stuck in his craw, so he didn't go overboard with a purchase for Vera. He knew that those preserved roses received A-list treatment in her bedroom, while his presents hung—sacredly—in the back of her closet. As such, he gave her a neat Shakespeare-themed card, and some chocolate turtles. She happily accepted them, and that was that.

Life remained relatively ordinary until a Thursday in early March, but the event was not a frightening one that involved the 49er or the Haunts.

It was still an unwelcome thing, though.

Jonah spent the afternoon writing in the gazebo when Terrence wandered to him, rounding up orders and money for a fast-food run. Before Jonah could make a request or yank cash from his pocket, though, the two of them got blindsided by Reena, who'd taken a personal day.

"Jonah, Terrence," she breathed. "Just the men that I wanted to see."

"Oh, really?" asked Terrence, wary. "I hope that you don't expect me to do a food run to that vegetarian place on Main. Lasagna without meat is a violation of nature."

"It's not that at all," said Reena. "There is an event going on tomorrow night in the Jade Room at the Milverton Inn and Suites."

"So?" said Jonah.

"Spader got me tickets, and no, I didn't ask him how," she said. "I got one for Kendall, but she couldn't come, so I have one extra. I got Spader to snag me one more, so it can be all three of us."

There was something expectant in Reena's voice. It was almost hungry. Jonah lowered his pen and pad. "Alright Reena, I'll bite. What is it?"

"You'll come with me?"

"What is it?"

"I want your word first," said Reena.

Jonah's eyes narrowed. "You want me to blindly accept something?"

Terrence shrank away from Reena just a bit. That look in her eyes was rather intense.

"Yes, I do," she said. "Now, your word. Both of you."

"Fine! Whatever!" Jonah didn't have much patience left. "Now, what the hell is this event?"

"Turk Landry—"

"Not available." Jonah grabbed his pen and pad, but Reena grabbed his arm.

"No, Jonah, listen!"

"I will not look in the face of that phony—"

"Hey Jonah, come on, man!" said Terrence heatedly. "That night was messed up, but he ain't a fake!"

Jonah glanced at Terrence. He was still in the dark about Landry.

"I mean that I might still have tainted vibrations," he invented. "I don't know if I want to subject myself to that again."

"This situation will be different, Jonah," promised Reena.

"How do you figure?"

"I got Spader to pull some strings by doing whatever he does, and I got these."

She pulled out the tickets, which were unremarkable save one thing. They were color-coded, rimmed with three braces that were blue, yellow, and burnt orange, respectively.

"What makes them special, other than the snazzy bands?" asked Terrence.

"They're Spectrum-coded," clarified Reena. "It's a promotion that the hotel runs when they have events to commemorate the spring season. It's usually done with raffles, but since *ScarYous* is a big deal, they implemented it here. Every Spectrum ticket has to be recognized. Landry has to give all coded tickets a spirit reading, and that includes us. All of us. He can't pull that tainted vibes crap on all three of us!"

Suddenly, Jonah loved the idea. Reena was absolutely right. Landry would be in an awkward place indeed if he tried to push that excuse on three people.

What would Mr. Secret Eleventh do when faced with three ethereal humans? Maybe then, Terrence would see the farce for what it was.

"Alright Reena." Jonah's tone was as devilish as hers. "I'm game."

The Milverton Inn and Suites buzzed with the same excitement it had when Landry first got into town. His game was so tightly interwoven into people's hearts and minds. He could take this show anywhere and achieve the same results. But Jonah only wanted one result tonight.

Just one.

As everyone filed in, took their seats, and waited for the man of the hour, he and Reena—unbeknownst to Terrence—trembled with a different type of anticipation. They wanted to see the man sweat. They wanted to expose him once and for all.

Landry stepped into his allotted space, and the Jade Room exploded into applause. Jonah felt his lip curl into a sneer. These people were like blind sheep. It wasn't a great thing to feel like one of the only competent people in a sea of ignorance. But the worst part was the person who took advantage of them.

A sharp whack on his arm turned his attention to Reena, who widened her eyes in warning.

"*Cool it, buddy,*" she mouthed, and pointed at Terrence, who painstakingly contained his own enthusiasm out of respect for his friends.

Jonah took the hint, and smoothed out his face. All in good time.

"A lovely evening to my fellow paranormal journeymen," said Landry in that dramatic voice of his that was just above a whisper. It made the sycophants hang on to his words even more. "As you all know, my time in this region ends in a month's time."

The feelings of disappointment were so profound that Jonah almost pitied the people. Almost.

"But our time is not yet over," continued Landry. "And I will prove my gratitude by offering a number of you here tonight special readings. You are indicated by special color codes, which are on your stubs. I have your colors here, and will call at random. Who is magenta?"

A black woman in the second row lifted her stub excitedly. Landry smiled.

"Very well, ma'am. We will begin our celestial traverses with you."

It was the same as before. Jonah shook as his head at the man's delivery. Turk Landry was a propaganda machine; a weapon of deception made out of flesh and bone. He knew what to do, how to do it, and when to do it. He impressed, he enlightened, and he moved on to the next.

Jonah spent almost two hours in Spectral Sight, which he had also suggested to Reena. He didn't bother advising Terrence, because it wouldn't have done any good. Each spirit and spiritess that Landry "communicated" with vanished as soon as he was done with them, just like last time.

And then he reached Jonah's color, blue. His helpers pointed him out, and Jonah and Landry locked eyes. Landry's eyes narrowed.

"Ladies and gentlemen." Anger and irritation robbed Landry's voice of some of its dramatic quality. "I have told you before that I have battled many enemies of the paranormal. They vary, and are many, just like ourselves. But those attuned to the ways of Spirit, such a myself, have no trouble discerning them from the truly open ones. Like that man there."

He actually raised a hand and pointed at Jonah. Everyone turned cold eyes on him. It happened in seconds. Jonah had to remind himself that Tenth authorities didn't take kindly to assault.

"Get him out of here," snapped Landry, "and take his fellow deterrents of peace with him."

He pointed at Terrence, who looked shocked and affronted, and Reena, who seemed to brace herself for an opportunity.

"Be gone from this place, adversaries of tranquility!" snapped Landry.

Security grabbed them. Jonah weighed whether or not he cared about an assault charge, but Reena gave Landry a supplicating look.

"Mr. Landry." Reena's voice carried a note of desperation. "I am not an adversary of tranquility. I merely seek answers from the beyond."

Landry gave Reena a look reminiscent of an inflexible parent. "You are in the company of debunkers, girl. Their lies have swerved you to skepticism. I cannot help you."

"But why not?" asked Reena breathlessly. "So what if I have been led astray by those who don't believe? What if I desire to be clear once more, if only to hear loving messages from those I've lost? Don't I deserve that chance?"

Jonah saw many people in the audience frown. Some nodded. Some even shed some tears. Landry noticed it too, and he looked uncomfortable with the shifting stance. Reena was amazing. Jonah even glanced at Terrence. Clearly, the man didn't know what to think, but he looked proud of Reena as well.

Landry tried a different tack. "You are right, beautiful one," he said kindly. "This is what I propose. Allow me to complete my event here, and then I will convene with you privately."

"No." Reena said it in such a pleading voice that even Jonah was almost moved by the charade. "A private meeting won't do. I've been so full of doubt and grief for so long. It has to be here. It has to be now, in front of everyone. Their positive energy and love will serve to elevate my spirits even more. Please, sir. Please."

Surprisingly, people in the crowd began to beg Landry to help Reena out. Jonah was pleased to see that he was hot under the collar. He was backed into a corner, and he knew it. If he shot Reena down, he'd lose face. If he "helped" her, he'd expose himself. Rock and hard place, much?

Landry raised his hands, which silenced the crowd at once. "I will help you, young one. Allow me to reignite the spiritual cogs in my mind. The interlude has interrupted my connection."

Good one, asshole, thought Jonah as Landry made quite a show of closing his eyes and placing his fingers to his temples. Seconds later, he opened his eyes with such a look of resignation that Jonah could have burst out laughing. He was about to witness history. He was about witness a cataclysmic fall from grace.

"There isn't much that I can do you," said Landry softly, "Reena."

Jonah froze. Did he just call Reena by name? But his was nothing compared to the mask of shock on Reena's face.

"You're right, Reena," Landry continued. "You have dealt with doubt for many years. It's eroded your self-esteem." He looked at the audience, whose expressions of pity reflected his own. "I also sense an intense heartbreak that has only recently begun to heal."

Jonah's eyes widened, as did Terrence's. But Terrence's reaction was because of shock. Jonah's was one of horror. This couldn't be real.

He couldn't see Reena's face anymore, because the security guards turned her so that Landry could get a better look at her. He couldn't imagine what he'd see on her face at the moment.

"Yes, I see it clearly." Landry nodded. "Your heart was broken years ago. I can't divine a full name, but I see the letter *J.*"

Jonah saw Reena tense. It burned him.

"Shut up, Landry!" he snarled, wrenching himself free of the guards grasp.

"But dude, Reena might need to hear this!" hissed Terrence.

"NO!" Jonah shouted. "End this now!"

"Why does it have to end now—" Landry narrowed his eyes, "Jonah?"

"Wow," whispered Terrence, but Jonah only felt fury. He had no words.

"Why does it have to end?" repeated Landry. "You wanted my attention, didn't you? And now you have it. Do not be angry that Spirit yielded truths that Reena was not yet ready to hear."

Jonah sensed that the crowd turned against him once more. He knew what this looked like, but he couldn't give less of a damn. He didn't know how Landry was doing this, but he had to stop. Reena didn't deserve to be laid bare this way.

"You're a liar," said Reena, and Jonah's heart sank. She sounded like she was in tears. "There is no way that you can have that information. There isn't."

"You're right," agreed Landry. "*I* don't have that information. I am merely the vessel. The messages given to me came from the spirit at your side, who has been looking out for you since he was so tragically taken away from you all those years ago."

Jonah felt numb. There was no way. No way in hell...

"He was looking out for you even before he was in spirit form," said Landry. A tear even slid down the bastard's face. "He was the family member that took you in when your family abandoned you. I can tell by your face that I'm right. It was your uncle. Uncle Kole, yes? He is so proud of you. Just the way you are."

Reena buried her face in her hands. Terrence's guard released him, and he wrapped an arm around her shoulder. Jonah would have attacked Landry right then and there if the shock hadn't numbed his body.

"Please escort them out." Landry's voice was full of emotion. "I think I've learned more about the bonds of spiritual love in this moment than I have in all my years of doing this. I thank you, Reena, for persuading me to aid you. But what you do with that information is up to you."

They'd been played. Jonah didn't know how, but Landry played them. Played them *well*. And because of that, some forty-odd people knew some of Reena's darkest secrets.

He didn't even protest when powerful hands guided him out of the Jade Room. It was just as well, because if he didn't get out this place fast, he was going to rip Turk Landry's balls off.

17

One Stupid Vigil

The trip back home was a silent one. Jonah allowed Terrence to drive because he felt that his emotions were too close to the surface to operate heavy machinery. A small portion of him feared that the Haunting taint might overtake him, but Felix claimed that he could do a Mind Cage, should the need arise. He had to trust that.

Jonah knew that Reena would never appreciate it, but he pitied her. Her plan was so brilliant. Or was supposed to be. She'd wanted to catch Landry in the act, just like he did. His "tainted vibes" copout was sure to fail if he tried it on three different people. But Reena got stripped bare in front of total strangers, Terrence's belief in the guy was probably irrevocable at this point—even though he was still angry for Reena's sake—and Jonah couldn't show his face in that hotel again.

How did Landry do it? That question coursed in Jonah's mind the entire ride back. He'd known his name. He'd known Reena's uncle's name. He knew about her heartbreak; he even knew the first letter of Julia's name. For a brief moment, Jonah wondered if Landry was a vampire with those psychic links, like the 49er had with the Haunts. But that couldn't be. Jonah had already seen him in broad daylight, and unfortunately, he hadn't burst into flames. On top of that, if Landry had been a vampire, all those spirits and spiritesses he worked with would fear him, not flock to him.

Reena shut herself in her room that night, and Jonah and Terrence didn't see her for four days. Everyone asked what was wrong with her, but what could they say? Everyone bought Turk Landry's shtick, and no one knew about her plans to purge herself of her ethereality sometime soon. In the end, Jonah and

Terrence made generic comments about Reena going too full-throttle lately, and needing to get rest. Since Reena was a well-known perfectionist, everyone bought it.

Terrence confided in Jonah that the whole experience brought Landry down a peg or two in his eyes. That was such a shock that Jonah actually forgot some of his frustration.

"How he did that was amazing," he conceded. "But something about it...just didn't feel right."

Jonah could have done a somersault, but his response was quiet. "How do you mean?"

Terrence pulled out a pack of sour jelly beans, his favorite pensive snack. "The way that he just owned her like that. It just seemed a little...convenient. A little too good, I guess."

Jonah nodded. He knew exactly what Terrence meant. Landry's reading was a little too perfect. And even after that, he still couldn't bring himself to tell Terrence that the man was an Eleventh Percenter. A part of him felt like he was insulting his best friend's intelligence, but Jonah remembered how Terrence hated to be let down. One way or the other, this whole thing would blow up in someone's face. Jonah was certain of it. But with any luck, that face would be creator of *ScarYous*.

"We'll figure it out sooner or later," he told Terrence as he snagged a few jelly beans.

When Reena finally came out of her room, Jonah didn't see a woebegone, depressed sap. She looked resolute and frighteningly determined. He was surprised by the change, and when he asked about it, Reena just smiled.

"Kendall helped me out," she explained. "She reminded me that it's not in my nature to hide within myself."

"Wow." That impressed Jonah. "Your relationship is so new, and she has picked up on that already?"

"Sure did. My woman is perceptive as hell." The fond smile faded, and Reena looked Jonah in the eye. "I want him, Jonah. I want to know what his game is, and how he knew about Julia and my family. He shouldn't have made an enemy of me. I will hand him his ass. It may very well be my last great act as an Eleventh Percenter."

While Jonah didn't need that last part, he was grateful that the old Reena had returned.

Another strange thing was how Felix treated Jonah now. He regarded him with wariness whenever he saw him. Jonah didn't what to make of that. He wondered if it had anything to do with that final Mind Cage lesson, but that didn't make sense.

Did Felix think he was dangerous? Did he think that Jonah's weapon of expression would be dangerous? He didn't see how that could be. The man didn't even let him complete the process!

It was yet another thing that Jonah could add to the list of things that made up the mysterious Felix Duscere. Honestly, Jonah wouldn't feel sadness when Felix moved on. He'd bless the day that the business with the 49er ended and *ScarYous* wrapped up filming their season.

But that had consequences as well. With all issues resolved, Reena would be free to take her little potion and purge herself of the Eleventh Percent. She'd be free to leave them behind.

Jonah put his mind on something else.

During all of this, Jonathan was like a Protector Guide with an iron-clad purpose. He was determined that there would be no further attacks on his students. He wasn't interested in doing another mass watch because he felt that too many eyes might spoil detections. So he sent residents out in herald-escorted shifts. This became the routine, and everyone liked it. When the night finally came for Jonah to have his turn—he'd had to reschedule it twice due to class—he pulled double duty with Bast. The patrol seemed like a good time to relax his mind.

The grounds were too vast for Jonah and Bast to patrol alone, so he wasn't surprised to see other residents and heralds on the grounds. Bast intimated no thoughts to him, so all he did was observe. He laughed when he saw that Bobby had taken a shift with Liz. But there was no fun to be had. They had a job to do, after all. Besides, the scout with them, an Abyssinian cat named Horace, was probably the worst third wheel on earth. On the west side of the grounds, Spader strolled around with his own scout, and edgy Tabby named Tara. Jonah was certain that Spader was ready for his shift to be over so that he could return to his usual questionable pursuits.

Jonah almost laughed at that when an acrid smell hit his nostrils. Cigarette smoke. He glanced down at Bast, who tensed as she faced the east. Following her lead, Jonah headed east, and came face to face with his least favorite person.

Trip stood with his back against a garage, with his right foot propped behind him. His expression was as cold as always, and that intensified when Jonah and Bast moved into his line of sight.

"What are you doing here?" he asked Jonah shortly.

"I'm on patrol, duh," Jonah fired back. "Don't you see Bast?"

Trip took a heavy drag from his cigarette. His accusatory glare never left Jonah's face. "Still doesn't answer my question, does it?"

Jonah rolled his eyes. "Alright, fine. I was curious about where the cigarette smoke came from. I didn't know any of the residents here smoked."

"Well, some do," said Trip. "Surprise."

Jonah ignored the sarcasm. "Why do you do that to your lungs? You're a saxophonist. Don't you need your lungs at full capacity?"

Trip sneered. "All the great jazz and blues performers—Ray Charles, Miles Davis, Nat King Cole—were all smokers, Rowe. Nicotine doesn't impede talent. It relieves stress."

Jonah shook his head. He really didn't need this right now. "Whatever, man. Bye."

"One second, Rowe."

Jonah turned back to Trip. "What?"

Trip finished off his cigarette before he threw it to the ground and stamped it. "You would do well not to befriend Duscere."

Jonah frowned. Random, much? Bast glared at Trip. It truly said something about a person's character when a sweet-natured cat hated them. "Where did that come from?"

"He is teaching you to repel Haunts, no?" asked Trip.

"So what if he is?"

Trip ignored the question. "No doubt that he's also dropping anecdotes here and there about his illustrious travels. Tell me something: Have you recovered from those ridiculous roses her gave Vera?"

Jonah gritted his teeth. That was still a sore spot, but he wasn't about to discuss it with Trip. "Where are you going with this, Trip?"

Trip lit another cigarette. It was at that point that Jonah noticed that there were no less than twenty butts at his feet. "Felix is a charmer, Rowe. That's his hook. You see how it's worked on Jonathan, the women at this estate—*your* woman included—"

"Vera is not my—"

"Don't cut across me," said Trip, who shushed Jonah with his cigarette-toting hand. "As I was saying, that's his hook. And, even if you don't know it yet, it's worked on you as well."

"What are you talking about?"

"I'm simply giving you a fair warning," said Trip in a cool tone. "Felix is heading for serious trouble soon. And the people that he has charmed…I suppose that it would suck for them to go down with him. That is all."

Trip tossed the butt away and left. Bast's glare remained glacial. But Jonah watched after him, unnerved.

Jonah wasn't an idiot. Was that a death threat? Or a—what would one call a death threat is death wasn't real?

"That was bold," commented Terrence with mock admiration. "He practically put a hit out on someone that Jonathan welcomed at the estate. He also promised that *you'd* get it too if you got in the way."

"Yep," said Jonah. "That's pretty much what I got from it, too."

Reena shook her head. "I just can't see Trip being that brazen. Jonathan told you that they were the best of friends once. And Jonathan even warned Trip about threatening Felix! Why would Trip risk good standing with Jonathan by defying that? Hell, losing good standing would likely be the least of his worries!"

"The bad blood between them must be intense," said Terrence. "But what the hell happened between them?"

The last Thursday in March brought about strange news for Jonah. He didn't pay too much attention to college life; he just went to class, ate, and went home. But when he went to turn in an assignment to Kendall, he saw a picture of two women in a few places. It said they were missing. He decided to ask Kendall when he reached her office.

"Here you go, Kendall. I have to ask something…who are those missing girls?"

Kendall took his assignment with a frown. "You don't know? Oh, wait. You don't spend a lot of time on campus. Those girls are Marybeth Peck and Pilar Contesa. They've been missing for almost a month, apparently."

"What!" Jonah exclaimed. "How did it go for so long?"

"Because no one actually knew they were missing," said Kendall. "They were supposed to be abroad. But, evidently, they never got to where they were going."

"Why didn't their families do or say anything?"

"Pilar is a foreign exchange student from Peru, I think, and Marybeth has no family. In essence, there was no one around to corroborate stories."

Jonah shook his head. "That's terrible. I hope that they're okay."

"Me too, Jonah," said Kendall. "Me too."

Jonah sipped on some coffee several hours later in the university shop, still thinking about those students. He had been a student at this university for almost a full year, and he hadn't laid eyes on either woman. But he still felt sorry for them. It seemed so unfair that their social circle was so non-existent that they'd been missing for a month, and no one had even noticed they were gone. He knew that locating two missing college students that were both under twenty-one might be too much to ask for.

He closed his eyes. If it were that worst-case scenario, then he hoped that whoever supervised celestial journeys welcomed their spirits gladly, and they had peace. It would only be fair.

Movement caught his eye from outside. It was nearly sunset, but he counted maybe a dozen people walking around the Britton Building. As he watched, one broke away from them, unmistakably shaking their head about something, and went back into the building. Jonah recognized that walk. It was Kendall.

He shouldn't have been nosy, but curiosity got the best of him. What was that all about?

He tossed his coffee cup in the trash, and headed for the building where he had his class. It was still unlocked because the campus police had to make their rounds, so entering was easy.

It was completely quiet, so he didn't want to make too much noise as he approached Kendall's office. But he was maybe five feet away when he heard her complaining to herself.

"Old idiots," she muttered. "Thinking that will help. I could halfway to Reena right now, but *no...*"

One of Jonah's steps sounded louder than the rest, which prompted Kendall to poke her head outside her door.

"Oh, it's you." Relief was in her every syllable. "Everything okay?"

"Yeah, fine," replied Jonah. "I saw you from the coffeehouse, leaving that group. You looked like you were so annoyed. What's up?"

Kendall sighed, and beckoned him into her office. "I *was* annoyed, Jonah. Mavis, Susan, Carrie, and the rest of the department are about to go downstairs to have a vigil."

Jonah shrugged. "A vigil for those missing girls? What's wrong with that?"

Kendall snorted in a cold sort of way. "If only. Apparently, they are about to do this thing they call a scandal vigil."

"A scandal vigil?"

"Yeah." Kendall leaned on her desk. "Hilarious. It's my understanding that they do it every two years or so, and thought it was necessary to do now."

That annoyed Jonah. *That* was their concern? "They think the missing girls could lead to scandal?"

"They don't know," said Kendall, who mirrored Jonah's feelings. "But they think that their little scandal vigil will ward off any new scandals. It's like the power of visualization gone wrong. Superstitious idiots."

"New ones?" Jonah regarded Kendall. "Does LTSU have that rich a history of scandals?"

"Don't have to have a rich history of them, Jonah," murmured Kendall. "It only took one to smear things for a very long while."

"What are you talking about?"

Kendall grabbed a mint from her desk. "Please don't fly out of the room and sing it from the highest mountaintops."

"I won't," chuckled Jonah. "You have my word."

"Thank you." Kendall still looked uncomfortable, but Jonah thought that that might have more to do with the subject matter and not him personally. "There used to be a prominent sponsor to LTSU. He was very charitable—was always coordinating events to help the school, and never hesitated to tell people that this was his alma mater."

Jonah nodded. He hadn't heard anything scandalous so far.

"Anyway," one of his undergraduate classmates became a music teacher here," Kendall continued. "They weren't bosom buddies or anything, but they got along fine, I suppose. About sixteen, seventeen years ago, the music department was about to lose funding or something, so the music professor went to the sponsor guy and begged for the funds to bail the department out. They met at the Carruthers House."

"You mean that frat house up the road that's been shut down and everyone avoids?" asked Jonah.

"The very same," said Kendall. "Well, no one knows what happened, the sponsor must have refused or something, because the music teacher flipped out, and killed him."

Jonah's mouth dropped. "What! Because the guy wouldn't give him some money?"

"That's what everyone thinks," said Kendall. "You know what they say about money, after all. But the story gets better—or worse, I should say."

"What's worse than killing?" demanded Jonah.

"*More* killing," said Kendall. "The sponsor guy's son went off in a drunken rage and killed the music teacher."

Jonah stared. "You're serious?"

"Oh yeah," said Kendall with a heavy sigh. "It wasn't even three weeks later. The messed-up thing was that the kid was supposedly a problem child anyway. But after he killed the teacher, he actually got off. I was told that it was temporary insanity, with a diminished mental capacity on account of drunkenness."

She offered Jonah a cup of water. He took it and simply stared at it. "Damn. That's soap opera material."

"Yes, it was horrible." Kendall sipped some of her water. "And the old people in the department have been doing that dumb vigil ever since. Like it's going to prevent new scandals."

Now Jonah laughed. They thought that they could ward off controversy? It was like the older women in his grandmother's church who told him that it was bad luck to whistle indoors. Ridiculous. "Do you know the names, Kendall?" he asked. "You only said that it was a music teacher and a sponsor guy."

"Oh, sorry," said Kendall. "It's just that every time I ever heard the story, the men were always labeled as such. It's like people tried to sweep away the names like they tried to sweep away the story. Now the sponsor guy—" she tapped her nails on the desk and gave it some thought. "Oh yeah. His name was Preston. Preston Duscere."

Jonah choked on his water, and he stared at Kendall in horror. "W-what did you say?"he gasped.

"Jonah! Are you alright?"

"Yeah, yeah, I'm fine," said Jonah hastily. "Water just went down the wrong pipe. Now, did you say Preston Duscere?"

Kendall looked Jonah over once more, just to make sure that he was actually alright. "Yes, I did. He left behind a wife, who died a couple years afterward. God only knows what happened to his crazy drunk of a son."

Jonah wasn't about to comment on that. "Kendall, what was the music teacher's name?"

"Oh that one's easy," said Kendall with a wave of her hand. "T.J. Rivers."

Jonah's body went cold. "What did T.J. stand for?" he asked in what he hoped was a calm voice.

"Titus Rivers, Jr.," said Kendall, oblivious to Jonah's struggle. "You want to know something funny? He's got a son running around loose in the world somewhere, too. God forbid he ever runs into Duscere's boy."

18

Faith and Knowledge

Jonah managed to keep himself in check enough to bid Kendall goodnight. Once outside, he tore off toward his car and sped down I-40 back to the estate. He knew Terrence would be eating, and Reena would be doing Pilates, followed by painting. He didn't want anyone to think of him as erratic, so he shot them both a text message when he took Exit 81: "*My room. Something HUGE to tell you.*"

Mercifully, they were both there when he arrived.

"Jonah, what's wrong?" asked Reena.

Jonah shook his head and closed his door. "Just let me get this out of my head."

He told them everything Kendall told him. Reena blinked in shock. Terrence looked away and muttered, "Well, ain't that a bitch."

"How could Jonathan, in good conscience, have that kind of volatility around us?" whispered Reena.

"He probably thinks that he can control them." Terrence still looked as if he'd been slapped across the face with a brick. "He's on good terms with both of them; shepherded them through some dark times in their lives. Maybe he thought kindness would prevail or something."

But Jonah barely registered either of their words. "Jonathan told me—he was going to tell me months back, I think. He probably would have modified it. Felix took Trip under his wing, and they were like brothers. Then he said an unfortunate incident happened between their fathers." Then he rounded on Terrence and Reena. "How could you not know? You guys have been here for years! You've been at this longer than I have!"

Reena looked defensive as hell. "Jonah, how many times do we have to tell you that we don't know everything about every occurrence in the ethereal world?"

"And my family has told me a bunch of stories, but it's not like they know them all!" said Terrence.

But Jonah wouldn't be denied that easily. "Reena, your girlfriend, who is a Tenth, knew the story. She even knew Preston and Titus, Jr. had sons! How could that be?"

"Kendall is a college professor, Jonah," said Reena calmly. "She is a professor at the setting of the scandal. If there is any field that is rife with gossip and miscommunication, it's teaching."

"She's got you there," admitted Terrence. "I work around teachers. I know."

Jonah deflated. He knew they were right.

He sat down in his computer chair so forcefully that it rolled from the desk by a few inches. He didn't even notice. "I told Jonathan to his face that Felix and Trip were powder kegs that could go up at anytime. And I have no doubt that the 49er knows the story inside and out. He's probably trying to figure out how to use it to his advantage."

Reena's eyes shot up to Jonah. There was a gleam in them that hadn't been present when she'd first heard the revelation.

"What?" said Jonah.

"I hadn't even thought about the 49er," she said. "But now that you mention him, I can't help but wonder whether or not this is all connected."

"What if all *what's* connected?" asked Terrence.

"Just go with me on this." Reena twirled one of Jonah's pens, because she had no paintbrush. "The 49er has been in your life for a little bit, Jonah. He monitored portals for Creyton's ruse at your old job at S.T.R. So he knows how important you are as the Blue Aura. He knows what that signifies. So he shows up in Rome, knowing that his presence would bring Felix, who had been tracking him. But the X-factor to people banding against him is Trip, with whom Felix has a very dicey history. Best friends, now mortal enemies. Trip has even hinted that he's planning to do something to Felix. What if none of this is random? What if this is all part of the 49er's plan?"

"That's an interesting theory, Reena," said Jonah. "Truly, it is. But nothing can be gotten out of it. I wanted to know *Trip's* situation, but Felix asked me to talk to Jonathan, who wouldn't even discuss it. In all fairness to Jonathan, I don't blame him for not volunteering that information. It's some sick shit. But it all comes to three dead ends."

"Trip wouldn't give us his opinion on anything to start with, Jonah," said Reena, unabashed. "I don't want to speak to Felix on the matter because—because it would probably do more harm than good. And Jonathan is a spirit. He is across two worlds, and is of two minds because of that. Far too many variables."

She stood up and headed for the door.

"Where are you going?" asked Jonah.

"Find Jonathan," answered Reena. "I need to get approval for the three of us to use the *Astralimes*."

"What?" said Terrence. "Why?"

"We don't need a person of two minds," said Reena mysteriously. "Just a man of two jobs."

Jonah had no idea what Reena told Jonathan, but in no time at all, they had focused on their destination, taken the two-steps across the Astral Plane, and ended up on the path of a specific address: 1017 Langston Drive.

The house there was a comfortable-looking brick one, nothing fancy. But Jonah was sure that was by design. It was just as well. Subtlety was a must.

Reena cracked her knuckles, walked up to the front door, and knocked three times. There was movement within the house, and the door opened to reveal an intimidating man with a burly build and boxer's hands. Despite that, none of them were afraid.

"Welcome to my home!" said Reverend Abbott, inviting them into the living room. "I would have prepared for you if I'd had more advance notice. I was a little surprised to get a call from you, Reena, but honored nonetheless." He looked at them warily. "I hope that you don't think me a poor host because I have nothing prepared."

"Oh no, Reverend Abbott. Not at all." Poor host? Please. Jonah couldn't say anything negative about Reverend Abbott. The man once saved him and Terrence from a dark spirit entity by bashing the thing with a spiritually-endowed bag of tools, forever earning Jonah's respect in the process. "We didn't even know that we were coming here until half an hour ago."

Soon, they were comfortably seated on the reverend's sofa. Reverend Abbott lowered himself into his recliner, pulled a huge bible onto his lap, and eyed them with interest.

"Now, how can I help you, Reena?" he asked. "You said you needed some advising?"

"Yes sir, I did," said Reena. "But not advising of a religious nature. I was hoping that we could take advantage of your…other area of expertise."

Jonah's eyes narrowed in confusion. He knew that Terrence was on the same wavelength. What was Reena talking about now?

"Ah."Reverend Abbott's smile faded, and he slowly closed the bible. "What do you need to know?"

"Do you happen to have information on the murder, and subsequent crime of passion, at the Carruthers fraternity house at LTSU?"

Reverend Abbott's mouth twisted. "Hmm. That one. Pardon me."

He went upstairs. Jonah followed him with his eyes the whole way.

"What was all that about?" Terrence asked Reena. "Now you got the preacher acting mysterious, too? These are ethereal crimes, Reena. What information could a man of God possibly have?"

"I wasn't always a man of God, Terrence." Reverend Abbott had returned with a lockbox in tow. "When I was discharged from the military, I had no idea I'd follow in my family's footsteps and join the clergy. I spent several years as a consultant for the Spectral Law Guild. I was in the department that handled crimes that resembled ethereal foul play."

"Wait a second," said Jonah. "How would Spectral Law information assist us? This scandal is known amongst the Tenths. It's public record."

"So true." Reverend Abbott seated himself and placed the lockbox on the table. "But you are aware that no Tenth law enforcement can handle crimes that are ethereal. A common practice of the Spectral Law Guild—let's just refer to them as the S.P.G.—was to approach Tenth police stations, pose as branches above their pay grade, and claim jurisdiction. That happened anytime that culprits or victims were Eleventh Percenters. Like the case that Reena mentioned."

Reverend Abbott returned his attention to the lockbox. Jonah noticed that it didn't have a locking mechanism of any kind. Reverend Abbott banged the left side twice and the top once and it popped open. It was filled with newspaper clippings, notes, and flash cards. All of the materials were discolored due to age.

"The S.P.G. took control of the matter after Felix killed T.J Rivers," said Reverend Abbott, and to their surprise, he made finger quotations when he said the word *killed*.

"You think Felix is innocent?" asked Reena.

Reverend Abbott sighed. "This case has troubled me for a long while," he said as he spread papers across the coffee table. "The official story—the Tenth one, I mean—is that T.J. killed Preston Duscere over funding issues, and then Felix vowed revenge and killed T.J. weeks later. Cute. It was enough to appease the Tenth justice system. But on the ethereal side…things just didn't add up. Things were far too perfect."

"Far too perfect?" repeated Terrence. "What would make a crime perfect?"

"I'll tell you what, Terrence," said Reverend Abbott. "A crime is perfect when all the puzzle pieces fit together on their own, without tweaking or extra work."

Jonah looked at the clippings. "I'm sorry, sir, but I don't get that."

"Allow me to explain." Reverend Abbott lowered his glasses. "When a person commits a crime, Tenth or Eleventh, they do not want to get caught. So they muck and muddy up the waters as much as they can. The puzzle becomes a mess, and there are far more questions than there are answers, assuming that you even have any answers at all. But I can assure you, the motive of every crime ever committed boils down to one simple question: Who gets something out of it?"

He pushed a newspaper clipping their way, which covered Preston Duscere's murder.

"Now, the S.P.G., being Eleventh Percenters, always had more information than those poor Tenth police," Reverend Abbott continued. "To the Tenth populace, Preston Duscere was a family man, sponsor, and jack-of-all trades. But in reality, he was a Networker."

"What?" said Jonah, Terrence, and Reena at the same time.

"Yes," nodded Reverend Abbott. "A phenomenal one. Depending on who you ask, he was the best Networker the ethereal world had ever seen."

"Wow," said Jonah. "That explains how Felix knows about Mind Cages."

"You know about Mentis Caveas?" said Reverend Abbott, distracted. "Are you taking lessons?"

"I'm—it's complicated—you know what, Reverend? Please continue."

Abbott smiled. "Alright, then. Preston had been stationed to investigate LTSU."

"Why was he investigating the university?" asked Reena.

"To see why Creyton planted the 49er around there," answered Reverend Abbott. "To have a lifeblood-looting vampire at LTSU was very ironic, wouldn't you say, Jonah?"

"Ironic?" said Jonah blankly.

"Aren't you enrolled at LTSU?" asked Reverend Abbott. "La Tronis State University? Haven't you discovered the meaning behind that name?"

Jonah felt more and more idiotic by the second. He hadn't even known that there was anything to learn in the first place. "No, sir."

"Don't even worry about it, son," said Reverend Abbott. "I'll fill you in. La Tronis is actually two Latin words, *Latro*, which means hunter of vampires, and *onis*, which means duty. That's why the mascot is Hunters, and the *T* in the word is fashioned to look like a wooden stake."

Jonah was intrigued, as was Terrence. It looked like Reena hadn't known that information, either.

"The school was supposedly founded by vampire hunters who were also Eleventh Percenters, but no book in their library will tell you that." Reverend Abbott laughed. "The Tenths believed that it was a cute little story, and a catchy name to match. But to vampires and Spirit Reapers, it was a threat to their agenda. It had always been that way. To this day, a dedicated group of vampire hunters are tasked by the Curaie to check in on the school at various points. Any Eleventh in Spectral Law enforcement knew that. Which is why a vampire's presence around that university raised red flags. So the Networkers sent Preston to find out."

"Did he ever find out that information?"

"The waters got muddied at every turn," said Reverend Abbott, "by one of Creyton's followers, who worked at LTSU."

Jonah raised an eyebrow, but Reena whispered, "*No.*"

"Oh yes," said Reverend Abbott. "I see that you've figured out who I mean, Reena?"

Reena nodded, wide-eyed.

"Well, I haven't!" said Terrence, frustrated. "Who was Creyton's man inside?"

"Titus Rivers, Jr.," said Reena. "Trip's dad was a Spirit Reaper."

Jonah's stomach tightened. "Seriously?"

"Yes, he was," nodded Reverend Abbott. "As was his father before, who took part in the Decimation."

It felt like the walls of the reverend's home had begun to close in around Jonah. "Two generations of Spirit Reapers? And Jonathan took Trip in?"

"Well, now." Reverend Abbott gave Jonah a stern look. "Trip didn't commit those atrocities; his father and grandfather did. T.J. tried very hard to groom his son for service to Creyton, but Trip wanted no part of Creyton, or his followers. He fled to Jonathan in his early adolescence, and Jonathan raised and protected him from that day on. Trip is—" Reverend Abbott's voiced trailed off, and Jonah suspected that he wanted to sanitize his thoughts, "—a troubled young man. So angry and bitter. But he is not the man that his father was. Nor the man his grandfather was. But we've strayed from the point."

He pushed another newspaper clipping their way, which illustrated people holding candles around Carruthers House. Some were on their knees in a praying position.

"Creyton was a monster, pure and simple," the reverend said. "But his plans were always complex. A plan within a plan is an accurate way to put it. So, if the 49er was conducting secret work for Creyton while being cloaked by Titus, Jr. and his cover job, then why would Titus, Jr. flip out and kill Preston Duscere? Preston was a very popular man, in Tenth and Eleventh circles. Such a murder would have all sorts of eyes where Creyton didn't want them. So it comes back to my simple question: Who gets something out of it?"

Jonah lowered his head and stared at his hands. After Reverend Abbott's tales, he had to admit that his feelings had become mixed. Obviously, he hadn't known any of this information. He only knew about the murders. For that reason, his judgment was compromised, because he knew that the grisly affair ended in physical lives lost. It was like watching a movie with a skewed outlook because you already knew the end.

"So what you're saying is that Titus, Jr. had nothing to gain from murdering Felix's dad," said Terrence. "But Felix would definitely have gotten something out of an act of vengeance, wouldn't he? Eye for an eye, right?"

"Seeking vengeance is playing God, Terrence, and I have no patience with that," said Reverend Abbott sharply. "But things were weird concerning that, too."

"Why?" asked Jonah.

Reverend Abbott yanked another story from the box, and handed it to Reena. "Read that," he commanded. "Read it all. Don't skim."

Jonah put on his reading glasses, and the three of them crowded in to read the yellowed page. It was not a pretty tale. It spoke of how Felix, seventeen at the time, had been found in Carruthers House with the body of Titus, Jr., which had been savaged beyond recognition. According to the news story, though, Felix had been discovered—

"—*unconscious, with a blood-stained knife in his hand*?" read Jonah aloud. "Unconscious?"

"Yes," said Reverend Abbott, with a stiff nod. "The Tenth authorities said he'd passed out due to a drunken stupor, or something like that. He stank of liquor; that much was true. But I think the truth ended there."

"You were there?" inquired Reena.

"Right again, Reena." Reverend Abbott's voice was solemn. "Titus, Jr.'s body was on the floor, massacred, and Felix was unconscious across the room, reeking of alcohol and lifeblood. It didn't make a damn bit of sense!"

Jonah's head shot up. "Whoa! Reverend!"

"You have to remember, Jonah," said Reverend Abbott, "that I didn't see this through the eyes of a clergyman. I saw it through the eyes an ethereal crimes consultant. Do you remember what I said about puzzle pieces fitting together too well? Well, wrap yourselves around this: Preston Duscere was murdered by a Spirit Reaper, who was supposed to be hiding the actions of *another* Spirit Reaper. Preston left behind a wife (who'd follow him into Spirit four years later) and a son, who was a delinquent with serious issues concerning authority, yet experienced breakthroughs under Jonathan's tutelage. I can see the rage the murder might cause. I won't dispute that piece. But tell me if the three of you can see the error in Felix throwing away all of his progress with Jonathan, and breaking his mother's heart, when she just became a widow. And that isn't all. Felix supposedly found Titus, Jr. at the three-week old crime scene, destroys him, and then conveniently passes out when he is done? He is also conveniently drunk. With the added bonus of the bloody knife still in his hand. I will ask again, who gets something out of it?"

After the monologue, Reverend Abbott calmed himself and fell silent. A long period of quiet ensued, which Reena broke with a gasp so sharp that Jonah thought she'd been attacked.

"It was the 49er," she whispered.

"What?"

"The 49er did it!" Reena hopped up from the sofa and pointed a finger at Reverend Abbott. "You said it, Reverend! Who gets something out of it? Whatever work that 49er was doing around LTSU could very well have ended. But Creyton always played things close to the chest, didn't you say? So he'd want to tie all the loose ends! Every piece was right there. Creyton must have known that Preston was closing in, so he got the 49er to kill him. Titus, Jr. was perfectly positioned to be a patsy. He would have done anything that Creyton said, especially if Creyton promised him protection for his loyalty. But that decision made him raw meat to be devoured. Like you said, Reverend, conveniently placed puzzle pieces. I'd bet anything that Creyton ordered Titus, Jr. to return to Carruthers House—what other reason would he have to return to crime scene?—and had the 49er kill him there. Titus wouldn't have put up a fight, since the 49er was an ally."

"Um, Reena?" said Jonah, who eyed her as though spoke in a different language, "How does Felix fit in there?"

"Easy," said Reena. "The 49er likes mind games, and it couldn't have been hard to manipulate and subdue Felix; he was intoxicated. So getting him there wouldn't have been a problem. So he deposits Felix, unconscious, at the crime scene, and puts the weapon in his hand. Creyton cut his losses by using perfectly positioned people. And his vampire could disappear, job done!"

Jonah didn't know how Reena put that together. Once again, Terrence looked as if his brain hurt. But Reverend Abbott worked Reena's data through mental cogs he probably hadn't used in years. His thoughts must have tallied with Reena's, because he smiled.

"That fits very well, Reena," he said, "but there is just one thing. Why did Titus, Jr., a loyal follower, have to be sacrificed?"

Jonah cleared his throat. He felt halfway intelligent again. "You answered that for us, Reverend."

"I did?" asked Reverend Abbott.

Jonah held up a yellowed flash card for them all to see. "You wrote that Titus, Jr. was trying to move Trip and his wife away. I read it earlier, but it didn't click until you asked why he had to be sacrificed. I'm guessing that Titus, Jr. wasn't stupid. He knew his family might be next in line if anything went wrong. He wanted Trip to be his heir apparent, but he didn't want him to be offered up like cattle. Reena, you're amazing, by the way."

"I'm just really good with connecting dots," she said. "Once we had the reverend's information in front of us, it wasn't hard."

"Speak for yourself," muttered Terrence.

"And don't you dare sell yourself short, Reena," said Reverend Abbott. "You are an amazingly brilliant woman. Connecting dots is only a small part of what you are."

Reena tried very hard not to look pleased with herself.

"So Felix and Trip have spent all these years mad at the wrong people." Terrence shook his head. "What does 49er plan to do with that information?"

An idea suddenly took hold of Jonah. Could it be? Had he figured out the 49er's grand plan without any help from Reena?

"Are you alright, Jonah?" asked Terrence, concerned. "You look like you need a toilet."

"What? Oh no, I'm fine. I think I know what the 49er plans to do with that information. But we'll need some help."

"Jonah, this has been a raw nerve for Tenths and Elevenths for almost two decades," said Reverend Abbott in a warning tone. "It could get ugly if you seek help in the wrong place."

"You're right, sir," said Jonah, "which is why I'll need a fresh perspective."

That gave Reverend Abbott pause. "I take it you already have an idea where to look?"

"I do."

"You do?" asked Terrence.

Jonah nodded.

"Who is this person?" asked Reena. "Where are they?"

Now it was Jonah's turn to be evasive and mysterious, but that had more to do with mental fatigue than a desire to be enigmatic. "Not tonight. Our brains have been through enough. But tomorrow night, we're going to see a man about a spirit."

19

The Five-Star Plan

Jonah barely touched on his plan with Terrence and Reena. That evening had been too full of information for him to force-feed them more. A good night's sleep remedied that, but the next day brought about a case of nervous adrenaline that even writing did little to help.

He spent the entire day going over his plan in his mind, so when Terrence and Reena got home from work, he knew exactly what to tell them, what holes to fill, and what arguments to counter. Terrence refused to do anything on an empty stomach, so after a quick dinner of rigatoni and garlic bread (Reena had Greek salad), they left.

"I'm really sick of this place," muttered Reena as they pulled into the parking lot of the Milverton Inn and Suites.

"Me too," agreed Jonah. "But we don't have a choice."

Terrence stared at the hotel in confusion. "You're certain this is a good idea? Why do you think this will be of any help at all?"

"Sorry, Terrence," said Jonah, "but you're just going to have to see it with your own eyes."

They were in the lobby in minutes. The first (and trickiest) part of Jonah's scheme was the decoy. She didn't know she was the decoy just yet.

"Have you given any thought to how you're getting past the guy at the front desk?" asked Reena.

"Yeah I have," said Jonah carefully. "Between the three of us, who is best suited to distract him?"

Terrence laughed under his breath. Reena frowned for a second, but then her eyes widened.

"Jonah! Are you serious? Tell me you're not serious!"

"Well, Reena," said Terrence in a thoughtful tone, "you *are* beautiful."

"Shut up," snapped Reena. "Jonah, you know better that anyone how much I hate trading on my looks!"

"For God's sake, Reena," spat Jonah, "I'm not asking you to let him whisk you away! Just give him a daydream or two, and meet us upstairs in ten minutes! Damn!"

Reena's eyes narrowed. "Jonah Rowe, You owe me. In the biggest way you can imagine."

"Duly noted," muttered Jonah. "Now, please go!"

With a final cold look, Reena manufactured a seductive smile and walked to the guy at the front desk. Jonah and Terrence didn't hesitate because they knew that they could trust Reena's powers of persuasion.

"You know that Reena's gonna get you for that, right?" said Terrence.

Jonah tried very hard to tune out the elevator's muzak. "Yeah, I know. But she'll just have to be patient."

The elevator paused on the ninth floor, and opened silently. This place was top notch; no squeaks here. Jonah and Terrence exited and hurried to the stairwell where Reena was to meet them. A few minutes passed before she arrived, slight out of breath.

"You know that I envy your speed ethereality," commented Terrence.

"You wouldn't if you had to run up steps." huffed Reena. "I tripped twice on those narrow things."

"Is the hotel clerk in love?" grinned Jonah.

"He called me an angel." Reena rolled her eyes. "A damned angel. Silly bastard probably believes that."

Jonah shook his head. The guy couldn't be that ignorant. But he moved forward, and beckoned Terrence and Reena behind him. After twenty paces, all Jonah could think about was his destination, so he was a little surprised, and annoyed, when Reena yanked him out of sight.

"Reena, what the hell?"

Reena put a tense finger to her lips, and mouthed, *"Bodyguards."*

Jonah peeped back into the hallway. Sure enough, there were two hulking men next to their destination. They were the same ones who provided security at the events. Two muscular hindrances to his goal.

"Jonah, dispatch them!" whispered Reena.

"Me?" whispered Jonah. "How?"

"Cut off their oxygen for thirteen seconds," suggested Terrence. "That amount of time constitutes a knockout."

"Did you learn that on the Discovery Channel?" asked Reena.

"Nah," said Terrence, "UFC."

Jonah poked his head out from his hiding place once again, and allowed his spiritual endowment to fine-tune his focus. Suddenly, he was much more mindful of his surroundings. He was also aware of the air around them, which his increased focused made clear to him. The trails of oxygen moved all around them, like traces of visible cloud. Once Jonah pinpointed the oxygen trails that flowed to the bodyguards, he isolated them with his mind, and made a clamping motion with his hands. *Thirteen... twelve... eleven... ten...*

Seconds later, the heavy bodies crashed to the floor. As he was hidden, Jonah didn't see it, but the huge thuds made him jump. The three of looked into the hall, and saw the huge men sprawled on the floor.

"Well done, Jonah!" said Terrence. "It won't be fun moving 'em, though."

"We're ethereal beings, Terrence!" said Reena. "Cloaking, remember?"

And with no further warning than that, she waved her hand, and her fingers gleamed with the yellow of her aura. Jonah no longer saw the slumbering behemoths in the hallway. He hoped that no one came walking through there. They'd trip over obstructions they wouldn't be able to see.

"Wow, Reena," he said. "Now we got to move!"

They raced to the door of the Apex Suite, and not a second too soon. It cracked, and an uncertain voice said, "Godrey? Alec?"

Having outstripped Jonah and Terrence, Reena grabbed the door and forced it open, knocking Turk Landry flat.

"What the—?"

Reena shut the door and locked it. Jonah glared at Landry as he scrambled to his feet. The man looked foolish in a monogrammed bathrobe and silk pajamas. His frightened face wasn't its usual esoteric mask, and his hair was a rat's nest.

"What do you want?" he cried. "I've got money, lots of i—" Then his eyes narrowed in recognition. "You three. Christ, can't you take a hint? I'm calling—"

"No one," snapped Reena. Landry had grabbed the telephone, but she caught up with him and seized his wrist, which still held the receiver.

Landry's expression loosened to become one of interest. "That's quite a grip, lady," he commented. "Why don't you ditch the boys there, and let's get cozy?"

Reena tightened her grip on Landry's wrist, which made him wince. "Keep it in your pants, bitch," she growled. "You don't do a damn thing for me."

Jonah stifled humor. He loved it when men flirted with Reena. Hilarity always ensued when she emasculated them.

Comprehension dawned on Landry. "Shame."

"Okay, Matchmaker?" said Jonah. "If you could kindly stop barking up the wrong tree, we all need to get on the same page." He glanced at Terrence, sighed, and went for the point of no return. "Reena?"

Reena nodded, used her free hand to extract her key from her pocket, and touched it to Landry's palm. The minute it hit his flesh, it shifted from Reena's yellow to a deep shade of purple. Terrence looked like he'd been punched. Jonah felt for him, but the charade had gone on long enough. For some reason, Reena looked at the purple aura in disgust, and let go of his arm as though it were diseased.

"You're an Eleventh Percenter?" said Terrence in a hollow voice.

"Yes, I admit it," shrugged Landry. "You caught me. Want a cookie?"

"This is not a joke," growled Jonah. If there hadn't been a purpose for this visit, Jonah would have broken his jaw with a baton. "Terrence here looked up to you for being a psychic medium, and you turned out to be an Eleventh. It's fucked up."

"More fucked up than you know," said Reena through gritted teeth. "He's a purple aura. That means he's a Gate Breacher."

Landry's attention snapped to Reena.

"What's a Gate Breacher?" asked Jonah.

"There are some Eleventh Percenters whose relationship with ethereality is woven far past interaction and influence," Reena explained. "Some spirits and spiritesses reach a point where they reconsider their decision to stay behind. So they seek out Gate Breachers, like this bastard. A Gate Breacher's aura allows them to actually dissolve portions of the gate to the Other Side itself, and they can grant burnt- out spirits and spiritesses their wish."

"Well, I'll be damned," said Jonah, but Reena wasn't done.

"So that's your game," she barked at Landry. "You've never been debunked because you locate spirits that are tired of walking Earthplane, and promise them an out. All they have to do in return is go into a run-down spot for you, and rattle chains and make spooky sounds. I don't know the name to call you right now."

"Rich?" suggested Landry. "Successful? Ingenious?"

Jonah had a dozen names on the tip of his tongue, but they wouldn't help matters at the moment. "Like I said, Landry, we need to talk."

"Certainly," said Landry, oddly welcoming all of a sudden. "Seat yourselves. I'll make tea."

"You got any Luzianne?" Terrence still wasn't over the bombshell. "Or Nestea?"

Landry turned a contemptuous gaze on Terrence. "I may have been raised in America, but I am English born, boy. You will not find cold teas here."

* * *

Jonah ignored the comfy sofa. Ignored the posh suite. It was all he could do to keep from shutting up Landry's ridiculous humming as he made tea. But there was no way in hell his plan could work if he didn't sit here and tolerate it. So that was what he did.

Terrence looked like he didn't believe in anything anymore. Jonah and Reena didn't even try to cheer him up. He simply sat between the two of them, contemplating his knees.

"How long have you known?" he asked Jonah.

"Since that night at Ballowiness," Jonah admitted. "He didn't have any spirits around him, and he said that tainted vibes bullshit because he didn't see any spirits around me, either. When you went to the can, I saw him deactivate Spectral Sight."

Terrence didn't lift his head. "I s'pose it goes without saying that you knew as well, Reena." It wasn't a question. "And neither of you filled me in because—?"

"Because you told me all that stuff about how you hated being let down," said Jonah, hoping against hope that Terrence would understand. "You told me about your stupid biological parents, and your stupid *adoptive* parents, and I felt like you didn't need anyone else to crush you."

Terrence laid his head on the back of the sofa. "It isn't like you were the one who is lying to America's face," he said. "I'll never figure out why I didn't see it. Goddamn, I'm stupid."

"That is not true, Terrence," snapped Reena, but before she could continue, Landry returned, complete with tea.

"Drink up," he said with a smile. "There is plenty extra."

Jonah frowned at the cups, but Landry just laughed.

"I've nothing to gain by poisoning or drugging you," he said.

Unmoved, Jonah looked at Reena, who lifted the dampener for a few seconds. "He means it," she said. "He hasn't done anything to it."

Landry eyed Reena again. "An essence reader, too? You are a like a human Swiss Army knife, Reena! You know, I could offer you a position with *ScarYous* Incorporated. I can triple what you're making now—"

"How did you find out about my personal life?" Reena demanded. "You're obviously not psychic."

Landry sipped his tea. "Money talks, my dear."

Reena's eyes bulged. "A private investigator?" she whispered. "You invasive prick!"

"Did you look me up, too?" asked Jonah.

"No," replied Landry. "You're a student name Jonah Rowe. It was a simple matter of looking in the university directory. Besides, I was fascinated by Reena, not by you."

Jonah swallowed the swear word that nearly flew out of his mouth when a better idea took hold in his brain. He reached into his pocket, and pulled out a baton. Blue essence shot up the entire thing. "Fascinated *now*?"

Landry lowered his teacup. His trembling hands rattled the glass. "B-Blue Aura? W-Why are you here?"

"Unfortunately, we need your help."

"My help?" said Landry. "But the Blue Aura is a supposed juggernaut. Why would you need little old me?"

Jonah laughed with no mirth. "Oh, don't downplay yourself now, Landry. You ever heard of Creyton?"

"Roger Creyton, you mean?" The father of *ScarYous* sounded fearful. "Every Eleventh Percenter has heard of him. But he's gone. That's why I'm here."

"Pardon?" said Reena.

"He got killed by the Blue Aura," said Landry. "I knew that, too. But I didn't know that that was *you*, Jonah. I would have treated you better during the spirit messages. Anyway, the damage he inflicted on the path to the Other Side is not yet fully rectified. There were bound to be spirits ready to kiss Earthplane goodbye. Who better to give them a reprieve than a highly accomplished Gate Breacher? They're frightened, stranded, and weak. I do them a service, and in turn, they assist me with the three R's of *ScarYous*."

"The three R's?"

"Absolutely," replied Landry. "Ratings, Revenue, and Royalties!"

"Son of a—!" Terrence nearly pounced on Landry, but Jonah and Reena grabbed his arms. Jonah was nearly off the handle himself, and he didn't need essence reading to know what was on Reena's mind. But he also knew that Terrence had it worse than all of them. He'd believed in the man, and now he saw him for what he was: A fraudulent, ambitious, self-serving turd.

Landry was unabashed by their anger. It did not faze him. "What are you so up-in-arms about?" he asked. "I truly do not understand. We all have paths in this world, don't we? Do you know how many jobs I went through to find my calling? The Eleventh Percent is not an infallible construct; it is a tool! You think *ScarYous* would survive if it were just a good show? No. That's not enough in today's climate. *ScarYous* needs to be a *great* show! I take my ethereal talents all across the nation and knock it out of the park, every single time! There are even talks about expanding *ScarYous* into Canada and Europe! I'm no Spirit Reaper. I don't pervert essences. I employ scores of people. I have built an infallible empire. I've blessed spirits with the opportunity to continue their journey when they tire of being confined to Earthplane. I have the perfect example for you. RUBEN!"

The silence that ensued was a blessing after all the garbage that Landry spewed, but Jonah found himself surprised when an elderly spirit materialized next to the man's chair. He resembled a retired bellhop, and had the softened look of a man who had enjoyed relaxed later years. But there was something about how he regarded Landry. He didn't grovel, or look like Landry was the answer to his dreams, like all those other spirits and spiritesses had. Truth be told, he looked like he didn't want to be there.

"Ruben is one of the spirits who found me when we researched Rome," Landry explained. "He agreed to scout three final areas for me that contained spirits and spiritesses that wished to be released. That will allow me to wrap up this season of *ScarYous*, and finally get the hell out of this backwater hole. In return for his kindness, not only will he receive his wish to cross to the Other Side, but I plan to grant him temporary tangibility so that he can actually touch and hold his newborn granddaughter. I'm a giver, don't you see? So tell me, where is the evil in that?"

Jonah was speechless. Tangibility was dark ethereality. Landry's plan was to use dark ethereality for a heartwarming cause. He had this spirit on the hook only because he'd infused his lies with just enough truth to appear charitable. It was such a flawless system that it sickened him.

Terrence, who'd been silent since he nearly tore Landry's head off, began to laugh, which puzzled Jonah. It puzzled Landry, too.

"What could possibly be funny?" he asked.

"You should have never shown us this spirit," Terrence told him. "He's only here because you needed an edge when you got to Rome. I wanna know something, Mr. Ruben: How long has Landry been holding that thing with your granddaughter over your head? You didn't find him, he found *you*, am I right? What did you do, Landry? Hire another private investigator to scour the obituaries?"

"Oh my God," said Jonah. "Terrence, you're on to something. You found names of people who'd recently passed into Spirit, and then found out things about their families, didn't you, Landry? You hitched this spirit to your little sideshow wagon because you found out he recently had a grandchild. You dirty son of a bitch."

Landry's eyes widened somewhat. His unshakeable demeanor cracked just a little. The spirit narrowed his eyes as he slowly considered Landry.

"Is that true?"

Landry didn't answer. Reena joined in.

"Yes, Mr. Ruben, it's true," she said. "Let me ask you something, sir. That little tangibility that he promised you? Was there a time frame on that? Or was it open-ended?"

"Jesus, man," said Jonah. "You were going to milk this guy for a while, weren't you? Were you going to make him your in-house spirit scout, or something?"

"ENOUGH!" shouted Landry, but there was more worry in his tone than anger. "These accusations are absurd! Why are you planting these lies into Ruben's head?"

"They aren't lies," said Jonah. "It sucks to know that someone has an edge over you, doesn't it? But don't worry, if you let Ruben off the hook and help us out, we might forget your little schemes."

Ruben looked at Jonah with something like hope. It didn't go unnoticed by Landry, whose eyes darted between them before he snapped, "Help with what, exactly?"

"With the lifeblood-looting, of course."

Landry's looked scared. "L-lifeblood looting? But that means vampires are present!"

"Two points for Turk Landry!" exclaimed Terrence with mock applause. "*Want a cookie?*"

Landry shook his head. "You lie. Vampires are hemocentric. Everybody knows that."

"Well, the 49er must have missed that," said Jonah. "Did you ever wonder why Ruben was only able to find you just three more locations? It's because spirits are running scared. They don't want to get attacked by vampires. That's why we want your help."

"I'm sorry?"

"Yeah, you've proven that," said Jonah, "but that's beside the point. Listen to me, because now we're at the point of this meet."

He told Landry an abbreviated version of everything they'd learned. Reena threw a nice cherry on top when she added the part about the psychic vampires who became Haunts. Terrence probably couldn't trust himself to speak without swearing, so he contented himself with emphatic nods in the right places.

Landry was pale by the end of their story. Ruben looked like he wanted to vanish, but he probably stayed in place because he didn't want to encounter a vampire outside. Landry didn't say anything for several moments, but then an odd determination morphed his face into its standard expression.

"I've reached a decision," he said in his on-camera *ScarYous* voice.

Jonah's eyes widened. Dare he believe it? "So you'll help us?"

"Of course not," scoffed Landry. "Your attempts at blackmail by scaremongering and reciting outlandish lore have not swayed me. But since this evening has been most entertaining, I've decided to give you a choice."

He moved the tea tray into their line of sight. He'd replaced the cups with a checkbook and a cell phone. Jonah didn't know how he did that so fast. Sleight of hand must have been one of his talents as well.

"You have two ways out of here," Landry announced. His voice sounded like that of a game show host who touted fabulous prizes. "The first way is with the police, who will have evidence of breaking and entering, as well as my two bodyguards you assaulted out there. And that's just the Tenth charges; the S.P.G will no doubt discover your violent ways, and will punish you further, for abusing your ethereal talents on two helpless Tenths."

Jonah tightened his fists. Was this guy serious?

"The second way," said Landry as he pulled the cell phone back and pushed the checkbook forward, "sees you walk out of here with three checks denoting more money than you've ever seen in your lives, autographed by yours truly. If you blab about me, the check is evidence that you took a bribe. If you remain silent, then your life becomes a Bond movie. You can abandon this stupid farm-boy town, and live like normal people. Choice meals, top-notch attire, fast cars, and even faster women, which I know appeals to *all* of you."

Reena's eyes blazed when Landry glanced at her.

"So what's it going to be?" he asked them.

"Mr. Landry?" said Ruben suddenly.

"Not now," said Landry with impatience.

"But—"

"I said, not now—"

"Sir, please—"

"Silence, you feeble echo, or you'll remain Earthbound!" snapped Landry.

"DON'T YOU DARE THREATEN ME!" shouted the spirit, which made Jonah, Terrence, and Reena jump. "They are not lying. The 49er is out there, with a group of vampires! They're right about everything!"

Landry snapped his attention to Ruben. He actually stood up. "Why are you saying these things to me? You were on the brink of blissful eternity, and then you get lofty and side with these children?"

"These children have more gumption in their palms than you do in your entire body!" said Ruben. "They want to eradicate a threat to Tenths, Elevenths, and spirits alike! You only want to buy your way out of a tight spot!"

Landry glared at the spirit. "You've blown it, Ruben!" he spat. "You're stuck on this plane forever! You won't get to hold your granddaughter, I promise you!"

"Turk Landry." Pensiveness infiltrated the anger in Ruben's voice. "Do you realize that you have threatened the Eleventh Percenters who are trying to curtail a hideous threat, attempted to fabricate ethereal crimes, and threatened a spirit who has the ability to go to the Phasmastis Curaie and tell them how you've built your empire?"

Jonah thought if Landry paled any further, they'd be able to see the bones beneath his skin.

"You wouldn't," he whispered. "The Curaie would ruin me!"

"Sounds like you got three new R's, you purple-gate pimp," said Terrence. "Refund, Ruin, and Run out of town!"

Landry looked disarmed and desperate.

"Like I said earlier," said Jonah, "you can consider all this forgotten if you use your ethereality the right way for once, and help us."

"I-I can't," said Landry. "I'm just an entertainer."

Jonah glared at him. "I thought you were a giver."

"Mr. Ruben," said Reena, "what made you see sense?"

The spirit looked ashamed. "I wasn't ever fully on board with this, but Landry hooked me with many promises, including the thing with my granddaughter. I knew the 49er was around, but your story made it scarier and truer than it had been before. It got me thinking that maybe I should stop thinking about myself, and do what I could to make this world safer for my granddaughter, even if I can't do anything big."

"She's lucky to have your influence, even if she never knew you," said Reena. "We thank you."

"I apologize that this coward won't help you," said Ruben, who threw a salty look at Landry's seated, blubbering form, "but there is something that you should know. It's April Twenty-Eighth. The young man Felix Duscere is headed to Carruthers House to pay his annual respects to his father's memory."

"Why doesn't he just go to his grave?" asked Terrence.

"His father was cremated," said Ruben. "But that is not the point. I've found out from other spirits that Titus the Third is going to demolish the place with his sound ethereality. Tonight."

Jonah closed his eyes. There was *no* was their luck was that bad.

"They still believe the original story," whispered Reena. "Trip is going to go to that house and see Felix's vehicle. They'll be in the same place. There'll be no Jonathan."

"No rules or reason," mumbled Terrence.

Jonah finished it. "And they'll finish what the 49er started all those years ago."

20

It Runs Cold

"Do you have any idea how to get there?"

"I know how to get there! I've just never come from the Milverton!"

"If you don't speed up, we'll be findin' corpses!"

"If you don't shut up so I can concentrate, I'll be dumping *your* corpse from this car!"

Terrence and Reena kept at it. It started the minute they left the Milverton. Jonah allowed Reena to drive this time, because she knew shortcuts and alternative routes better than anyone. It was true that they didn't have time to waste, but Jonah didn't want Reena to floor it. The last thing they needed was a speeding ticket.

Jonah didn't care too much for Felix, but he had come to respect him. Trip could go to hell in most situations, but not in this one. Not one where everything he believed was completely wrong.

Felix and Trip couldn't kill each other. It couldn't happen. They had to stop it. But how the hell was that supposed to happen?

It took a long time—too long—to reach the next exit, but the Carruthers House was in sight. Jonah had always ignored the place because it wasn't his destination, and was about two and a half miles from LTSU. But it had his attention tonight. Reena turned off the headlights, even though it was pitch-black dark. Jonah reached for them in alarm, but she batted him away.

"Reena, are you crazy?" Jonah didn't ask so much as proclaim.

"We don't want to be noticed, do we?" said Reena.

"We don't wanna be killed, either!" cried Terrence.

"Spectral Sight, Terrence!" said Reena impatiently. "I can see in the dark if I focus. Now shut up and let me!"

They pulled into an area near an outer rim of trees. Jonah steeled himself. His words had to be pristine, otherwise this wouldn't be pretty.

"Remember, give me time to get in there," he told his friends. "Look out for Trip. When you see him, high-tail it in after me. Hopefully, we can stop the hell before it even starts."

"We got this, Jonah," said Reena. "Please, *please* be careful."

"Resort to balancing moods with your aura if you have to," threw in Terrence. "I don't know how well it'll work with these guys, but it's worth a shot!"

That wasn't the most heartening notion, but Jonah nodded, and hurried to the abandoned fraternity house.

These grounds were new to him. Jonah couldn't be aware of his surroundings even if he waited for night vision to fine-tune his eyes. Three times, he tripped in the thick grass, and then he nearly wiped out over a stump. He stopped about ten yards from the back door, and did a quick scan. Felix's mobile bunker was there (he appeared to have just barreled through all the brush and tall grass), but he didn't see Trip's car. That was great.

But then Jonah heard a twig snap, which made him tense. After a sharp breeze, Trip stepped out of thin air, right on the back porch. Jonah could have cursed. How could he have forgotten about the *Astralimes*? Of course Trip wouldn't bother to drive, especially if he had clandestine plans!

Jonah abandoned all pretense, and ran to the back door. Trip hadn't closed it.

He didn't care about the layout, but he idly noted the kitchen was empty of everything, save a wooden china cabinet. He kept moving until he reached the den, which gave him a clear view of the living room. There were remnants of a rocking chair, a caved-in sofa, and broken liquor bottles. Felix was there, but Jonah didn't see Trip. He saw him walk into the house, so why wasn't he there?

Felix knelt at a seemingly random spot on the floor, and dropped some flowers on it. That must have been where they'd discovered the corpse of Preston Duscere all those years ago. Jonah wanted so badly to warn Felix that Trip lurked about somewhere, but he felt like it would disturb a sacred moment. Stifling his impatience, he remained in his hiding place out of respect.

"You're on the Other Side, so I don't even know if you can hear me," Felix said to the floor. "These are tiger lilies. You know, Mama's favorite."

Jonah watched Felix reverently spread them out, and then bow his head.

"Dad, Mom wanted me to keep up visiting this place." he continued. "But I can't do it anymore. I don't know if total peace is possible, but I've got to try. I brought the flowers for Mama's sake. I know she is with you wherever you are, and I hope she understands."

Felix paused. It sounded like he just bit back emotion. But he cleared his throat.

"I hope I made you proud, Dad. Despite everything, I hope I made you proud."

"Nope," said a voice from nowhere.

Felix scrambled to his feet and looked around in alarm. Trip willed himself into visibility, loathing in every iota of his being.

Jonah shut his eyes in frustration. He sat there—out of some misguided respect—and waited too long. Now the powder kegs—his own damn affirmation—were face to face, without Jonathan there to be moderator. And Terrence and Reena were outside, still awaiting Trip's arrival.

"You didn't make him proud, F.D.," said Trip. "Remember that nickname? F.D.? From back when I was stupid enough to call you my brother?"

"Why are you here, Trip?" demanded Felix.

"Funny you should ask." Trip place his hands in his pockets. "See, I'm ready to move on as well. I came to level this cursed place."

"What?" said Felix. "How?"

Trip pulled out a Mason jar that looked empty, but Jonah knew better. By the look on Felix's face, he did too. It was a Ghost Wave. Concentrated sound vibrations designed to cause ethereal disturbances. They were Trip's specialty. But what good was it here?

Trip answered the question that Jonah didn't even ask. "Ghost Waves can send a signal up to a hundred and fifty miles," he revealed. "They can also pulverize a sixty-year old house more efficiently than dynamite."

Felix eyed the Ghost Wave with scorn. "You expect me to believe that you'd level a house with you still in it? You wouldn't do that. You're too far up your own ass."

"That's what the *Astralimes* are for," said Trip. His calm façade seemed to diminish with each word. "This house ruined my life. But tonight, it provided a gift. The bonus of you being in it. Finally, you murderous, back-stabbing bastard… goodbye."

Trip raised his hand. Felix stepped forward to thwart him.

"NO!" Jonah emerged from his hiding place, consequences be damned. He placed himself between them, both batons aloft. "STOP!"

"Jonah?" Felix looked incredulous as hell. "What are you doing here?"

"Jonah Blue." Trip's eyes hardened as they moved from the blue crackling baton to Jonah's face. "I warned you. I had the decency to *warn* you, and you couldn't leave well enough alone."

"Trip, you need to listen, you don't understand—"

"I UNDERSTAND PERFECTLY" shouted Trip. "If you don't want to get crushed, you'd better get out! Or stay, I don't give a shit!"

He raised the jar again, but Reena sped out of nowhere and snatched it from him. Terrence lassoed Trip with Jonah's jumper cables, and boy scout-knotted a length of rope around his wrists. He then shoved Trip onto the old sofa.

"Where did that rope come from, man?" asked Jonah.

"Got it from Liz," answered Terrence. "Don't ask."

Jonah didn't. At this particular point in time, he didn't really care. He turned his attention to Trip and Felix. "There are a lot of things that you both need to know."

Trip growled in fury, and struggled against the bonds. "You bastards have NO right to stick your nose in business that doesn't concern you!"

"It was necessary," Jonah fired back. "And you need to shut up. There are things you need to know, like I said."

"Know what?" demanded Trip. "You don't know what's going on! None of you! This piece of shit killed my father!"

"Your poor excuse of a sperm donor murdered *my* father first!" roared Felix. "And I've told you a million times that I don't remember what happened that night!"

"Convenient moment to have a blackout, don't you think?" barked Trip. "Your dad was a stupid Networker, always on my father's case—"

"That was because your father was a goddamned Spirit Reaper!" snarled Felix. "Right in Creyton's inner circle! He killed more people than you've had gigs—"

"SHUT THE HELL UP!" bellowed Jonah. The venom in his tone actually had the desired effect. "Felix wasn't who killed your father, Trip! Felix didn't kill anyone that night! And Felix, T.J. Rivers didn't kill your father! He might have killed a lot of other people, but not Preston Duscere! It was the 49er. It's always been him."

Trip's face twisted. Felix's went slack.

"What are you talking about, Jonah?" he asked.

"It was the 49er," Jonah repeated. "He is the spider at a very intricate web of lies."

"You don't know what you're talking about, Rowe," snapped Trip. "His asshole father was playing a glad-handing citizen at LSTU, when he was actually breathing down my father's neck—"

"Your father was using his teaching position to provide misdirection from the 49er," interrupted Jonah. "Now just hang on." He returned his gaze to Felix. "Felix, did your father ever tell you why he spent so much time at LTSU?"

"No," said Felix. "He shared Networker techniques with me, but never official business."

"Sounds about right," said Jonah. "He was stationed there by his superiors to figure out why the 49er was around. They were suspicious of a vampire's presence, because La Tronis means—"

"I know what it means," said Felix with impatience. "Keep talking."

"Whatever the 49er was doing must have ended," continued Jonah, who felt more like a bard of old, telling a tale of deceit. "Creyton ordered Titus, Jr. to cloak the 49er's activities, but then he deemed him expendable. Mr. Duscere was closing in, so Creyton gave 49er the job of cutting the fat, and Titus, Jr. was ordered to take responsibility."

Felix looked on, but Trip's eyes narrowed.

"Do you expect me to believe that my father took the fall for that Networker's murder? Seriously, do you think I'm totally stupid?"

"Yes, actually," answered Jonah, "but as the son of a Spirit Reaper, you know the hold that Creyton had over his followers. If Creyton told Titus, Jr. to do something, he either did it out of fear, or considered it an honor. I don't think I'm wrong in guessing that there wasn't really a grey area. I bet he didn't go on the run because Creyton ordered him not to. He must have trusted Creyton to protect him from Tenth and Eleventh justice."

"But he must have known that something didn't smell right," threw in Reena, "because he tried to move Trip and his mother away somewhere."

Trip straightened. "How did you know that, Katoa?"

Reena took a deep breath. "Holy men tell no tales."

Trip glared at her, but she turned her back on him.

"Please." There was supplication in Felix's voice that Jonah hadn't ever heard. "Are you certain that I didn't kill Titus, Jr.? I was angry and drunk. I woke up covered in blood and holding the knife. How do you know I didn't do anything?"

"It's your turn to think back, Felix," said Jonah. "Do you remember anything from that night? Anything at all?"

Trip laughed. "You're asking a drunk to remember that far back? Great day in the morning, Rowe, you really *are—*"

"I tried to comfort my mom," recalled Felix in a hollow voice. "There wasn't anything I could do for her. I went to a hideout that I had, and started drinking. I had twenty bottles of Distinguished Vintage. I don't remember anything more until I woke up in this house."

"You drank twenty bottles of that shit?" said Terrence, horrified. "That's ninety-proof alcohol, man! Forget a lapse in memory; you're lucky you didn't pass into Spirit from alcohol poisoning!"

Felix started to say something, but Reena beat him to it.

"Alcohol wouldn't have killed him, Terrence," she said quietly. "He is made of tough stuff. All sazers are."

Jonah's eyes snapped to Reena and Felix, while Terrence cried out, "WHAT?" Felix ignored them both. He only had eyes for Reena.

"Let me guess," he grumbled, "you figured it out after Trip's purposeful slip of the tongue before Christmas, right?"

"No, actually," said Reena. "Trip had nothing to do with it. I researched sazers after one attacked me years ago. You have a public record of juvenile delinquency, Felix. I also found out that you have a childhood diagnosis of Oppositional Defiant Disorder. You have an almost encyclopedic knowledge of anger management, plus the first thing that you do when things get tense is employ diaphragmatic breathing. You father was one, too, right?"

Felix shook his head. "You are a maven, Reena. Why the hell do you do clerical work again?"

"Quit ass-kissing, Felix," said Terrence. "I'm thinking about that locker room incident with the vampire snitch. You wouldn't let us talk to him because he probably would have exposed you as a sazer. Am I right, or am I right?"

Felix's silence was all the answer they needed. Trip laughed once more.

"So the nosy children realized that Santa isn't real." His voice was full of fake pity. "You're damned fools. All of you. You should have realized by now that you can't count on anyone, 'specially some nutcase that's prone to Red Rage—"

"Wait." Felix straightened, and all eyes went to him. "Shut up, Trip. I remember something. I didn't think about it until you mentioned Red Rage. A man showed up after I was drunk. It seemed so odd, because he was covered. Completely covered— hooded, everything. I seem to recall thinking that he had bad skin."

Jonah looked at Felix intently. "What did he do?"

"He…He knew me," said Felix. "He said that he knew my dad had *died*—that word alone would have been a red flag had I been sober—and he also knew the man that cut the head off of my family. I got pissed. More pissed than I already was. It was a scary thing combined with the Vintage. The man told me that if I wanted to fulfill the Hydra, or something, then he knew where I could find the killer. I don't remember anything past that. I reddened out."

"You mean blacked out?" said Terrence.

"No." Felix shook his head. "Reddened out. Red Rage."

Jonah stared off into space. "The head of your family was cut off—wow. It was the 49er, man. I'm sure of it. He waited till you got drunk, pushed you over the edge, and then probably whacked you in the head. After that, he went to Carruthers House and killed Titus, Jr. Man probably didn't even fight him. That was his buddy, after all. What do you want to bet that the 49er savaged the body the way a sazer would? Then, it was a simple matter of dumping you next to the remains, deposit some blood, and then gift wrap the case by putting the blade in your hand. The Tenths had their motive, which was crime of passion, and the Elevenths had their motive, which was drunk, Red-Raging sazer who gets even with his father's killer. Perfectly-placed puzzle pieces."

He looked at Trip, whose face had loosened from its usual sneer for the first time since Jonah knew him. He would have pitied the bastard if he weren't, well, a bastard.

"There you go, Trip," he said, not wanting anymore counterarguments. "Your dad had proven a liability by trying to spirit you and your mom away. Preston was getting too close, and the 49er needed to fade to black. Three birds, one stone. You guys have spent all of these years hating the wrong people. It was the 49er, and by extension, it was Creyton."

Terrence focused on Jonah after several moments of silence. "Okay, Jonah. The truth is out. Now please tell us what the 49er is planning? You said that you knew. Why did he rehash all of this crap?"

Jonah took a deep breath. The suspicion came to him the very first time that Terrence asked what the 49er planned to do with the old information. He'd hooked them all. It was the bard-like quality again. But Jonah didn't do it to milk them for dramatics at all. He just knew that his answer had to come after every single fact was known. And now it was time. "The 49er wants to take Creyton's place as Public Enemy Alpha," he announced. "The way he sees it, his boss is gone, all the followers are scattered in the wind, and he wanted to end the vacuum period. He already had all the Haunts he needed; making new ones all over the Astral Plane was just misdirection so that Spectral Law wouldn't focus on what he was really doing, which was making a small army of vampires. Bringing up the old scandal was a way to cut loose ends, just like Creyton did when he ordered him to kill Preston and Titus, Jr. He wanted me out of the way because I'm the Blue Aura. I think the three of us were supposed to kill each other. The embittered son, the guilt-ridden sazer, and the Blue Aura. We aren't supposed to make it out of here. Like I said before, three birds, one—"

Jonah's last word got drowned out by a feral roar of rage. Before anyone could utter a question, a warning, or an exclamation, many windows shattered, and the front door banged off of its hinges. Jonah had ruined the 49er's plan, and he and his army were out for blood.

No. *Lifeblood.*

Jonah's head spun. They had gone from yet another revelation to a white-hot and furious fight in the course of ten seconds. It was a blur of vampires descending, Eleventh Percenters reacting, and the aged floorboards groaning under increased weight. He got bowled over by a vampire that burst through the window behind him, and fell flat on his ass.

All Felix's emotional upheaval evaporated, and the vampire hunter was back. He fought off two vampires at once, a silver blade in one hand and a foot long silver nail in the other. He had been prepared. Good for him. But none of the rest of them had any silver.

Trip dispensed with the rope and cables that bound him (Jonah didn't know how he did it) and altered the sound around himself, which damaged the equilibriums of the vampires that charged at him. A vampire attacked Reena, and she pushed him away, which made him lose his balance on the broken glass.

Another vampire went for Terrence's throat, but he managed to block her, and now they looked like they were in some type of wrestling match.

But Jonah knew that those reprieves wouldn't last, and he didn't think Felix could do it all by himself. They'd be done for if they didn't find some silver or wood.

Wood. The ragged china cabinet in the kitchen.

He scrambled to his feet and took off.

"Jonah, what the hell!" shouted Terrence, still locked with his own beast. "Get back here, man!"

"Shut up and hang on a second!" Jonah threw over his shoulder.

The damned kitchen didn't seem this far away when he first got in the Carruthers House, but Jonah saw the cabinet before he reached the room. It looked prehistoric, which meant he could break it without issue—

Then something heavy hit Jonah in the back, and breaking the cabinet was no longer necessary. He and the vampire that jumped him crashed into the thing, which stood no chance against their combined weights. It was sheer dumb luck that Jonah didn't get impaled by shards of glass or broken wood, but it didn't prevent splinter wounds and cuts. That crap hurt like hell, but Jonah made himself as oblivious as possible. He had a vampire to worry about.

The vampire had had too much momentum when she'd jumped Jonah, so she hit the ground as well, and rolled a few inches away from him. But her eyes were back on Jonah—and his fresh cuts—in seconds.

"I haven't fed in so long," she rasped. "Your lifeblood is mine!"

Jonah detached a baton and brained the bloodsucker to buy himself some time. She staggered into the sink, and he grabbed a jagged-edged piece of wood. It might make a serviceable stake. He charged her, but she reacted fast and got her hands up to the stake's edge.

Jonah roared through gritted teeth. He wasn't prepared for how strong she'd be. This was a mortal struggle. The vampire pushed against him with every ounce of strength she had, and even tried to break the edge off the stake. One such yank cleared her hair from her face, and with a jolt, Jonah recognized her. Not this anguished, emaciated version, but with a sweet smile on a missing poster...

"Pilar Contesa?"

Shocked, she slackened her grip on the stake, which made Jonah's stake drive home uncontested. Pilar's body spiked as the wood lacerated her heart, and she cried out. For the tiniest of moments, he saw a trace of the innocent girl that she used to be, but then she withered to a husk and collapsed.

Jonah stared down at her as a backlash of emotions flooded him. He'd killed her. He'd killed an innocent girl, a foreign exchange student who left her home and came to LTSU to get her feet wet in America—

No. *That* girl was killed when the 49er bit her and turned her into a lifeblood-looting shell of her former self. The 49er was the guilty one.

Anger corroded his guilt. He gathered a pile of strong wood pieces into his hands, and returned to the fight.

"STAKES!" he shouted. "OR SKEWERS, WHATEVER!"

Reena, Terrence, and Trip pounced on them before he'd finished the word.

"JONAH, WATCH OUT!" screamed Felix.

Jonah whirled around, but never got the chance to defend himself. A vampire was seconds away from biting his neck from behind, but a figure crashed through the last unbroken window, and collided with the beast. He impaled the vampire's back with a tree branch, and the thing withered to a husk. Jonah looked confusedly at his savior, but then caught a strong whiff of B.O.—

"You!" he exclaimed.

The sazer boy looked up at him. "Me, friend! Heard the noise and wanted to help!"

Trip vanquished his vampire. "Two sazers. How nice."

With sufficient arms, they were able to finish it. Felix assisted Reena with two vampires, while Terrence staked one. Trip wrenched a stake from the chest of another withered husk, while Jonah and the sazer boy killed the two remaining ones. Soon, all that was left was their sweaty, exhausted band. But Jonah was far from relieved.

"This isn't over, is it?" he asked in an anxious voice. "The 49er has an army. Was this, like, the first wave or something?"

"Jonah, pull you head out of your ass." Trip looked at him with scorn. "A vampiric army does not need to be large in order to be a credible threat. A dozen of them can be as dangerous as the 82nd Airborne if you aren't prepared for them."

"Uh-huh," said Jonah. "Well, screw you very much. Everybody alright?"

"Got a slice on my arm from some glass, but other than that, I'm great," said Terrence.

Apart from a bloody nose and bruises on her arms, Reena looked fine. It seemed that the sazer boy's only problem was his smell. Trip crossed his arms and looked away. But Felix didn't respond. He didn't even appear to have heard Jonah.

"I don't see him," he said as he looked over the husks. "I don't see the 49er."

"You wouldn't, friend," said the sazer boy. "He sent his buddies in here, but he ran off somewhere."

Felix stared at him for several seconds, and then stalked off toward the door. "He isn't getting away. I'll get him."

"To hell with that!" Trip blocked Felix's path. "That son of a whore is mine!"

"Back off, Trip," muttered Felix. "This isn't about you."

"Who made you the Avenging Angel?" demanded Trip. "Leave it to someone who can get it done. You're liable to fail, just like your Daddy."

Reena looked at Trip in horror.

Felix stiffened. "What did you say?" he whispered.

Trip didn't show the slightest bit of fear. "You heard me, or is your sazer hearing going down? Face facts! None of this would have gotten this far had your father handled his business and killed 49er way back when. But *no*. He had to investigate, and follow the evidence like a good little houseboy. He played by the rules, and he got dropped. What makes you think you can do any better?"

Jonah's mouth fell open. What did Trip think he was doing?

"Shut up, Trip," said Terrence. "You gotta shut up!"

But Felix and Trip no longer seemed to realize that they weren't alone.

"Shut up about my father, Trip," said Felix in frighteningly calm tone.

"What, do you expect me to sanitize it?" Trip's voice elevated as much as Felix's had lowered. "No way in hell. You father dropped the ball. And you're just as big a fuck-up as he was."

Jonah saw Felix's eyes flash red. Fear of the unknown engulfed him. The sazer boy tensed.

"Oh no," he whispered, "oh no no no..."

"He's in Red Rage!" cried Reena. "Get away from him!"

"Oh, for God's sake!" Trip went across Felix's face with his stake, and he fell to the floor. He looked at the rest of them with a sneer.

"See, you little punks? He's nothing. Nothing at a—"

Felix lifted his legs and nipped up. Trip's facial strike hadn't even fazed him. He grabbed Trip, and threw him through a wall. He literally threw Trip *through a wall*. Trip landed in a heap in the room beyond.

"Oh my God!" shouted Terrence, but for some reason, Jonah's fear fell from him. All he could think of was the damage Felix might do out there in Red Rage while he hunted his father's true killer. He had to stop him. A straight-up fight was out of the question, because Felix was damn near unstoppable when he was lucid, let alone now. But he had an idea.

"Boy!" he barked at the sazer kid. "Help me!"

Thankfully, the boy was quick on the uptake. Felix had two silver knives aloft and was on his way to the door when Jonah and his new friend upturned the ruined sofa on his unsuspecting form. Felix roared in primal fury, and his knives clattered away from him. He was facedown underneath the sofa, but already trying to muscle his way out from underneath. Jonah placed his weight on top of the upturned sofa, and the sazer boy followed suit. Terrence compounded Felix even further by adding his own weight, and Reena (after struggling with herself because she didn't want to be near a crazed sazer) joined them.

"You goddamned BASTARDS!" Felix bellowed. "You would do well to run, because when I get free, I won't try to control myself!"

"Yeah!" Jonah retorted. "Because you're doing swell with that right now!"

"Boy, you're out of your league!" spat Felix. "You're untested, weak, and unsure of yourself! You aren't even enough for Vera! You haven't even completed a Mentis Cavea!"

"But I am in control of my emotions!" countered Jonah. Those comments cut, but he filed them away. "Can you say the same?"

"This is who I am! I don't need control! I embrace this!"

Jonah was suddenly furious. He jumped off of his place on the couch, ignored Reena's warnings, and lowered to Felix's face. "That is bullshit! We have a choice! Always! You told me anger was a tool, and now you elect to stew in rage! Your dad had this same weakness, but by all accounts, he mastered it and was known for his greatness, not delinquency like you. So stop with the justifications and show some damn responsibility!"

Felix's eyes flashed again. "Jonah Rowe, I swear I'll—"

CRACK.

Jonah had had enough. He bashed Felix in the head with his baton. He was out cold.

Reena looked at him. "Wow, Jonah."

Jonah shrugged. "He'll be fine. Made of tough stuff, right?" He looked at the boy. "I saw a shed out front. Can you put him in it, please? And break off the doorknob afterwards. He needs to cool off."

"Sure, friend," said the boy, "but what will *you* be doing?"

Jonah took a deep breath. "I got to deal with the 49er."

"What, Jonah?" breathed Reena.

"Have you lost your mind?" demanded Terrence. "Let's summon Jonathan! He can contact some Networkers, let them handle it!"

"They won't get here in time," dismissed Jonah. "Besides, I have a bone to pick with that bastard. He got in my thoughts. Screwed around in my head. He'll pay for that."

"Listen to yourself, Jonah!" exclaimed Reena. "This is not the time to be a badass!"

"Who else can do it, Reena?" demanded Jonah. "Felix in Hyde mode, not to mention unconscious at the moment. And Trip just got thrown through a wall. The 49er can't go somewhere else and start all this over. I'll stop him."

Reena glared at him, but there was a trace of respect in her eyes. A small trace, but it was there. "Fine. Be careful."

"Kick his ass, man!" said Terrence, who coughed suddenly. Jonah raised an eyebrow, but Terrence shrugged.

"All this dust and mold put a little tickle in my throat. Go handle your business!"

* * *

Jonah cautiously walked out of the house, mindful of the wood and age. His batons were in his pocket, because not only would they give him away, they were steel, not silver. He'd lifted two of the long silver nail-things from Felix's belt.

He passed Felix's mobile bunker and his own car, and crossed the road to another stretch of woods. It had been a little while since the 49er took off, and Jonah didn't really know where to go. But he trusted his gut. He was on the right track. What he found at the end of said track was another matter.

After about forty more yards, Jonah came to an opening in the trees. A thread of moonlight illuminated something that moved on the ground, which caught Jonah's attention.

"Looking for me?"

Jonah turned, but was caught across his chest with a hit that felt like rock. He slammed on his back, breath knocked out of him. The nails flew out of his hands.

"You've ruined everything," growled the 49er, who kicked Jonah's side a few times for good measure. "Why couldn't you just die? *WHY?*"

"Death isn't real," gasped Jonah. "I'm here to stop you."

"Are you, now?" sneered the 49er. "You think I'd let you do that after you wrecked my plans?"

Tired, disoriented, and hurting, Jonah got up off the ground. "You did everything you could to help Creyton when he wanted the Time Item," he said. "But now you're all ambitious. Now you've got aspirations. If Creyton were here, he'd kick your ass."

The 49er's eyes gleamed. "But he *isn't* here, boy. They are, though."

Jonah felt them before he saw them. A chill went down his spine as he looked behind himself.

There were at least fifty Haunts. The 49er had turned many spirits and spiritesses into Haunts, and clearly, Spectral Law didn't kill all of them. They were sequenced like an army, all growling and baring their ethereal steel teeth. It was Jonah's worst nightmare come true.

Almost like clockwork, the front few interlinked with the 49er, and he smiled.

"Felix is right, you know," he said. "You are a weak, untested novice. How many people must you fail before you realize that you have no chance? Why not just die. You'll never be man enough to take Altivera for your own, so why don't you just die, and let Felix have his way with her, sazer-style?"

The bile was almost sentient in the way it rose in Jonah's body. He doubled over and grabbed his head. His very brain hurt. He hadn't mastered the taint he'd received the first time, and now he had another piled on top of it. Through his squinted eyes, he saw that Haunts advancing, and the 49er's look of disappointment.

"I told Creyton you didn't look like much back at that bookstore, and I stand by that," he said. "Look at you now. A mistake on two legs that can't seem to recognize his betters."

Jonah focused on closing the mental cage door. Felix told him that he could do it, but then he said not even a half hour ago that he couldn't. It was up to him. He had to beat his body before his body beat him.

The 49er was still speaking. "But you're learning that now, because *I* taught you. Next, I'll teach Titus the Third and Felix, just like I taught their fathers. And then I'll finish up with your dear friends, starting with pretty little Altivera."

Still working on the cage, Jonah screwed his eyes open once more. He saw the 49er give him a cold smile, motion to the Haunts to take him, and then turn his back on him. He turned his back on Jonah like he was nothing. No threat at all. It pissed Jonah off.

So much so that the fresh anger slammed the cage door in his mind.

Jonah straightened, his mind and body clear of all Haunting taints. The ground underneath the Haunts began to rumble and crack, and unless he was much mistaken, blue shone through cracks just like it did on his batons when he had a spiritual endowment. When the object shot out of the ground, every Haunt was trapped.

The 49er, who'd turned in alarm at the rumbling, looked at the object in horror, and Jonah almost laughed.

It was a massive cage, blue like Jonah's aura. Almost electric blue. His weapon of expression was an actual cage. He also noticed something else. Every time a Haunt grazed the sides of the cage, it would yelp, and its body would steam. Hmm...

Experimentally, Jonah stretched out his hands and tightened them. The cage complied with his hand motions, and tightened in a very claustrophobic manner on the demon dogs. He saw the 49er's eyes widen in dread, which let him know that he was on the right path. He made fists, and the cage closed in on them. The predators quickly devolved into a sorry bunch as they yelped, howled, and stumbled across each other. But there was no escaping the cage. In seconds, they were totally consumed, and the cage vanished along with them. The 49er just stood there, dumbstruck.

"My pets," he rasped. "You—You—"

The 49er was stationary, but Jonah didn't take any chances. He threw a baton, and bashed him right between the eyes. When he fell backward, Jonah retrieved the silver nails (the Mind Cage had illuminated the place where they fell), hurried to the 49er, and plunged them into his heart.

The 49er's scream would have awakened the world. But there was one problem.

He writhed in agony. His skin took on a translucent, weakened quality. Lifeblood flowed from his mouth and nose. But he didn't wither and hollow out. He didn't devolve into a husk like the others vampires had. Jonah didn't know what to make of that.

The 49er spat blood on the ground, managed to turn on his side, and fixed Jonah with a malicious glare. "Y-Y-You've not won anything boy...storm's coming...you'll see."

He reached into his coat with difficulty and pulled out what looked like an oversized card. He threw it as best he could, but the wind caught it and landed on a rock. It never hit the ground.

"C-Consider it—" the 49er spat out more blood, "—a parting gift."

The wind picked up sharply, and Trip stepped out of nothingness. His nose was bleeding and he favored one side, but he looked like a man on a mission. He didn't even acknowledge Jonah's presence as he walked up to the 49er and pushed the nails further into his heart with his boot. The vampire screamed even further.

"Trip, I hit him with the silver, but he didn't hollow out," said Jonah. "Why hasn't it worked?"

"The 49er is unique," said Trip with no emotion. "A vampire who is formerly an Eleventh Percenter. You have to neutralize both of his natures simultaneously."

"I don't have any ethereal steel blades!" said Jonah. "I can't stab him with my baton!"

"Don't concern yourself with it, Rowe."

Trip reached into his own pocket and pulled out two more Mason jars. He uncapped one and pointed it down at the 49er. The Ghost Wave rumbled the soft earth so much that it actually lowered the vampire into the ground. Trip then burrowed the other jar into the dirt and stomped it. Jonah's ears popped when the Ghost Wave got released into the ground, but after a minute or so, it faded. There was silence.

"What did you do?" asked Jonah.

Trip stared at the ground as though he could still see the 49er. "The sound waves will repeatedly disturb the earth. He'll shift underground at intermittent points. He might be only halfway killed, but it doesn't matter. No one will ever find his body."

Jonah almost regarded Trip with admiration. The man got thrown through a wall. The fact that he was on his feet was a miracle. "The 49er mentioned a parting gift," he told him. "That mean anything to you?"

"No," said Trip.

"We probably ought to get back—"

"There is no *we*, Rowe," snapped Trip. "Tonight doesn't change a damn thing."

Jonah stared. "Are you an idiot? First, you send Felix into a frenzy, and now you're still acting like a—EVERYTHING has changed, Trip! You've been mad at the wrong person for years! The 49er killed your father, not Felix! You can reconcile things now."

"This didn't do me any favors, Rowe," said Trip lazily. "I hated my father."

"What! Then why—?"

"Didn't I already warn you about staying out of business that doesn't concern you?" asked Trip.

Jonah slowly shook his head. "I don't get you, Trip. I can't understand you at all."

Trip lit a cigarette, took a long draw, and returned his gaze to Jonah. "Don't even try to figure me out, Rowe," he said. "I'll always be two steps ahead of you."

He dusted ashes from the cigarette, and left the scene via the *Astralimes*. Jonah just looked at the open air where Trip had been.

"The hell with you, too," he muttered.

He turned to head back to Carruthers House when the moonlight illuminated the card the 49er threw. The card looked very strange to Jonah; it seemed an odd thing to discard. He picked it up and held it close to his face because he didn't have his reading glasses.

The card had an illustration of an exposed sword above an open eye. At the bottom was the word *SCIUS*. It didn't mean anything to him, so he shrugged and tossed it down. Then something strange happened.

When the card made contact with the earth, it began to smoke, and then caught fire. The card itself didn't burn; its outer layer burned away, and the ground rumbled through the entire area, like a random pocket of Trip's Ghost Wave returned to make a last hit. Jonah picked the card up once more. It had a new illustration on it. The old illustration was an exposed blade above an open eye and said *SCIUS*, but this new illustration showed a sheathed blade above a closed eye. There was even a new word there in the place of the old one.

The new word was *INIMICUS*.

Jonah returned to Carruthers House with every intention of forgetting what had just occurred. Scius…Inimicus…didn't anyone speak English?

Then he saw something that almost wiped it from his mind.

The shed where Jonah asked the sazer boy to imprison Felix no longer had a door. It was completely smashed. Terrence, Reena, and the boy were nowhere in sight.

What had happened? Had Felix not come down from Red Rage? Was he still out of control?

Christ alive, if he'd broken free and hurt Jonah's friends…

He yanked both batons out of his pocket, and ran to the shed…to find Felix still seated there. His eyes, which had previously contemplated the ceiling, lowered to Jonah.

"What do you expect me to say?" he demanded. "I'm sorry?"

Jonah was so relieved that Felix was no longer in Red Rage that he simply shook his head.

"Well that's a shame." said Felix. "Because I am."

"Huh?" said Jonah.

"I'm sorry," said Felix, with full sincerity. "I let my anger get the best of me, and made an ass of myself. You were right; I do have a choice. Which is why I decided to sit right here after I destroyed the door, and employ my breathing techniques until I cooled down."

He offered Jonah a hand, and Jonah shook it. Just then, Terrence, Reena, and the sazer boy came to the door, all pleased to see Jonah back healthy and whole.

"Hey, Jonah!" Reena was not only relieved to see him back safe, but also relieved to see that Felix had calmed. "Is the 49er gone?"

"Well that's an interesting story," murmured Jonah. "See—"

Terrence coughed a dry hack, and Jonah saw smoke.

Wait. Smoke?

Then Terrence roared like he was in pain, and collapsed. Jonah hurried forward, Felix right behind him.

"MY INSIDES ARE ON FIRE!" shouted Terrence. "IT BURNS! *IT BURNS!*"

"What the hell?" demanded Jonah. "Why would his insides feel like that? Bad acid reflux or something?"

"Acid reflux doesn't make your mouth smoke, Jonah!" said Reena.

Felix had a look in his eye that Jonah didn't like.

"What are you thinking, Felix?"

Felix ignored the question. "What has Terrence eaten this evening?"

"The usual garbage," replied Reena, "but what's that got to do with anything?"

It looked to Jonah like Felix choked back a sarcastic comment. "Bit more specific, please?"

"They had rigatoni and—" Reena's eyes bulged, "—and garlic toast."

"Garlic is burning—" Jonah didn't even finish. Realization hit him like direct sunlight. Garlic was burning Terrence's insides...

He thought about the blood he'd seen on Terrence's arm earlier, which he'd attributed to a glass cut—it must not have been a cut—

"Felix." Desperation infected Jonah's whole being, much like a Haunting. "What do we need to do? Tell me!"

Felix looked pained. "Call Terrence's family," he said quietly. "Tell them they need to say goodbye."

21

Blank Slate

Jonah hadn't ever felt such a collection of emotions in his entire life. Anger at the 49er for the lives he destroyed, which included Pilar Contesa. Fear for Terrence. Annoyance that Felix didn't have a ready-made solution to the problem. Anger with himself for not preventing the problem in the first place. And a bizarre relief that the need for a Mind Cage had passed.

They used the *Astralimes* to get back to the estate. Reena didn't use subtlety or discretion; they traveled directly in the infirmary, where they deposited an unconscious Terrence (Jonah's new sazer friend performed another brutal kindness, and punched Terrence out) onto a bed.

"Felix, I need you to find Jonathan, Liz, Ben-Israel, Alvin, and Bobby," she ordered. "You, boy, go round up every cat that you see. If you can, locate a calico named Bast. Go!"

The boy hurried off like he knew the layout of the estate or something. Felix followed him, but not before throwing Jonah and Reena another futile look. Jonah looked at Reena in confusion.

"I get calling Jonathan, Liz, and Ben-Israel," he said, "but what you do need the heralds for?"

Reena barely looked at him as she felt for a pulse in Terrence's wrist and neck. "The heralds monitor the spirits, and make certain that they don't depart their physical bodies before their time. I hope that they can keep Terrence's spirit right here."

Jonah looked down at Terrence with another stab of dread. He looked like he was in a pained sleep. He knew that Reena had a thorough understanding of many things that concerned the Eleventh Percent, but he also knew that all her know-how might not be enough this time.

"Reena, has a resident here even been bitten by a vampire before?" he asked.

"No," said Reena, who attempted to keep fear out of her voice. "These are uncharted waters, Jonah."

Jonah made a sour face. Weird things happened in the ethereal world all the time, but this particular one had to be unique? Seriously?

The infirmary door burst open, and all of the requested presences filled the place. Jonathan materialized next to Bast and seven of her herald friends (Jonah was thankful and awed by the sazer boy's efficiency), and Liz and Ben-Israel were at Terrence's side in seconds. Felix stood apart from them, his face an impassive mask. Jonah tried very hard to ignore him, but he was smart enough to know what Felix's demeanor signified. No doubt he'd seen numerous situations identical to this one, and simply didn't have the heart or nerve to tell people that curing vampirism couldn't be done.

"How long ago did the bite occur?" asked Liz.

"Little less than two hours," said Jonah. "What's that got to do with any—?"

"Did the bite occur on his neck?"

"No, it was his forearm."

Ben Israel grabbed Terrence's arm and turned it over to discover the tell-tale bite mark just inches below his elbow. Jonathan winced.

"Since it wasn't a direct bite, Elizabeth," he said, "you have an opportunity—"

"Wonderful, sir!" interrupted Liz. "Tell me what to do—"

Liz's excitement faded because the somber expression on Jonathan's face hadn't wavered.

"You have an opportunity to postpone the spread of the vampirism," he finished.

Every face in the room fell except for Felix, whose businesslike countenance really infuriated Jonah. Apparently, Bobby, too.

"You need to do something, Duscere!" he barked at him. "You're the one who knows all about vampires!"

"Vampirism isn't a disease that you can just catch and have cured," said Felix. 'It's a curse. Nothing in those Green Aura healing satchels will do anything."

"Don't give me that!" snapped Alvin in a harsh tone that Jonah had never heard before. "This is our brother, man! You had damn well better fix this, and you'd better do a better job with it than you did protecting us from the 49er!"

Felix's eyes flashed, which prompted Jonah to scramble to his feet.

"Stop," he said to Alvin. "We're all scared here, man. Let's use our energy on finding a solution and not pointing fingers."

Jonah knew that Alvin may have been a little justified in his stance, but he'd also seen Felix pushed over the edge. That wasn't going to happen again. Red Rage had no place at the estate, let alone the infirmary.

"Jonah's right." Jonathan's voice carried that iron authority it sometimes had. "Felix, harsh reality helps nothing. As long as Terrence has not turned, there is hope. And Alvin...you need to call your parents."

Alvin paled, but Bobby stood up.

"I'll go with you, big bro," he said, and then he looked at Liz. "If anyone's capable of a miracle, you are, Lizzie."

Jonah winced. He wished Bobby hadn't said that. He was unaware of the pressure he just placed on his girlfriend's shoulders. Liz didn't answer, but she blinked a couple times. Reena glanced over at Bobby.

"Liz is not alone," she said to him. "Now, please give us room to work. Go call Mr. and Mrs. Decessio."

Alvin and Bobby left, which decreased the tension, if only by a fraction. Jonathan went to Ben-Israel's healing satchel and grabbed a clear vial full of something that looked like lemonade, and another vial full of something purple.

"Ben-Israel, this one—" he indicated the yellow fluid, "—goes on Terrence's bites. Five drops on each wound. Then put a teaspoon of this purple tonic into his mouth."

"Certainly, sir," said Ben-Israel. "But, if I may be so bold, what will this accomplish?"

"It'll slow the vampiric blood's progression to a snail's pace," answered Jonathan. "It'll buy us more time to organize options."

"How do you know that, sir?" asked Liz.

"It's my duty to know how to protect my students, Elizabeth," said Jonathan.

Liz asked no more questions, and followed Jonathan's instructions. A tense expression tightened Terrence's face for a second, like he'd had an uncomfortable dream. Liz splayed her green-gleaming fingers from Terrence's torso to his throat.

"That couldn't have happened at a better time," she breathed. "The internal burns from the garlic were already beginning to heal."

At that moment, Felix's and the sazer boy's heads shot up. Jonah felt more and more useless with each passing bit of information.

"What does that mean?" he asked.

The sazer boy looked really tense. "Means Terrence done started regenerating like a vampire."

Jonah clenched his fists. He saw Reena's eyes lower to the ground. Despite the temporary boon, tears fell down Liz's face, and Jonathan pulled her over to the side and told her words that only she could hear. "Is there anything *I* can do to help?" he felt agonized by this. "Just give me something to do!"

Jonathan turned from Liz for a second, and eyed Jonah in a curious way. "You *are* helping, Jonah. Haven't you seen your fingers?"

Jonah unclenched his fists with a frown, and was surprised to discover that his fingertips glowed with the blue of his aura. Huh. "What does this mean? How does it help Terrence?"

"You're using your balancing power to filter away excess tension," Jonathan explained. "You've leveled out to the infirmary greatly."

"Oh, have I?" said Jonah a little coldly. "We are worried sick, Jonathan. Liz is in tears. Reena is about to break something. And this infirmary is *level?*"

"Have you ever been in a sickroom with full, unbridled emotions?" asked Ben-Israel. "It's not pretty. This situation is almost calm compared to what can happen."

"This is driving me crazy!" said Liz angrily. "We are supposed to be organizing options, but I can't think of any! If I had to fail, why did it have to be now?"

"Don't you dare do that to yourself, Liz," said Jonah. "It's not up to you to fix this by yourself. No one here blames you, and I have no doubts that Terrence wouldn't, either."

"There has got to be something that can be done," whispered Liz.

"Don't hurt yourself like that…Elizabeth, was it?" said the sazer boy. "We slowed it up. Got ourselves some extra time. But if he turns, don't blame yourself. This ain't in your control."

"Wrong answer," said Liz, defiance in her tone. "I can't accept that."

"Elizabeth," said Ben-Israel after he poured more slowing tonic in Terrence's mouth, "I'm as much a Green Aura as you, but we might have to accept defeat here. Besides making him comfortable, there may very well be nothing we can do."

Reena suddenly stood up. She'd been silent for a while now. "There is something we can do," she said.

She walked out of the infirmary. Everyone stared after her. Jonah had half a mind to follow her, but Jonathan noticed and shook his head.

Reena returned with a medium-sized box in her hands. She took a deep breath, and seemed to steel herself. "Felix, Ben-Israel, Liz, kid—leave. Jonathan, I know I can't make you do anything—"

"Reena, you are one of my most talented students," interrupted Jonah, who clearly understood something that Jonah still didn't. "I trust your judgment, and support you wholeheartedly. Everyone, you heard her."

Jonathan walked out the infirmary as opposed to vanishing, and Ben-Israel, Felix, and the sazer boy followed suit. The heralds remained, but Liz hadn't budged.

"Liz," said Reena, "please leave."

"No," said Liz as she wiped away her tears.

"Am I missing something?" asked Jonah. "It's been a long night, and my mind's gotten quite a workout. Maybe that's why I'm not following right now."

Liz and Reena ignored him.

"Elizabeth," said Reena slowly, "I am asking you nicely to—"

"I'm not leaving, Reena," said Liz flat-out. "I know what that is."

Reena's eyes widened, and Jonah finally figured it out. But no. Reena couldn't be!

"You know?" she asked.

"I've known all along, Reena," said Liz. "You came to me for plant research. You think I wouldn't know if someone was making a nullifying agent?"

"Reena," breathed Jonah. "Are you really—?"

Reena opened the box and revealed the long vial of red liquid. Both he and Liz moved closer to her. Reena still had her eyes on Liz.

"I can't believe you've known all along," she told her. "What were you planning to do with that information?"

"I was creating an antidote," Liz confessed. "You know, in the event that you realized you'd made a mistake."

Reena stared at Liz for five straight seconds, and then snorted. "Destroy it."

"Are you sure about this, Reena? asked Jonah, who brought a hand to her wrist. "I never wanted you to go through with it, but—are you sure? That is your joy—your freedom. Your shot at being a normal woman."

Reena took another deep breath. "Normal is overrated, Jonah. This is who I am, just like you said on Christmas Day. Liz, do you have a sy—?"

Liz surprised her by holding a syringe under her nose. "I had an idea where you were going when you left," she explained.

Jonah couldn't believe it. Reena had been so adamant, so set on purging her ethereality. Now her plan was to sacrifice it. It brought about conflicting emotions.

"Will it work?" he asked her.

"Yes." Reena sounded so confident that it wasn't even funny. "This solution is meant to purge one of an existing nature. If it would have turned me from an Eleventh to a Tenth, then it will purge Terrence of the vampirism and return him to a full ethereal human."

She looked at the heralds, who'd observed this entire thing. "Two of you on the left of the bed, two of you on the right, and two of you at the foot."

"What do you need them to position themselves like that for?" asked Jonah.

"The heralds will keep Terrence's spirit stationary," said Reena, "for when Liz resets him."

Liz blinked. "Excuse me?"

"It makes perfect sense," said Reena, who drew up the entirety of her solution into the syringe. "I still remember your computer reboot metaphor from last year. Computers restart for the benefits to take effect. When Terrence is reset, the solution will take hold. But it has to be when he is a blank slate. When his functions resume, he will be Terrence again."

Jonah didn't understand it all, but he got enough of it to be concerned. "Are you sure this will work?"

"Yes," said Reena.

"Why are you so sure?"

Reena looked Jonah in the eye. "Because it has to."

"Huh." Jonah was dubious, but didn't argue. "Okay. Liz, are you sure that the resetting thing will work?"

"Oh yeah," said Liz. "I'd bet it on everything I own."

Jonah nodded. He had to trust them. "How can I help?"

"Just keep on maintaining the balance like you've been doing," said Reena.

"Can do." Jonah tried to intensify his focus. If he'd already been doing such a great job unconsciously, it could only improve if he actually focused.

Reena nudged Terrence. He stirred, and opened his eyes, which shocked them all for a moment. The brown of his irises was significantly diluted. It was almost gone. His pupils seemed a bit sharper, much like the beasts they'd fought hours ago.

"R-Reena," he mumbled. "You guys gonna have to put me down?"

Jonah noticed Terrence's teeth when he spoke. The incisors were longer than usual.

"Not today," said Reena, lifting the syringe. "We are going to make you better."

Terrence's discolored eyes moved to the liquid. "That's your joy stuff, ain't it?"

"Yes," said Reena.

"You're giving that up for me?" murmured Terrence.

"No," said Reena. "I'm giving it up for *me.*"

She nodded at Liz, who gave a specific spot on Terrence's torso a hard press. Terrence exhaled, and relaxed as his whole body ceased. The process was almost instantaneous.

"Here we go," said Reena, and she emptied the syringe into Terrence's chest.

Jonah looked around to see the heralds concentrating hard on keeping Terrence's spirit in place. He hoped his balancing power helped them, too.

"Twenty seconds and counting," said Liz.

Jonah gritted his teeth. Those twenty seconds could have been twenty lifetimes.

Then Terrence took in a slow, smooth breath. His chest began to rise and fall in a rhythmic pattern.

"How do we know it worked?" asked Jonah.

He needn't have asked, because when Terrence took in another breath, his eyes opened slightly. The irises were brown again, and the pupils had filled out to their original state. For further reassurance, Liz checked his incisors to discover that they'd shortened to their normal size.

Reena and Liz clamped hands and grinned at each other. Jonah sat back and let relief alleviate all the tension in his body.

"I know one for sure," he said as he leaned back in his chair.

"What's that?" asked Reena.

Jonah raised his fingers to his temples. "I don't ever want to see a vampire again. Not ever."

22

The High Road

Terrence's recovery was a much steadier one after Reena and Liz chased away the vampirism. Liz insisted that he remain in the infirmary just a bit longer so that his recovery hit no snags, but luckily, all was well. The only change that anyone saw was a taste aversion to anything with garlic in it.

"It sucks something awful, too," he lamented one day after his parents came to check in on him. "Never again can I eat garlic toast. It was one of my favorite things."

"Terrence," chided Reena, "that crap is laced with so many impurities that it can only be classified as toast by the loosest definition."

Jonah and Terrence glanced at each other, but neither of them was annoyed so much as relieved that Reena was back to her old self. Still.

"Reena," said Jonah in a cautious tone, "do you have any regrets?"

Reena looked out of a nearby window. "Want to know the funny thing? No. I don't have a single one. I remember that argument that we had on Christmas. Specifically the part where I spoke on the things that I said I'd be glad to lose. But if I hadn't had those gifts, I couldn't have aided you in ending the 49er's threat. I never would have reached Trip in time to snatch away his Ghost Wave. I might have had issues making connections with Reverend Abbott's information. There are so many things that I could have lost. I just didn't think of them when I got caught up in that moment. Don't get me wrong. That sazer attack years ago, the dampener incident, and the Haunting were all horrifying, but they didn't justify purging who I am. I'd have done myself a great disservice by taking that solution."

Terrence hoisted himself up on his pillow. "And Kendall? 'Cuz let's face facts, Reena…it had to do with her, too."

Reena didn't even argue the point. "If we're meant to be, and I truly believe we are, she's going to have to love me for me. That doesn't seem to be an issue so far. I haven't had to change anything."

Reena grinned, and Jonah shook his head. Who would have thought that underneath all Reena's hard exteriors, she was a hopeless romantic?

"I can't thank the both of you enough," she said to Jonah and Terrence. "You guys never wavered, and didn't abandon me when I lost my way. You are true family."

Jonah smiled to himself. He was glad to hear Reena say that.

"You do realize what this means, right?" she asked Jonah.

"Um…what?"

"You're going to have to teach Terrence, Douglas, and me how to do Mentis Caveas so as to get the Haunting taint out of us!"

Jonah's eyes widened. "It's a highly emotional process, Reena. It ain't easy."

Reena scoffed. "What else is new? But if you try to slap me, I will kick your ass."

Jonah just looked at her, and then laughed. "Fine. I think I can do that. Glad you're back, Reena. And I'm glad you've found a kindred spirit that has no issue admitting to anyone that she's in love with you. Right, Terrence?"

Terrence's lip curled. Jonah eyed him with a bit more intensity.

"*Right,* Terrence?"

"Yeah," sighed Terrence. "Yeah, right."

"Speaking of spirit," Reena was suddenly annoyed, "Bast brought me this early in the morning. Got it from Mr. Ruben."

"Mr. Ruben?" frowned Jonah. "But that means—"

Sure enough, the rather thick letter was embossed with the *ScarYous* imprint.

Jonah's face hardened. Turk Landry's season wrapped up filming a week prior, and all things *ScarYous* were gone. Jonah could have declared the day that Landry left Rome a national holiday. But what was the deal with the letter?

Moving nearer to each other, they read:

Mr. Aldercy, Miss Katoa, and Mr. Rowe,

I pray that this letter finds you well, and of sound mind.

I have thought at length of all the superficial trappings that my endeavors have granted me, but in light of my experiences with you three, I find my selfish justifications have been shaken.

"Shaken?" Jonah frowned. "What the hell does that mean?"

"Don't know, but I imagine we'll find out soon enough," said Terrence tersely. They read on:

I wish that I could have assisted you, but I pray that you understand the complicated situation in which I am so tightly placed. I wish to atone, but that process will take time. Thank you for this clarity. I have enclosed a small gift to illustrate the initial stages of said atonement. Please enjoy.

In spirit and all things paranormal,

Turk Landry

Jonah pulled a second folded piece of paper out of the envelope, and opened it. Three blank checks fell out of it.

"Atonement," muttered Jonah. "When the hell has atonement ever included a blank check?"

"I'll be damned," said Terrence, "even his apology is arrogant."

Reena picked up one of the checks and shook her head. "That letter was such farce. I could sum it up in one sentence: I'm scared that you might expose me, so I'm prepared to compensate you if you keep my secret."

She made to tear the check in two.

"NO!" shouted Jonah and Terrence at once.

Reena started at their reaction. "What? It's dirty money, even *if* the check is blank. It's blood money. *Lifeblood* money."

"Reena, all money that is in circulation has been spent on at least one dirty deed at some point or another," reasoned Jonah, who picked up one check, and handed Terrence the other. "So here is what you do. You take this lifeblood money, and do something good with it." He looked at Terrence again. "I'm really sorry that Turk Landry turned out to be a—whatever he is. The situation is too complicated to simply label him a fake, but... you know what I mean. I'm sorry."

Terrence made a face, but then smiled. "It's not your fault," he said. "Punk doesn't matter. Besides, he isn't the only paranormal show that's in the game. I've already found another show."

"Have you, now?" asked Jonah.

"Yep," said Terrence. "It's called *Grave Messages.* It's even better that *ScarYous,* and it's hosted by a woman. A hot one at that!"

"Okay, Terrence." Jonah glanced at Reena, who rolled her eyes. "I'm just glad that you're back to normal as well."

Surprisingly, the sazer boy was a hit with the residents of the estate (save Trip and his buddies, but whatever). He had a remarkable sense of humor, and was fascinated by the aspect of so many people comfortably congregated in one place. He was pleasant company, particularly after a bath. Regular showers and clean clothes made him a brand new creature.

"Will you please tell us your name now?" Jonah asked him after Terrence's recovery dinner, where the boy almost outstripped Terrence in food consumption. "Because personally, I'm tired of calling you Boy."

The boy slowly put down his fork and raised his eyes to them. "Don't know," he said quietly. "That's why I didn't answer you the night I first met you. I had a name back at the foster home when I was little, but I never heard it again after I ran away. I don't remember it. All of the people I met on the road called me *kid,* or *pal.* I got nothing else for you."

"Oh, man," said Terrence. "We gotta come up with a name for you."

Jonathan looked thoughtful. "Jonah showed him kindness, and that resonated with him. He always managed to find his way back to people whom he could help, or people who could help him."

Reverend Abbott smiled. "Kind of like the prodigal son."

"Huh." The boy glanced up at Reverend Abbott, and a smile lit up his features. "Prodigal. I like it!"

"You don't understand," said Reena patiently. "That isn't an actual name."

The boy looked at her like he didn't understand the argument. "I still like it."

"What the hell," said Terrence, spreading his hands. "Prodigal it is."

Jonah turned it over in his mind. It sounded better and better the more he thought on it. "So what are you going to do now, Prodigal?"

Felix spoke before Prodigal could. "I can help him out, no problem."

"What are you talking about?" said Terrence. "Like adopt him, or something?"

Neither Felix nor Prodigal looked amenable to that.

"That might not be the best course of action," said Felix. "He's a runaway, not in the system, and doesn't have a proper name. But I can see to it that he has what he needs."

"Hate to be a downer," said Jonah, "but needs require money."

Felix pulled out the lighter that once belonged to his father and lit it a couple times. "Money isn't an issue for me."

Reena raised an eyebrow. "What does that mean? Do you have an panic stash, or something?"

For some reason, Jonathan laughed to himself. Felix still looked rather awkward.

"It's not exactly *panic*, but I do have a stash."

Jonah got burned out on Felix's enigmatic words a while back. "Come on, dude. You have some wads in your sock, a lockbox in the ground—?"

"I'm loaded, okay?" Felix blurted out. "Second-generation rich kid. I have more money than I'll ever spend. You happy now?"

Jonah blinked. Terrence dropped his fork, and Reena looked like she'd been shot. Felix didn't seem smug about it. He actually looked embarrassed.

"You're second-generation rich?" asked Jonah.

"Yes," said Felix. "My parents left me money. Plus, bounty-hunting can be fortuitous as well. The point is I can help Prodigal out, and see to it that he has essentials for the foreseeable future. Prodigal, let's talk."

The two of them left the kitchen. Reverend Abbott excused himself, and Terrence followed Felix and Prodigal. Reena went after him, and Jonah suspected that she did that to curtail Terrence's nosiness. It took Jonah a few seconds to realize that these departures left him alone with Jonathan for the first time in a while.

"I'm proud of you, Jonah," he said.

"What for?" asked Jonah. "The 49er didn't even get vanquished. Don't get me wrong, I'm glad that everyone is okay, and that the spirits and their lifeblood are safe. But that thing is still out there in the ground somewhere."

Jonathan nodded. "Very true. But if Titus employed Ghost Waves to disrupt the earth, we may never lay eyes on the 49er again."

Jonah half-shrugged. Small comfort, that. Jonathan took a step closer.

"You exposed the 49er's plan, Jonah," he said. "You provided your friends with the necessary weapons to defend themselves against a cabal of vampires. You mastered a Mentis Cavea, which is Networker-level defense, and most importantly, your actions led to the clearing of innocent names, as well as resolution to an age-old scandal."

Jonah scoffed. "It wasn't like Titus, Jr. was innocent. And after all that's happened, I thought that Trip might have changed somewhat. But he said he hated his father. That didn't explain why he was so keen of avenging his killing."

Jonah lowered himself into the seat that Prodigal vacated. Jonathan remained standing.

"Jonah, Titus's life has not been a pretty one," he said. "I'm not making excuses for some of his unsavory behaviors, but I can assure you that negative feelings that have inhabited one's mind for years won't just evaporate with one revelation."

Jonah had to admit a feeling of surprise. That actually made sense. Jonathan didn't wrap it in a riddle. But still. "Jonathan, Trip said he hated his father."

"It was still his father, Jonah," said Jonathan. "He was indeed a follower of Creyton, and an evil man. I am not disputing that. All I am saying is that the complexities of blood ties make a situation a very grey area. There can be no black and white. The 49er brought a great deal of trauma on both Titus and Felix, whose lives were complicated, anyway. There are factors and variables in their lives that simply wouldn't be undone in a night."

Jonathan's words triggered something in Jonah's mind. "The 49er caused trauma, which all went back to Creyton."

He stood up and looked out of the window, where he allowed himself a laugh at Liz running around with Bobby's football.

"Speak your mind, Jonah," said Jonathan. "Don't be afraid."

Jonah sighed. "I didn't want to bring this up around everyone, because they're so relieved, which is just fine. They should feel that way. But what the 49er did...there was just something odd about it."

Jonathan didn't say anything. Jonah took that to mean that he could continue.

"The 49er's plan to wipe out his biggest threats and take Creyton's place as top dog—I get that part. I would have been completely satisfied with that story, but one thing didn't smell right."

"What was that, son?" asked Jonathan.

"The lifeblood," said Jonah. "In the very beginning, right when Felix first showed up, he told us that the 49er was collecting lifeblood, hoping to get his samples up to a certain number. I know things went sideways from there, but I never forgot that piece about the lifeblood samples. It made me think that—that there might have been another plan in place before the 49er hijacked things and tried to take Creyton's place."

To Jonah's surprise, Jonathan nodded.

"So you thought that, too?" the Protector Guide asked him.

Jonah frowned. "You suspected that?"

"I did," said Jonathan. "The 49er is a dangerous being, but he wasn't ever bright or calculating. I never forgot the lifeblood samples, either. But what I do know is that the 49er's plan—hijacked or otherwise—was thwarted by you and your friends. We may never know the full rundown, but all that matters is that the schemes came to naught. So that is what we will take from the experience."

There was one other thing that bugged Jonah, but he had no interest in sharing it with Jonathan. He just didn't need the cryptic riddles. He wanted a direct answer, and luckily, he knew where to get it.

"Malcolm?" he called as he knocked on the door of the woodshop. "Malcolm, you in here?"

Seconds later, the familiar buzz-cut head poked out from behind a half-finished archway. "Hey, Jonah. What d'you need?"

Jonah stepped inside the shed, and shut door. "Your Latin expertise."

Malcolm laughed and returned to his carpentry. "Okay, shoot."

Jonah cleared his throat. "I came across some Latin terms—somewhere—and I had never of them in my life."

"Yeah?" said Malcolm idly. "What were these terms?"

"One was Scius, and the other one was Inimicus."

Malcolm looked at Jonah with a frown. "Have you been in Jonathan's study?"

"No I haven't," said Jonah. "Why?"

"Those terms are on two of the Spectrology cards."

"Spectrology cards? What are those?"

"It's an eighty-four card deck," explained Malcolm. "Kind of like spiritual Tarot."

"Really?" said Jonah. "Well, what do they mean?"

"I won't bore you with the whole deck," said Malcolm, "but the two you mentioned are called the Gloved cards."

"What the hell does that mean?" asked Jonah, baffled. "You have to wear gloves to hold them or something?"

"Not at all," said Malcolm. "They are called Gloved cards because, like gloves, they come in a pair. The first one is Scius, and that's supposed to be the obvious enemy. The one you can see. The other one, Inimicus, is the embedded enemy. The one you can't see."

Jonah felt a slight chill. "So Scius is basically the devil you know, and Inimicus is the devil you don't?"

Malcolm lowered his chisel so that he could focus better on Jonah. "It's not that clear-cut. Inimicus is not quite the devil you don't know. It's more like the devil you *don't* know you don't know. The one you never saw coming in a million lifetimes. That's why they say embedded enemy."

Jonah didn't like the thought of that at all.

"But it's just a stupid myth," said Malcolm. "A game."

"Okay," said Jonah delicately. "How would you play the game? In regards to Scius and Inimicus, I mean."

"According to what I read years ago, Scius goes out to handle some business or whatever," began Malcolm. "If Scius succeeds, then great. But if Scius fails, then they're supposed to take out the Scius card, and touch the ground with it. The card touching the ground alerts Inimicus that Scius failed, and it's time for them to take over the business."

Jonah stared. That's exactly what happened that night with the 49er.

"But you need to forget that game, Jonah," said Malcolm, who returned to the archway work. "I don't know where you heard those terms, but it doesn't even matter. It's just a game."

"Yeah..." mumbled Jonah. "Just a game."

"By the way," said Malcolm, "you might want to say goodbye to Felix. He's hitting the road in a few."

"What?" The cards flew to the back of Jonah's mind. "He can't go yet! I've got something for him!"

Jonah left Malcolm's woodshop, raced to his room, and then back out onto the grounds.

Not a moment too soon. He caught Felix as he slung a bag into the back of his mobile bunker.

Felix saw Jonah's hurried approach and threw him a cautious look. "Jonah? You're not coming to attack me, are you?"

"No, of course not," panted Jonah. "I have something for you."

He handed Felix a folder. Felix took it, curious.

"What's this?"

"It's information," said Jonah. "It'll clear that crime of passion charge off of your record on the Tenth side of things."

Felix's eyes widened.

"We all knew that Jonah would present the new information about that night to the Phasmastis Curaie, which would clear you on the ethereal side," said Jonah. "But this'll please the Tenth justice system. It will make all the old evidence circumstantial."

Felix regarded the file as though it were a diamond. He even tightened his grasp on it. "How did you get this? How did you find this?"

"Reverend Abbott did me a favor," Jonah explained. "He thought the whole situation was—ah—gift-wrapped a little too perfectly. Those were his exact words. But he always knew something didn't smell right."

"Ahhh." Felix nodded. "The Reverend was involved in ethereal crimes before he took over at Serenity Road."

"Yep," said Jonah. "I knew that Reverend Abbott hadn't always been a holy man."

Felix focused on Jonah. "You really are a remarkable Eleventh Percenter, Jonah."

Jonah's eyes bulged. Did he hear the man right?

"Oh, don't look so surprised," scoffed Felix. "I admit that I wasn't so sure about you that first night, when you were blubbering and Haunted, but you've shown me a lot since then. Not to mention your mastery of the Mentis—oh, the hell with it—Mind Cage."

Jonah chuckled in a nervous sort of way. "Praise? Humor? I'm going to slowly back away now…"

They laughed. It was good to see another piece of Felix's personality.

"Okay, now I'll let you go," said Jonah.

He made to back off, and Felix headed to his Jeep. Then he wheeled around.

"Hang on a second, Jonah." He grabbed something from the driver's seat. "I almost forgot. Luther Coy."

Jonah blinked. "Are you speaking in code or something?"

"No," said Felix. "Luther Coy was the name of your father."

Jonah flinched. He was that stunned. Of all the things that Felix might have said, he didn't expect that one. "My…father?"

"Funny that you brought me a file," said Felix. "I've got something for you, too." He placed a thin manila folder into Jonah's unsteady hands. "Luther Lane Coy. Born July 27th, 1947 in Washington, D.C."

1947. He always knew that his parents had been nineteen years apart. The man was forty when Jonah came along.

"I didn't bother looking up your mom," Felix went on," I assumed your grandmother gave you all the information that she felt you needed on her. But I remember you told me that she hadn't been all that forthcoming concerning your dad."

Jonah shook his head numbly. "She didn't even tell me his name. She hated him. I think we had maybe one conversation about him, and that lasted maybe two minutes."

Felix nodded. "Figured that. Open it up."

Jonah opened the folder, and just stared at the picture. It was like an aged picture of himself. Everything was the same: Brown hair, hazel eyes, slightly pointed nose—even his ears were the same as this guy's. If he hadn't had a full beard, Jonah would have said that he was this man's twin on a forty-year delay. "Wait," he said suddenly. "You said Luther Coy *was* his name. Is he in Spirit?"

Felix nodded. "It's my understanding that he couldn't cover a gambling debt. You would have been fifteen, give or take."

Jonah didn't know what to think, or how to feel. Nana had hated this man's guts, so the picture that he painted in his mind was far from a great one. The thoughts had always been bad. But now, there was only confusion. He always wondered how he'd react if he met his father, what he'd say. And now he'd just discovered that his father, Luther, had been in Spirit for nearly ten years. "How did you find all this?"

"I have my ways," replied Felix.

"Why did you do it?"

Felix squared his shoulders. "So that you could make your own choice."

"What?"

"Remember what you told me about choice that night I went into Red Rage?" asked Felix. "Well, you didn't have a choice concerning Luther. All you had were feelings of anger, inadequacy, confusion, and the handful of words your grandmother gave you. She made the choice for you, which I completely understand. But now you get to make your own choice. And now you have a name and a face to put that mass of emotions to. All the necessary pieces to take the high road, and make your emotions finally work for you."

Jonah let that sink in. It was going to take a minute. Or an hour. "Was he married?" he asked. "Was I the product of an extramarital affair?"

Felix sighed. "Yes. His widow is now remarried, and lives in Rhode Island. He had a daughter with her. But he had other children outside of his marriage as well. In addition to that sister, you have another sister, and at least two brothers. I have the page with their information here—"

"No." The certainty in Jonah's voice was so strong that he even surprised himself. "Burn it. You can burn this picture of my father, too." He pointed to the estate. "The people in there are my family. *They* are my brothers and sisters."

Felix half-smiled, pulled out his father's lighter, and incinerated the page, along Luther Coy's picture. Jonah watched them burn, with a nary a regret or doubt.

"I'd better be going now." Felix shook Jonah's hand, and climbed into the mobile bunker. "It's been a pleasure, Jonah. I have no doubts we'll see each other again. Until then."

He gave a two-fingered wave, and went off down the gravel drive.

"He's gone?" said a familiar voice.

Jonah turned to see Vera behind him. She had on the *Wicked* T-Shirt.

"Yeah, he had to head on out," said Jonah. He filed away what he just learned. The past was what it was. "You're wearing my gift?"

"Of course I am," said Vera. "It is sacred, but it's too damn special to hide."

Jonah had to stifle the grin that almost illuminated his face. "It is? Because I thought—you know—the roses Felix gave you—"

Vera's eyes widened with comprehension. "Oh, Jonah—you've gone all this time thinking I was partial to Felix's Christmas present?"

"No," said Jonah too quickly. "Not at all."

Vera rolled her eyes. "I heard that you got an A in your creative writing class," she said, "so you better be glad that you're a better writer than you are liar."

Jonah felt his face warm, yet again. She'd nailed him.

"Let me explain, Jonah," said Vera. "You know I'm a stage actress, but events in my life have kept me off the stage for a while now. I like it here at the estate, but I still miss it. Anyway, when my friends and I started, we were starving artists. Some of the places we did plays in were so low-end that the male actors got paid in McDonald's coupons, and we actresses got paid in roses. Like I said,

I miss the stage, and Felix's roses were a nice reminder. I didn't act like that to blow you off! I loved your gifts!"

Those words pushed Inimicus, Luther Coy, and any remaining jealousy of Felix away.

"Jonah, you needn't impress me," said Vera. "I'm a simple woman. I'd be just as pleased with a nice dinner, followed by a show."

Jonah grinned as Turk Landry's blank check burned in his pocket. "Really, now?"

About the Author

T.H. Morris was born in Colerain, North Carolina in 1984, and has been writing in some way, shape, or form ever since he was able to hold a pen or pencil. He relocated to Greensboro, North Carolina in 2002 for undergraduate education.

He is an avid reader, mainly in the genre of science fiction and fantasy, along with the occasional mystery or thriller. He is also a gamer and loves to exercise, Netflix binge, and meet new people. He began to write *The 11th Percent* series in 2011, and published book 1, *The 11th Percent*, in 2014, followed by book 2, *Item and Time*, in May of 2015.

He still resides in Greensboro with his wife, Candace.

Connect Online!

Twitter: [@terrick_j](https://twitter.com/)
Email: Terrick.Heckstall@gmail.com
Author Page: www.facebook.com/authorthmorris
Website: 11thpercentseries.weebly.com

By T.H. Morris

The 11th Percent (The 11th Percent Series, Book 1)
Item and Time (The 11th Percent Series, Book 2)

Coming Soon
Lifeblood (The 11th Percent Series, Book 3)
Grave Endowments (with Cynthia D. Witherspoon)

Lightning Source UK Ltd.
Milton Keynes UK
UKHW041909031120
372650UK00001BB/136